A/F
December 2019

A SMALL TOWN

Also by Thomas Perry

The Butcher's Boy

Metzger's Dog

Big Fish

Island

Sleeping Dogs

Vanishing Act

Dance for the Dead

Shadow Woman

The Face-Changers

Blood Money

Death Benefits

Pursuit

Dead Aim

Nightlife

Silence

Fidelity

Runner

Strip

The Informant

Poison Flower

The Boyfriend

A String of Beads

Forty Thieves

The Old Man

The Bomb Maker

The Burglar

THOMAS PERRY

A SMALL TOWN

A NOVEL

The Mysterious Press
New York

Published simultaneously in Canada
Printed in Canada

This book is set in 13-point Arno Pro by Alpha Design & Composition of Pittsfield, NH

First Grove Atlantic edition: January 2020

FIRST EDITION

ISBN 978-0-8021-4806-3
eISBN 978-0-8021-4807-0

Library of Congress Cataloging-in-Publication data is available for this title.

The Mysterious Press
an imprint of Grove Atlantic
154 West 14th Street
New York, NY 10011

Distributed by Publishers Group West

groveatlantic.com

20 21 22 23   10 9 8 7 6 5 4 3 2 1

To my wife, Jo

A SMALL TOWN

1

As Beth Tiedemann packed Jack's lunch, she occasionally looked up from the kitchen counter and out the window at the town. Most of the important parts of it just peeked up above the roofs of the small two-story houses like theirs. She could see the spires of the five churches—Catholic, Presbyterian, Methodist, Lutheran, Baptist—all lined up on the circular drive around the city park, and the old Tivoli movie theater, tall because it had a loge level high in the back where high school couples like her and Jack used to sit and misbehave. It wasn't the sort of thing that she'd heard kids did now. That was still a time when a lot of people in town got married so they could have sex. She and Jack hadn't been that way, but there wasn't much indoor privacy available. She could also see the upper levels of the Holiday Inn outside town and the tower of city hall right in the center, but those were partially obscured by the thick summer foliage of the big trees along the parkway.

She cut slices from the roast beef she had made for dinner yesterday, picked the best ones, and put them on the bread for Jack's sandwich with the layers of lettuce and mayonnaise and some black pepper, then wrapped it in wax paper with perfect folds, like a present. She put two small thermoses in the box, one with cold milk and the other with hot coffee, because Jack was going in for the night shift, 7:00 p.m. until 7:00 a.m. Having him get sleepy was a huge worry to her.

She hated that he worked at the prison. He wasn't the sort of man to work as a prison guard. He was big and strong, and he had played left tackle for Weldonville when they were in school, but he wasn't mean or a fighter. It was hard on him to be in the punishment business.

It was hard on the whole town to be in the punishment business. She and Jack had been about thirteen when the men from the Federal Bureau of Prisons came to hold an informational meeting at city hall, but she remembered it, and if she hadn't, her parents had talked about it enough so that she couldn't misremember it. The government men had talked about Weldonville being one of the competing sites for the new federal facility. They knew a lot about the town—that the cattle grazing and mining that had given people a livelihood were long gone. Lots of people had taken to working away from town, driving long-haul trucks or commuting once a week from Denver or Colorado Springs. The prison would employ over a thousand people in government jobs in a facility that didn't need to make a profit and could never go out of business or move to another country.

A few days later the mayor had asked that the city have a vote to tell the local politicians what to do. People were eager for the jobs, so the politicians lobbied for the prison. Whether there really was a competition or not, the town of Weldonville got the prison. The government selected a contractor, and the contractor even included a few local people in the workforce, which kept them employed for five years. By the time they were laid off, the big, bright, brand-new prison was taking applications.

Beth had been a little concerned when Jack Tiedemann applied for a job, and that concern only got worse with time. The money was good—Jack was twenty-eight and making more than her daddy had ever made working at the department store. But she felt the job was costing them something, just as it had cost the town. Weldonville didn't really have an identity now that was separate. When people in surrounding cities and towns mentioned Weldonville, they didn't mean the nice little Colorado town with the round park in the center and the old trees shading the grid of residential streets. They meant Weldonville Federal Penitentiary; just like when people said "Leavenworth," they didn't mean a city in Kansas.

Since the subject had become important to her, she had noticed that the government seemed to prefer to build prisons in places like this, where the ground was flat and covered with fields of grain or weeds for miles in every direction. That was so if a prisoner ran away, he would have no place to hide.

She loved Jack so much it hurt, and if she closed her eyes and pictured him in his guard uniform going inside the high-walled complex, she could make herself cry, even though she wasn't a crier.

The Bureau of Prisons men had said this would be a modern, limited-security facility for white-collar and nonviolent offenders. But a few years after the complex was finished and Jack was working there, something had changed. Or maybe just their story had changed. The supervisors said there were many more violent criminals and fewer tax evaders and insider traders and computer hackers than they had planned for. Some of the other prisons in the system were old and out-of-date, not suited to house more difficult prisoners. Because Weldonville was new and had been built to a higher standard, it was one of the only places they had that would work.

Jack had found himself on details in the general prison population with a couple of other guards, all of them carrying only extendable batons and pepper spray because the thing prisons feared most was an inmate getting his hands on a guard's gun.

There were snipers in the guard towers and on the catwalks with M4 rifles, partly to protect those unarmed guards. Sometimes the man on the catwalk who had to be prepared to kill prisoners was Jack.

She put the apple and the cupcake in Jack's lunch box and was nearly ready to shut it. She looked up at the window again and saw that the pinks, oranges, and reds on the white wisps of cloud were losing their fire, and the night blues and blacks were waiting behind them. The night shift was coming, and she had only a few minutes.

She reached into the drawer where she kept things like buttons and needles and took one of the invitations from a small stack. She carefully blotted her lipstick on the inside, and then looked at it. There was a clear impression of her lips. She knew it was a corny thing to do, but she didn't care. She took the ballpoint pen lying next to her shopping list and wrote on the invitation, "Date at seven a.m.?" beneath the red kiss. She could feel herself blushing as she closed the invitation and put it in its small envelope and pushed it under the coffee thermos. She knew that would keep him awake. She shut and latched the lunch box.

Jack came into the kitchen and gave her a gentle hug and a kiss on the back of her neck. She shivered and spun around to face him. "Your lunch is ready," she said. He was wearing the blue pullover shirt she had bought him a week ago. It looked great on him. "Be careful," she said. "Keep your eyes open and stay alert."

"No argument from me," he said. "But it should be an easy night. After a couple of hours they'll all be locked in their cells, and most of them will be asleep by midnight."

She kissed him, then pointed at the wall clock above the kitchen table. "You'd better get going."

She watched him lift the hanger from the coat hook on the door. It held his uniform, all starched and pressed by the cleaners: the tan short-sleeve shirt suitable for July 19 and the razor-creased green pants. The embroidered patches on the shoulders made him look like he was an important man.

"See you in the morning."

"Bye," she said. She got a little pleasure out of making it sound routine. In a few hours he'd open the little invitation and learn what she'd been thinking.

2

It was evening. The Weldonville Federal Penitentiary was down and quiet now, the head count finished and the inmates in their cells for the rest of the night. The day-shift guards were on their way to their cars, and the relief process was complete.

Putting the inmates to bed at night and making them get up again in the morning were done during the overlap when both shifts of guards were inside the walls at once, because those were the times when friction was most likely to occur and the largest number of inmates were outside their cells. In the evening, inmates had to get up from what they were doing—sitting in classes, watching television, playing games—and as they filed along the cellblocks past one another, there was an opportunity for the kind of accidental jostling that caused resentment or even fights. All of them were about to be locked into their cells for the whole night alone with their thoughts, and at Weldonville, as in all federal prisons, the thoughts often ranged from tragic to insane.

All of that was over for this day, July 19. The appropriate lines on all the papers on clipboards in the administrative wing had been checked and signed by the responsible duty officer in each section.

The night shift consisted of fewer officers than the day shift because little supervision was required for the 2,500 inmates when they were locked up and asleep. Nobody had to be overseen or conducted anywhere or reprimanded or protected. Only forty-two officers were on duty during the night shift. There were also a doctor and two nurses and a staff of seven non-sworn personnel, who did things like ensure that the food and other supplies ordered for the next few days had been received, sorted, stored, and paid for, and administrative tasks like checking time cards to ensure that the workers' hours were being reflected on the payroll and making employee schedules for the next month.

Captain Gene Humphry, the executive officer for the night shift, made his first rounds at ten o'clock. He found that all inmates were accounted for and the prison staff was present. This hadn't surprised him, because there were few absentees in July. The guards in the towers were alert, and the roving guards were patrolling the catwalks at appropriate intervals. He held a surprise locker inspection for the guards and was pleased.

He always dreaded these locker inspections because he felt they were intrusive, but even more because he was afraid that someday he would find something—contraband for a prisoner or an unauthorized communication being smuggled outside, for instance. It would be easy to take the attitude that if you didn't look, you wouldn't see anything you didn't want to know about. That was the way ranking officers at some correctional facilities he'd read about operated. That was also the way they got guards selling drugs, alcohol, and cell phones to inmates. He'd even heard of guards bringing in weapons. It was hard to fathom stupidity like that.

Once again, Weldonville was clean. Humphry loved being the boss of a shift that had some professionalism to it. Every locker had the man's personal belongings—car keys, cell phone, wallet, watch, the occasional pocketknife. That meant they weren't carrying them on the cellblocks. He and his deputy, Scott, had gone through all of it, from the shoes on the locker floors to the pockets to the stuff on the shelves at the top, and found nothing that would cause him to make a comment in anyone's file.

When Humphry had taken the job, Weldonville had been planned as a low-to-medium-security prison for nonviolent offenders—people embezzling from the government and tax cheats. But that wasn't who they had now. The vast majority now were violent criminals, the overflow from high-security facilities. He suspected that when the Bureau of Prisons had asked wardens to send Weldonville their excess, there had been quite a few inmates hand-selected from their worst-behaved lists.

Humphry marched along the broad walkway in the center of the ground floor that the staff called Main Street. He walked with his head up and his shoulders back. His heels made a bright, hard click when they hit the polished concrete. He wasn't going to tiptoe along. If any of the inmates in their cells could hear it through the steel doors, then it would do them good to hear the sound of honest, unapologetic strength. Weldonville was not the old-fashioned kind of facility that was designed to be ugly and threatening, but Weldonville was still a prison. If you resisted it, what would break first would be you.

He reached the open stairs that rose toward the administration levels. There were only a few elevators in the complex. They were made for moving freight, not people, and they were isolated from the cellblocks and other areas where inmates roamed. In the hall at the top of the steps was a set of bars across his route. He walked to the electronic lock, inserted his key card, and tapped his code number into the keypad, and the bars moved aside almost silently, rolling on well-oiled wheels into a pocket in the wall. After he passed, a sensor in the mechanism triggered the motor and made the gate roll back across the hall again and lock. He went through another gate at the top of the next set of stairs.

After that barrier, he entered a hallway. He could see the Operations section office, where he worked. Often the section reminded him of the bridge of a ship, partly because of its location and partly because it was full of monitors and other instruments for watching and controlling the prison. As he approached the office, he heard an alarm beeping and a female electronic voice saying, "Disturbance on Cellblock C. Disturbance on Cellblock C," over and over.

He heard a crash bar disengage a lock, a steel door swing open, and then the sound of boots hitting the concrete floor. He ran toward the noise and turned the corner near Operations in time to see a squad—three in the vanguard and then two and two— running out the door and away down the hallway perpendicular to his. They were six guards and a sergeant to supervise them. He couldn't help appraising their appearance. They wore uniforms like his, the starched khaki shirts and green creased pants, black boots, and black belts. They looked sharp, and they looked formidable. He felt proud.

He turned away from them toward the Operations office and stepped inside. Before the door swung shut he heard the squad clattering down the stairs toward Cellblock C.

Humphry stepped into Operations just as the intercom system went quiet again. He asked Paul Scott, "What's up on Block C?"

Scott was younger, only thirty-one, but he had an air of competence that reassured people, even Humphry, who was aware the quality had to be a good temperament and not extensive experience. Scott was a good man to have on a night shift because he was responsible. Night shifts at Weldonville consisted of very few men, so most of the time just Humphry and Scott were in Operations.

"We're not sure, sir. We could see on the monitor that two men were out of their cells. It looked like they somehow slipped out between the bed check and the general door lock. They looked to me like they were squaring off to fight. The trouble squad took off a minute ago."

Humphry said, "This is really too bad. I've been afraid that some-day one of them would find a way to hotwire the locking system. I hope this wasn't the day. They're like one big organism with stuff like this. By next week all of them would know how, and we'd be dealing with something like this every night."

"Sir?"

"What?"

"Something else just happened." He pointed at one of the other television screens on the big wall of monitors. "Now the cameras on Block C aren't showing anything."

The seven guards reached the gate at the end of the hall before the entrance to Cellblock C. Pelletier, the sergeant, inserted his key card into the reader, punched in his code, and stepped back. The bars rolled out of the way into the wall, and the seven charged past—first McGovern, Ciccio, Decker, Yashinsky, Tiedemann, and Polk; and then, in accordance with procedure, after he'd stayed long enough to see the gate across the corridor roll shut and lock, Pelletier pivoted and ran to catch up.

Pelletier was through the door to the cellblock before he saw that the disturbance wasn't a couple of stupid inmates who had arranged to fight over some insult. It was something else entirely. The steel cell doors on all sides of the semicircular block abruptly opened and three prisoners dashed out of each one and threw themselves on the guards from all directions.

The first two men out tackled the nearest guard, one high and the other low, so the guard was sure to go down. The third piled on and made sure the guard stayed down, using impact, weight, and strength to disable him. In some fights the third man's dive onto the guard's torso broke ribs, and in others a guard's arm would be broken. Within ten seconds all seven guards had been swarmed and put down, but it wasn't over, because there was a fourth man.

The fourth man carried a ligature made of shoelaces or twine or braided leather attached to a pair of wooden handles. He sat down, slipped the ligature over the guard's head, braced himself by placing his feet on the guard's shoulders, and tightened the ligature around the guard's neck.

The guards of the trouble squad had been chosen for their size, strength, and athleticism, but they were all dead within minutes. As each guard died, his assailants removed his uniform. While one of the inmates put on the guard's uniform, the others dressed the guard's body in his prison clothes. They dragged each guard into a cell, lifted him onto a bunk, and arranged him to look as though he were sleeping.

The seven prisoners dressed as guards hurried out the cellblock door to the gate that prevented prisoners from entering the corridors and stairways. Martin Ortega, the one who was now dressed as a sergeant, used a key card to make the gate of iron bars roll aside into the pocket in the wall. He held the card there while Ed Leonard, the first man out after him, reached the hallway side of the gate, took out a screwdriver made from the sharpened handle of a spoon, and removed the screws from a maintenance panel in the wall to reach the electric motor and gears for rolling the heavy gate aside. He tore the wires out of the motor, took out a tube of epoxy cement stolen from the prison repair shop, and jammed the gears by sticking the tube of epoxy cement between them and moving the gate a few inches manually to burst the tube.

Cellblock C was now open and could not be closed again remotely or manually. The seven inmates in guard uniforms moved on, using the same method to jam open the gate at the bottom of the steps to the second tier, the one in the second-tier corridor, and then the one by the third-tier steps.

They split up into three groups of two and a lone sergeant. They emerged from the last steps onto the system of catwalks that ran above the cellblocks and Main Street.

The first pair to find one of the riflemen patrolling the catwalks came striding up together, both looking concerned. One of them said, "We're filling in from the day shift tonight, and we've got to make an extraction from a cell. They warned us he's a badass, and he's got a history of fighting back. Would you mind helping us out? If you'll stand by with the rifle where he can see you, things will go a lot easier."

"Sure," said the catwalker. "Where is he?"

"D Block, cell eighty-nine." The first one set off ahead, and his companion let the catwalker go next while he followed. He took a couple of steps before he had the metal baton from the dead guard's belt extended. He swung it downward into the rifleman's head. The impact made a hard, hollow sound, and the guard collapsed. As he started to fall, the first man pivoted and wrenched the rifle out of his hands, took the guard's spare magazine from his belt, and set them on the catwalk. Both men hoisted the guard by the arms and draped him over the railing. Then they squatted to lift his legs and released him headfirst.

The second and third pairs of inmates found the other two catwalkers within a few minutes and let them drop to the pavement of Main Street too. Now the seven uniformed inmates had three military-grade rifles and six loaded magazines. They came together at the door to the passage to the outer wall and climbed the steps.

Three guard stations overlooked the outer yard of the prison. They were referred to as "towers," but they were fixed concrete turrets built along the top of the wall. Each held two men with scoped rifles, mounted spotlights, and binoculars. These men were the deterrent of last resort, the certain way to control the open yard, the top of the wall, and the entrances and exits of the prison if everything else went wrong. The towers were fortified against most kinds of attack, and they contained large caches of ammunition in case of a lengthy standoff. Prison policy, ever since the mission of the prison had been revised, was for the tower guards to lock themselves into their towers for the whole shift, not opening the door for anyone until they were replaced at 7 a.m. The lights inside the guard towers were dim, like the dashboard lights of a car, to keep their vision of their targets bright.

The north tower was the first to come under attack. One of the inmates in a guard's uniform climbed to the top of the wall and crawled along beside the inner railing of the walkway so he couldn't be seen. He verified that the description of the tower was correct. The steel entrance door, the bulletproof-glass windows, and the reinforced-concrete structure of the tower were not vulnerable. The ventilation system was.

The tear gas–and–pepper spray combination on the guards' belts was occasionally used to get a barricaded inmate out of his cell, and the mixture had always worked. When the uniformed inmate reached the right spot beside the tower, he found the ventilation outlet where the fan pushed out stale air. It was a pipe that extended out and down, so rainwater couldn't seep in, and had a screen so insects couldn't creep in. He plugged the outlet by inserting a layer of paper under the screen. But there was also an intake for fresh air, and he found it by listening for the whirr of a fan on the opposite side of the tower. The intake pipe also faced downward and had a screen over its opening to keep out insects. The prisoner removed the screen.

The design included a carbon filter that looked like a can of charcoal chips with screens on both ends, to provide some protection from tear gas that might drift all the way up there during the quelling of a prison riot. The prisoner simply pulled the filter out of the pipe and set it aside. He was carrying the gas canister from his belt and the canister from the belt of his partner, and had another piece of paper folded in his pocket. He unfolded the paper and formed it into a funnel, with the larger end covering the intake. He took the two canisters out of their leather cases, pushed the first one into the small end of the funnel, and began to spray the gas into it.

For a minute or two there was nothing but the sound of the aerosol spray. Then there were noises from inside the tower. There was a voice, and then a thump, something like the sound of a chair being kicked over, and then two voices. The prisoner left the canisters and the paper and ran around to face the tower door.

The door of the tower flew open, and the two snipers burst out, coughing and rubbing their faces. They staggered a few paces from the door before they saw the uniformed inmate.

"Guys, come this way," he called. "We'll get you help."

The two seemed to see only that he was wearing a guard uniform, and that he was trying to get them to follow him, so they hurried behind him as he trotted toward the stairwell.

"Did you have a tear gas grenade go off in there?"

"Nothing went off," said one of the men from the tower. "It was coming in through the vent."

The uniformed prisoner opened the door to the stairwell and ushered them inside. He knew that there were inmates with strangling cords, backed up by his partner with the rifle in case things went wrong.

By the time his partner emerged from the stairwell, he had the door of the tower propped fully open and the ventilator fans turned on high and clearing the air of the poison he had sprayed in.

In the stairwell, the inmates who had strangled the two men from the north tower were busy dressing two prisoners in their uniforms. At the same time, other prisoners were executing identical attacks on the southwest tower and the southeast tower; the four guards stationed there were killed and their uniforms taken. The three towers yielded six rifles with scopes, 2,100 rounds of ammunition for them, six more expandable batons, and six more tear gas–and–pepper spray canisters. There were now sixteen armed prisoners dressed in guard uniforms.

3

Captain Humphry was worried. The seven-man trouble team that had gone out twenty-eight minutes ago had not returned. He left his desk and went out to the Operations room where Paul Scott was watching the monitors. "Have you been able to bring up C Block yet?"

"Yes. It looks like there may have been some kind of power glitch. It looks all quiet there, with all the inmates in their cells and nobody fighting or anything."

"Do you see the trouble team?"

"There hasn't been any sign of them since the visual came back. They could have taken somebody out of the block to the infirmary or isolation. Turning off the power for a minute or two could have been a part of that."

Captain Humphry lifted one of the handheld radios from the counter and pressed the talk button.

It was too late to use the radio. An inmate named Albert Weiss, a life-sentence offender from Florida, had already turned on an electrical device he had made in his cell over the past few months. He could have done the work in a few hours if he'd had the proper parts delivered in a single order from an electronics supply distributer. Instead he'd had to get other prisoners to let him take apart their radios and various other possessions, and to ask their relatives to send other approved items he could cannibalize. He had also taken pieces from many devices in the prison—television sets, toasters, a microwave oven, disc players, and other appliances had all contributed to his radio jammer.

This was a familiar project to Albert Weiss. He had made his first radio receiver at age ten and his first transmitter at twelve. The most effective jammer was simply a more powerful radio transmitter working on a particular band. He had gone to college at Florida State to become an electrical engineer and learned to complete much more complex and difficult projects.

He had built his transmitter as a clone of the walkie-talkies the guards used. He had started with some experimental work. Two-way radios intended for recreational use could be tuned to a wide variety of channels, but the pro models worked only on certain channels on reserved frequencies. Once he had made a crude, toy-like receiver, he had used it to find and listen to the frequencies and channels the guards' radios used. Next, he simply built a more powerful radio transmitter that could transmit on the same ones.

Over several months Weiss had assigned other inmates to use their cassette recorders to record the voices of guards walking up and down the cellblocks talking into their radios. He had used three recorders so there were at least three different sets of guards talking simultaneously on his master tape, all of them using standard prison radio codes and jargon. Some of them were from the night shift, so there would be familiar voices among them.

When Humphry turned on his handheld radio in the Operations room, what he heard was a powerful transmission of several voices talking simultaneously about routine operations, emergencies, questions, observations, and things that took place months ago or days ago. Some voices were mumbled or slurred, others loud and insistent, but no speech was comprehensible beyond three or four words. Humphry tried to break in by pressing his talk button several times and speaking. He tried saying, "This is Operations," and then, "This is Captain Humphry," but nothing interrupted the flood of words. He tried switching to the first alternative channel, but there was the same cascade of meaningless chatter. The second alternative channel was the same. He set the radio back on the console. "Now the radio system is screwed up too. Did we take a lightning strike or something?"

"I don't think so, sir."

The arsenal had no markings on its door, and no inmate was ever allowed on the corridor where it was located. Plenty of inmates probably didn't know it existed. The key that the man wearing the sergeant's stripes carried wouldn't open the steel door. The only key that worked was kept in the Operations section in the warden's desk. The steel door was too sturdy to be battered in by force, so the man in the sergeant's uniform said, "Go get Joe Lambert and tell him to bring the thermite." One man went and the other two got busy cutting off the electrical feed to the security cameras.

In a few minutes Lambert was there carrying a large plastic bottle made for laundry detergent. He set it down and fitted a metal trough over the door handle so its end was held against the door lock, and then poured a generous portion of the dark powdery substance from the plastic bottle into the trough so it slid down to gather around the lock and bolt.

The substance was a mixture of aluminum powder filed from the under parts of a folding chair and common rust from an iron dumbbell rack in the exercise area that had its paint chipped off a few months ago so the rain would corrode it, the undersides of several iron benches bolted down in the yard, and a few other rust-production areas. The final ingredient was magnesium in the form of thin strips that had reached the prison inside the bindings of several books.

Lambert produced a flint-and-steel spark lighter, stolen from the welding kit in the maintenance shop, and lit the magnesium. It took a few seconds to get the sparks to start the magnesium, but then he succeeded and the thermite caught.

The tray sent out bright flying bits of metal, as though that part of the door had been transformed into a big sparkler. The uniformed inmates stepped backward, with their hands up to protect their eyes, but the reaction intensified, heating the steel door and the hardware attached to it higher and higher.

"How long?"

"Until the color is right."

Ortega, the man with the stripes, stood eye to eye with Lambert. "This is going to work, right?"

"Yes. The hard part is getting the reaction to start, and we've done that. Metal burns at incredibly high temperatures. We could melt the whole door if we had enough thermite."

In five more minutes, the door was so hot it radiated like a furnace, and it was hard to stand near it. Lambert stared at it some more, then quickly stepped up and gave the door a stomp-kick beside the door handle. The door swung inward into the room. They could see that the lock had stayed where it was, with the bolt still stuck in its receptacle and the hinges still attached to the jamb, but the thinner steel of the door had softened and melted away from them.

The uniformed inmates formed a single file and stepped around the door into the arsenal. There were dozens of rifles in racks along the walls, olive drab steel cans of ammunition, and twenty-round magazines. On one whole wall was a display of identical semi-automatic pistols. The men armed themselves as heavily as possible, most with a rifle and two pistols, and then they were joined by some of the other uniformed inmates, who took extra arms and ammunition for others who were occupied in different sectors.

* * *

Humphry came out of his office and looked over Scott's shoulder at the monitors. "Keep looking for them. Check each sector, one at a time, until they turn up. Start with the infirmary and isolation if you want, but let me know." He went away again.

After a few minutes, Scott came to Humphry's office. "I've been looking, but I haven't found them. And now I'm getting these intermittent outages. I'll check on a place and it all seems fine. Then I'll come back to it and there's no visual. I'll go off it and look somewhere else, and then the visual is on again, and there doesn't seem to be anything out of place, but the seven men never show up."

Humphry said, "Is there anything off right now?"

"One of the hallways. And the infirmary."

"Not the front gate or the yard?"

"Not so far. It's all random places."

"Great. That means nobody's trying to get out. The only serious problem is that the trouble squad hasn't come back yet. How do you propose we could solve that?"

"I tried calling them again and the talk button didn't get me an override." He knew what Humphry wanted and he was reluctant, but Humphry was staring at him, waiting. He gave in. "Do you think I should go out and look for them?"

Humphry shrugged. "That might do it."

"Would you mind holding down the office by yourself while I go, Captain?" It was his only way of retaliating. He knew Humphry hated being alone in the office running from phone to phone and watching the monitors.

Humphry said, "I don't expect you to answer the phones when you're not here. When you find them, tell Pelletier to come see me."

"Yes, sir." Scott turned and left Humphry's office. By the time he passed his work station at the monitors, the outage at the infirmary had been restored. A glance showed him the reception desk and the secure area where the sick or faking inmates waited to be examined, and the dimly lit ward with sleeping inmates on narrow beds. He reached for the handheld radio. Maybe everything was working again. It wasn't. The continuous chatter of guard voices was loud, if not clear. He set the radio down and hurried out.

Scott was thirty-one years old and had worked at Weldonville since he was twenty-six. The job of commander's deputy was not at all what he had thought it would be. He had worked for a while in a state facility, where crimes were ugly—murder and armed robbery, child abuse, assault. He had always assumed that a federal prison would have a lot of men who were easier to be around. He'd expected the people in federal prisons had committed federal crimes, like counterfeiting, stock and bond manipulation, or postal fraud. He couldn't recall having seen any of those offenders at Weldonville. They were all hard cases now.

He used the logic of elimination to decide how to attack tonight's problem. It would do no good to look in Cellblock C for the seven men, because whatever had happened there was over. Order had been restored, or had returned on its own because everybody was locked up. The same was true of the infirmary. The patients on camera were all in their beds. The yard was empty and the towers that oversaw it were manned. The best remaining idea was that maybe the squad had taken the two offenders to the solitary holding cells away from the cellblocks so they could be interviewed separately and the arguments sorted out before they were either disciplined or returned to the general population. When he reached the first stairway, he opened it with his key card and began to climb.

He took a route along the catwalk above Main Street. He told himself that it was a shortcut, but the prison was a place of straight lines and right angles, so whatever route ran the length of the place was the same distance to the inch. The truth was that the catwalks were above the cellblocks and the prisoners and the routes they could use. If he met anyone up here, it would be one of the roving guards armed with rifles, and that thought was comforting.

He trotted along the catwalk, trying to make good time. Captain Humphry was a fair boss, but he felt it was his job to evaluate everyone. It was essential for Scott to dispel any suspicion that he was lazy, incompetent, or fearful, a man trying to keep his place in an office so he wouldn't face the danger the guards had to.

He didn't like being out alone this way in the prison, especially when there was an odd breakdown in the surveillance and communication systems. He was determined that after this lonely scouting mission, Humphry would be pleased. At least for the present, Humphry would approve of him.

He saw one of the roving riflemen coming along a catwalk that was perpendicular to his. He was coming from the west side of the prison. Scott adjusted his speed so they would meet at the intersection. The man had his rifle on its sling over his shoulder, and not in his hands. He obviously wasn't aware of anything wrong.

Scott didn't recognize the man. He hoped he would come up with the man's name soon. This was one of the bad things about being isolated in Operations. He wasn't close with the rest of the prison guards. He smiled broadly and waved his hand as he approached. The other man smiled and nodded, and when they were about eight feet apart, his hand came up too. By the time Scott saw and understood that it held a canister of CS and pepper spray, it was already propelling its pressurized stream of liquid into his face, blinding his eyes and making them burn.

"Stop it!" he shouted. "I'm a guard like you. Can't you see I'm a guard?" He was bent over, his hands rubbing his eyes. "I'm the deputy commander."

The uniformed man used the butt of his rifle to knock Scott senseless and prone on the catwalk. Then he put down his weapons, slipped his hands under Scott's armpits, dragged and hoisted him up to the railing, draped him there, and then squatted and clasped his thighs and lifted him up and over.

He watched Scott's unconscious body fall eighty feet toward the polished concrete pavement of Main Street. His body sprawled out full-length, his arms and legs out, like a gingerbread man. When he hit, his body bounced slightly before it settled. He was facing upward, and his head had a circular splash of blood around it like an aura. He was dead, and there had not been enough noise to be audible on the next cellblock. The uniformed man picked up his rifle and aerosol tear gas–and–pepper spray and walked on along the catwalk.

4

Humphry had a moment when his mind ran through the most alarming possibilities. What if the seven men of the trouble team had arrived at the Cellblock C hallway gate, gone in and closed it behind them, and then had the power go off? Judging from the blackouts on the monitors, there had been an outage. During a circuit failure and then the surge afterward, the gates could have shorted out or lost their programming and become inoperable. The seven men could be trapped between the outer gate and the gate to the inmate housing area. With the glitch in the radio system, they couldn't even call for help.

There were certainly inmates in a population of 2,500 who had some training as electricians. Some could even have degrees in electrical engineering. One of them could have tinkered with the circuitry and stranded the seven men.

The seven could be there all night. It was the sort of predicament the inmates all relished. Whenever a guard got injured or got locked in somewhere, they would celebrate it, hurrying to tell all the other inmates and, if possible, bringing them to see the poor guard in there waiting for rescue. That kind of event was a disruption in the ecosystem of the prison. It undermined the guards' sense of themselves as the superiors of the inmates, and it reminded the inmates that the guards were vulnerable and could be hurt. He hoped that what had delayed the trouble squad wasn't as dire as that.

He hoped it was nothing, even though he knew it couldn't be nothing. Almost any problem would have been reported to his office within a minute and a plan could have been selected within two more. But there had been no report.

He thought hard for a moment. There was no sight or sound from Paul Scott either. He walked to the wall of monitors at Scott's workstation and began to study the segments of the screens. Each monitor represented a section of the prison, and each square on a screen was the feed from a single camera in that section. A couple of them were still blacked out on the first section he checked. Three were blacked out on the next one. That meant something. Probably the electrician Humphry had posited was playing another trick.

Humphry hated to call for help, but he felt he had to. The normal procedure was to pick up the phone at this point and make three calls, in order. The first was to notify the warden, then the local police, and then the state police that something disturbing was happening inside the prison.

He went to the nearest phone, which was sitting on the desk that Scott had vacated. He lifted the receiver, but there was no dial tone.

He caught a movement in the corner of his eye. The door handle was moving. Thank God, he thought. It was undoubtedly Scott and the seven men. They were fine. The door opened.

Six men in guard uniforms burst into the room at a run, saw Humphry, and veered toward him. The first pair collided with him, knocked him to the floor, and overwhelmed him.

Minutes later the dozen uniformed prisoners who had led the break reunited and were on the move again. Now they had the watch commander's key card, which would open any and every lock in the prison. There were only two of those keys, and the other one was at home with the warden.

They made their way toward the guards' locker room, led by Paul Duquesne, the man with the captain's key card. He ran ahead of the other men, stopping at each gate to open it and then run on while two of the others jammed the mechanism so the gate could not be closed again.

It took five minutes to reach the guards' locker room. As soon as they were inside, they took off their guard uniforms and put on the civilian clothes that were hanging in the lockers. They took the dead guards' wallets, keys, phones, and other belongings.

They left the uniforms in the lockers, but took with them the firearms and ammunition they had stolen from the arsenal. Each man had an M4 rifle capable of firing on the settings for semiautomatic and fully automatic, two Glock 17 pistols, and as many loaded magazines as he could carry in his pockets, jacket, and belt.

They made their way to the out-processing area on the ground floor, where prisoners were held while being prepared for release. They shot the two guards on duty there and used the watch commander's key card to open the building doors and the outer gate. Then they streamed out through the gate and left it open for the inmates they knew would follow.

They trotted out to the staff parking lot outside the prison walls, and quickly figured out which sets of keys went with which cars and trucks. Most of the car key fobs had brand logos on them, and all of them could unlock a door and light the dome lights with the press of a button.

Within minutes each of the twelve had a car, and by then most of them had found the addresses of the guards, either from a driver's license or a car registration. Each of these addresses was a place where a man about to start a new life might find things that would help him on his way.

The guards' houses would contain more clothes and maybe a suitcase or two to carry them. The houses would also contain some cash, some food and water, and some valuable items that could be sold or traded later. There could be many additional attractions at any one of those houses, and the seven-to-seven shift was not even close to over. It was only 1:12 a.m.

None of the escapees had ever been outside the walls of the prison before, and the U.S. marshal's vehicles that had delivered them at the start of their sentences had carried them directly from the interstate highway to the prison without passing through the residential neighborhoods of Weldonville. Some of the twelve escapees used the guards' cell phone apps to get directions to the dead guards' addresses.

Beth Tiedemann was upstairs asleep when the car crept up the street. The evening of July 19 had been such a hot, still time that she had the bedroom windows open and the ceiling fan running. The doors and windows downstairs were all locked and bolted. Those were the only ones that mattered, because the upstairs windows were too high to reach without an extension ladder, and there were no big trees close enough to the house to use as a way to climb up to a bedroom.

The bass-range hum of the engine woke her. It sounded exactly like Jack's Mustang to her. She knew that sound so well because she'd listened for it for three years, and she'd heard it every time he'd come home from work, so it gave her a warm, happy feeling. She opened her eyes, but it was still dark. Maybe it was a different car, because Jack wasn't supposed to be home until after seven in the morning. She sat up and listened. It sure sounded like Jack's Mustang. She looked at the red numerals of the clock on the stand beside the bed. It was only 1:28.

She looked out the window. It was Jack's Mustang. And what would he be doing arriving at the house just after one? Was Jack coming home sick or hurt?

She got up, stepped into the slippers by her side of the bed, and ran out into the hallway. Because it was a hot night, she hadn't worn the sweatpants and football shirt she often wore. She'd put on a pair of shorts and a tank top. She hurried down the staircase.

When she was almost to the first floor, she heard a key in the front door and the doorknob turned, but the door didn't open. She had set the deadbolt because she was alone, and that didn't open with the key. She hurried to the entrance, turned the lever that made the deadbolt retract into the door, and tugged the knob. As the door swung open, she said, "Jack, what's—"

The door was pushed inward hard and as it hit the wall, a man was already charging inside, reaching out for her like a creature in a nightmare. The man was wearing Jack's new blue shirt.

5

Leah Hawkins was six feet two inches tall and bony, with unruly, wiry hair the color of clover honey that she had confined in a tight bun. Tonight she wore her navy blue version of the suit that many female cops wore. The jacket was tailored to hang from her shoulders without curving in much at the waist, so the sidearm she wore on her belt wouldn't cause a bulge.

She drove her personal car from her house on Calloway Street on the east side of Weldonville to city hall. As she went, she passed empty lots that had once been the homes of people she knew, burned the night of July 19 two years ago but never rebuilt or even sold to new people or builders. Most of the charred wood and the standing remains of chimneys had been removed, and the holes that had been basements were filled in, but the work had not been done by the owners. Many of the owners were dead, and the survivors had abandoned the lots, and the city had assigned the Department of Public Works to use its two bulldozers and four dump trucks to clear the ruins.

Whole blocks on the east side had been leveled, and the wood, bricks, concrete, and pipes hauled off. Two or three houses on nearly every other block had been removed, from where the federal highway met the town at a tangent all the way to Main Street, where the fire damage had been stopped.

Near Main Street in the commercial district there had been a slower kind of damage. More than half the small stores and restaurants that had been alive two years ago now had plywood sheets over their windows and doors. Leah could look along Main Street and see the handiwork of the employees of Clay's Hardware Store. The plywood was all cut accurately to size, placed over each opening, and screwed—not nailed or stapled—in place. The boarding-up job would probably last longer than the other parts of some of those buildings. You couldn't get hired at Clay's Hardware if you didn't know your way around a toolbox, and you wouldn't stay long unless you took pride in doing things right. The older Clays, the brothers who had run the business, had died that night two years ago, but those standards hadn't changed.

Leah had heard that the work of boarding up storefronts and offices and gas stations had actually given Clay's a year of better-than-normal profits before things had begun to taper off from people leaving. But that was typical gossip. People in the area beyond the periphery of a disaster did a lot of talking, while the ones in the center seemed to lose interest in it. The talk wasn't even about anything most of the time, just people's way of claiming a small share of a big event.

She parked her car in the lot of the Public Safety Building next to the big, black unmarked car she'd had assigned to her when she'd returned to Weldonville from her years with the Colorado Bureau of Investigation in Lakewood. She looked at it for a second and wondered who would be driving it next.

She walked from the employees' parking lot by the Public Safety Building to the Main Street sidewalk and then across from the park and up the eight steps to the front entrance of city hall, taking them two at a time. The big set of double doors were clad in a dark metal that was supposed to look like bronze, unlike the glass doors from her childhood they had replaced. The glass had allowed kids like her to stare inside down the long corridor and watch people on their way to and from official affairs. The bronze ones reminded Leah of the doors of a church, but an ugly church.

She tugged the right door open and headed along the mirror-polished marble floor to the place where Sergeant Tim Munson stood waiting to operate the metal scanning machine. When she was close enough, Munson said, "Evening, Lieutenant."

She said, "Evening, Sergeant," as she took off her utility belt, with her badge, sidearm, and handcuffs on it, and set it in the plastic bin on the metal table. "Everybody in there waiting for me?" She put her phone in the bin and stepped through the metal detector.

"It's not eight o'clock yet, but I think they're ready for you." He picked up the bin holding her equipment and said, "You know I have to lock these up while you're in a council meeting, right? No firearms, no phones?"

"Sure," she said. "I've been to the council." She knew the gun ban was a tradition that dated to the city's founding in 1873. As he put the belt and phone into the lock box below the table, she started in the direction of the council chamber. "See you later."

She walked to the door of the city council chamber and opened it. The seven council members were not in their semicircular row of seats facing the audience, the way they were at open, official meetings. They were sitting around the big table where the citizens who had business before them sat. As Leah walked down the aisle between the two halves of the chamber, the mayor said, "We saved a seat for you, Lieutenant."

"Thank you, Mr. Mayor." She sat in the empty seat at the foot of the table.

The mayor said, "You all know Detective Lieutenant Leah Hawkins."

Of course they did, and if they hadn't before, they would have learned in the past months. Tonight was their third closed meeting with her during that time.

Linda Harris said, "Yes, of course." She and most of the others gave Leah a wave or a nod.

But Mayor Donaldson persisted. "And Lieutenant, you undoubtedly know City Attorney Phil Haymes. He wasn't here for the other meetings."

She said, "We went to high school together. Hi, Phil."

"Hi, Leah."

"Okay, then," said Mayor Donaldson. "Since we've dispensed with all of the routine issues before the council, and the lieutenant is here, the agenda lets us turn to the police issues. We've all read the FBI's report we received at our May 12 meeting. As far as I can tell, they have made no progress in two years locating, much less arresting, any of the twelve men who caused, planned, and directed the July 19 prison break. I'd like to ask the lieutenant this. Is the destruction of Weldonville now a cold case?"

"Nobody is saying that," Leah said. "But in my experience, no law enforcement agency, even the FBI, keeps hundreds of people working on a case after the public's safety is no longer threatened and there haven't been new leads for them to follow. There will be a few agents keeping the files current. If there are tips from informants or chance sightings, they'll act. But barring that, our case is a piece of history. One big indicator is that the expert special agents in charge that we worked with at first have all been reassigned."

The mayor said, "Since our May meeting each of us has been making quiet inquiries of our districts and pulling on the threads each of us has out in the community—neighbors, relatives, close friends, members of our clubs and churches. Mark Stein has completed a list of the people we've consulted and what they said. Mark, can you summarize for the lieutenant what we've learned?"

Mark Stein was a tall man with dark hair thinning at the top of his head. He was still dressed in the white shirt and tie he'd worn in his insurance company office all day. It was wrinkled and a little gray, and that was a sad sight to Leah. His wife had died during the prison escape two years ago, or she would have made him put on a clean shirt.

He said, "We've only got about three thousand citizens left on the voting rolls, but we've talked to three thousand four hundred and eight. Once you sort out the doubles and the triples, it looks like we got to about everybody in town who is young enough to be of sound mind and well enough to chat with his councilperson. There's pretty much a consensus."

He cleared his throat. "If you live here, you lost family or friends or both. Everybody feels the town is wounded, and a bit over eighty-five percent say that after giving it two years to recover, the wound is probably fatal. The town's morale is at a new low and sinking. Twenty-five hundred were asked specifically if they thought it was time to leave, and two thousand and twelve said yes, and just over three hundred said they didn't know but were leaning that way. A hundred and sixty-two said if we were going to do something about it, they wanted to put their names in to volunteer. Sort of a vigilante thing, I guess." He held up a neatly typed sheet of paper. "Here are the names."

"May I see that?" asked Leah.

He handed the sheet to her. "I made it for you. Keep it." He sat down.

"Thank you." She put it into her inner coat pocket without looking at it.

"The next issue on the police segment of the agenda is Lieutenant Leah Hawkins's request for a sabbatical leave of absence to last up to one year. It will be spent studying the operations of a number of other police forces through on-the-job training and management studies. I propose that the city pay for her travel, living, and equipment expenses out of the federal grant for the rebuilding of the city's police force. Any discussion?"

Donald Hall said, "How much money are we talking about?"

"For the travel and expenses, probably not that much," said Nell Hoagland, who acted as the council's comptroller. "I would guess it will be under two hundred thousand dollars, and the grant is for four million. She would also continue to receive her police department salary during her training, of course."

"Thank you," Hall said. "I'd like to second the motion."

"More discussion?" asked Mayor Donaldson. "No? Then ayes? Nays?" He made a note on his yellow pad. "The motion passes unanimously." Then he looked up and said, "Mr. Haymes, I believe you have a related motion?"

"Yes, I do," he said. "What Lieutenant Hawkins might discover is that there are pieces of equipment, vehicles, weapons, surveillance, communication, or other items that will have to be part of the federal grant's use. She might need to purchase prototypes or the services of consultants. I would like to ask that Lieutenant Hawkins be given the power to spend additional money up to a limit at her own discretion."

"I so move," said Linda Harris.

"Discussion?" the mayor said.

"Once again, how much?" asked Donald Hall.

Haymes said, "I propose that one quarter of the grant, or one million dollars, be at her disposal."

"Isn't that a little high?"

"Yes," said Haymes. "But since the commander of the police department will, in effect, be our main expert in deciding how to spend the entire grant to make the city safer, it seems that entrusting her with a quarter of the sum is not excessive. And there's an incentive not to spend unwisely, since if she wastes any of it, she'll have less to spend later. It can only be used on law enforcement, and we've spent exactly none of the grant so far."

"Okay," said Hall. "Just wanted to know."

"Any more discussion?" said the mayor. "No? Ayes? Nays? The motion passes unanimously. Mr. Haymes?"

Haymes stood up, took a folder out of his briefcase, and set his briefcase on the floor. He opened the folder and took out four sheets of vellum paper with the city's crest embossed on them, a buffalo and an antelope in a blue circle with points around the edges, like those of a gear, and gold lettering saying, "The City of Weldonville, Colorado, 1873."

He set them on the conference table, then set his fountain pen beside them. "I took the liberty of producing two documents to record the two unanimous resolutions the council has just made. I ask that the mayor and council sign your names on the lines at the bottom of each sheet now so that Lieutenant Hawkins will be able to take a copy of each with her. We'll retain the other copy, of course."

The council members each got up and signed where he had indicated, and then the mayor signed with a flourish. Haymes was the last to sign. Then he waved each sheet back and forth to dry the ink, and put two in one file and two in another.

"Any other new business?" Mayor Donaldson asked.

There was silence.

"Motion to adjourn," said Stein. Four voices called, "Second."

"Meeting adjourned."

Linda Harris said, "Leah, we'll miss you around here." She got up and hugged her. "You and Kathy were such good friends that to me you seem like a relative. If you ever need somebody to talk to while you're far away, I'm available."

Linda Harris's mentioning Kathy was a complicated gesture, and Leah Hawkins saw all sides of it. Kathy had been one of seven civilian workers at the prison on the night of July 19 two years ago, and she had not lived through it. In high school Kathy had been one of Leah's special friends, a member of the league championship basketball team with her, and a great spiker on the volleyball team. Sports had been part of their solution to being two extra-tall girls in a small town. Boys were too self-conscious to ask them out, but they were invited to everything. Linda Harris was reminding Leah why she didn't want Leah to go, but Kathy's death was why she was right to learn to make people safer.

"Lieutenant Hawkins?" Mayor Donaldson said. "Can you stop in my office so we can get the paperwork done?"

"Sure," she said. "Thanks, Linda."

The other council members shook her hand or hugged her, and then she followed City Attorney Haymes and Mayor Donaldson down the hall to the mayor's office. They went inside and the mayor shut the door. They kept going into his inner office and sat in the old oak chairs upholstered in green leather.

Haymes took the first piece of vellum out of the file folder. He said, "This is the resolution composed and unanimously approved by the council and signed by the mayor and council and me. It transfers the first million dollars of the federal government's four-million-dollar disaster grant into a second fund accessible only to Weldonville PD commanding officer Lieutenant Leah Anne Hawkins, to be used at her sole discretion to fund additional law enforcement efforts necessary since the escape from the federal penitentiary at Weldonville."

"I didn't ask for anything like that. I asked for a leave of absence. Is that even legal, Phil?" Leah asked.

"It's legal enough," Haymes said. "The city council gets to say how the grant money is spent. You just watched them do it. If the feds were to audit it, they would be forced to find that we used it in a public effort at restoring the rule of law. The fact that the town is speeding up the process of quietly dying is not something they can prove or punish. It may also mean the rest of the money will probably never be spent. That will make the accountants among them happy."

Leah said, "All I asked for was a leave of absence. What you two did was present the council with a fiction and get them to pay for it."

"The city has turned your request for a leave of absence down," Haymes said. "It has decided instead to make sure you have resources to do what all three of us know you're planning to do anyway. The million dollars has been deposited in the five largest banks in the United States. It will be accessible to you by five debit cards in your name. They're in the white envelope. Use them like credit cards, or make withdrawals in cash. If you need to pay for something by check, any branch can issue a cashier's check. Don't keep financial records. The banks will record every expenditure as a matter of course. Any explanations will come from the city."

He took out the second sheet of vellum. "This one is your commission from the council, essentially. It says you are engaged in enforcing the state laws of Colorado, and have the full support of the police force, the district attorney, and the city government. The city will cover any matter of legal counsel, bail, and criminal or civil liability for you and your deputies."

He put the two sheets in the folder and handed it to her. "That's everything we want in writing. The more you say, the more you might have to explain. The police department will remain open, partly to keep writing tickets and maintain order, and partly to back you up and send you anything you need. With the department still open, you're a sworn police officer on assignment. If it's closed, you're a civilian."

"I understand that. What I don't understand is why you two want to become accessories to murder."

Phil Haymes said, "Stein said it. We all lost people. Two years ago, we both heard you say that if the FBI didn't find those twelve killers within two years, you were going after them yourself. Now, exactly two years later, you tell us you're leaving. We know what you're doing. We want you to succeed. We want them dead and you alive. What we're doing is trying to make that more likely."

Mayor Donaldson said, "Do you have any questions about anything, Lieutenant Hawkins?"

"How could I?" she said.

"All right. You can still think about it while you're getting ready over the next few weeks. During the time while you're gone, more people—ones you grew up knowing—will probably be packing up and moving away, but you're working for them too. It's up to you if you want to say goodbye to anybody. No matter what, City Attorney Haymes, Sergeant Tim Munson, Sergeant Art Sprague, and I are committed to staying at least another year to wait until you get back here. After you return we'll each still have time to start deciding what we'll do with the rest of our lives. If you change your mind, just let us know and we'll make up another story."

Leah put the folder under her arm and said, "It's probably best if I'm gone in the next couple of days. The story you just spun is fine. I'd appreciate it if after I'm gone nobody contradicts that lie."

Haymes said, "You can count on us. Even the council has no idea what they just approved, and we won't enlighten them. Have you given any thought to who you're going to take with you?"

"Yes," she said. "I'm going alone." She got up and shook their hands, then accepted a hug from Mayor Donaldson. He had been a good friend of her father's, and she had been reminded tonight that they had a lot of the same mannerisms. He even hugged like her father. She took a last look, turned, and walked out the door of the office.

Leah walked back along the marble floor of the corridor past the council chamber toward the entrance where Sergeant Munson was taking her phone and her belt with her gun and badge out of the steel box.

6

As Leah drove past the apartment building where Bill Halvorsen lived, she was tempted to stop her car, get out, and ring the bell. She could see a light on behind the curtain in a second-floor window. She kept going.

Halvorsen was a marine who had been out of the country more since high school than he had been in it. She had been about eight years older and had watched him growing up. Two years ago, when he had come home from Afghanistan, he had gone to the police station and knocked on her door. When she said, "Come in," he had stood in the doorway for a moment.

She said, "Bill! Come in. I'm so sorry about Nick." She got up and went to the door, closed it, and gave him a hug. He was shorter than she was by about four inches, so his chin was on her shoulder, but he was muscular—even more than when he was young—and she sensed he could pick her up with one hand. Nick was his older brother, who had worked in the prison.

Bill hugged her back, then released her. "Hi, Hawk. I'm sorry about—hell, everybody."

On the basketball court they'd called her the Hawk, but she hadn't heard it in years. "Did you just get back?"

"I flew into Denver last night and made it here this morning."

She accepted that the responsibility to bring it up was hers. "You know most of it, right?"

"Some," he said. "What I saw was a week-old television report that lasted maybe five minutes, and a couple of newspapers. I figured the only person who would know everything and still tell me the truth is you."

She told him. "There were two thousand four hundred and ninety-eight inmates housed at the prison. About twelve hundred left the prison that night. The FBI, the state police, and our department managed to account for nine hundred and sixty-two of them during the first night and most of the rest within forty-eight hours."

"Pretty impressive. You did a good job."

"Not really. Those were all the easy ones. What happened was that there were a dozen men who broke out of prison. On the way out, they jammed the gates and doors and left the gun room open, so the others would go too."

"That was to make it harder to find the twelve?"

"I think so. The smart inmates stayed in the prison and waited. About half of them saw what was going on and went back into their cells to wait it out."

"And the other ones?"

"The stupid ones who used the opportunity of the prison break to make a run for it came out and found themselves out there in the middle of twenty miles of wheat and alfalfa fields. Most of them were city boys. They were wearing orange prison jumpsuits, and sandals and white socks instead of shoes. None of them had any civilian clothes when they ran out of the prison. None of them had a dime, and probably none of them had a clear idea of where they were or which way to run. By daylight we had nine hundred sixty-two in custody. The problem for us wasn't capture. It was transport and incarceration. We used any trucks we could commandeer, and then had to lock them in areas that could be closed off and chained shut with padlocks because the electronic locks were sabotaged."

"How did Nick die?"

"He was working in the out-processing area near the main gate. The twelve came through on their way out, saw him and Dave Culbert, the man working with him, and shot them."

"Good," said Bill. "I read that most of them were caught and strangled. Strangling would have been worse."

"They had full-auto M4s, so Nick and Dave went fast."

"What happened in the town?" Bill asked.

"Well," Leah said, "first the twelve ringleaders came into town. They were wearing the street clothes from the lockers of twelve guards they had killed. They had guns from the armory of the prison. They were driving the cars the guards had parked in the lot. They had the addresses of the guards too. And they had the cell phones the guards left in their lockers. In other words, they had directions to a dozen addresses where the man of the house wasn't ever coming home."

"What happened?"

"Pretty much everybody's worst fear. There were a dozen brand-new widows raped in their homes. Four of them were killed afterward. A couple of the inmates went to the warden's house and made a big production out of making him see what they did to his wife and daughters before they killed him."

"Why do all that stuff?" said Bill. "They had a limited time to get as far away as they could."

Leah shrugged. "I wondered at the time, and I still do. At first, I thought they were just a bunch of psychopaths who had found each other in prison, and that's the kind of thing psychopaths do. Now I think they had two things in mind. One was practical. They wanted to pillage those houses to get everything they could—more clothes, food, money, and any valuables. In order to do that, they had to at least silence the families in the houses—tie them up and gag them, cut the phone wires, and take the cell phones. After that, they had the opportunity to do what they wanted. But there was something else."

"What?"

"They were trying to kill the town—to ruin it for the people who lived here and make it into someplace where nobody would ever want to live again. They wanted people's houses to be places where horrible things happened, so the families couldn't bear to be there anymore, to sleep there, knowing what some member of the family went through in the next room, or even in the same room. They wanted to demonstrate to the people of the town that as long as there was a prison here, the idea of being safe was an illusion.

"The prison is actually between three and four miles from Weldonville, which the Bureau of Prisons considered enough of a margin for safety. If somebody broke out, they couldn't get on a road and hitchhike, because the road there went right from the interstate highway to the penitentiary, so it missed the town. The only people ever on that road were guards, supply trucks, and families trying to visit a prisoner."

Leah shrugged. "That night the twelve leaders had cars, but the other escapees didn't, at least at first. A few saw the mountains in the distance and went toward them on the theory that forested high country would hide them. But the mountains look much closer than they are because they're so huge. Quite a few inmates have learned how to hotwire a car, and these prisoners saw the other cars that belonged to dead guards and workers. There were forty-two guards and ten civilians there that night, and eventually the forty other cars in the lot got started and driven off."

"Where did they drive to?"

"Whenever an inmate got one started, five or six others would pile in, sometimes even more, and the first place all of them headed was to town. They wanted the same things the first escapees did— civilian clothes, money, food and water, credit cards, keys for the cars that were parked in people's garages. And by the end of an hour, the first escapees on foot began to arrive. As I said, there were about twelve hundred men in all. They were like an invading army."

"What do you mean?"

"They came in waves. They broke windows and kicked in doors and stormed houses. The ones who had taken guns from the prison armory shot householders, but even the ones who hadn't gotten guns found things to use. Every kitchen had kitchen knives. Many of the houses had guns in them. But anything would do—there were claw hammers, monkey wrenches, hatchets, and axes."

"How many?"

"Three hundred and seventy-six houses. Ninety-seven murders —sometimes everybody in a house, and sometimes none. Sometimes the people on a street heard a commotion and abandoned their houses to avoid the escapees. When the escapees killed somebody in a house, sometimes they would set the place on fire to destroy evidence. After the first gunshots, we got calls and we went to work. Firefighters deployed to fight the fires, but they were shot at right away and had to retreat while we fought the escapees."

"Did you lose any officers?"

"Eight. That's twenty percent. We concentrated on stopping them on the east side of Main Street, because none of them had made it to the west side yet. We killed seventy-eight of them there and wounded a hundred more, but we held. Fortunately, the average violent offender isn't as good at violence as he might be. We were far better shots. In the end, the sun came up, and it was over. It was like a horror movie, where the zombies just turn to dust in the sun. The last ones who could get cars to move did it then. The state troopers and the FBI were on their way here, and they caught most of them at roadblocks. The ones still on foot we rounded up and locked in the school gym with armed guards at the doors and on the baseball field. We drove them back to the prison in trucks starting around noon."

"That's a terrible story."

"It sure is," she said. "They murdered Weldonville. People started packing up, locking their houses, and driving away before we had even taken all the escapees back to prison."

"Jesus."

"That night didn't help His popularity. Some people came back for the funerals, or stayed for them. Since then the churches have been practically empty on Sundays. The congregations are mostly gone."

"What's being done now?"

"Right now, we're doing basic police work. It's a federal prison, so the FBI is the lead agency. The state police are working on it, and we're working on it."

"What does 'working on it' mean?"

"I'm the senior officer of the Weldonville Police Department right now, since Chief Roberts was killed. But the department doesn't need much administration, and I'm a homicide cop. What I'm doing right now is investigating and collecting evidence. Most of the crime scene stuff is secondhand from the FBI labs, which are about the best. I want to connect every bit of DNA from each of the victims to the DNA of whatever prisoner raped or killed them. I want to know which prisoners burned a house, stole a car, or picked up a gun. And I want to know which of the guns were fired, by whom and at whom. And I'm compiling a collection of all the records any police agency anywhere has on each of the twelve men who were the real escapees."

Bill Halvorsen stared at the desk for a few seconds and nodded. He pointed at the pen and pad she had on the desk by her phone, and she nodded. He said, "I'm writing down my cell phone number, my mailing address, and my email. If the FBI and the others get tired of looking and give up, and you're ready to go after the men who killed Nick, I'll be available."

"You're not a cop, Bill."

He looked at her, his sharp brown eyes unmoving. "No," he said. "But I'm not offering to arrest anybody." He set the folded paper on her desk. "Thanks for telling me the truth, Hawk. I knew you would. Don't lose my information." He gave a sad smile. "Or maybe it doesn't matter. I'm sure you're good enough to find me without it if the time comes." He walked out the door.

She had seen him around town a number of times over the next two years. They had talked, but she had never called his number or told him what she had decided she would do if the twelve men weren't caught in two years.

Before she'd brought her suitcase out to the car, she had looked over the rest of the list of people who had volunteered to go after the missing killers. It had contained some names she had expected: Ray McClellan, the ATF agent who had come back to town to retire and worked a few nights a week bartending at the Parkman House because he liked the company; Marjorie Clay, whose family owned the hardware store but who had been working as a private investigator in Denver; and her business partner Kristen Green, who often served as bait in traps because she was strikingly beautiful. There had been some surprises, including a man named Kenneth Long, who had never been to Weldonville but whose ex-wife had been born there. She had moved back to town with their son and daughter and all three had been killed on July 19. He owned a security company in New York that she'd actually heard of. They provided protection for important people. She had torn up the list, put the pieces in her garbage disposal, and washed them away before she'd left. Taking those people along would have been a terrible waste. She had always been a great homicide cop. She didn't need anybody's help to commit a few murders.

7

The drive was over a hundred miles along Interstate 76, heading over low, flat plains that slowly rose in altitude until the Denver airport. It was late night now, and much of the other traffic on the interstate highway consisted of long-haul tractor trailers grinding along at a constant speed. There was no rain and not much wind, so the trucks would probably make good time and be able to get into safe spots where the driver could park and get some sleep, then drive the last few miles into Denver to unload. Leah would hold out until morning and sleep after the plane took off.

As she drove, she thought about the men she was hunting. She knew most of their lives by heart. All twelve of the men she was looking for were transfers from one or another of the 122 prisons in the federal system. They came over a period of about a year, most from different prisons, and none of them at exactly the same time.

She had compiled a great deal of information about these men from their prison records and their trial records and the joint FBI and police investigation of the July 19 prison break and the crimes they committed that night. Weldonville Penitentiary had supplied fingerprints, DNA, photographs, and medical records of the inmates. They'd kept track of the names and addresses of the people who wrote to them, accepted telephone calls from them, or visited them. If they committed infractions in prison, there were investigation records. The Justice Department's original trial records contained the names and testimony of witnesses, and she had paid special attention to defense witnesses. The police and FBI investigators had filed reports, including the names and addresses of everyone they'd interviewed. Leah had been collecting these things and studying them for two years.

The man she had selected as her first target was Albert Weiss, age thirty-seven. He had been convicted of federal kidnapping and hostage-taking charges five years before the prison break. He had actually committed the same crime twice before he was caught, and each time received a million dollars in ransom. He was caught only after his third attempt. At the time of his arrest he was suspected of conspiracy to commit murder but not charged because the actual killing of the kidnap victim occurred after he had been arrested. Evidence that he had planned the murder didn't meet the conspiracy standard. He was originally sent to Terminal Island in California, but after two and a half years he was moved to Weldonville to ease overcrowding.

Weiss had been the one to build the radio signal jammer and use it on July 19. DNA showed that at some point he was wearing the guard uniform of Harry Costa. The Costas were a big Weldonville family, the children of two brothers, each of whom had four or five kids. Harry was a son of the older brother. When the group of twelve inmates broke into the guards' locker room, Weiss changed into Costa's clothes. He took Costa's car keys and stole his car, but since the car hadn't been recovered and tested, there would probably never be any proof. He had done so much of a more serious nature that it didn't matter.

The FBI had pieced together what happened during the prison break using the fragmentary video from the surveillance cameras, witnesses from among the prisoners who didn't try to escape, and times when the electronic locks on doors and gates were opened and jammed. Albert Weiss was certainly a participant in the murder of Harry Costa, because he touched both Costa and the handles of the ligature used to strangle him. Costa's body was found wearing Al Weiss's prison jumpsuit and placed on the bed in his cell.

Weiss's prints and DNA were also present in Costa's house. Costa's eighty-one-year-old father was found unconscious from being beaten with a blunt object, and he died in the hospital a few hours later. Weiss had sexually assaulted and killed Costa's wife, Megan. Costa's car left town, heading south past the cameras on the Parkman House restaurant and the gas station at the Stillwell interstate entrance. No police agency had reported a sighting of Albert Weiss since then.

Leah wasn't sure, but she thought she saw in the mass of information about Weiss a vulnerability. When he first entered the prison system, he filled out a form listing the people he wanted to be allowed to visit him. On the list were his mother and five women who weren't relatives. The FBI had this information, interviewed each of these women a few times, and came to no conclusion. At first, the FBI had a thousand escaped prisoners to capture and investigate, charge and prosecute, so they were stretched thin, and even when the number was down to twelve, they had hundreds of other leads to follow.

In the investigation of Weiss's mother, the FBI learned she had never lived anywhere except Naples, Florida. The records showed Albert had lived a few other places for brief periods, but had always returned to Florida. His crimes had been committed in Florida. All five of the females on his list of visitors to the prison had provided addresses in Florida. Where was Albert Weiss likely to be after two years? She had a guess.

Al Weiss decided it was late enough at night to go out to get some air that hadn't been through an air conditioner. He had been born in Naples, and had always succeeded in staying on the Gulf side of Florida when he wasn't imprisoned. July had a daytime temperature of ninety-three and a nighttime temperature of seventy-four, which he had always thought of as right, and every other climate as wrong. July was also the rainiest month, with an average rainfall of over nine inches, but he didn't mind that either. It gave him an excuse for carrying his special umbrella. The steel tip was ground down to a point and covered by the end of the hollow steel shaft from an old umbrella that he'd fitted over it like a sheath. A six-inch spike was better than a gun to a fugitive because it was silent and nearly invisible.

He could feel the humidity building even as the breeze from the Gulf brought the cooler air in over the city. He knew that if Mother had been awake and aware that he was going out, she would have told him not to, and she would have been right, of course. The July rains could be torrential sometimes, and a man walking around in it was asking for attention. Weiss would stay out tonight at least until things got definitely wet. It was the only time he could go out for a walk. During the day, people were always watching and staring at everyone on the street. Walking around was risky.

He had excellent fake identification in the name of Michael Hooper, but if somebody recognized his face, having identification in another name was not enough to protect him. The cards he had for the purpose were more than two years old now, so he couldn't be sure they were so excellent anymore anyway. False identity cards should not be too fresh and unworn, bearing new starting dates and expirations far in the future. But they shouldn't be too old either. States changed the formats of their licenses, and credit companies modernized their logos, their safety features, and their designs. The photographs of the supposed driver that had been taken three or four years ago and had seemed fine two years ago could suddenly look ancient. Worst of all, the debit card accounts that had started with big deposits a couple of years ago could die from starvation. It didn't matter that the card was genuine if the genuine account was empty.

The reason Weiss had gone to a federal prison was that members of his crew had botched a kidnapping. He had already executed two perfect kidnappings and collected the ransoms, but the third had netted him nothing, and defending himself in court had cost a large portion of the money from the first two.

Weiss had begun to think about working again. He didn't have an immediate, desperate need for money, but the way money had been drained away from his savings in the past two years had alarmed him. He had been living almost entirely from his mother's accounts for a while, and that could not go on forever.

His walk wasn't one of the most scenic. He couldn't openly stroll along Fifth Avenue in Naples, a street filled with shops, restaurants, and bars. There was too much light, and too much life. He was hoping to go down to walk along the beach for a distance, as he sometimes had, but there had often been drunks and street people lurking down there, and he didn't want to have to stab a couple of them to get home. He also didn't want to be on the sand in the open when the ocean breeze brought the rain.

His kidnappings in the old days had been well planned. He had spent time out in the nightlife scene looking for rich people who weren't observant or well protected, and shopped for victims at real estate open houses, nice hotels, oceanfront bars, and even golf courses. When he had selected candidates, he had put in the time and effort to learn all about them: Who could be expected to pay a ransom for their lives? How much money would that be? Where did they live? Who else lived there, and what were the security features? It had gone on and on.

Now that he had been to prison, he couldn't do it that way anymore. If he wanted to get back into kidnapping, he would have to think much smaller and operate without his helpers, who had been unreliable anyway. He would have to do it all himself. That meant working by stealth and taking someone who was sure to be unarmed and unable to put up much of a fight. The best place to find someone like that would not be in bright sunshine by their pool or at their country club, or in the bright lights of the nightclubs or on the streets in front. It would be in the dark parking lots behind the buildings very late at night.

What he envisioned was a lone girl walking out to her car in a lot after an evening of heavy drinking. As he formulated the idea, he further defined the victim he was imagining. It would probably be a college girl. That was the age when a girl might be alone late at night and drunk. He could perform something like a screening process by walking in the lots behind bars and nightclubs, searching for a suitably expensive car that had been a present to a young single woman. It would be something small and a little bit sporty, but not hard to drive. It wouldn't be a Lamborghini or Ferrari. It would be something like a small Mercedes or BMW with an automatic transmission. It would be painted a light color. It probably would have a license plate holder or a window sticker with the name of a college. It might even have a vanity license plate that said something like PRINCESS or CUTIE. He could stay nearby, waiting to see who came to claim it, and simply take her away.

Other refinements began to occur to him as he walked. He could abduct her and not contact her family for a few days to give them the time to imagine terrible things were happening to her, or even longer, to persuade them that she might be dead. Then, when they heard her voice, they'd be delighted to pay whatever he asked. The circumstances would dictate whether he freed her or actually killed her, but that would be a decision for after he had squeezed them for money.

As he strolled beside the parking lots, he raised his eyes to the rear corners of the buildings that faced Fifth Avenue. Electronic devices had always been his special talent. He would use his skills to make the recordings from security cameras disappear, or maybe the opposite. He could take control of the system to send the security footage to the parents as proof that he had their little girl in his possession.

The first raindrops arrived with a slight increase of the wind, so he put up his umbrella and turned his steps toward his car. Probably he would kill the girl. That was always safest. But before he did, maybe he would take the pleasure of making the parents' bad dreams come true.

8

Leah Hawkins, like other cops, had spent years of her life doing surveillance, so she knew how to make the job easier. The apartment she had rented was on the Gulf shore side of Mrs. Alma Weiss's house, so the afternoon sun was behind her and not shining into her eyes. In the morning, from the back windows of the bedrooms, a person could see the Gulf of Mexico and the beach.

The beaches here were among Leah's favorites on the continent. Their white sand looked like sugar, with tall swaying palm trees along the margin. From this apartment house a person could simply stroll down the sidewalk for two blocks to the west, where the street ended in a narrow path through a stand of leafy trees. After no more than twenty feet on the shady path, she would emerge on the sand, looking out over the blue water at tiny, distant white clouds just above the horizon.

Leah had known that she would have to do much of her reconnaissance after dark. The person she was interested in was likely to be nocturnal, and the landscape of a town was often markedly different at night. In hot places, some buildings that during the day seemed unused and unoccupied had people coming in and out all night. Bars and restaurants that had few customers in daylight were teeming once the sun was down. Even in a prosperous residential city like Naples, there were sure to be places that reached full live-liness after midnight. The man Leah Hawkins was watching for knew that he was being hunted, and that it would never stop until he died. He had done too much, and committed the wrong kind of crimes, for the interest in him to end. He would be reluctant to show his face at any time, but particularly in daylight.

If he had to go out in daylight, he would drive rather than walk. He would try to stay off the busiest downtown streets, where the popular stores and restaurants were. He would be a man who used back entrances. He would favor additions like facial hair, sunglasses, and hats.

Weldonville Penitentiary was thousands of miles away, but Weiss would not be under the illusion that distances mattered to the people who were after him. He would be on his guard at all times, scanning for strangers who seemed too interested in him or seemed to have nothing to do but stare at passersby.

Some of the FBI agents had worried that Weiss might have altered his appearance with plastic surgery, but Leah Hawkins wasn't concerned. The techniques were all intended to correct injuries or flaws or make the subject's face look younger. And while the best practitioners could do those things well, they weren't able to make fundamental changes to the shape and metrics of a face. The eyes were the same distance apart, and no plastic surgeon seemed to add anything that didn't look added.

Leah was not worried that Albert Weiss would go to see his mother and Leah would fail to recognize his features. As a homicide detective, she had spent many hours studying faces, photographs, drawings, and reconstructions of faces to match them to murder-ers or victims. Her biggest concern was that she was planning to commit murder, which was something a decent person did alone rather than involving others. That meant she was limited to what one person could see, and to the number of hours one person could keep looking.

She had brought some devices from Colorado to help with her work. She had a box of pinhole cameras that could be operated on their own batteries or plugged into an AC outlet or a laptop USB outlet. They would transmit photographic images to her laptop computer or phone. At the end of her first day, she placed one of them above the curtain rod of her back window, aimed it at the back of Mrs. Weiss's house, and left it there. Then she got ready to go out to explore the streets of Naples in darkness.

She was aware that in many situations her height would make her stand out to a man like Weiss, who would be watching everyone. She was a head taller than most women and a forehead taller than many men, so she stayed away from the light and the people. She had rented a car at the airport, and she did much of her exploring by driving slowly along the main streets or parking to study the pedestrians. After the people went home, she drove around exploring the geography of the city.

When she went back to her apartment, she kept the lights off, ran through the recordings of Mrs. Weiss's house from her pinhole cameras, and went to sleep.

The next morning Leah Hawkins sat at the dining room table thinking about what a person would need in order to live in a city like this. He would need a supermarket, a pharmacy, a doctor, a dentist, a gas station, a barber. As the list grew, she began to write it down.

"A bank," she added. He'd been out for two years, and if he'd spent that time here, he would have a bank. She wondered if she could find a way to see the security footage of banks. The cameras in banks were the best. Anytime there was a robbery in a store, even part of a big chain or a store that sold cameras, the surveillance footage was crap. On the recordings from cameras over the tellers' windows, a cop could see whether the suspect had shaved recently. The problem was, if her attempt to get Weiss turned ugly, she didn't want to be on record as having asked institutions for help finding him.

* * *

Seven banking companies were listed online as having at least one branch in Naples. The first one that attracted her attention was part of a small corporation that had only nine branches, all in southern Florida. The branch in the center of town was large, probably the flagship. She took out a dozen pinhole cameras connected to transmitters. It took her several days to leave one camera aimed at the door nearest to each bank's parking lot.

Over a period of weeks, Leah acquired many hours of bank surveillance recordings and watched them at high speed whenever she had unoccupied time. Photographs of the twelve fugitives were taped to the wall by the computer, on the theory that if one of the twelve was here, others might be too.

When she had tired of looking at the mother's house, she explored the possibility that Albert Weiss had a house of his own. Naples had a population of about 21,500, with a median age of 65.2 years. Among them, 94.2 percent were Caucasian, 90 percent spoke English, 85 percent were born outside Florida, and 80 percent owned their houses. The best neighborhoods were mostly along the shore. The Old Naples neighborhood, where Weiss's mother lived, was home to about four thousand people. Leah walked the district once a day. The first day she walked beginning at dawn, and each day she made her walk an hour later. She also drove the district for about two hours a day, going up and down streets in roughly a circular pattern with the Weiss house at the center. If Albert Weiss had come back here to be near his mother, then near his mother's house was where to look for his place.

Late one night she installed a pinhole surveillance camera high on the trunk of a tree across the street from Mrs. Weiss's house, and a second on a tree in the house's backyard. Her career had taught her patience. If the batteries began to wear out, she planned to go around again and change the batteries on all the cameras.

As Leah walked and drove and watched, she worked on identifying the occupants of each house in the Old Naples neighborhood. Some had names on their mailboxes, and others received mail with addresses that could be read through a slot or on a package that was left in front. She would simply photograph with her phone anything she found and then look at it closely later.

Whenever she saw a man from a distance who appeared to fit Weiss's general description, she followed him until she could eliminate him as a possibility. Leah had formed the theory that Weiss did not have a job, or he would already have been found by one of the various police organizations that had been looking. He was more likely to have a fake profession of some kind so he could pay himself a salary out of a secret cache of money from his days as a kidnapper.

His record showed no periods of employment before he was caught, tried, and convicted of kidnapping. Since it was hard to imagine anyone who hadn't had a source of income before age thirty, when he'd gone into kidnapping, he had probably committed a few crimes before then and hidden those proceeds too.

Leah was out most of every day and night looking for different places where a thirty-seven-year-old career criminal and occasional murderer might be found, and spent the rest running through recordings looking at perfectly normal scenes of life in a nice Florida community. There were times when she felt like a stubborn ornithologist waiting in the long-deserted habitat of a bird that the science world was almost certain was extinct. Then one day there was a possible sighting.

9

At first Leah couldn't be sure. All she had was an image from one of the cameras she had placed in front of a bank, a man pushing the door open, stepping outside onto the pavement, and walking across the facade toward the corner of the building and out of frame. As soon as she spotted him, she stopped the playback and held him there. To her, he looked like Albert Weiss, but he probably wasn't Weiss. Then, as she considered the question, she realized the only reason he seemed unlikely to be Weiss was that he had appeared on one of the cameras she had planted precisely to find Weiss. What if it was Weiss? This could be her only sighting.

She ran the sequence again and again, and compared the face on the screen with the pictures she had stored on her laptop. He looked like Weiss, but Weiss wasn't unusual-looking. She froze him again. She took a piece of paper and a pencil and looked at him as he came out of the building. He was leaning forward slightly, his right arm extended to push the glass door open. She drew his exact stance and counted the rows of bricks of the bank wall from his feet to his head. She estimated the distance from the top of the door to the top of his head. She noted that the length of his step was roughly one and a half per block of pavement.

She could see from the side that he had a widow's peak. She looked at the profile pictures in her computer file and measured how far the side hair had receded as about two inches. She translated the sight into a proportion of his head from forehead to back—about one-fifth. The proportion for the man on the recording was about one-fifth also. She got into her car, parked off Fifth Avenue, and went for a walk. As she passed the bank door, she took a phone picture of her own reflection in the glass and kept going.

When she got home, she used her own height to tell her the height of the door and used that to give her an estimate of the man's height. She put it at almost exactly five feet eleven inches. His slim body and his hair matched Weiss's. She spent another half hour finding, stopping, and enlarging the man's profile. She compared the profile with the profiles on Weiss's mug shots.

These operations required trying to copy the shape of the face with her pencil and paper, and while she was doing this, her recording was running. Other pedestrians walked past the bank's doors; some went inside and others didn't. Traffic on the street in front of the building was moving slowly, and when the traffic signal somewhere to the left turned red, the cars stopped and waited. When she had finished her comparison of the chin and nose shapes and positions, she looked at the screen. The cars had stopped again, and the man she could see in the lane headed from the right side of the screen to the left was the same one. She paused and held him there.

He must have retrieved his car from the back of the bank and now he was leaving. She let his car inch forward and then expanded the image. The logo in the center of the trunk was a horizontal winged oval. She couldn't make much of that, but the number to the right of it was 300. He was driving a blue Chrysler 300 sedan.

She still couldn't be positive that the man was Albert Weiss. He was Weiss's age and size, had a profile that looked like Weiss's, and had similar hair. As she strained her eyes to see better, she realized that the car seemed familiar. It was dark blue and very shiny. The more she looked at it, the more she felt the familiarity.

Leah pulled up the many hours of recordings she had made at Alma Weiss's house. For weeks she had gone quickly through each day's recordings and determined that nobody visited Alma Weiss. Nobody ever pulled a car into her driveway, never drove into her garage. But then she saw the blue car. Somebody had driven it past the house not once but a number of times. Each time Leah saw it, she checked the time and date of the recording and wrote it down. Sometimes after the car went past, it parked. It was never parked in front of the house or beside the house. Sometimes it would pass and then reappear on the street behind the house.

Leah saw no pattern for the timing of the car's appearances, and she never saw anyone approach the house on foot. But the coincidence of the man's resemblance to Weiss and the reappearances of the car were enough. Albert Weiss was hiding in or near Naples, and he had, at least occasionally, been near his mother's house.

It was night, time for Leah to visit her too. Leah surveyed her belongings, laying them out on the bed. There was a compact burglary kit that she had put together from things she'd learned arresting burglars—a pick and tension wrench, a set of bump keys, a very sharp folding knife made of tough 440 steel, and a pry bar. She had a small, powerful flashlight that could be mounted under the receiver of her service pistol.

She also had a second Glock 17 pistol that had been fitted with a silencer and drilled to remove the serial number. It had been confiscated during an arrest at a motel off the interstate during Chief Roberts's time. For some reason it had not been destroyed after the trial. Leah had looked at the transcripts and the evidence paperwork and discovered that the gun was listed as having been destroyed eight years ago, but there it was in the evidence room. She had left it there until a few months ago. Then she had taken it out, cleaned it, fired it at the range, and then cleaned it again and put it away.

She had placed it in the metal carrying case where she kept her own service weapon and flown with it, listing it with the serial number of the spare Glock she kept at home. Tonight she removed it from the case, loaded it, took out the silencer that went with it, and brought them with her when she walked up the street to the house.

Leah Hawkins walked quietly around the side of the house, looking for the best way in. As she came around the house, Leah saw something that might help. This was Florida, so the backyard pool was inside a screened enclosure to keep the area free of pests and leaves.

She knelt at the edge of the screen, studied it, and peered through it at the house. The pool was meant to be entered directly from inside the house, as if it were another room. The entrance to the pool from the house was through a sliding glass door that was closed.

She opened her folding knife, cut an opening at the lower edge of the screen, extended the slice about three feet, and then crawled through the opening. She moved quickly to the sliding door and tried opening it, but it was locked. She inserted the knife blade into the space between the door and the jamb. She wiggled it and forced it upward a couple of inches to the hooklike latch that dropped over a bar. She pounded the knife upward with her other hand and it moved. She hit it again and the latch unhooked.

She slowly opened the door, slipped inside, turned on her flashlight, and walked quietly toward the front of the house, scanning the space ahead of her. She stopped at the edge of the living room, where she had a clear view of much of the first floor.

Leah remained still and listened. She couldn't detect any sound. There were no lights anywhere, not even the faint glow of a low-voltage nightlight from a bathroom, the kind some elderly people used to prevent falling. She went up the stairs to the second floor.

At the end of the hall, where a master bedroom might be, she saw a bedroom with the door closed. She stopped, went low, turned the knob, and then pushed the door inward. The room was what she had expected. There was a four-poster queen bed with a thin white fabric canopy, a duvet with lace around the edges, and a few big decorative pillows. Nobody was sleeping there, and she could not imagine anyone had in some time. There was a distinct old-lady smell that was a combination of stale perfume, cold cream, and maybe a hint of Vicks VapoRub, but the accumulated scents seemed to be mixed with dust.

Now that she was up on the second floor, Leah was more aware than before that the house was hot. The lower floor had been a bit warm, but up here the sensation was much stronger. The warm air had collected on the upper level, and all day the intense, unmediated sunshine had burned onto the roof, and the heat hadn't had time to disperse. She didn't feel or hear air-conditioning, and there were no fans running to at least move the air around.

Leah had already formed a theory about the house. She moved from room to room verifying it. Three of the four bedrooms had beds in them. One held another queen bed that was made up and looked as though it had been slept in recently and remade. She bent and sniffed the sheets and pillow without touching them. It was a male smell. Someone might have been here a week or two ago, since she had come.

Leah went directly down the stairs and looked in the kitchen. It was marginally clean, but nobody seemed to have used it today. She felt the sink and drains, and they were dry.

As soon as she opened the refrigerator, she knew. There was beer—eight bottles—but little actual food. There was cheddar cheese and some olives. In the freezer were ice trays and a bottle of vodka. She unlocked the door and went outside. She used her folding knife to jimmy the small side door of the garage.

It was a two-car garage with a car parked on one side, but it wasn't the blue Chrysler 300. It was a ten-year-old Toyota Corolla. On the far side of it was a row of stacked and tied newspapers, and on the top of them was a long bundle made of something wrapped in a tarp, with a couple of other tarps folded on top of it.

Leah had no doubt, no hesitation. She went right to the bundle. It might have been because she had been a homicide detective for more than ten years, and had gone to look at so many victims, especially when she had worked at the Colorado Bureau of Investigation. This one was way past the worst stages, and had moved into the realm of archaeology, but Leah's nose was sensitive to a remaining hint of the distinctive smell.

The woman had been old, a small person, about five feet three and quite thin. Leah could tell from the fit of the woman's tracksuit that she had probably weighed about a hundred pounds or less at the time of her death. The usual decomposition process had completed itself a long time ago, probably a year or more. She was now mostly desiccated, dried and leathery. Leah looked closely at the visible parts, the fabric of the tracksuit and sneakers, and decided the woman probably had died a natural death.

She rewrapped the body and went back inside the house. She climbed the stairs back to the man's room. It looked to her as though Weiss must be using the room only occasionally, or only for short periods. A few pieces of clothing were in the closet—jeans, a stack of folded T-shirts, underwear, socks in a cardboard box. She went into the next room, which shared a wall with the man's room. It was smaller and nearly square. But something very odd had been done to the room. All four walls, the floor, and the ceiling had been altered.

She took out her flashlight and went over the place. There were no windows, but there was still a closet. All the room's walls and the floor had been covered with particleboard sheeting, and it gave a bit when she walked on it. She pushed on the wall, and it moved inward a little too. She went to the side where the edge of the false wall was visible and saw under the particle board a layer of insulation almost three inches thick. There was a small bed made of steel with a single mattress on it, like one of the two components of a bunk in a barracks. Everything was clear. There was no possible misinterpretation. The walls, floor, and ceiling had been remodeled to be soundproof. The insulation and sheeting had also covered the windows. She examined the things she could see, and then she walked to the closet and opened it.

Inside the closet was an unopened cardboard box that contained a portable toilet for camping. There was also a plastic water pitcher and some cups that looked as though they'd come from a hospital-supply store. Draped over the clothes rod at the top of the closet were lengths of thick, silvery chains, and clicked onto them to keep them neat and easily stored were padlocks with the keys still in them. Hanging on the pole beside them were two pairs of hand-cuffs. Other odds and ends were on the shelf and on the floor—rolls of duct tape and a few boxes of electronic gear, including a set of six closed-circuit television cameras with mountings and a couple of reels of coaxial cable.

After about five years in prison and two years of living with first his mother and then apparently with the remains of his mother, Albert Weiss was once again preparing to go into the kidnapping business. As she glanced around her, she realized that he was just about ready. The bed, the chains, the soundproofing were all set. The reels of cable had been used and snipped at the ends with a wire cutter, so he had undoubtedly run the cable for the surveil-lance cameras under the wall surfaces or ceilings. All he had to do was mount the cameras and then monitor them remotely with a mobile phone or a computer.

And then she had a feeling that was either instinct or a new sense of Weiss's pace. He was out right now searching for the person who would be chained in this small, windowless scream-proof room while he waited to collect the ransom.

Leah went down the stairs, out of the house, and walked down the street to her apartment. She got into her rental car and began to drive. She had not seen anything that would tell her exactly where Weiss was doing his hunting, but she knew that she had to try to find him right now. He could not go out in the daytime to overpower and kidnap some rich businessman. He was a fugitive. She had been looking for him full-time for weeks and had never caught sight of him until the footage at the bank. It was probably because he seldom needed to go out during the day. He would want to take his victim at night.

10

As she drove, she let her cop instincts begin to take over. Part of being a good homicide detective was putting herself into the mind of a suspect. This time she had to look at the world as a collection of places that were mostly dangerous for a killer and others that were crowded with possible victims. Right now, Weiss wouldn't be wasting his time in the dangerous places where there were too many witnesses. He would be in the ones where the hunting was easy.

She drove to the beach, parked, and then walked, trying to see every person who passed within range of her eyes. Weiss hadn't been doing any kidnapping here since he'd been out. Any crime of that sort would have come up during her research and in the FBI reports. In the old days he had worked with two accomplices, and then with three. But his dungeon for kidnapping was new. He hadn't even completed the finishing touches. He hadn't taken anyone yet, and she'd seen nothing in his preparations that implied more people would be involved when he did.

He was alone, and he was planning a kidnapping that he could do alone. She felt sure that he was going for the easiest kind of kidnapping—a child or a young woman. She walked along the beach and looked. It was too late for children to be playing, or for their parents to be distracted so Weiss could snatch one. There were four young people, two couples who were probably on a date, strolling along and enjoying the cool air and the beauty of the night and the ocean. She sat and watched. It was too late even for them to be out on the beach. They veered toward the place where the beach rose up to street level and disappeared.

Leah was alone again. She stood and brushed the sand off the back of her pants, went up through the trees to the street, and got into her rental car. She drove along the streets from Twelfth Avenue to Fifth searching for places where she might have lain in wait if she were a kidnapper. As she looked and thought about Weiss, it occurred to her that the trick was like being a spider. He would be in the darkest spot he could find, watching the edible creatures moving around in the lighted spaces until he found one that was alone and off guard.

She kept driving, studying the clubs and restaurants that were still open, and then scanning the curbs and parking lots for the blue Chrysler 300. She parked her rental car among the other cars in each lot, waiting for him in each place while she studied the people coming out of each establishment. Most of the restaurants stopped serving food at ten or eleven o'clock, and the people who stayed to drink and talk tended to be members of celebrations—engagements, birthdays, anniversaries. They were well dressed and mostly happy, and few had obvious signs of inebriation.

The places that were still crowded at this hour were something else. The younger the crowd, the later they stayed and the more they drank. The bars stopped serving at 2:00 a.m., and at the ones she thought were most promising, a last burst of liveliness began around 1:00.

What she was looking for was not somebody who left with friends at 2:00. The person Leah was watching for was not going to be in a crowd. It would be a girl. She would be alone. She would be somebody who probably didn't have much experience in navigating her way along the far border between tipsy and hammered and had pushed it too far. That meant she was probably going to be on the younger side, either just twenty-one or carrying false identification that said she was. She would be the one who was left behind.

The car that caught Leah's eye was not the Chrysler 300. It was an Audi convertible. It was white with a tan leather interior and a tan canvas top that was folded down at the moment. To Leah, the open top meant that it hadn't been driven until after sundown, because the sun today had been too harsh for an open top. But leaving the top down in this parking lot hinted to Leah that the person was not thinking clearly. Rains here tended to come with no warning whenever the right cloud passed overhead.

Leah's headlights were reflected back by a sparkly frame around the rear license plate. She drove a little closer and saw something that was a familiar sight to cops late at night. There was a pool of liquid on the pavement beside the driver's door. Most of the time that meant a drink had been poured out, either from a glass or from the driver's stomach.

Leah turned off her headlights and kept her distance while she studied the rest of the lot. She was sure that if she walked over there, she would find a young woman lying in the car, slumped over, her butt in the driver's seat and her head and shoulders on the passenger seat, just the way she'd been since she passed out. Leah craned her neck and straightened her long legs to raise her body so she could see the car better. From a foot higher, she could see down into the convertible. Between the bucket seats of the convertible she could see a part of the girl's back in exactly the position Leah had expected. Leah slid back down and stayed there.

Her cop's mind began to work on the situation. She couldn't very well drive away and leave this girl lying there. People, particularly small people, sometimes died of alcohol overdoses. And she could easily choke to death. Even sleeping off her intoxication unprotected in a convertible in a dark lot was dangerous. There were sure to be other men besides Albert Weiss in town who would be glad to find a girl unconscious and alone late at night.

But Leah was torn. It was just after closing time, precisely the perfect time to find drunken potential victims. If she left the girl here, she could drive from lot to lot for another fifteen or twenty minutes, scan fifteen more establishments, and maybe spot the Chrysler 300. It was possible she could even get Weiss tonight.

No, she knew. It wasn't even a decision. Leah would have to get Weiss some other way, some other time. Having discovered this stupid girl, she could not undiscover her. Leah would have to get her to safety and then see what was left of the night. She pulled her car around the corner of the nearest building and parked on the street so the girl wouldn't see instantly that her car wasn't a police model. She got out of her car and opened the trunk. She had put a towel and bathing suit in there a few days ago, planning to spend time on the beach watching for Weiss. All she knew right now was that she was probably going to need the towel. She picked it up, closed the trunk, clicked the lock on the doors, and began to walk around her car in the direction of the Audi.

She stayed in the dark, shadowed area where she was difficult to see. She didn't want to have a local police cruiser enter the lot and stop so the cops could ask her questions, and she didn't want to have bystanders watching her attend to the girl and get a good look at her. She walked about halfway to the Audi, heard a car door shut, and then saw another shape moving along on foot from the other direction. Leah stopped and stood beside a parked van, so her silhouette dissolved into its shadowy side.

The man was walking along quietly but not slowly. He was definitely heading toward the Audi. Her eyes found him in the dim glow of light from the cloudy sky. She held her breath. It could be. He was about the right height and the right build. He was wearing a baseball cap tonight, so she couldn't see the receding hairline if it was there. The bill of the cap came down from his brow so she couldn't make out much of his face either.

Leah reached into her jacket pocket and extracted the pistol that had been drilled to remove serial numbers. She screwed the silencer onto the threaded barrel. Then she placed the towel over it and began to move.

The man was walking faster. Then, suddenly, he heard the sound of a car engine, louder than most, come up the alley toward the lot. He stopped, and Leah stopped. For a full second, then another, the man remained frozen in place, listening. Leah heard the car turn and pass out a driveway between buildings and onto the street in front.

The man began to move again. Leah let him get a few more steps and calm himself down before she walked too. She reached under the towel and grasped the slide, then pulled to cycle it and put a round in the chamber.

She saw the man stop at the passenger side of the Audi. He leaned over the girl and craned his neck to see her face. Leah still couldn't be sure it was Weiss, but she was sure she wasn't going to let this man take the girl. As the man walked around the back of the convertible to reach the driver's side, Leah began to run.

The man looked up and saw her, then stopped in place. His face contracted into an imitation of a sincere smile. "Oh, good," he said. "I'm so glad you came along. This girl seems to need help. Do you think you could give me a hand with her?"

Leah kept going until she was about fifteen feet from him, which was when she was sure. This man was Albert Weiss. She stopped and said, "What's wrong with her?"

"I don't know for sure. I think it's probably alcohol. If you can help me get her into my car, I'll drive her to the hospital and they'll check her out." While he was chattering, he reached in and got his hands under her arms, then lifted her.

"Don't move her."

"I'm pretty experienced with these things," he said as he raised the girl to a vertical position.

"Put her down."

He lifted the girl, holding her in front of him like a doll. One arm was across her body, and the other arm was under her neck. He began to walk backward toward his car, holding her up between them. "What are you talking about? You can't leave an unconscious person lying there where her own vomit will block her airway."

Leah let the towel drop from the silencer and aimed the pistol. "Put the girl down, Mr. Weiss."

His eyes widened, and then narrowed. "Are you willing to shoot me?"

"Of course I am."

"I can break her neck, kill her before you can—"

Leah fired, and the bullet went through Weiss's forehead. He fell, his muscles limp, his limbs instantly deprived of strength. "Stupid," she muttered. Any cop in the country would have taken the shot, and a criminal like him should have known it. Cops were all trained to take the shot, never to let the hostage taker decide.

Leah stared at the scene for a moment as she made some decisions. While she walked toward Weiss, she removed the silencer and put it and the gun in her jacket. She lifted the girl off Weiss's body and carried her to her own rental car. She laid the girl across the back seat and then rolled the towel and put it under her head like a pillow.

She moved to Weiss's body and patted it down to find his keys, then got into his car and drove it close to Weiss's body. She opened the trunk, strained to hoist the upper part of Weiss's body into it, then pushed the legs in, closed the trunk, and parked the car back in its spot.

As she walked past the girl's car, she picked her purse off the seat, took it to her rental car, then opened the wallet to find the license.

She used the map on her phone to get directions to the address on the license, then drove the girl to her house.

The house was a sprawling single-story building at the end of a curved drive. She opened the back door of her car, lifted the girl, and walked with her to the front lawn. She placed the girl on the grass a few feet from the front steps with her head still propped up, rang the doorbell until she saw a light come on, got into her rental car, and drove back to her apartment.

She parked in the carport, walked along the alleys back to the lot where she had left the Chrysler 300 with Weiss's body in the trunk, and cautiously studied the area from the street. She saw no signs of cops. She could see that two buildings in the alley had surveillance cameras, but their servo controls had aimed them up at the sky. That had to be Weiss's work. She got into the Chrysler 300, drove it to Alma Weiss's house, put it into the garage beside the old Toyota, and closed the door. She walked around the outside of the house to the back.

She entered through the slit in the pool screen and the sliding door into the living room and began to search. The prison break at Weldonville had been one of the most carefully rehearsed crimes she had ever seen. Was it possible that they had all simply turned their backs on the others that night and driven in twelve different directions, never been in contact with each other again, and all successfully avoided a national manhunt?

She put on her surgical gloves and began to look for anything that might give her a lead on any of the other escapees. She looked for phone numbers, addresses, computers, thumb drives or discs, or anything else that might hold a list. She had searched a thousand homes in her career, and she looked everywhere in this one. This was going to be her last visit to this house. She whispered to herself, "Find it now or it doesn't get found."

There were hardly any books in the house. There was Alma Weiss's old family Bible, but it had no marks in it other than the print and a register of births, and nothing was stuck between the pages. There was also an old photograph album that started with Alma's parents and ended when Albert Weiss was about thirteen. Leah looked behind each photograph to see if anything was written in the book or on the backs of photos.

She found a den with a desk in it, and among the papers found the answers to questions she had no interest in asking anymore. Albert Weiss had been living for most of the past two years by using Alma Weiss's checking account to pay the bills. At some point she had died, but he had never notified anybody. Her social security and pension payments kept appearing electronically in her account, and he kept writing checks in her name to pay bills. When he ran out of checks, the bank sent more. The reason he had begun to think about returning to kidnapping must have been that the payments hadn't been enough. He had nearly finished depleting her savings and soon would have been living month to month.

Leah found nothing that could be a list of the names, phone numbers, or addresses. But she did find something that Weiss had left in the closet of his new dungeon upstairs. It was a list of tasks to accomplish in preparation for his return to kidnapping. On his list were things to buy: "gloves, insulation, soundproofing, cameras, cable, chains, duct tape, hats, glasses." There were also reminders: "Get cash from bank, keep tank full, Buffalo ID, burner phones."

She had what she had hoped for. Even if she was wrong, the time she had allotted to searching was gone. She was done. She had to get moving before first light. As she walked back to her apartment just before 5:00 a.m., it started to rain. In ten minutes, the town was in the midst of a full-fledged rainstorm. Leah was glad. The rain would wash away the pool of Albert Weiss's blood in the parking lot.

11

Leah made a reservation for a late-afternoon flight from Tampa to Buffalo, New York. While she waited, she cleaned her small apartment, throwing into trash bags anything that she didn't expect to need again. She vacuumed the floors and emptied the dirt into the trash bags too. She packed her suitcase as she cleaned. She wiped off every doorknob, every faucet, every light switch, every flat surface. She poured drain cleaner in every drain and ran hot water afterward to be sure every hair was altered and sent to the local water treatment plant. She washed the sheets, pillowcases, towels, washcloths, and cleaning rags, folded them, and put them in the linen cupboard. When she had finished, she locked the door and left the key and a note in the rental office mailbox saying that she'd been called away and that she understood she had to forfeit the rest of her rent for the month.

She drove to Tampa, returned her rental car, and waited for her flight to Buffalo. While she waited, she thought about her decision to go to Buffalo. To most people, Albert Weiss's to-do list would have seemed insane. But Leah had seen these lists before. All homicide cops had seen them. Many killers would write them out in the days before a murder, and sometimes she had wondered whether any of them had seen the grim humor in them. They would actually write down a list that read, "Duct tape, hunting knife, sharpener, hacksaw, chlorine bleach, spade, three bags of lye, plastic tarp," and sometimes even include "gun, ammunition." They would leave the list lying around their houses or in their cars, often with the receipts for these items.

When Weiss left his list, he hadn't been quite as stupid as some of the others. He had known that if anybody got that far in a search of his mother's house, they would find a trove of incriminating evidence, including his mother's body. But he was long past worrying about evidence. There had never been a question about his guilt. The only issue had been finding him. But the list was important to Leah. An entry with "ID" and "Buffalo" told her where to look for Viktor Panko.

Viktor Panko was another of the twelve. At the time of his federal arrest and conviction, he had been living and operating a business in Chicago. At first, he had been arrested for credit card fraud, because he had been caught selling counterfeit credit cards—mainly to fugitives who were actively being sought for crimes. The first sign that he was more came when the investigators discovered that many of the cards were printed with the names of real people. Then they discovered that several of those real people were dead, and their deaths had not yet been reported. By the time of his trial, there were enough fraud, forgery, and counterfeiting charges to send him away for just over forty years, with some expectation that he might later be charged with a few of the murders.

Leah had spent many hours going over the records of each of the twelve men, and she had been intrigued by some of the facts about Viktor Panko. He had been selling very high-end pieces of identification, including driver's licenses, credit cards, key cards, and picture identification cards to gain admission to businesses. There were many exhibits at trial, including each of these kinds of fakes. But the authorities never found the factory or shop where these things had been made. They had raided the homes and businesses of people all over Chicago, eventually interrogating anyone who had any known connection with Panko, but had never found any equipment, blank cards, or anything connected with the counterfeiting. He'd had fake IDs and sold them, but the rest of the logistics remained a mystery.

It was one of the things that Leah had wondered about. She had noticed when reading his file that Panko's roots in Chicago weren't very deep. He had known a few other people who sold things that were illegal, a few shady lawyers, a few customers who were eventually caught for things they'd done. He had no relatives in Chicago, and nobody who seemed to be a friend, particularly any women friends. All his relatives seemed to live in the place where he had been born and raised—Buffalo, New York.

Some interviews had been added to Panko's FBI file after the escape. Prisoners said that during his incarceration he had made a business out of offering inmates who had served their time a chance to buy new identities they could use in the free world. If it was true, his identity card and forgery workshop had not shut down just because he was imprisoned. Maybe the reason the FBI never found it was that it wasn't anywhere near Chicago, the place where he had been caught. Maybe it had been in Buffalo, the city where he had grown up and where he had connections that meant something. All she had was Weiss's notation "Buffalo ID," but if her theory was correct, Buffalo was where one of the twelve would go for a new fake ID. If so, Buffalo was where Viktor Panko was most likely to be.

Leah reviewed Viktor Panko's history in her mind. In the course of the prison break he killed a guard named Mike Forest, put on his clothes and stole his car, then drove it to his house, robbed the place, raped his wife, Debbie Forest, who was a teacher in the elementary school, and left her there tied up for the next wave of escapees to find. Panko hadn't been the escapee she had planned to go after next, but he would do.

12

Buffalo Niagara International Airport was not a giant hub. Leah was relieved not to be jostled by crowds. She could stand straight and take full, long-legged steps on the concourse and take the stairs down to the baggage claim without feeling like she had to step around anybody. She noticed a sign that said, "BUFFALO, THE CITY OF GOOD NEIGHBORS," and thought, "Show me the bad neighbors." She picked up her suitcase and walked to the car rental.

She drove to downtown Buffalo and checked into a Hyatt hotel for two nights. She didn't know what part of town she was going to have to explore, and the hotel seemed to be in the middle of things. There was also the fact that being in a big, upscale hotel provided a certain amount of safety and anonymity while she prowled around a new city.

That night Leah used the throwaway cell phone she'd brought from Colorado to make its only call. She dialed the number of Molly Walker, whose daughter Megan had been the wife of the guard Henry Costa. After Albert Weiss had killed Costa at the prison and Costa's father at home, he had killed Megan too. Leah said to her, "I wanted to tell you that Albert Weiss has been shot to death in Florida. The FBI doesn't know about it yet, but you deserve to know that Weiss isn't out there somewhere. He's dead."

When the call was over, she took apart the phone, went for a walk, and threw away the pieces. Before she went to bed, she put her next burner cell phone into service and tried directory assistance to find phone numbers for the Panko family, but wasn't surprised when none were listed. Fewer and fewer people had listed numbers.

Leah spent most of the next morning reviewing Viktor Panko's criminal record, trial record, photographs, and other information that she had assembled during the two years since the prison break—newspaper articles from the *Chicago Tribune* and the wire services, confidential memos that the FBI investigators had written to share information with other police agencies, and television news footage from Panko's trial.

Panko was shown during his perp walk with the FBI when he was arrested, and then walking in and out of the courthouse with his attorneys over the length of his trial. Leah studied the way he walked and refreshed her memory of the way his face looked during the movements of speech and how it looked reacting to the sights around him. There was even a bit of voice recording when he said, "No comment," and when he pushed through the reporters saying, "Excuse me, excuse me."

The files said that Viktor Panko, father of the criminal, had emigrated from Hungary in the early 1950s and came to Buffalo to join some cousins, who had vouched for him. The file said that Viktor junior had some knowledge of the Hungarian language. In Leah's experience, language was a huge indicator of ties to a culture. She searched for Hungarian clubs or festivals. The list was thin, so she decided to start looking for him in restaurants that served Hungarian dishes. She had sometimes observed that men who had spent extended time eating prison food were eager for the food that they had grown up eating. They particularly seemed to be drawn to food that had some spice or distinctive seasoning, because prison food was bland. She looked up restaurants that advertised Hungarian food and came up with a few restaurants that offered it—the Black Sheep in Buffalo, and the Black Forest in Amherst, and the Red Chateau across the bridge in Niagara Falls, Canada. She had no idea why the names all had a color, but it didn't matter.

Leah decided to start with the Red Chateau. Like most police officers, Leah didn't mind a long drive. She drove over the South Grand Island Bridge, across the island to the North Grand Island bridge, over the Rainbow Bridge, and into Niagara Falls, Ontario, where she gave her passport to the Canadian customs officer, got it back, and drove on.

The restaurant was in a small red house from the 1850s on Main Street in Niagara Falls, and it served a selection of Middle and Eastern European food. There were groups and couples she guessed were probably from both sides of the border, all of them unthreatening and, to Leah, disappointing. Leah had been hoping that Panko would love a place on the Canadian side, where he wouldn't run into American law enforcement people. The food was good, but the hunting was bad. She showed her waiter a picture of Viktor on her phone and said he'd recommended the place to her, but there was no recognition in his eyes. "I can't remember seeing him," he said. She showed him a couple of photographs of friends, just so he wouldn't remember her as asking after this one man.

Leah made similar visits to the other restaurants in the area that advertised Hungarian food, but didn't see Panko or find any waiters or waitresses who recognized him from the pictures on her phone. There was no progress, which was a situation she had long ago learned to reinterpret as cops did. Every search that came up empty eliminated a place or an approach or a person. She wasn't wasting her time; she was making a list of places where he was not.

She switched her search to one of her other favorite hunting grounds—churches. Colleagues had sometimes been surprised when Leah turned her attention to churches to find fugitives.

She remembered one of her early cases at the Colorado Bureau of Investigation. When the lead detective Bill Jansen had asked what she thought would be a good way to find a suspect named Mike Decker, who was believed to have arrived in Denver a week or two earlier.

She said, "Tomorrow I'll start hitting churches—young people's discussion groups, confession, church choirs, whatever there is."

Jansen had smirked. "You think a man like Mike Decker is going to be hanging out at church?"

"He is if he wants to get laid." Her smile was angelic. "It's an easy place to meet people."

"Oh, of course—yes," Jansen muttered.

"I can see you've been inspired by the divine spirit yourself," Leah said.

"Shut up," he said. "Just don't wait too long to call if you need backup. And take somebody with you."

She had recruited an attractive young detective named Julie Musgrave to go with her to several churches, and they had found him in a couple of days.

Leah knew that the majority of Hungarian families were Roman Catholic, but that a sizable minority were Calvinists or Lutherans, so she tried some congregations of all three in the southeastern part of the city where Panko's parents had lived and he had grown up. She started by looking at bulletins that were left in the vestibules after church each Sunday. They often contained schedules of events with the names of people to contact to participate. There were lists of people who were hospitalized and could use a visit or a prayer, and names of people who had died recently. There were names of choral directors and organists, and sometimes whole choirs. None of the churches she tried had any Pankos listed. The bulletin boards in church buildings were often useful, but there were no Pankos there either. She went to a few weeknight events at each church, talked to people, and showed her picture of Viktor, always pretending not to know his name. Sometimes she said he was a man she'd met but had erased his information on her phone, or a man who had given her a ride from a party and had accidentally driven off with her keys or glasses.

Between her church expeditions, Leah followed other lines of inquiry. She searched the county records for houses or apartment buildings owned by Pankos in Erie County. Viktor's parents had died early in his incarceration, and their house had been sold by his siblings. She wanted to see if one of them had rental property and let him live there under a false name.

Leah moved from hotel to hotel in downtown Buffalo. She still had trouble getting herself to sleep each night. She couldn't help thinking, retracing things that had happened and how they could have worked out differently, how the relentless inevitability of the steps of the disaster could have been derailed and the death of the city of Weldonville could have been stopped. Two years after July 19, her night thoughts were still about that.

It was as though time had been shunted down a different tunnel on July 19 at 11:52 p.m., when two inmates lifted and held inmate James Holliman, the former electrician, up to the surveillance camera wiring box in Cellblock C and two other inmates started fighting. He watched them for just a few seconds and then disconnected the cameras. The moment that happened, the rest of it was all going to follow.

The trouble squad of guards was going to come to investigate. The twelve escape planners were going to get loose inside the prison. More guards were going to die, and the prison was going to open up and spill over a thousand angry, half-crazy men out onto the road to Weldonville, some armed and others not yet armed but determined to be.

The plan was like a piece of machinery designed so that each step happened in order. It had been formulated and then spread to every one of the inmates needed to execute the steps. Over the past two years Leah had watched hundreds of hours of prison surveillance recordings, some of them dated as much as six months before July, in early January. There were recordings of inmates rehearsing their roles in the prison break as they went about their daily routines. Three men would simultaneously converge on a spot from three different directions and recite what they were going to do to subdue a guard in approximately that spot and hold him still for the fourth man, the strangler. Sometimes there were gestures, slight arm motions and half turns to practice the movements. Then they would part without looking back.

She had seen a few sequences of men in the exercise yard demonstrating for others the tricks of leverage and momentum to bring down a guard. There were other segments when an inmate would stand before several others and appear to be reciting a list of things to be done in a particular order. Now and then another inmate might correct him or add a step and he would begin again.

If anyone in the command center noticed the oddness of these interactions, none of them interpreted what the motions meant, any more than they interpreted the steady increase in the endless weightlifting in the yard or the growth in the number of inmates running along the walls together, or the pull-ups and push-ups inmates were doing in their cells during the lockdown hours.

During the night of July 19, most of the surveillance cameras were blacked out for periods of time and then restored, but Leah had noticed that the key to understanding the phenomenon was simple. When a camera was blinded, something bad was happening in that location for those minutes. This gave her an unassailable record of the timing for each step in the plan. After watching the footage dozens of times, she could stop the flow of time in her mind and say what was going on in each part of the prison for each minute of the night. For each crucial event, she could name which of the twelve men were in that spot at that time.

And after all this time, she could also remember exactly what she was doing. At no moment had it been what people assumed. Leah knew that the mayor and council, her police colleagues, neighbors, and parents had all held roughly the same view of her. They had all formed that opinion based on years of observation and the free-flowing gossipy exchange of information that went on in places like Weldonville. They all had missed something.

Leah Hawkins was the longtime mistress of Mark Ballard, the city manager. On July 19 she and Mark were both thirty-four and had been together for about seven years. He had come to town after college and five years of working in city government in Denver. He was handsome, about an inch taller than Leah was. He was steady, and he was married.

His wife was a beautiful, sweet, and adoring person named Marcia. Mark had met her in college at the University of Tennessee, and they had married at the end of their senior year. Shortly after their move to Denver, Marcia was in a car accident that left her hospitalized with a couple of broken bones in her legs. She seemed to be doing well for a time, but when the schedule called for her to begin physical therapy, she couldn't do it. She had a continuing weakness unusual in a young, healthy woman. The doctors began doing tests, and one of them revealed the presence of creatine kinase in her blood. Her biopsy, neurological tests, and imaging were consistent. She had muscular dystrophy.

When Leah Hawkins was a state police officer in Longmont, she and her partner brought an injured suspect to the hospital in Denver where Marcia Ballard was receiving treatment. While Leah was in the cafeteria getting coffee for herself and her partner, she met Mark Ballard. He told her about his wife in the first few minutes, so there had never been a second when their relationship had been the familiar one—no cheating husband pretending to Leah that he was single until after she was in love, no extenuating circumstances, no pretense that he would ever divorce Marcia and marry Leah, or that Marcia's death was imminent. Marcia was young and had excellent medical care, so there was every chance that she would be around for a long time. When Leah stopped by the next week to get coffee for herself and her partner, Mark even took Leah into Marcia's room to introduce her.

Leah had seen all of it, and her police officer mind had not been a place where illusions could flourish. Mark Ballard was permanently married to a beautiful young woman. It was true that she was so weak and frail that sex was already a fading memory, and that he functioned as her friend and caregiver, but that wasn't what he was. He was her husband. And sometimes it seemed to Leah that the absence of physical contact between the married couple made them closer because they both so intently missed and desired it. The atmosphere of erotic despair around them was so thick that Leah felt it with them.

When Ballard got the job of city manager in Weldonville, Leah was upset and angry. Weldonville was her hometown, and his arrival seemed to her to put her family home in a forbidden zone. But six months after the Ballards had moved to Weldonville and Mark was managing the public works, water, power, and buildings, Leah applied to the Weldonville Police Department and was hired as a detective sergeant, her rank in the state police. A couple of years later she was promoted to lieutenant.

The night of July 19, Leah was awakened by the sound of distant gunfire when the first twelve escaped inmates arrived in town driving the cars of dead guards. The gunshots were single events— maybe a shot or two, and then no more shots for a few minutes— because they were the sounds of an escapee shooting an unarmed person in a dead guard's house. There were no gunfights, no rounds of return fire at first.

A complication was that July 19 was one of the regular nights when Mark Ballard slept at Leah Hawkins's house instead of at home. The story for the benefit of others was that he was in Denver on those nights working on Weldonville's relationship with the state government and consulting on public projects for the city of Denver for extra money. On those nights, his car was parked at the train station and his wife, Marcia, had a visiting nurse scheduled to be with her.

Leah was up in a second, and was at her dresser stepping into some underpants and hooking a bra in front of her, spinning the clasps around to her back and putting her arms under the straps, and then pulling on a black long-sleeve pullover. She tugged up a pair of jeans, stepped into some black running shoes, then knelt and tied them. She put on her utility belt with the police equipment, took two extra loaded magazines from her dresser, and only then looked in the direction of the bed.

She expected to see him still lying there naked with only his feet under the sheet, and the blissful look he often had when he had fallen asleep after sex. He wasn't there. He was up, buttoning his dress shirt with his sport coat already over it and his belt buckled. Then he was at the side of the bed with the drawer of the nightstand open, taking out her spare Glock 17.

"Hold on," she said. "I'm just going out to see what it is."

"You know what it is." He stuck the pistol into his belt at the small of his back. "I'll just borrow this and go along for the ride. That's all."

"Mark—"

"You know I can shoot and I can see behind you."

It was true that she had taken him out to the police range a few times because she had to find time to get in her own practice, so she had let him come and shoot too. She had been prepared to tell anyone who asked that she was doing it because he was a city official, but nobody had asked. This was different. It wasn't paper targets.

As she tried to force her distracted mind to formulate a refusal that wouldn't permit a rebuttal, there was a volley of gunfire—three pistol shots, then a series of louder reports that must have come from a rifle. The shots were very close.

She ran to the front of the house and looked out. Two uniformed police officers she recognized as Willenz and Gutierrez were sheltering behind their police car with their pistols drawn. They were under fire from three men, two carrying what looked to her like military-issue rifles and the other armed with a semiautomatic pistol. The shooters had taken a position behind the concrete steps of the bandstand in the park about fifty yards away. In the seconds while she was watching, the three men opened fire on the police car, a barrage that exploded windows, pounded holes through the sheet metal of the doors and roof, and flattened two tires.

She opened the gun cabinet in the den, took out the M4 rifle that she carried in her car trunk at work, inserted a magazine, pulled the charging handle, and went to the corner window at the front of the house. She slid it open and took aim.

The first man rose slightly so his rifle was no longer resting on the bottom concrete step. He held the foregrip in his left hand and rested his elbow on the third step. Her shot went through his head and he collapsed. She adjusted her aim to the second prone rifleman and fired. Her shot was low, but she saw it spark on the surface of the concrete and ricochet upward into the man's face. He went down.

The man with the pistol had scrambled away and been crouching with his back to the bandstand. When the second man fell, he sprinted across the park, trying to keep his back among the trees. Leah had no shot, so she shut the window and went out the front door. "Willenz! Gutierrez! It's Hawkins. Are you all right?"

They both waved in her direction, staying low. She ran to their car and crouched by the front wheel. "What happened?"

Gutierrez said, "We were responding to a 'shots fired' call. We came around the park, and they opened up on us."

More gunfire was coming from the east side of town. It had not yet occurred to Leah that one of the things on the east side of town was the road to the prison. She said, "We'd better go get those rifles from the bandstand. And any ammo lying around. Are you up to it?"

Gutierrez said, "I'll go." He moved to the rear of the police car, looked and listened for a moment, and then ran toward the bandstand. Leah rested her M4 on the hood of the police cruiser to cover him, but she saw no targets.

Willenz reached into the broken car window and took out the microphone. "This is Three Zebra One. We've been under rifle fire at the city park. Lieutenant Hawkins shot two of the suspects, but a third is running up Calloway Street to the north. He is armed with a semiautomatic pistol. He's wearing dark clothing, probably blue jeans and a work shirt. Average height and weight, dark hair."

Instead of the soft reassuring voice of Emma Giles, the night dispatcher, the voice of Chief Roberts came over the speaker. "Is the lieutenant still with you?"

She took the microphone. "Yes, Chief. I'm here."

"The whole prison is out. I'm not sure how it happened yet, but there are at least hundreds on foot coming toward town. A lot of them have been seen with guns."

"I can verify that, Chief," she said. "Gutierrez is recovering two rifles from the men I shot."

"They're coming into town from the east, from the prison highway. We're going to try to set up a barrier at Main Street. I think we can hold them at Main and keep them from getting to the west side of town."

"We're on our way, Chief," she said. "Out."

Gutierrez returned from the park carrying two M4 rifles just like Leah's. He had stuck eight loaded magazines in his jacket, his belt, and his pockets.

Mark Ballard came around the corner of the street, where he must have gotten by cutting through Leah's neighbors' yards. When he appeared, the two uniformed cops raised their pistols. "Hold your fire," he said. "It's only me, Mark Ballard. I thought I heard shots." He was walking toward them, but his hands were in the air.

Leah's jaw clenched, but she ignored him for the moment and talked to the two uniformed cops. "You two get these rifles and your Glocks reloaded while I get the car. Come with me, Mr. Ballard."

The two cops released the magazines and inserted full ones while Leah ran to her driveway to get her unmarked black police car. Ballard got into the passenger seat. She saw him and said, "You're really being stupid. You're not paid or trained for this, and you're going to leave Marcia a widow."

"I can't watch these guys take over the town."

She backed up quickly and spun the car around to pick up Gutierrez and Willenz. She saw them step toward her car and called, "Don't leave the shotgun."

Ballard got out of the car, stepped to the disabled police cruiser, and took the shotgun out of its vertical holder. He returned with it and sat down. She glared at him. "Thank you."

Leah drove fast with the windows open, and they heard more distant gunfire. It sounded like it was coming from the northeast. She drove faster but slowed nearly to a stop at each intersection, looking up and down the streets to see if she could spot any escaped prisoners. The quiet night streets still looked empty and benign, not much different from the way they had looked when she was a teenager walking home late from a party, slowly if she liked the boy she was with, or fast if she didn't, using her long legs to stay a step away from him.

She reached the broad intersection with Main Street in a few minutes. She looked to the north along the wide street. It was marked for diagonal parking on both sides and had two more lanes for traffic, but the only cars there now were a row of police cruisers facing outward from the curb on the west side with their doors open. Cops—some in uniform and others in various kinds of civilian clothes that they'd thrown on—walked up and down the sidewalk behind the cars, some of them just hearing what had happened and others settling into firing positions.

Leah pulled the black car into line with the others, and she and her passengers got out and walked to the spot where Chief Roberts was giving his men and women their orders. "We'll try to stop them right here," he said. "Use the cars as well as you can. The engine block is the best barrier. Always stay low. And if you use the door as a shield, open it only halfway so rounds will ricochet past you instead of piercing it and hitting you. When they arrive across the street, turn your high beams on. Any order to fire will come from me."

As Leah approached the chief, she appraised the situation. There were only eight cars, all in the line with fifteen or twenty feet between them. The small town's whole fleet didn't constitute a barricade, just a few firing positions along a two-hundred-foot stretch of Main Street.

"We're here, Chief," she said.

"Who else?"

"Gutierrez and Willenz. And we picked up Mark Ballard on the way. He was coming home from meetings in Denver and heard shots. I gave him my spare Glock and the shotgun from the wrecked unit on Calloway Street."

Chief Roberts pointed at Gutierrez and Willenz. "Where did they get M4s?"

"From the bodies of the two shooters. They've got to be from the prison."

"And you have the one from your car. I've got the one from mine too. So we've got four. That's quite a bit of firepower if we need it."

"Should we station the rifles at both ends of the line so the escapees can't outflank us?" she asked.

He raised his voice. "Gutierrez, take a spot at the end car up there. Willenz, take a spot at the other end. Don't let any of them get around us." He turned back to Leah. "I want you near the middle, so you can help me take the heart out of them if they come at us hard." He saw Mark Ballard a few feet away with the shotgun resting on his forearm and pointing down at the pavement, like a pheasant hunter.

"Hey, Mark," he said. "Nice to have you with us. I hereby deputize you with a rank of field marshal."

"Thanks, Chief. Anything special I should know?"

"Just stick with the lieutenant. If you do what she does, you'll be fine."

It was only a moment later that Leah saw the dark mass of men moving up Constitution Street toward Main. They were still a block away, but they were a long, shadowy, moving thing, like a monstrous animal crawling along the street. They stretched from one sidewalk, filling the street, to the other. They must have come from the prison on foot, trotting or walking the three or four miles of alfalfa fields. She strained her eyes and estimated that there must be at least five hundred men. As the throng streamed along Constitution Street, some of them would climb or be lifted by others to the level of the old-fashioned streetlamps. The top man would lift off the glass cover of the lamp, leaving the big bulb bare. Then he would smash the bulb, leaving that section of the street in darkness. When they were still a hundred yards from Main Street, they looked like they were emerging from a tunnel.

The first three or four ranks of escapees were armed with what Leah later confirmed were weapons from the prison arsenal. The next ranks carried looted weapons from houses that had been hastily abandoned by their owners or stormed by the mob. There were hunting rifles, shotguns, a number of revolvers, and compact semi-automatic pistols. There were even three men carrying compound bows and quivers full of steel-tipped deer hunting arrows. Behind them the crowd was still in deeper shadow.

Chief Roberts stood beside his command car and used the built-in loudspeaker. "This is the chief of police of the city of Weldonville. We don't want any unnecessary violence. If you will stop and place any firearms or other weapons on the pavement, raise your hands, and walk up Main Street to your left, you will be permitted to surrender peacefully without having anything to be afraid of. You will be kept comfortable and safe while we arrange for your transport back to the prison."

Joseph R. Roberts was a brave man, and his bravery was one of the tools he had used to exert power during a thirty-five-year career in law enforcement. He stood in the open beside his command car with the microphone in his right hand, his feet planted apart, and his left arm resting comfortably across his chest. His voice held no hint of fear, no uncertainty or hesitation.

His approach should have worked. But there was a growing murmur, like a hum, coming from the escapees. It moved forward from the rear to the front, the impatient crowd wanting to know why their progress had stopped. Then, like a wave subsiding, the sound went from the vanguard to the back as the men who could see ahead passed the word of what was happening. One of the men in the second rank who had made it almost to Main Street raised an M4 to his shoulder and fired.

The chief dropped to the pavement, the microphone he had been holding swinging freely against his car on its curly cord. Every chest inhaled once while it was silent, and then the police officers on the west side of the street opened fire. They cut down the shooter and the five or six men nearest to him in a wave. The murmur from the column of escapees on Constitution Street rose to a roar of rage and ferocity.

By then there was no certainty, not even about what had happened. The police officers had fired at the man who had shot their chief, but it was probable that the other men were hit by rapid and poorly aimed shots, or by rounds that had gone through the culprit's body. The escapees back on the darkened street and sidewalks of Constitution Avenue knew that people had been shot, but they could not possibly know who or why.

The escapees at the front of the column who had firearms from the prison crouched, knelt, or lay prone and fired on the police officers across the street. The escapees immediately behind them were armed with whatever weapons they could find or improvise. The ones who had taken guns from homes fired them. Others lit the rag fuses of Molotov cocktails—the bottles scavenged from garbage cans and the gasoline siphoned from parked cars—and threw them at the police cars. Some threw stones or bricks.

Leah reached into the chief's car to hit the high-beam headlights and put the escapees into the glare. When she had done that, so did many of the other officers, but it was less effective because some of the police vehicles were now enveloped in fire from the flaming bottles.

Escapees charged forward between the shooters at the mouth of Constitution Street, sprinting to take the seventy feet as fast as they could to kill or disable police officers distracted by the fires that flared up and the fusillade from the shooters. They wielded hatchets, hammers, kitchen knives, crowbars, or baseball bats. Some threw broom handles that had been sharpened into spears.

Leah rested her left elbow on the chief's car and fired the M4 rifle into the charging men. She listened to the bangs of the rifles of Gutierrez and Willenz, the booms of the shotguns on both sides of her, the *pop-pop-pop* of the 9mm Glock pistols.

In the first five seconds the police had shot down nearly all the armed men in the vanguard, but as they fell, the ones behind came up to take their places. They flopped onto the pavement beside the bodies to take up the weapons and keep firing.

Four of the eight police cars had been hit by Molotov cocktails and were burning. In the light from the flames and the headlights Leah could see five police officers on the pavement severely wounded or dead. The loss on the other side was much worse, but escaped prisoners kept streaming to the mouth of Constitution Street to take up the fight. Leah looked to her right and left and wondered how much more ammunition the police officers still had.

She ran to the nearest burning car, got in, felt the motor idling, straightened the wheels, and threw it into gear. It moved, slowly at first, but gained speed. When it was twenty feet out, she stepped harder on the gas and rolled out. As the flaming car glided into the mass of advancing men, she ran back in its wake toward the chief's car.

As she did, she saw Mark Ballard. He was standing one car over, firing the shotgun. She saw it kick against his shoulder as the muzzle flashed, and then his left hand pump the slide to eject the shell and bring a new one into the chamber, and then the kick and flash again. And then she saw the end, the prisoner's bullet pound into his forehead and through it, the puff of red mist in the air behind him, and his tall, strong body falling backward, no longer occupied.

She knew in the first instant that Mark was dead. She searched for the shooter, for any man on the east side of Main Street with a gun. She fired rapidly, moving efficiently from one to the next, putting a bullet in each one to hold him where he was until the twenty-round magazine was empty. She reloaded, aimed, and fired, but the energy of the attack had been exhausted.

The psychopaths and the desperate lifelong fighters and the suicidal fatalists had become scarce. The ones who had been content to take places in the main body of the throng, the ones who hoped to escape, were all starting to slip away to try it on their own. The ones who had stayed in the rear, far from the fight, were beginning to break and run away.

At the north end of Main, she saw colored light from the roof bars of the state police vehicles as they flashed past. Two of them closed off this block of Main, but the others kept coming, speeding to get ahead of the retreating prisoners.

As soon as the last of the prisoners had fallen back, she gathered the four intact police cars and drove slowly with them along Constitution Street, executing a sweep to be sure no stragglers stayed behind. When she and her officers reached the end of Constitution, she found that the state police had diverted the mob of escapees onto the baseball field, which was surrounded by high fences on all sides. At dawn they began the long process of transporting the prisoners back to their prison.

At the funeral, Mark Ballard's casket was closed to keep his wife and others from seeing what the rifle shot had done to his head.

A week after the funeral, Marcia Ballard wrote a note to Leah Hawkins thanking her for being Mark's beloved friend and saying that Leah had made his life a thousand times better. She had typed it on Mark's computer, a task Leah knew had taken a huge effort for her. By then she could not have written a word by hand. After Leah had read the note a few times, pausing over the word "beloved," she burned the paper. She knew she wouldn't forget the words, and what the two women and the man had said to each other about their private life was not ever going to be anybody else's business.

About six weeks after that, the police department received a report from the FBI that the bullet that killed Mark Ballard had been found and identified by ballistics analysis and blood DNA found on and around the bullet. The bullet had gone through the victim's head and lodged in a maple tree on Main Street. The bullet had been matched to a rifle stolen from the prison by an inmate named Earl Detweiler. His fingerprints and DNA were found on the foregrip and the lower receiver. Detweiler had been killed by a bullet from an M4 owned by the Weldonville, Colorado, Police Department and issued to Lieutenant Leah Anne Hawkins. Leah made a copy of the report and sent it to Marcia Ballard.

13

Leah had reviewed the various photographs of Viktor Panko, read his interviews with the Buffalo Police Department when he was young and the FBI when he was older, and read the court transcripts from his four trials and the police reports going back to his first adult arrest at age eighteen. She had searched for nuance, for small, seemingly unimportant details about him. She had looked at the way he dressed, his preference in cars, his use of figures of speech—any peculiarity that would direct her to some particular place or group of people. After the prison break, the FBI had done interviews with inmates who had known him.

They learned from the inmate transcripts that Panko's conversations were filled with nostalgia about women he had seduced, paid for sex, or raped. Two of them noted that the women in the stories often sounded very young.

The stories emerged again about how Panko had told other inmates that he could help them after they were released by obtaining new identities for them with no criminal histories. He said he had contacts he could talk to from inside the prison who had remained in business after he'd been caught.

All telephone calls inmates made from Weldonville prison were taped and monitored, so that could not have been his way of placing orders for identity documents. He had to be using a messenger or go-between who visited him in prison. The people on his visitor list were the only ones who could come and go, so they would have been the only possible messengers. She began to spend more of her time pursuing this possibility.

She still made visits to community and church groups in the parts of Buffalo that had been settled by immigrants from Eastern Europe. Poles, Serbs, Hungarians, Slovakians, Ukrainians, and others had come there to find work, built neighborhoods with churches and schools and stores that sold traditional food and drink. Most of the factories that had drawn immigrants there and employed them were long gone, and many neighborhoods had changed ethnicities or been gentrified or torn down to make something new. But she had found plenty of people who were descendants of the old owners. Often, they lived in the suburbs but came back to the old neighborhoods for visits.

One night, Leah was at St. Stanislaus Church pretending to be waiting for a women's club meeting in the school building. She would chat in a friendly way with other women when she could, and as soon as she had a promising woman alone she would find a way to show the pictures of Viktor she had on her current burner phone.

After a number of tries, she found one woman who seemed to hesitate. She stared at the picture for a few seconds, and then said, "The meeting is going to start in about five minutes, and I need time to think about this. Can you write down your number for me so I can call you another time?"

"Sure," Leah said. "It's not a hurry. I just wondered if he was still around after all these years." She gave her a slip of paper with the name "Sue" and her number.

Leah had made similar attempts with other people in the southern and eastern parts of the city, but all of them had said they didn't know the man. This one seemed promising. Her name was Stella Wizshinski, and she was about sixty, with curly blond hair that she had certainly been dyeing for a few years to hide the gray. Age and living had broadened her body, but she wasn't soft or fat. She seemed to have done a great deal of physical work over time.

In the next few days Leah let the contact fade and merge with the others she had made in over a month in Buffalo. But then one night her phone rang. She said, "Yes?"

As soon as the voice came, she saw the woman in her memory. "Sue, this is Stella Wizshinski. We talked for a minute a week ago at St. Stanislaus."

"I remember you," said Leah. "Curly blond hair—"

"Yeah, that's me. My brothers used to tell me I looked like Harpo Marx."

"I hope you didn't put up with that," Leah said.

"They're all forgiven," said Stella. "I got each of them back years ago, and they've got the psychological scars to prove it. But the reason I'm calling is that I thought about the picture you showed me, and I managed to place him and remember the name. It's Panko. The man whose picture you showed me was Viktor. To tell you the truth, the reason I called tonight is that I want to warn you, even if it's out of place. Viktor is not a nice man, and his family isn't any better. If this is a romantic kind of thing, I would get as far away as—"

"It's not," said Leah. "I appreciate your willingness to give this to me straight. Can I ask how you met them?"

"I didn't call to talk about me. It was a long time ago."

"Please, if you could just tell me what you can, it might matter a lot."

"I used to be a cop," Stella said.

Leah clamped down her nerves and made her voice sound as though she were smiling. "Let me come clean. I'm a cop too. I need to meet with you in person. Would it be all right if I drove to your house for a brief talk? I promise the second you tell me it's time to leave I will. You won't have to hint. I'm not tender."

"Interesting," Stella said. "You've got me curious. Let me give you my address." She recited the address as Leah typed it into her phone.

Leah said, "Can I come now?"

"What the hell is keeping you? I expected to hear a car starting by now."

Leah was already walking toward the dresser in her hotel room where she had set her purse. She said, "The map on my phone says I'll be there in twenty minutes."

Leah took the elevator to ground level, went across the street to the hotel's parking structure, and took her car. She followed the phone app's instructions until she found herself on Fillmore Avenue near the Broadway Market. She looked at the location of Stella's house on her phone's map and decided to park and walk the last block to the house.

She trotted across the street and then walked, looking around her at the area. The houses were all two stories and narrow, with roofed front porches. They were built so close together that Leah wondered how cars could fit up their driveways and into the old one-car garages.

When she found the right house, Leah climbed the front porch and rang the bell. Through the glass in the door she could see Stella walking toward her to open it. Stella walked with a slight limp, which Leah diagnosed as an old injury in her right knee. It was possible that it had been bad enough to end her career.

Stella opened the door and said, "There you are. I figured you'd beat that twenty-minute figure. Come on in."

"Thank you," said Leah. She stepped in and held out her identification with her badge on it.

Stella waved it away and walked from the door into the parlor, which was the first room past the small foyer. "I don't need to see that. I could hear it in your voice. Come and sit down."

They sat in the small parlor, which was furnished with a couch and two large armchairs, all of them positioned to provide a view of the big television screen on the wall. Just as Stella sat down, there was the sound of a teapot whistling. She got up and said, "I made us some tea."

Leah followed her along a narrow hallway, past the staircase to the second floor and a small dining room, and into the kitchen, where Stella poured the tea into big cups with two teabags in each one. Leah said, "Where were you a police officer?"

"Here," Stella said. "I retired as a sergeant thirteen years ago. I was one of the first cops in Buffalo who sat down to pee. And I can tell you we weren't exactly welcome at first. It was tough life for a while."

Leah nodded and waited. Any cop who had lived through the bad old days had a right to go on a little bit. She took her tea and said, "Thanks very much for the tea."

"It's a pleasure. I like coffee better, but there's no point in my being up all night anymore."

Leah sipped the tea. "I like it."

They sat in the parlor and Stella said, "I knew the Panko family professionally. I ran into a couple of them as juveniles. Their age was also the reason I ran into the old man a couple of times too. It was not a pleasure. He was involved in a lot of small-time stuff—smuggling things to and from Canada, combined with a little fencing of stolen goods both ways. He did a little forgery, mostly in service of car theft—pink slips and registrations and stuff. After I'd met a couple of the kids and their father, I was not happy to notice that they lived a half mile from here at the time. They were another reason to look over my shoulder. The father died a few years ago, and the house was sold. The wife may be alive, but I think I remember something about her going to an old-age home. There are about five kids, I think. They'd all be in their thirties at least, and a couple of the boys as old as forty-five. Viktor would be in his late thirties."

Leah said, "I've got to open up a little with you. I'm in Buffalo trying to find Viktor because he committed some murders while participating in an escape from the federal penitentiary in Weldonville, Colorado, a couple of years ago. Nearly all the escaped inmates are in custody or dead. He isn't. I've been trying to find local people who might have seen him."

Stella said, "Interesting. I'll ask around and try to find out what I can."

"I appreciate that, and I thank you. But I don't want you to return to police work. If you had happened to know something current—an address for him, a place where he hangs out, I would have run with it. But I don't mean to get you involved in my investigation. I don't know about the rest of the family, but Viktor is a violent psycho who has committed several murders. If you recall anything else about him later, great. Call me. But please don't draw any attention to yourself."

"I was a cop a long time, and this is not only my hometown, it's my home district. People here know me, and they like me. I can tell you that you're more likely to make a mistake here than I am. People here are not nasty to strangers, but they won't tell you anything about a local boy, especially if he's a rotten local boy."

"I can't ask you to take a risk."

Stella sipped her tea. "Don't get ahead of yourself. I may come up with zip. There's nothing safer than not finding the bad guy. I'm just saying I'll ask some people. If anything useful turns up, I'll call again. If it doesn't, I won't."

"Thank you," Leah said.

"I read about that prison break, but I had no idea that Viktor Panko was in it. I didn't even know he was in prison at the time. Do you mind if I ask you a prying question?"

"You're entitled. Ask away."

"What's left of your hometown after two years?"

Leah took a second drink, a sip this time. "Not much. New people will probably come to Weldonville after we're gone. There are good roads and sewers and water lines and electricity. And the prison is already being remodeled by contractors who fooled the government into thinking they're making it escape-proof this time. But the people who lived in those houses up and down those quiet streets before the prison break are about half gone already—the people I grew up with and their families. A lot of them had jobs in the prison, and a lot more sold things to the prison itself or to the people who worked there, and that's been choked off for two years. Others left because somebody they loved died and they couldn't stand to look at the place anymore."

"If your town is ruined, what are you doing here looking for Viktor Panko?"

"The town I knew is over. It took one night. What I'm doing is not trying to reclaim the place. It's about who we were, the kind of town our families had built over about six generations. The town didn't die off, the way some do. These twelve guys just got together and made a plan to kill it. They took something that belonged to all of us that we can't get back. Your past is your identity, and they took that. I could make you a noble speech that I'm only taking part in the search so they won't do it to some other little place. But I don't think they would anyway. It was a onetime thing. I just don't want them to walk away from it."

"I understand," Stella said. "I'll get on this in the morning. Can I pour you another cup of tea?"

"No," said Leah. "I'll be working tonight, so I'd better get going. Thank you for everything, Stella."

As Leah walked along the street toward her car, she considered her new circumstances. She had never planned to tell anyone who she was or what she was doing. Now she had another cop on her side. Maybe Stella would help, but now Leah had another burden. If she got to Panko, she would have to make his death happen without the body ever being found, or she would have to make it look like self-defense, or Stella would certainly turn her in.

*   *   *

Leah Hawkins went back to work on the fourteen names that Viktor Panko had placed on his list of people he wanted to be allowed to visit him in prison. He had filled out a form when he entered the system at the federal penitentiary in Beaumont, Texas. He had listed his father, mother, three brothers, and two sisters. The other seven were his defense attorney, three cousins with the surname Halasz, and three cousins with the name Varga.

The list of actual visitors he received was the next thing Leah studied. The most likely go-between for a federal prisoner would be a relative, the closer the better.

The brothers were Istvan, Sandor, and Gyorgy, and the sisters were Viktoria and Dorina. The sisters had never visited him in Beaumont Penitentiary, and never visited him in Weldonville either. Maybe they didn't approve.

She scrolled down the list slowly. His parents had visited him three times a year at Beaumont, when they'd still lived in Buffalo. It wouldn't be efficient for them to carry messages or job orders from Viktor to some remnant of his organization at four-month intervals. It had to be someone else.

Leah scrolled farther down the list. Istvan never visited. Sandor came twice, once in Beaumont and once in Weldonville. Gyorgy came once, to Beaumont.

So much for the siblings, she thought. What about his lawyer?

She came three times during the Beaumont years. The notation on the record said it was to confer about his appeal. The appeal failed in his third year, and there were no visits from her after that.

The cousins, then, she thought. There's nobody else. Of course he could have been bullshitting about still being able to get people new identities. But none of the twelve had been caught, and that meant they all had acceptable identification from somewhere.

She decided to begin with the Halasz cousins. She scrolled to the end. No. None of them ever came. The Varga cousins then. The Varga cousins were named Denes, Attila, and Regina.

Regina came a few times while Panko was in Beaumont, Texas. She gave her address as Houston. How far was that? She checked her laptop. About ninety miles. That was close enough.

Leah went back to the visitor list. Regina saw him about once a month in Beaumont, but it wasn't a regular routine. She came on random days of the week. He could have called her when he had information to send out about a customer.

She had visited Weldonville prison too, after he was transferred. She came about as often as she had to Beaumont at first, but then more often near the end. She gave an address in Denver. She had to be the go-between. Neither of her brothers ever visited Viktor.

Leah began using the common search engines to find the addresses of the Vargas. Regina was not listed anywhere, but Denes and Attila were easy. They both lived in the town of Orchard Park, southeast of Buffalo, in large houses set far back from highways. When Leah found the addresses and looked at them on Google Street View and Google Earth, she began to pack equipment for her visit.

Late that night, she drove to Orchard Park. Denes Varga lived off Route 20, the old highway that predated the New York State Thruway to run the length of the state from Lake Erie to the Hudson River. His brother Attila had a house on a side street about a mile north of the highway. Leah went past Denes's house, taking video with her phone, and then drove the car to the lot of a diner on Route 20 and went back on foot.

She walked into the trees away from the highway to study Denes Varga's house. The house was huge, a white mass at the end of a driveway that ran straight back at least two hundred feet and then curved so that it disappeared behind a stand of trees, where it passed the front porch and then split. The right branch hooked around to the rear of the house, where there was a four-car garage, and the left hooked to return to the highway.

Leah selected a tree, then crouched in the woods and took out the equipment she expected to need. She didn't want to wear climbing spikes, because they made holes in the bark that would be noticed. She took out the climbing belt she had bought in the afternoon and hoped that she could keep her footing with her treaded walking boots. She slung the belt around the straight, limbless trunk of a hardwood tree that looked like an American sweetgum, leaned back against the belt, and began to climb. She would take a step up with each foot, then use both hands to make the belt hop upward to that level, take two more steps, and shift the belt upward again. In a minute and a half, she was up to the level of the first big limb, about twenty feet off the ground. She took out the safety rope she had tied around her waist, slung it over the limb at the trunk, and clasped a carabiner around it to hold her there. She took out the pinhole camera, attached it to the top of the limb, where it was hard to see from the ground, and aimed it at the front of the house. She took care to be sure the frame included the front porch and its windows, and the section of the driveway where a car's license plate would be clear enough to read. From her perch she selected another tree that had a good view of the garage and the back of the house. Then she unhooked her safety rope and used her belt to inch her way down.

She climbed the second tree and placed another camera on its first big limb, and then climbed down again. Then she took a cross-country shortcut to Big Tree Road, where Attila Varga's house was.

The building was even bigger than Denes's house. Attila's had a rustic look, with a faux–log cabin facade on the front and a large door that looked like it was made of thick, solid planks with black iron braces and studs so that it could probably resist a battering ram. When Leah moved closer, she realized that the facade wasn't a surface layer of half logs, but real ones about ten inches thick, fitted so tightly that the mortar between them was nearly invisible.

Instantly Leah promoted Attila to the most likely Varga to be doing something illegal. The house looked like a place a rival could not fire a weapon through except at the few windows, and one that the police would take at least fifteen minutes to break their way into. Fifteen minutes was a lot of time to shred and burn evidence of forgery.

Leah placed four cameras in the area around the house, attempting to take advantage of every window and record any vehicle that came up the long driveway. When she had finished installing the cameras, she walked to the parking lot of the diner and drove back to her hotel. She used her laptop to check the images from the cameras and verified that they worked, but she had no idea if her efforts had put her any closer to Viktor.

14

Leah kept patrolling, searching for Viktor Panko or for anyone who recognized his picture. In her experience as a homicide detective, she had seen many times when simply talking to people in the neighborhood of a case and asking questions had brought unexpected benefits. But here she had to be careful, and do more observing than talking. Tonight she decided to try the theater district. The theater district in Buffalo was small and manageable. It seemed to consist of Main Street from Chippewa Street to Tupper, with a few satellite businesses on the parallel streets—Pearl, Franklin, and Delaware. About five big hotels were downtown within a few blocks, including the Hyatt where she'd stayed the first few nights and the Westin, where she had moved to keep from getting too familiar, along with several good restaurants.

Shea's Performing Arts Center was a landmark theater and seemed to be where the main attractions appeared, and there were four or five smaller theaters that presented plays and shows. The concentration of these places would be helpful. If she made the rounds, she would have a pretty good chance of seeing anybody who frequented the bars and restaurants and clubs. If Viktor Panko came here, she would have a much better chance of spotting him than she would in a larger district.

She went for lunch at a restaurant on Main Street that had been a big bank around 1910, when Buffalo was thriving. There was a modern hotel next door, and the opening between the two buildings was a monumental arch that had been one of the bank's original entrances. It was impressive, and that kind of amused her. The old bank must have looked like a temple for the worship of money.

Leah never thought much about money. Part of her indifference had come from being raised in a family supported by her father's pay as a police officer, and then living on her own pay as a police officer. A cop would never starve to death, but she wouldn't get rich either, so it had seemed best not to think about it much.

In her personal experience, the people who had money to share were nearly all men. She'd heard it pointed out many times that this was unfair and was changing. To Leah this process was simply one of the features of the planet Earth as she had found it. Unfairness was like the Rocky Mountains, west of where she grew up. She never doubted that the mountains were being eroded away, but in the meantime, when she'd climbed there, she'd reached about the same altitude as she would have if she'd arrived with the first Indians tens of thousands of years ago.

Lots of other problems were built into the planet, and she was always striving decisively to mitigate them instead of devoting much time to resenting them. Leah Hawkins was a woman who met freezing weather with warm clothes instead of complaints.

Leah had taken on a dangerous and difficult job, but for the first time in her life, she had what amounted to an unlimited budget— the million dollars the council had diverted from the government grant. She knew that if she was going to search the theater area where the expensive and fancy bars were, she was going to have to spend some money on clothes. She had the debit cards with her today, so when she finished lunch, she was going to search for the right outfit.

She liked the dress that the restaurant hostess was wearing, so she asked her where she bought her clothes. The hostess gave her a quick recitation of the boutiques in the area—Brassard, Adrianna Marsh, Montrose, Enfer—and the blocks where they could be found. Leah thanked her, but the implied compliment seemed to be a sufficient reward. Leah spent the next hour picking out a couple of outfits that would get her noticed favorably in expensive restaurants, and some flat shoes that wouldn't exaggerate her height or incapacitate her if she needed to run or fight.

There was a dark blue dress that looked elegant on her. It was short, but it flowed, and it emphasized her blond hair and long legs. The style made her feel like somebody important—maybe a diplomat. The other outfit was a pair of tight black pants, a black jacket that was cut like a sport coat, and a dark gray silk blouse. She looked at herself in the two outfits and then hung the elegant blue dress on the dressing room hook. The woman at the store said, "I hate to see you put this back. It's perfect for you. If it's the money, we have very flexible credit terms."

Leah said, "It's not the money. It's the time. If I take them both, then tonight I'll waste time putting on that one first. But what I'll wear is this one."

15

She was out for the evening and she was glad now that she had not been tempted to get the blue dress too. It was interesting, she thought, how having an unlimited supply of other people's money made self-indulgence seem like a real option. As she walked, she let her mind settle into its police mode, and her eyes began to scan. This section of Buffalo looked promising to her. It was full of people just out of a revival of *Sunday in the Park with George* that was playing at Shea's Performing Arts Center, and a lot of people were heading for bars and restaurants.

She followed a promising-looking group to Le Saucier on Delaware. The online restaurant reviews listed it as one of the best restaurants in the city. Leah was not convinced that Viktor Panko would be interested in that kind of restaurant, but she knew that most women would, and he probably knew it too.

Leah got to the door after a stream of couples and waited her turn for the maître d' to seat her. She could see that a table for one would require a wait, so she headed to the bar. The bartender was tall, so he seemed to think they were both part of a secret society of tall people, and he took her order for a gin and tonic right away.

While she waited, she studied the room in the big mirror over the bar. She approved Le Saucier as a good place to start the evening.

The food was expensive, and people were dressed well enough to assure her that the evening wouldn't end in a bar fight.

If Panko was back in Buffalo and he was still in the illicit businesses that had sent him to prison, this was an environment where he would feel at ease. He wouldn't be likely to meet any of his business associates or the purchasers of his false identities in a place like this. It was too quiet and tasteful. It was also too expensive for an honest cop to visit very often.

While Leah watched for the return of the bartender or the approach of Panko, she also devised a plan to glance at the reservation book for the names of any of the Varga cousins. They would be even more likely than Panko to haunt nice restaurants, because during the years he was in prison, they were still here making money, and they still had no reason to think anyone might be searching for them.

Her eyes passed over a very young couple as they came in the door and then returned to them. They were both well dressed, and the girl was pretty. The maître d' listened to the boy's name, looked at the reservation list, and then told the hostess which table; she led them there and gave them menus. Leah tried to guess. It was too late for graduation, and there weren't any holidays in the summer after the Fourth of July. It might be the girl's birthday. Or it might be one of the many anniversaries that young girls feel should be marked, even if the boy didn't seem like anything to celebrate.

Leah saw the bartender coming and accepted her gin and tonic. Then she glanced up at the mirror again and watched a waiter come to the table where the new couple was seated. They looked up from their menus to order drinks. The waiter smiled apologetically at the girl and asked what Leah knew was "Can I see some ID?"

The girl opened her purse and handed him what appeared to be a driver's license. He looked at the picture on it, looked at her again, turned the license over, and then said, "I'll be right back."

The girl looked alarmed, and that interested Leah. After she had scanned the room for Panko again, she let her eyes return to the young couple. The waiter was back with an older man, who was holding the driver's license. He handed it back to the girl and said something.

Leah slipped off her bar stool and stepped away from the bar. She was carrying her drink, and as she walked, her eyes passed over the girl, but she kept walking toward the ladies' room.

Leah and the young girl stood in front of the big wall mirror, freshening their makeup. Leah moved her eyes slightly to her left to look at the girl's face in the reflection. "Fake ID, huh?" She smiled. "I got caught at that."

The girl winced and then met Leah's eyes in the mirror. "I know— I'm stupid. I feel so idiotic. I was trying to look mature and stuff. Now I feel, like, so embarrassed."

Leah said, "It happens all the time. In a few years you'll be hurt if they don't ask you for proof. Can I see the fake one?"

The girl took it out of her purse and handed it to Leah.

Leah glanced at it. "No, the fake."

"That is the fake."

Leah looked harder at it. "It is? Oh my gosh. It's so good. It's perfect." She turned to look at the girl directly. "Except the picture. That's not you, is it?"

"It's my sister. She bought it and loaned it to me."

"Then it is real, right?"

"No, fake. She's got her real one with her." She rolled her eyes. "Oh my God. All I wanted was to have a glass of wine with my date. It's not like I even like the taste. But it relaxes me—takes the nervousness away."

Leah handed the license back to her. Then she picked up the short glass she had brought in and set on the marble counter. She had been planning to pour it out to remain sober. "This is a gin and tonic. I never leave a drink anywhere because of Rohypnol and GHB. I haven't touched it yet. Take a good, healthy sip of it. You'll take the edge off, and your teeth won't turn purple like they do with red wine."

The girl looked at it, then at Leah. She accepted the glass and sipped from it, then held it out.

"That's okay. Finish it if you like," said Leah. "I can get as many as I want."

"Oh God. Thank you," she said and took another sip.

"That sure is a good fake license. Much better than the one I used to use. Where did your sister get it?"

"There's a woman. I guess she works at a mailing and print business in Kenmore."

"Do you remember the address or the name of the store or anything?"

"I wasn't with her. She's the only one who talked to the woman. Her name is Reggie."

"Do you have to know her or something?" Leah laughed. "Know a secret password?"

"No. But you have to pay a lot. My sister said it was three hundred, and that was almost two years ago. Now she's over twenty-one, so she gave it to me. We look kind of alike, and I was thinking it would be darker in here than it is."

"If it had been, you might have gotten away with it." She went back to her makeup while the girl watched her. "You're both very pretty."

"You're beautiful."

Leah laughed again. "Maybe the drink was too strong." She looked at the glass. "Done with it?"

The girl looked at it. "Oh. Yes," she said. "Thank you so much."

Leah took the glass. "You're welcome. But it wouldn't look good if you went out there carrying this."

They both left the ladies' room and walked back toward their respective places. Leah could see the waiter had left a glass of wine for the date and a glass of ginger ale for the girl.

Hours later, after Leah had been to three different bars and returned to her hotel, she thought back on the conversation with the girl. Fake licenses for underage drinkers didn't seem to be the kind of business a professional would take. Three hundred dollars wasn't what pros got paid. It was tip money. Still, the work was too good for anybody but a pro. It had magnetic tape on the back, perfect printing and sizing.

And she had seen odder things in her career. Sometimes dishonesty had no limits, either on the high end or the low. Crookedness wasn't just a bad quality. It was a disease that acted like a philosophy. And there was also a name, and the name had been Reggie. What did Regina Varga call herself?

16

Leah went online that night to find the business that had produced the girl's driver's license. She had said the place was in Kenmore, a small suburb pressed up against Buffalo that called itself a village. Leah found no businesses called Varga's This or That, or Regina's This or That. There were a few printing shops and a couple of stationery stores that advertised printed wedding invitations and business cards and advertising mailers. There were photography shops that offered specialty printing of the sort that might extend beyond passport photos into the rest of the passport, but the girl had said a print shop, not a photographer.

Leah knew she was going to have to go from one to another asking questions and hoping for answers that she couldn't quite ask for. She knew that when she had been to all of them she probably still wouldn't know if any of them were making fake identification, because all she would see was a counter and a cash register and a woman who would not volunteer any information. There were no photographs of Regina Varga in the material the FBI had shared with her department.

Leah made some of these visits the next day, and they went just about the way she'd expected. Nobody appeared to know what she was talking about when she asked about getting licenses or other identification, and the only Reggie who turned up when she asked for one was a Canadian man.

When she was back in her hotel room, she tried Facebook. She typed "Regina Varga," but got no result. Then she began the process of eliminating variations. There was no Reggie, no Reggie V, no Regina V, no R Varga, no Buffalo Reggie, and the initials RV brought thousands of possibilities, most of which were vehicles. Just the name Regina stimulated another avalanche. She spent hours trying to look at every one, but found none that could be the right woman. Before she gave up for the night, she spent a last hour on the variations of Kenmore and printing.

The tension was rising. After several nights of not hearing from Stella, Leah had begun to check her phone frequently to see if she had failed to hear a ring.

Her next two nights were spent in Black Rock, another older area, this time on the northwest side of the city, much closer to Kenmore, where Reggie's print shop was supposed to be. There were a few Eastern European enclaves, but she got nothing out of her explorations except to taste some unfamiliar savory dishes with reddish sauce. As she was on her way to her third restaurant of the evening, she felt her phone vibrating in her pocket. She took it out and saw she had an email. "Where have you been? I've been trying to reach you. Don't call or text. Come see me. Stella."

Leah typed in an email, "I'm heading for your house now."

She drove quickly to Stella's neighborhood. She had a feeling she hadn't quite identified as she drove along the old residential street. The trees were big along Stella's block, and the houses were small. They were all about the same—two-story houses that were so narrow they looked as though they were shrugging their shoulders. There was always a wooden porch up about six feet, and a door that opened from there into a small entry area. Beyond it in the hall were stairs to the second floor on one side and the entrance to the parlor on the other, with a straight hallway between them that led past the dining room to the kitchen. The second floor was always a landing with three very small bedrooms around it.

Stella's house was easy to pick out, because Leah had noticed Stella had installed a rattan shade over the left side of the porch to keep the afternoon sun off her favorite sitting spot. Leah slowed some distance before she reached the house. She couldn't say there was something wrong. She could only feel that Stella's email didn't seem right. She hadn't said the right things. It didn't seem like a retired cop to include the complaint that she'd been trying to reach her. By training and experience, an old sergeant would have no use for complaints like that. The worst days of a cop weren't about not getting a prompt return call.

Leah looked at the street intently, paying close attention to anything that looked like a hiding place or a firing position. The moment brought back the sense of menace she had felt on certain nights looking for homicide suspects. Each doorway, each wall, had to be noticed and evaluated. If she knocked on the next door, would a puzzled and cautious householder open it, or was there somebody on the other side who would hear the knock and fire through the door?

As Leah stared along the row of houses, she noticed the way the roots of the big old trees had lifted the concrete sidewalk squares and tilted them, so what had started as a perfectly straight walkway had become like a path in a forest.

Leah kept her speed constant, not wanting to appear to have reacted to something. She went on for another block and then turned left to get out to the business district one street over. She parked in the big lot behind a bowling alley and then trotted back across the street and past it to the front yard of the house she judged to be the one behind Stella's. She kept moving along the side of the house to the backyard, went over the back fence, and reached the yard behind Stella's house. Maybe she had allowed herself to become overly tense and nothing was wrong, but it wouldn't hurt to perform a welfare check, just as she'd done hundreds of times at her job.

She went up the concrete back steps to Stella's kitchen door and looked in. She saw nobody. The lights were off, but there was a glow from somewhere toward the front rooms, so she could tell the kitchen, the hallway leading to the stairs, and the parlor were empty. Would Stella sit in the dark to wait for her?

She descended the steps, walked around the house to the driveway, and moved forward beside the house toward the street. At the front corner of the house where the clapboards ended and the side of the wooden porch began, she paused. The porch was about six feet high, so the floor of it was almost at eye level. As she crouched and crept forward beside the porch, she noticed an access hatch on the side of the structure that was about three feet high and two feet wide. She went past it to the side of the steps to see if there were any suspicious cars parked at the curb.

There was room for only two cars in front of the narrow house, and neither of them had anyone sitting inside that she could see. There was a cough, and Leah froze. Someone was close by. Then there was a squeak as a person's weight came up off one of the wooden chairs on the porch. There were footsteps moving away toward the far side of the porch like a man pacing. Leah knew that the person up there would reach the far railing and walk back toward the railing just over her head.

She retreated backward to the hatch at the side of the porch, opened it, crawled inside, and then pulled the hatch shut. She stayed still and reached into her coat to take out the Glock 17 pistol with no numbers on it. She took out the silencer and screwed it onto the threads on the muzzle.

"Jesus." It was the voice of a big man. "Where the hell is she?"

Leah could hear that the man was just above her, leaning his elbows on the railing of the porch above the spot where she was crouching.

"She'll be here," said a second man's voice. "She's a cop, and if she thinks her old lady cop friend needs her, she'll come if she has to run barefoot over broken glass."

"I'd like to see that."

"Me too. But I don't think we can add any extra requests, and Stella's too dead to do it. Now will you please sit down where she won't see you when she drives up? You're making me nervous."

"You could get on Stella's phone again and text her to hurry up."

"No."

"Why not?"

"Because I'm not a fucking moron. Just get your mind off your fear. Think about getting off one perfect shot when she gets here. Visualize it."

"The cops could get here before she does. What then?"

"Then they must be psychic, because nobody called them yet. That's why I made you use a knife on Stella."

Leah Hawkins sat in the dark, dirty space beneath the wooden porch. The only light came from the glow of a streetlamp leaking in through the crack where the hatch met the side if the porch, but when she'd moved inward she'd felt spiderwebs against her face.

Leah thought about the situation. She was in a dark place listening to two men admitting to murdering Stella Wizshinski and discussing their plan for murdering Leah too. One of them was stupid and frightened. If he got startled into the realization that Leah had already arrived, he would fire off his whole magazine, imagining every shape on the dark street was an enemy. While all that metal was flying around, the other one, the calm one, was probably capable of killing Leah himself.

Leah crawled a few feet, feeling the way ahead with her hands. She stood with bent knees and touched the boards above her head. She could feel two boards were slightly bent under a weight. She heard a creak as the man sitting in the chair shifted. Leah waited and listened.

"Damn. I got the old lady's blood on my pants when her neck spurted. I didn't see it before. How am I going to get that off?"

Leah raised her pistol nearly up to the floorboards and touched the surface with her free hand to determine where the weight was.

"Wash," said the other man.

Leah fired three rounds up through the porch floor, then stepped quickly to the place where the other man was sitting. She fired three more shots, heard the man's body thump on the boards as he fell, and fired another round up through the floor to be sure she'd killed him.

She dodged to the hatch and stayed there for a few seconds, but there was no return fire from either man. She opened the hatch, and while she used her sleeve to wipe it for fingerprints, she listened for footsteps of other enemies. When none came, she crawled out and pushed the hatch shut. She walked around to the front, climbed the steps, and saw the two men, one lying almost at the rattan blind lashed to the front railing and the other lying beside the wooden chair near the wall.

Leah squatted, patted down the two men, and took their guns, wallets, telephones, and keys. There was a third phone, and she recognized it as Stella's. Then she stood and walked down the side of Stella's house the way she had come. She kept going to the backyard, over the back fence to the neighbor's, then out to the wider, busier street, and into the bowling alley parking lot to her rental car. She got in and drove.

When she was five miles away from Stella's house, she stopped in the parking lot of a supermarket in a lonely space under a high light fixture and examined the identification in the wallets of the two men. One was Attila Varga. The other man was Alex Halasz. She remembered that Halasz was the surname of the other set of Panko's cousins. Stella had been asking around about the family. She must have asked the wrong person. Leah put the wallets under the seat of the rental car and drove toward Orchard Park.

The Vargas and Pankos and at least one of the Halasz cousins seemed to be a criminal family, so maybe they wouldn't be in a hurry to report these two men missing. Leah hoped that the silencer on her pistol had been quieter outside than it had seemed under the porch, so people nearby had thought it sounded like firecrackers or something and didn't call the cops. Once the Buffalo police were called, the time for certain things would be up. She had taken the men's car keys, wallets, guns, and phones, but at least one of them must have parked a car nearby.

Leah drove as fast as she dared, trying to stay on the smaller, darker streets that had stop signs she could ignore instead of bright lights and traffic signals. As she drove, she used her phone to bring up the pictures that her surveillance cameras were seeing at Attila Varga's house. The cameras were all still in place and all still transmitting. But what they saw was unchanging—a big wooden house with very few lights burning and no movement. She put the phone away and concentrated on her driving. She got onto the southbound branch of the thruway and sped up again.

She spotted a state police car lying in wait beyond a viaduct ahead, exactly where she would have waited for speeders, but she slowed down by taking her foot off the gas and coasting instead of touching the brake pedal. She didn't want her car to give the characteristic nose-dip that happened when a speeding driver braked. It was impossible to miss at night when the car's headlights tipped down to aim at the pavement for a few yards. She kept her foot off the brake long enough for the cop to aim his speed gun at the next car, and then she sped up again.

Leah didn't know how strict the cops in the area were late at night, but she didn't want to get a ticket as she sped away from a double murder on her way to her next crime.

For the next few miles, Leah drove just a few miles an hour above the posted speed limit, making sure not to go too slowly, because that was what a certain kind of drunk driver did—the ones who were so impaired that they could barely keep the car between the lines.

When she reached the stretch of highway near Attila's house, she stopped and looked more closely at the footage recorded by the surveillance cameras earlier in the evening. All she saw was the front door opening and then the two men she had killed coming out, getting into a car in the garage, and then driving out past the camera.

Leah allowed herself to think about Stella and feel the regret and guilt for causing her death. Stella must have asked around about Viktor Panko in the community, and at some point had asked the wrong person. The two men had spent the early part of the evening killing Stella and then prepared to kill whoever had asked her to find Viktor Panko. Probably they had simply looked at Stella's phone and seen whom she had been calling lately.

Leah walked around Attila's house and found a wooden basement door set at a forty-five-degree angle to the house, to cover a set of concrete steps. She pried up the hasp to disconnect the padlock that held the door shut, opened it, and descended the concrete steps to the standard vertical door into the basement. The door was sturdy wood with a small glass window on top. She had to assume that this door would be connected to the alarm system. She studied it, looked inside through the window with a flashlight, and saw a keypad on the wall across the basement room.

She climbed the steps and looked around her. There was the garage.

She managed to get into the garage through the side door and returned with a battery-operated electric drill, a Swedish harp saw with a cross-cut blade, and a crowbar. Over the next few minutes, she drilled holes in the lower door panel, removed the blade from the saw, inserted the blade into the holes, and used it to saw out the panel.

She crawled through the opening into the basement. Using her flashlight to light the way, she climbed the stairs to the kitchen hallway and began to search.

She searched as quickly as she could, looking for hiding places, opening filing cabinets, drawers, cupboards. In each room, after searching the simple, obvious places, she removed the grates over heating and cooling ducts, looked at the spaces behind paintings and inside closets, and pulled back rugs to look for false floors.

She kept her phone connected to the surveillance cameras to be sure that they hadn't recorded any new arrivals, but the driveway remained clear. After two hours she had found four rifles and three shotguns of various configurations and purposes, three handguns, a pornography collection, a supply of marijuana and a smaller supply of cocaine, and almost four hundred thousand dollars in hundred-dollar bills. She interpreted the cash as proof that Attila had been involved in something he wasn't interested in explaining to the IRS—probably the forgery business with Viktor.

Among the things that Leah didn't find was an address for Attila's sister Regina, a list of customers, or any other piece of information that could lead to the other ten fugitives.

Leah took one more pass at the den, a room she had searched before, and in a stack of papers she found a yellow receipt about seven inches long and five inches wide. It seemed to have been torn from a pad of them, and it was written in pen. "Received from: Attila Varga. Item: Rent, second quarter. Amount: $9,000. 59950 Colvin Boulevard, Village of Kenmore, New York."

Leah took the receipt with her and went out through the hole she had made in the door. Before she went to her next stop she drove to the airport rental lot and traded her rental car for an SUV that looked nothing like it.

17

The building on Colvin Avenue was small, and it seemed to be from an earlier era, when the main roads of the northeast had lots of businesses set far apart in single wooden buildings—hot-dog stands, ice-cream stands, and stores offering souvenirs, personalized signs and light hardware, tickets, maps, and pamphlets for tourists. They were usually set back from the gravel shoulder of the road, with parking in front.

This one looked as though it had grown at some point, with a disproportionately large section added in back and parking on a paved lot behind. Leah Hawkins noted that the layout kept the parking spaces partially invisible from the street, which was ideal for a business with an illegitimate side.

No lights were on in the lot or in the building. A sign at the front above the entrance seemed almost intentionally pale. It read, MAILBOXES, COPIES, FAX. The sign seemed to Leah to be a list of dying technology. It might as well say, "Things you don't need much anymore."

Leah drove up the driveway and around the building to one of the hidden parking places and stopped. She got out of the car and walked around the building. She was fairly certain the back door could be jimmied, but she was sure an alarm would go off if one of the doors or windows were opened. Most alarm systems had a delay of forty seconds or so after the alarm began sounding before the signal went to the police station or the rent-a-cop dispatch. If she could open the control box in that time and switch the system off, it wouldn't get sent at all. This building was small and simple, so she might be able to spot the box from outside.

She went to the nearest window and shone her flashlight inside. Within about thirty seconds she identified it, attached to the wall at the back of the shop, but it had a large padlock attached to keep it shut, and the lock looked too sturdy to hammer off. She would have to find another way. Alarm systems wired the places that were supposed to open—doors and windows, usually. She would have to look for things that weren't supposed to open.

She took out the keys to the SUV, climbed in, backed the vehicle up to the building, stopped, and set the brake. Then she got out, took a rope out of the climbing kit at the back of the vehicle, and tied the rope to the trailer hitch. She walked around to the front of the vehicle. She climbed on its hood and stepped up on its roof and then walked to the overhang of the building's roof and stepped up.

The roof was nearly flat, with a slight slant so the water and snow would slide off. She saw vertical vent pipes, but what interested her most was the HVAC unit mounted on the roof. It wasn't huge, so she tried rocking it. Screws held it fast though, so she took out her folding knife and unscrewed the ones she saw. When she tried rocking it this time, she was able to tilt it much farther. She tied her rope around the upper part of it and walked back along the building to the roof of the SUV and slid down its hood.

She started the vehicle, put it in gear, and let it drift ahead until the rope was taut. She gradually pushed down on the gas pedal until the car pulled the unit over onto its side. Leah backed up to the side of the building again and climbed back up to the roof.

The unit had exposed a gap where the warmed or cooled air was supposed to blow into the building. She untied the rope, pulled up the slack until it was tight, and then tied a loop in the end, held it, and lowered herself into the building.

Leah used her flashlight to see what was beneath her. She found that she was coming down only a foot or so from the front counter, where the customers came for service. She swung on the rope a little so her feet would reach the counter, and then stood. She took off the rope and jumped to the floor. There was a wall of mailboxes with combination locks in the front. She walked around it to the backside, where the clerks were supposed to stick the mail for postal box renters. She reached in one and looked at the pieces of mail.

They were old. One held a copy of *Newsweek* from 2009. Most of the letters in the boxes needed dusting. The wall of mailboxes looked good from in front of the counter, but it wasn't real.

She moved on to the back of the room, where there was a door. She tried the knob, but it was locked. She stepped back, raised her right leg, and gave the door a stomp-kick of the sort that she had used in raids. The door cracked on the first try and swung open on the second.

She let the beam of her flashlight play across the shapes in the back room.

There was a large photocopier, or maybe it was a scanner. There was a long tablelike machine that appeared to be a four-color printing press. She walked the room, past workbenches that had machines on them attached to computers. She read the riveted-on metal plates that gave the model and serial numbers. One was an embossing machine. Near it was a machine that said it was a seventy-two-character stamping machine for use with 0.03-thickness plastic card stock, with magnetic-stripe coating.

Credit cards, Leah thought. They didn't just make driver's licenses like the one the girl in the restaurant had. They could make credit cards.

She kept looking. The plate on one machine said it was sold by Miss Ling of Beijing, China. No address, no company name. She assumed it must be illegal.

The next one was a few sizes bigger, from desktop size to desk size. The label said it was an "instant issuance system." It said this one had not only mag-stripe but also chip data coding, and it could embed holograms. It said it was compatible with Windows, Mac, and GNU Linux.

She had found the source, the shop where Viktor Panko and his friends—and an unknown number of other people—had gotten their new identification documents.

Leah looked around her. There was so much to see, but it conveyed little to her. The machines had been used, and most of them had computers plugged into them, which probably was where the information about the imaginary owners of the new licenses and credit cards had been typed and stored and transferred for printing, coding, and recording in chips and mag-stripes. She needed that information. Even if all she could get for each of the twelve was an address, she would be immeasurably ahead of where she'd been at the start of the night. But the machines all had metal plates that said client data was encrypted.

It occurred to her that she had a valuable advantage. She knew the address where Weiss's mother had lived in Naples, Florida. If she could find any list that contained that mailing address, the others would be the addresses of the other killers. What she had to do was find the hypothetical list of mailing addresses, or a computer that was attached to a printer loaded with mailing labels.

She began to look for the label printer she had just imagined, but it didn't seem to exist outside her mind. Then she went to the only place that looked as though it might contain a mailing list, which was the file drawer of a big old oak desk near the windows. There was no customer list in any of the manila folders in the desk. There was no billing record either. She remembered the four hundred thousand dollars in cash she'd found in Attila's house. Of course there was no billing list. People paid in cash, and in return nobody kept a list of their names and addresses lying around.

She knew that she was accomplishing nothing in this workshop, and that the time was passing. Even if the police didn't connect the bodies she'd left at Stella's with this shop, some member of the family would probably be here to open up in the morning, a few hours from now. She had spent half her life studying crime scenes—looking, drawing, photographing, and interpreting them. Coming in with a limited list of specific things she needed to find was the wrong way to do this. The right way was to look at the whole scene and let it tell her what it had to say. She stood still in the middle of the room and slowly turned her body, looking for a long time in every direction at the items arranged around the walls and in the center of the concrete floor. There was almost certain to be something useful and accessible in these two rooms. What was it? If it was hidden, where was the hiding place?

Leah became aware of a bright blinking yellow light coming through the window. She wondered why she had just noticed, and then realized it was the first time a light had stopped there all evening. There was a car in the left-turn lane, preparing to turn into the parking lot where she had parked the SUV.

She turned off her flashlight. She had to get out. She ran to the counter in the front room, held the rope hanging from the hole in the ceiling, and jumped upward to grasp it as high as she could. She shinnied up the rope and out onto the roof, pulled up the rope, and lay down. She stayed in the dark area beyond the peak of the roof on the side away from the street. She saw the car in the left turn lane waiting for car after car to approach and go by. The driver was patient and determined to make the turn, and that meant he was not abandoning his plan to come into this lot. She threw the rope off the roof to the back of the SUV, where it would not be noticed.

Outside, the car made its left turn and swung into the lot. The driver, Denes Varga, said, "You know, this is one of the two or three worst nights of my life. Maybe it's actually the worst."

"I know," Viktor Panko said. "Losing Attila is like cutting off an arm. Georgy Halasz is a loss too, of course, but it's not the same. Attila was your brother, but he was always like a brother to me too. My own brothers treated me like crap. I practically supported them. They wouldn't have had gas money without me, but they looked down on me even before I went to prison. You and Attila and Reggie never wavered, never let me down. I feel terrible about this. It's my fault that he felt he had to protect me." Viktor was looking into the lot as his cousin drove in. "What the hell? What's that SUV doing in the lot?"

Denes looked at the car parked by the shop. "It's probably somebody from one of the restaurants in the mall across the street. The owners never want the waiters and dishwashers to park where the customers might. We're closed at night, so they're probably always parking here. We just don't know it."

"I'd like to give him a real surprise when he comes for his car tonight."

"It could be educational." Denes pulled his car into a space near the rear door of the building.

The two men got out of their car and walked around to the trunk. They took out four shiny rectangular metal cans filled with kerosene. "I'm sorry we have to do this too," said Viktor. "I don't want you to get in a mess with the insurance people or the police."

"Not likely," said Denes. "We often keep a little kerosene around for cleaning the grease and ink off the printer rollers and things like that. The insurance people know that."

The two cousins walked to the door, and Denes unlocked it. He stepped in and reached up to the alarm keypad to punch in the code so the alarm didn't go off. "Remind me to turn that back on when we leave," he said. "Finding it off is the kind of thing the inspectors might wonder about."

"Sure thing," said Viktor.

"We should start in the front of the building and then work our way back here to go out the same door," said Denes. "You'd better follow me. I don't want to turn on the lights." The two men walked through the doorway to the front area. "I guess Reggie must have left that door open. But I guess that won't happen again after tonight."

"We better get started." Viktor lifted a can, twisted the cap off, and began pouring the liquid on the counter, the walls, and the doorway. The smell was thick and spread quickly.

"Stop!" Leah stepped into the doorway behind them with her pistol aimed in their direction and the small flashlight mounted under the muzzle shining brightly on them. "Police officer. Set the cans down."

The man who had the half-empty can set it down. The other froze where he stood beside the counter. There was a second can in front of him.

Leah said, "Come into the back of the shop, and bring the unopened cans with you. Leave that one where it is."

The two men walked into the back room. Leah turned on the overhead lights. The man closest to her was Victor Panko.

Somehow in the dark, Panko had managed to get a knife out of his pocket and stab a hole in the lower part of the second can. Now the clear odorous liquid was glugging out of the can onto the concrete floor and spreading, some of it running toward the business machines and work tables. He already had a windproof lighter in his hand, and he spun the wheel and dropped it in the pool of kerosene. There was a rush of hot air as the liquid ignited and flames rose toward the ceiling. Panko pivoted and dashed through the spreading flames toward the front of the building.

Leah shot him just as he reached the doorway, then sidestepped to the other man and held her pistol to the man's head. She clicked one handcuff on the man's right wrist and the other on the handle of the file drawer of the desk, locked the drawer, and took the key. She patted him down for weapons, but found none.

"What are you doing?" he said. "The place is on fire."

"Not really my problem. I didn't start it."

She went to the wall of the shop, took a foam fire extinguisher, and sprayed the flames. It took a few minutes for her to get the flames under control, but she succeeded. When the fire was almost out, she dragged the canvas dust cover off the top of a large machine, threw it over the last burning spot, and stamped on it to smother the flames.

Then she walked to the prone form of Viktor Panko, knelt to feel his carotid artery, and verified that he was dead. She stepped past him and looked into the front of the building but saw no more flames.

She remained out of the second man's sight in the front room for a moment, trying to think. When Leah had seen the car turning in, she had climbed onto the counter and pulled herself up to the roof with the rope and pulled the rope up after her. She had hoped that the two men wouldn't look up and see the hole, and apparently they hadn't, probably because they hadn't turned on the lights. She had simply stepped from the roof of the building onto the roof of the SUV and then the hood and slid down, then walked in the same door the two men had opened, and come up behind them. At the moment she was glad Viktor Panko was dead and she was alive. But there was still the second man.

Leah stepped past the spot where Viktor Panko lay and into the workshop.

Denes Varga said, "Is Viktor dead?"

"He has no pulse." She walked toward her prisoner. She said, "I might as well kill you too. You're worth nothing to me."

The man said, "Hold on. You got no reason to kill me. I was just helping Viktor."

Leah said, "You're his cousin Denes, aren't you?"

"Yes."

"Then I'll give you an opportunity to earn a full pardon. Here's how you do it. We want the new names and current addresses of the other eleven men from the prison break that got him out. If you can give me those, you're safe. If not . . ." She shrugged.

"I can get them," he said. "They're in the computers."

"Fine. Once I've got them, you're free. You can finish burning this place down or go home or leave town or whatever you want. Does that sound fair to you?"

"Yes."

She moved close to him and unlocked the handcuff with one hand. She kept her pistol in her right hand aimed at his chest and stepped back.

He straightened and walked toward the big machine Leah had uncovered to smother the fire. The machine had a cable running to a computer on the nearby workbench. He pulled a stool from under the workbench and sat at the computer. He turned on the computer, and when the opening screen appeared, he typed a few commands and began to scroll down a list of names and data. The list began to scroll faster, but he was still moving his fingers as though he were typing commands to find something.

Leah was watching him. "You're not doing it. You're erasing the file."

She grabbed his wrist, trying to pull his hand away, but he elbowed her aside and launched himself toward the two remaining cans of kerosene. He snatched one up and began swinging it around, throwing the fuel on the card printers, the floor, the benches, and computers.

Leah shot him once in the chest and he fell to the floor.

She sat on the stool he had just vacated and stared at him. The whole thing was a disaster. She was here in the place where everything she needed to know was stored. Tonight, she had shot all three of the men who could have given it to her.

Leah's eyes strayed along the computer's cable to the big machine. That was the one that made the licenses and cards. Beneath its stand was a tub about the size of a bathtub made of galvanized steel. It caught her eye partly because all of the machines were high tech, but there was this humble object, like something from a barnyard. She noticed that it was full of pieces of the plastic material of credit cards and licenses. Some pieces she could see were just trimmings, but others had mag-stripes or chips. Some bore parts of photographs, and some had whole pictures. She recognized a couple of logos from banks.

Leah moved closer. The tub seemed to be the scrap bin for the rejects and the experiments. She knelt beside it and began to reach in and pull out pieces of plastic. Leah began to look at cards and pieces of cards, taking them out of the bin, shuffling through them and dropping them in piles on the floor.

The Vargas had apparently not thrown their mistakes away and burned or shredded them to keep from being arrested for counterfeiting credit cards and licenses. They had simply dropped them into the tub.

She went through hundreds of cards, scanning them as she removed likely ones from the bin. Some of them had obvious flaws. About a year earlier, the machine must have gotten a scrap of plastic stuck to its printing surface, and it prevented a small section of each card from accepting a stamp or a print. There were at least twenty-five like that. There were other cards that were supposed to have a chip embedded in them, but the chip was protruding from the surface. In others the design proportions of a set of cards were wrong, or the photo of the supposed owner was crooked or improperly cropped at the top of the head.

As Leah dug down through the rejected cards, the start and end dates got older. There was a moment when Leah reached the two-year mark. The dates were in the spring two years earlier, and she slowed her searches and looked more closely at each photograph.

And then she found something. It was a New York State driver's license that looked perfect to her. There must have been something wrong with it, but she didn't see it at first. What she saw was that the picture was the face of Alan Becker, but the name on the license was Michael R. Miller, and his address was on 54th Street in New York City. "Got you," she whispered.

They hadn't been throwing out the mistakes. She supposed nobody dared to leave a couple thousand fake credit cards in their trash. Probably they had planned to destroy the scrap plastic in some prudent way, but had put it off because the tub wasn't full. She took another double handful and poured them on the floor. Her arm shot out like a snake striking and plucked out another license. "Brian Summers," she said. "I'd know you anywhere, even if your license is from Mars. Your name is Paul Duquesne."

There was Martin Ortega's picture, but the name was Juan Javier Martinez. It seemed to be a prototype for an ID badge for a company in San Diego—a security company.

Leah realized why she was suddenly finding failed attempts to make identification for the twelve fugitives. She had dug her way down to the level of March through June two years ago, so this layer of the pile was rich. She knelt there and took out double handfuls of partial or badly printed cards. Some had the pictures of convicts from Weldonville. Others had no pictures, or pictures of other men or women. Sometimes there were driver's licenses in a false name and then four or five identical credit cards in several names, all of them flawed in some way. She found a few identification cards, Class A driver's licenses for truck drivers, even pilot's licenses. Whenever she found any remnant or relic of these attempts, she slipped it into her pockets and kept looking.

Denes Varga had been shot at least fifteen minutes ago. His blood was on the concrete floor under his body and dribbled away from it in rivulets that had found their way into low parts of the concrete surface and pooled. In the mind of Leah Hawkins, he was dead, like his cousin Viktor Panko. He was not.

The smell of kerosene had been in every breath Leah had taken since Varga and Panko had poured it in the front section of the building hours ago, so she had almost stopped smelling it. She had not noticed that it had become stronger in the past few minutes, so she didn't look around and notice that Denes Varga had opened the last can and let it begin to drain, running along the same track as his own blood toward the galvanized tub where Leah was working.

There was a sound of the metal wheel rasping against the flint, and then a flash that lit most of the air in the building into flame, and then as it subsided into a fire along the floor, Leah had a second of deciding. Move now or die. The fire was about to engulf her and the tub, but Denes Varga was alive. He was trying to burn her to death, but she couldn't leave him to die in his fire.

She stayed low, grasping his wrists and hauling back, her arms extended and body leaning backward, dragging the wounded man to the door, trying to see through the haze of smoke that was filling the shop from the ceiling down. She stopped and dragged him to the threshold. Then she saw his face and chest. He didn't seem to be breathing now. She touched his neck to feel for a pulse. He was dead too.

She stepped past him and ran toward the tub. There were almost sure to be more cards that would tell her things. She reached the tub just as the flames engulfed it and the plastic inside became something else, a black, bubbling mess. She felt searing heat and pulled her hand back. She had chosen wrong, dragged a dead man out and left the evidence to burn. She retreated to the doorway, switched off the light, and closed the door.

She ran to the SUV. She untied the rope from the vehicle's trailer hitch, threw it inside, and scrambled into the driver's seat.

She turned and looked in through the windows of the building. In the shop in the back and the customer area in the front, flames were now licking the ceilings. Fire had engulfed the stamping, cutting, and printing machines and the counter, workbenches, desk, and chairs. The flames were all the way to Denes Varga's body. It was clear the building and its contents would be a pile of charcoal, ash, and unrecognizable metal parts in minutes. She knew the two bodies and the kerosene cans would give the investigators something to think about.

She turned to look ahead through the windshield. She had made some terrible mistakes tonight, but the two or three things she hadn't done wrong she had gotten really right.

Leah drove along a side street, hoping to stay away from the big north-south streets like Colvin, but finally took a chance on Delaware for a few hundred yards to reach the expressway entrance to get far from the scene of her crimes. She glanced in the rearview mirror and saw that her face was blackened by soot from the fire she had just escaped. She spotted her purse on the floor in front of the passenger seat, snatched it up, took out some antiseptic wipes, and washed her face and hands.

She drove to the Niagara section of the thruway, got off in downtown Buffalo far south of the burning building, and drove to her hotel. She pulled into the parking structure, went up the elevator to the second floor, and walked the rest of the way to her room so she wouldn't meet anyone.

Leah ran a bath and soaked in the tub until the water got cold. Then she went to bed. As she lay on the tight, clean sheets of the bed and closed her eyes, she knew that in this city at the moment, there were at least two manhunts under way, both searching for her. She'd had a busy day.

18

She decided her next visit should be to Alan Becker. He was now Mr. Michael R. Miller of New York City. She had his new name and address, and he couldn't possibly know it yet. He was on the other end of the state, but it was the same state. She could fly there in a couple of hours. The minute he learned of what had happened in Buffalo, she could lose him. The escapees in other states probably wouldn't see news of Viktor Panko's death. News organizations seldom reported murders in other states unless the victim was a celebrity.

She reserved her flight to New York City. She spent the rest of her time in Buffalo cleaning her hotel room and her rental car and packing. She was determined that if an enterprising homicide detective had a description of the car she'd been driving, he wouldn't be able to lift her fingerprints from the rental car. She returned the car and made it to the airport terminal early, already thinking about Alan Becker.

That morning Alan Becker was thinking about a job he was doing today on the north side of Long Island, in Rocky Point. He drove across the Williamsburg Bridge to Queens and along the interstate toward the turnoff at Route 347. He had done very well since the end of his prison existence. The original problem that had gotten him sent to Memphis Penitentiary and then to Weldonville was a job exactly like the one he was doing today. He had gone out to a quiet, prosperous suburb—that time near San Antonio, Texas—to pay a visit to a lady who was in the early steps of obtaining a divorce from a man named Chester "Chet" Grenville.

Mr. Grenville had made a significant fortune by selling what were called "notions" to sewing stores, supermarkets, and drug-store chains. When he had spoken with Becker, he had told him notions were things like needles, thread, buttons, zippers, snaps, pins, collar stays, and seam rippers needed for making minor repairs or alterations to clothes.

These items were all very simple and cheap, and could be manu-factured in any country on earth where people weren't shooting one another at the moment. To Grenville, that was a meaningful distinction, because his specialty was buying out whole warehouses full of this type of merchandise in countries where there had been wars or disasters and the owners wanted to leave. If the situation was sufficiently dire, the owners would take not even a pittance, but the promise of a pittance to be paid later. He would make the deal and ship that day, and sometimes the owners would not get out alive to collect, so his profits could approach 100 percent.

Mrs. Grenville—the former Star Macklin—was an attractive blond woman about thirty-five years old who was restless by nature. She had married Chet at twenty-two when he was fifty. She met a man at her tennis club during the first year of their marriage, and had met many more in many places since then. If Chet suspected, he had paid no attention, but a short time ago Star had announced that she was divorcing him and mentioned that she was expecting to take with her half of the money he'd made in a lifetime in the notions market. He had called his personal attorney and asked him to recommend a divorce specialist. His attorney had recommended

Alan Becker. Chet had asked, "Is he a good lawyer?" and his attorney said, "You didn't ask for a lawyer. You asked for a divorce specialist."

Becker had resolved their marital differences promptly and efficiently with a twelve-gauge Remington pump shotgun. What he had not noticed when he'd gone to visit Star was that Star had a visitor that afternoon, because the visitor's car was parked out of sight in the section of the horse barn where the caretakers often parked stake trucks to unload hay. When she came down to answer the front door, the visitor, a young waiter named Darryl Mosher, was upstairs in the master bedroom. He had looked out the window and seen Becker doing his job. He'd made a great witness in Becker's murder-for-hire trial.

Today's job showed that Becker had emerged from prison a changed man. He no longer used a shotgun, as he had in his early jobs. Now he carried a .38 revolver. He had come to this change after trying out a .45 Colt Commander for one of his first jobs after prison and having to crawl around afterward searching for the ejected casings. The .38 was not as powerful as the .45, and its power was a tap compared with that of a shotgun blast at four feet, but so far everyone he'd shot was dead, the revolver didn't eject any brass, and that was sufficient.

The woman he was going to see today was his favorite kind. Her husband was having an affair with a replacement for her that she didn't know about, but the husband had sufficient foresight and knowledge of his wife to know that she would be angry when she found out. He knew that when she was angry, she could be vengeful and punitive. He was avoiding all that unpleasantness by hiring Becker early. She would not ruin her last moments with a lot of amateurish attempts to hide, run, call for help, or fight back. That would also make Becker's day easier. She would die happy, secure in the belief that her husband still loved her, appreciated all her efforts and virtues, and wanted to stay with her until they both died of congestive heart failure at ninety-two.

Becker found her at home, reading a book in the porch swing in her back garden. He came around the house, stepped up behind her, and fired his .38 pistol into the back of her head. He returned to his car smiling. He was wearing a baseball cap, a pair of shorts, white sneakers, and a yellow shirt. If anyone saw him, they didn't think what they'd seen was a killer.

Leah had her laptop on the table of her hotel room. Alan Becker's name was now Michael R. Miller. He lived in a two-bedroom, two-bath apartment at 6122 West 54th Street. There were windows on the south side and on the east side. The other two sides were walls, one shared with another apartment. Leah had already checked to see if either that one or another was vacant or for rent, but they weren't.

Since he was on only the sixth floor, she might be able to get a shot at him through a window, but that would require finding a place that was nearby and a floor or two higher up so she could sight a rifle down into his unit. That was very unlikely. It was hard enough to find any apartment in New York, let alone one that was the perfect spot to shoot an escaped murderer.

Leah was over her temporary disappointment that she had found only four new names and addresses at the Vargas' shop. It would have been too much to expect that the Vargas ran tests or made mistakes on all twelve men's identities. Leah had to feel lucky to have found any, let alone four. But she was determined that when she got into Becker's apartment, the first things she would look for were contacts—names, addresses, numbers—he had for other men in New York or elsewhere. Any of them could easily be the new names of other escapees. But first she had to figure out how to get into Becker's apartment.

This time she would also have to take into account the competition. At the moment, the New York Police Department had forty thousand sworn officers, five thousand auxiliary cops, six thousand school cops, and fifteen thousand non-sworn employees. They also had eight helicopters, six thousand CCTV cameras, and an unknown number of license-plate readers, and probably all those numbers would climb by the end of the day. There were also outsize contingents of FBI, ATF, and other federal officers in the city. She did not want any tiny part of that army of righteousness to open a sleepy eye and notice her.

She reviewed what she knew about Alan Becker.

The murder he had been imprisoned for was that of the wife of a rich guy in San Antonio. Before that he'd killed the wife of a real estate developer in Seattle. He'd used a twelve-gauge shotgun that time, and there had been several similar killings with similar weapons before that. The FBI were convinced he had been making a business out of killing the wives of men in ugly divorces for some time. It was possible he would be out of money and doing it again. If he'd been paying the rent on a decent apartment in that part of Manhattan for two years, he was doing something lucrative.

She made a visit to the neighborhood near his current address, staying far away from his building so she wouldn't be picked up on a security camera.

It was a nice place. For a fugitive, it was worth putting out a little extra money to live in a better neighborhood. Being a victim of petty street crime could be dangerous. Even a criminal was better off in a neighborhood where nobody would rob him or pick his pocket or steal his car or start a fight.

Becker was smart, but smartness had its limits. He was up in that apartment today not knowing there was a cop walking around outside his apartment building waiting to kill him. She had found her way to this apartment through no mistake he had made, no miscalculation or rash action. It was just a bad break.

The next question she had was when she should take him. The answer was obvious. One day. No longer. Surprises and advantages were temporary, like ice cream. They had to be enjoyed quickly or they melted away.

The next afternoon at five o'clock, a white van arrived behind the building and parked in an improvised parking space with its blinkers on. A tall, thin figure wearing wraparound sunglasses and the jeans, hard hat, hooded sweatshirt, and green reflective vest of a workman went to the van's back door, put on gloves, lifted out a stepladder and a black canvas tool kit, and walked into the building carrying them. The new arrival went up the back stairway nearest to the door and climbed to the sixth floor. The sunglasses, hood, and hard hat blocked any cameras' view of the face beneath them.

On the sixth floor, the new arrival set the ladder under the first surveillance camera in the ceiling and climbed up. In a second, the outer surface of the camera's clear protective shield had a sticker pasted over it that read, "CAMERA UPGRADE PROJECT" in big letters and "PLEASE BE PATIENT" beneath it. From the hallway, the sticker was not noticeable because the outer side was the same dark gray as the tinted plastic, but it was white on the inside and perfectly legible on the building's security monitor. The sticker limited the camera's entire field of vision to its printed message.

Within seconds, the tall, thin worker was down the ladder and moving it up the hall to the next surveillance camera. There were eight small camera domes mounted along the ceilings of the sixth floor, and they were all covered within a minute or two.

Leah leaned the ladder against the wall so it would be out of the way, took her tool bag, and walked to the door of Michael R. Miller's apartment. She set the bag on the floor, knocked on the door, and knelt beside the bag as though she were retrieving a tool.

She waited for a minute and then knocked on the door again, this time harder. Nobody came to the door. Finally, she studied the lock on the door, picked a bump key from her ring of them, inserted it into the lock, turned it as far as possible, hit the door with her shoulder, turned the key when the pins jumped, and unlocked the door.

Leah went to the place where she'd left her ladder, brought it with the tool bag inside the apartment, leaned it against the wall, and then closed and locked the door. She took her silenced pistol out of the tool bag and turned to look into the apartment.

She passed the long curtains at the first set of tall windows, then moved rapidly from room to room, clearing each one as she reached it, looking for the man who now called himself Michael Miller. As she moved through the apartment, she took care not to leave any unexamined rooms behind her. Nobody was in either bedroom or hiding in the closets, the bathrooms, or the kitchen.

Leah made it all the way to the far end of the apartment, where there was a living room with a second set of tall windows that looked out over the street and the buildings nearby. The windows and the long curtains were the same size as the ones she had seen when she'd entered the apartment, but the first set had been closed. Something about that bothered her. She wondered if what she felt was just the basic human desire for balance and symmetry. That would be unspeakably fussy and stupid. The man who lived here wasn't an interior decorator. He was somebody men paid to kill their wives.

What was bothering her wasn't the pettiness of the discrepancy between the windows; it was that she hadn't looked closely enough at the windows as she had passed them. She was drawn back toward them now. She would take one look and then come back to begin searching his papers for the names and locations of the other killers.

As she moved through the kitchen, she heard something that made her stop because she couldn't identify it, and it seemed to have come from inside the apartment. It had sounded like something heavy rolling on wheels for a moment. She followed the sound toward the door and saw that one of the curtains across from the entry had been opened a few inches, and that what she had thought was simply a tall set of windows included a sliding glass door, which had now been pushed aside. Visible beyond the window was a balcony.

Her eyes turned away from the balcony toward the front door just in time to see the doorknob turn a half inch, as though a hand had just released it. He had to be on the other side of it, just moving off. He had been on the balcony when she'd come in, and she had walked right past the sliding door and missed him.

Leah stepped into the hallway and looked both ways. He was not visible, and she couldn't hear him. She clutched her pistol under her left arm in her hooded sweatshirt and began to advance. She walked quietly along the sixth-floor hallway, pausing for a second or two at each door to listen and to look at the fish-eye lens in the door to see if it showed light from the windows of the apartment or was darkened by the eye of Alan Becker looking out.

She heard a steel door open around the next corner and hurried in that direction. She stepped out past the corner into the next hallway. She had turned two corners, so this area was exactly opposite the stairwell she had used to reach Michael R. Miller's apartment. She went toward the stairwell on the new hall, opened the door, and saw him.

The man going down the stairway was wearing an open long-sleeved yellow shirt in a coarse-grained tropical fabric, a pair of sunglasses, and white tennis shorts. His feet were in sandals, and his skin was shiny from sunscreen. She knew he was Becker. She also knew what had happened. He had been sunbathing on the balcony beyond the sliding door, which was hidden by the closed curtains. She had walked past, thinking it was just a big window, but he had heard his door opening and knew of the arrival of an enemy. He had waited until the intruder was out of sight at the other end of the apartment and run for the door. Did he have a gun? If he did, it must be stuck in his waistband behind his back.

She came down the stairs fast and caught up just as he arrived on the fifth-floor landing. He was reaching behind him, and she knew he was grasping for the weapon under his shirttail.

Leah stepped to the side behind him, and her left hand grasped Becker's wrist and held it down behind his back. Her right hand snatched her own silenced pistol from under her arm, brought it up, and fired it into the back of his head. As his body began to collapse, she shot him once more in the head, then released his arm and let him fall.

She turned and climbed back up to the sixth floor. She kept walking to his apartment, picked up the ladder and tool bag, and went down the opposite stairwell she had taken to get up to the sixth floor.

She put her equipment in the van and drove out of the city and up the Hudson. As soon as she was heading north, she took off her hard hat, the vest, hooded sweatshirt, and jacket. When it was fully dark, she passed a series of small towns where she could dump the ladder, tool kit, and work clothes. Then she drove to the airport car rental and returned the van. She took a cab to her hotel, showered, and dressed for dinner. Then she went down to the hotel's restaurant.

It was late, so she was able to get a table in a corner of the dining room where she could think without being distracted by nearby diners. At this hour they were mostly couples who spoke quietly and paid attention only to each other.

It was time to go to California. Leah had just murdered enough people in the state of New York to qualify as a serial killer, and California was as far from New York as she could go without getting wet. She had addresses in California for three fugitives that she'd found in the Varga family's workshop. She had a California driver's license with Martin Ortega's picture on it, and a new name and an address in the San Fernando Valley. She also had one with Paul Duquesne's picture and one with Matt Bysantski's. She was lucky that California had changed the design of its licenses, and so they had become harder to make than they'd been the last time Leah had seen one. They'd always had two pictures of the driver and some bears that appeared under UV light. Now they had a gold miner on the right, poppies on the lower left, and under UV light was a third picture of the driver with his birthday printed on it, and pictures of a bear with a star on him, Coit Tower, and a few other sights. Every one of them had probably been a trial to the Vargas and a gift to Leah Hawkins.

19

When Paul Duquesne walked along the sun-warmed pavement of Wilshire Boulevard near his office in Hollywood, he seemed overcharged with energy. There was an elasticity to his step, a comfortable rolling from the heel to the toe, ending in a push from the ball of the foot that propelled him about six inches farther than the steps of the other people on the street. He was straight-backed and hard-bellied, so his suit coat hung perfectly from his squared shoulders. The long days at Danbury and then Weldonville he had spent in motion. In the slow times he did push-ups on the floor and pull-ups on the bars or hanging from the upper bunk. When he saw inmates doing something he didn't know, he would try it—Brazilian jujitsu, Krav Maga, tai chi, yoga, Pilates, anything. He divided the single hour of outdoor time each day into running and weightlifting.

For a while during his first year, inmates tested him. He had the look and the speech of someone raised as a rich kid. They guessed he had spent his youth playing tennis and swimming and riding horses, not fighting or scrambling for survival. There were some ugly one-on-one and two-on-one fights. He acquitted himself about average—not afraid to fight and not falling apart when he'd been hit. What had made his reputation was not the fights but the ensuing peace. As soon as a fight was broken up and everyone was caught, they were put in punishment for a few weeks. When they all got beyond the fight, he didn't forget it. He waited for his chance and killed his opponent.

One of them was stabbed, a sharpened toothbrush thrust up under his rib cage into his heart. The second victim was choked out and then drowned in a mop bucket. The third had his throat slashed with something that left cuts clean as a razor's, but was never found.

After these incidents, other inmates began to reinterpret the fact that Paul Duquesne was from a wealthy family. They decided the money should have been a warning. The rich protected themselves and each other, even if their efforts had to be blatant and obvious. If they had let this one be caught, convicted, and sent to prison for life, he must be a kind of throwback who frightened even them.

Duquesne made a few allies over time—selected them, really. They were men whom other inmates feared. There were rumors that he kept their loyalty by having his family send money to support their wives and children. There were observations that made this theory seem accurate. He didn't talk to his companions much. They would simply be around while he followed his routines—passing from place to place, reading books from the prison library, exercising, and practicing his skills. During an especially long stay in solitary confinement, he taught himself to walk on his hands like a circus performer. After that he would spend time each day in his cell walking upside down. His arm muscles grew strong and thick.

Once a prisoner in Danbury saw him walking on his hands and said aloud, "What's he doing?" His companion said, "Training himself to kill you quicker." Now that the inmates understood him better, that didn't seem unlikely.

Today as he walked along Wilshire Boulevard from his office, he was Brian Louis Summers, and he had no plans to harm anyone again. He had no plans at all beyond today. The plans for the long term had been made and were not alterable. The Duquesne family had transformed one of its many shell corporations into an entity devoted to his welfare. It was called 467 LLC, after the suite number of its Los Angeles office.

They had begun the transition as soon as he was convicted in federal court. At first 467 LLC had made investments in the stocks of reliable companies, corporate and municipal bonds, real estate that provided rental income, and other quiet activities. In time the family had 467 interact with other Duquesne corporations, buying from them, selling to them, or merging with them to increase the company's assets.

The employees of 467 LLC were all lawyers and accountants at first, since the company produced no goods or services, only collected profits and grew. Brian Louis Summers was its president and only stockholder. He was allowed to do nothing except receive a salary, which 467 paid directly to his bank, and which he spent through his credit cards, automatically paid by his bank. On the one occasion when he'd wanted anything more expensive than things people usually bought with credit cards, it had been a car. One of the lawyers paid for it with a cashier's check, then picked up the vehicle, registered it, drove it to Brian Summers's house, and parked it in the garage.

Paul Duquesne had been born in Philadelphia and raised at his great-great-great-grandparents' country estate on the Main Line west of the city center, which was no longer in the country, and in the city mansion on Rittenhouse Square. Even when he was a small child, his time spent in each place did not coincide with the time spent by his mother. She was an Englishwoman who saw him as shaming evidence that she was not as young and untouched as she wished to appear. It was an offense that only got worse as both grew older. His father, the formidable businessman Mark Duquesne, was the one in charge of the extended family's holdings, and this left him little time for either of them.

Paul went to college in Boston and then spent years building his own business in New York. He developed a service that helped people who wanted to avoid paying taxes move money offshore. He had twenty-eight employees who handled every aspect of the issue, from filling out tax forms to physically transporting money or other physical assets to other countries and putting them in secret accounts. Paul attributed his success partly to this business model, which prevented amateur mistakes by never involving the amateurs, his clients, in the process. He depended entirely on word of mouth for new clients, so theoretically nobody would learn about it who wasn't known and vouched for by people in his own social stratum. He miscalculated drastically, and it was only six years before one of the people who heard about the service was an Exeter and Harvard man married to a U.S. attorney.

When the raid came, several people traded testimony for leniency, so evidence that might have been difficult to find was not. He was charged with money laundering, tax evasion, wire fraud, forgery, counterfeiting legal documents, and a number of ancillary infractions. Ultimately, he was convicted of all of them, and of murdering a federal officer, which he had done during his troubles mainly as a piece of theater, meant to embolden the employees who performed that sort of work, and to cow the others into silence. He received a life sentence and enough additional years to make up two more at the actuarial male life expectancy of 78.7 years.

The Duquesnes were an old family with wealth founded on profits made in the days of French exploration in the sixteenth and seventeenth centuries. They had been traders, meaning speculators and smugglers, and they were good enough at it to have been accused of profiteering after every war since the War of the Spanish Succession. At the onset of the French Revolution, this branch of the family had been sent to America to exert closer supervision over the family's holdings there, and had brought a great many of the other branches' movable assets with them. Some of these assets were later accounted for and returned to their owners, but most were not.

When Paul had been tried for his crimes, a strong minority of the extended family in the United States and Europe felt he should be cut off from funds for lawyers and left to die in a federal prison. Family reputations were not something one selfish fool should be allowed to destroy. Paul had not threatened or vilified any of these relatives, but he was hurt that one of them was his mother. She was the younger sister of a British earl who was gay and not likely to produce an heir; so depending on who else lived or died, she might have passed a title to her male heir, Paul. There was no money involved, which was why she had married Paul's father, Mark, over thirty years earlier.

Mark was this generation's manager and the caretaker of the family's fortunes. His intellect consisted of an ability to hold on to many facts at once and recombine them in different ways until he perceived temporary imbalances or could create them. He would use them to make profitable exchanges quickly before normal conditions reasserted themselves.

Mark was able to see clearly from the beginning that no condition was ever going to change in a way that would exonerate his son. There was no solution in the courts. He continued to think about his son's predicament for a couple of years. When his son came up with the idea of assembling a team of specialists from within the prison system and breaking out, he experienced one of the few moments of pride in his son that he had ever felt. Mark Duquesne began to work on the idea.

His first act was to get to know a high-ranking official in the Federal Bureau of Prisons named Mundt. The Duquesne companies, and Mark Duquesne himself, had friendly and mutually beneficial relationships with many government officials, including appointees to the commissions that regulated mining, timber, trade, domestic commerce, pharmaceuticals, energy production, banking, and communication. He cultivated Pentagon officials, particularly those who had influence over purchasing and logistics. But he was especially welcoming to congressmen, who were in the regrettable predicament of having to raise the millions of dollars it took to run for office every two years. He often invited these people to parties, held dinners for them, even took them on trips. He added Mr. Mundt to the guest list for a few parties where he could meet people who impressed him.

After a time Mundt was included in some events where guests were provided with theme gifts—pheasant hunts where the guests were expected to keep the expensive shotguns they used, trips on a yacht to a company-owned resort where other guests included some unusually attractive younger women with foreign accents who were more appreciative and playful with older men than American women ever seemed to be. This phenomenon was explained by the suggestion that foreign women were simply less spoiled, but Mr. Duquesne was aware that they needed to be spoiled as much as anyone to ensure both receptivity in the present and loss of memory in the future. If Mr. Mundt ever wondered whether he was behaving recklessly, he could simply look to his right and his left and see men with much more to lose than he had.

During this period of a year or more, Mark Duquesne was waiting for his son's list. When it came, it was encrypted in a code the family had commissioned more than two hundred years earlier for situations when one of them was held for ransom or doing business in an unfriendly country where he didn't want to be understood. There were eleven names and the prisons where they were incarcerated. Paul had collected them patiently using the prison-to-prison system of gossip and rumors. He asked that he and the other eleven all be transferred from the prisons where they were to the penitentiary in Weldonville, Colorado.

These were special inmates. Three had escaped from prisons before. One was a chemical engineer, and another an electrical engineer. Two were Special Forces veterans with combat experience and extensive training who had both committed murders during their last enlistments. One was chosen because he had been known to sell impeccable identification to prisoners who were being released and wanted to start again with no records. Three were killers held in high regard by the major prison gangs that infested the prison system.

Mr. Mundt had never been surprised that Mark Duquesne would seek his acquaintance. In return, he had done a few small favors over a year's time for Duquesne's son—small improvements in his facilities, having infractions removed from his record, allowing him to have a cell phone. These were privileges usually reserved for prisoners who snitched on other inmates or provided information about crimes on the outside, but Mundt didn't care. He considered the favors to be to his own advantage. Doing well for Paul Duquesne only proved that he had power over him. If he could help him, he could harm him. He knew Mark Duquesne was intelligent enough to see that. Mr. Mundt became comfortable and confident in the feeling that he had this very powerful family at his mercy. He began to find new ways to monetize the friendship. Twice he asked Duquesne for large contributions to law enforcement charities that they both knew didn't exist. On three occasions he asked for large loans and got them, knowing that regardless of what papers he signed, he would never be asked to repay them, because Paul would be in prison forever.

The day came when Mark Duquesne took Mr. Mundt aside and talked to him in the privacy of his billiard room. He handed Mr. Mundt the list of inmates, and when Mr. Mundt understood what he was being asked to do, his heartbeat doubled. He said that this was a big favor, one that could get him into trouble.

Mr. Duquesne had never been unpleasant in Mundt's presence. This time he said, "I'll be very grateful if, as my friend, you will do me this favor." It was said in a quiet, even way.

Mundt said, "It's not that I don't have power in the system. For instance, I can pretty much dictate what your son's life will be like."

Mark Duquesne said, "Then use the power to help him."

"I don't know, Mark," Mundt said. "That kind of move could be risky for me personally. What keeps a public career viable is reputation."

"You should know I have audio and video recordings of every moment you have ever spent on my property, my boats and my aircraft, my country houses, and my resorts. Sending copies to certain officials would land you in the same institutions as my son."

"I can have your son killed in prison."

"I can have you killed anywhere in the world outside prison. I do lots of favors for friends, and once in a while I ask for one in return."

The transfers were done over a period of nine months. They were among many transfers from crowded maximum-security prisons after Weldonville had been reclassified to accept prisoners convicted of more-violent crimes.

Mr. Mundt continued to be on the guest list for various events hosted or sponsored by the Duquesne family's companies. After a lull he attended some of them, but he seemed to be testing the temperature and found it had cooled, so his visits tapered off. After July 19 two years ago, he never attended another, and never called, wrote, or emailed anyone connected with the Duquesne interests.

On July 19 Paul Duquesne also learned that his situation had changed while he was away. When he arrived at the rendezvous in Denver driving a car stolen from a murdered prison guard, he was met by an emissary of the family, his cousin Charles, son of his uncle Philip. Charles explained the rules and conditions of Paul's new life, set by the elders of the family who controlled the family money and, therefore, its power.

Paul would live in Southern California, a place he had never visited in his life except for airline terminals and hotels during stopovers while traveling to and from Asia or the Pacific. He must never go near any of the family homes in the Northeast and Europe, and never attempt to contact any member, friend, or employee of the family for any reason, either in person or through intermediaries. In return, the expenses incurred in defending him in court, freeing him from prison, and maintaining him for life would be forgiven.

The elders had selected Charles as the one to deliver the family's message because he and Paul had been companions in childhood and adolescence before Paul had disqualified himself from attending any of the schools and colleges where the family sent its sons and, increasingly, daughters. Paul and Charles had remained on speaking terms long after most others had begun pretending Paul didn't exist, simply dropping him from the lists, which became easier after he had gone to prison and wasn't likely to show up at a family event. But Charles shared a quality with Paul, being a pragmatist who believed that it might be to his advantage to keep a cousin's friendship—a small, nonperforming asset that cost him nothing. The two shook hands and thumped each other on the back when they parted the morning of July 20.

Paul was now thriving in Los Angeles, which he had found was in nearly every way superior to places in the East. He was bathed in sunshine and cooled by breezes from the ocean twelve months a year. He had a good house high in the hills between Hollywood and the Valley, slightly on the valley side of the crest line. The location, landscaping, and architecture made the house very private. He could activate the automatic door of his garage, drive out and down the quiet, winding street behind the tinted glass of his BMW, and go anywhere. His neighbors, who had also paid millions to live on this secluded street, had no more desire to notice him than he had to be noticed.

467 LLC retained three assistants to do things for the man they called Brian Summers that most people had to do for themselves. They brought him food from restaurants, ensured that his car was maintained and clean, and answered his door and his phone. Twice

a week two of them would go to pick up an escort from her apartment, drive her to Summers's house, and later pay her and drive her home.

This morning while Summers was in the middle of one of his exercise routines in the privacy of his secluded backyard, the assistant in charge of Summers's phone came out to the patio and handed it to him. When Summers answered, he recognized the voice on the other end as Charles's. "Brian," said Charles. "I have some news, and I don't think it will be especially good news. A man named Matt has called your emergency number."

"Did he say what was up?"

"He left a number."

Brian held out his hand and fluttered his fingers, and the assistant handed him a pen and a small pad. "Okay, go ahead."

Charles read the number, and Paul repeated it.

"Correct. I do have to remind you that whatever it is, you've got to abide by the rules the old men have dictated. They won't help again."

"I know. Thanks," said Paul. "I don't suppose there's any news about the family for me."

"No. I don't know if it occurred to you before, but they have rules for me too. That's one of them."

"I figured. You were always better than I was at the rules. Thanks again. If we don't get to talk again, have a good life."

"You too. Goodbye."

"Goodbye." He handed the phone back to the phone assistant. This wasn't the first time it had occurred to him that his assistants weren't only servants. They were also jailers. He said to this one, "Get me a phone I can use to call out."

The man turned and went back into the house, then returned with a cheap-looking cell phone. Brian tested it, got a dial tone, and dialed the number Matt Bysantski had left. Matt came onto the line almost instantly.

"Paul?" After two years it was a jolt to hear anyone call him Paul. "Hi. What's up?"

"Reggie Varga called me, trying to get the word out. Her cousin Viktor Panko and her two brothers and another cousin got killed a few days ago."

"Who did it?"

"She doesn't know. She said there was a retired female cop in Buffalo who had been asking about Panko, and after some poking around, her brothers figured out the old cop was working with some other investigator, a woman who wasn't local and had been asking around too. They were afraid she was FBI or state police or something. Right after they killed the retired cop, they set up an ambush at the old woman's house to get the younger woman she was working with. The ones who got killed were Attila Varga and his cousin. Then her other brother and Panko decided they'd better burn down their workshop to get rid of evidence. When they went over to do it, there were people waiting, and they got killed."

"It just sounds like they killed some old woman for nothing, and her relatives didn't appreciate it. A local thing."

"No. Once Reggie started calling, she learned that it wasn't just Panko and her family. Weiss has been missing in Florida for a while, maybe a month."

"Another thing that could be nothing."

"Could be but isn't. Two days after her brothers and Panko got it, she says Alan Becker got killed in his apartment building in New York City. Somebody called the police, and when the police came, they found him in the stairwell. It was in the papers there."

"Jesus."

"That's all you can say?"

"I just found out. Give me a second and I'll do better. Is there anybody else, or is that all?"

"Reggie was in the middle of calling people, and I decided I'd better help get the word out. I think somebody has been out there hunting us down, and I'm trying to be sure that everybody who's left knows about it."

"Gee, I don't know about this," said Paul. "I picked these guys for a lot of reasons—knowledge, skills, and so on, but some of them were a little bit temperamental. In two years any of them could have made a lot of new enemies, or gotten pissed off at somebody and then found out the other guy thought faster."

"I'm not doubting that. But this is a big country, and these guys had everything they needed to stay hidden for years. They were all living right where they said they would to be. They didn't decide to run for governor and get recognized."

"I'm not sure that proves they did everything right."

"Reggie thinks somebody got our new names and addresses."

"Didn't you say her workshop got hit this week? How does she explain Weiss? He disappeared before then."

"She doesn't explain it," said Bysantski. "She was doing us a favor by calling to tell us there's a problem. That's all."

"What are you trying to get me to do?"

"I think we've got to get ready for some people to show up in California."

20

Martin Ortega located the special cell phone after it had rung several times. After two years he had gotten used to the idea that it was never going to ring, just sit there plugged into the wall until he died. He was sure this would be one of those calls from people offering him a vacation at a special low price as a reward for having stayed at one of their hotels. He never stayed at hotels.

"Yeah, what is it?"

"This is Paul."

Ortega paused. "I'm surprised. You told me this phone was only for an emergency."

"We think we've got one."

"What kind?"

"Somebody has been taking our people off the count. Weiss, then Panko, and Becker so far. Reggie Varga says that when they killed Panko, they also killed her two brothers and another cousin and burned their bodies in their shop. She thinks that they somehow got a list of the new names and addresses."

"From the shop?"

"I don't think so. They got to Weiss before they found the shop, and killed Panko in the shop."

"What do you want to do?"

"Bysantski thinks we should pick a place—one of our addresses—and get together there to wait for them."

"Wait for who? To do what?" asked Ortega. "Is this Colorado state cops who don't want to bother with a trial? FBI? If any of them had us sighted in like that, why wouldn't they just call the California cops and have a hundred of them roll in and scoop us up? And if it's not cops, who is it?"

"Look, I only heard about this from Matt about ten minutes ago. I haven't thought it through. I'm just helping Matt make sure everybody finds out. I started with you because of where you live. Give yourself and me some time to think about it. Take a look around in your life to see if somebody seems to be watching you or anything else has changed. I'll call you again tomorrow. Is this a good time to call?"

"Yeah. I'll talk to you then."

Brian Summers hit the screen to disconnect. He set the phone down and the phone assistant took a step toward it, but Summers held up his hand and the man stopped. "I'm going to make another call on that line. No more than two. Then you can get rid of it."

"Yes, Mr. Summers."

The phone assistant turned.

Summers said, "Wait. Get the others. We're going to have a little meeting in the living room."

When the others assembled in the living room, Summers was sitting in an armchair facing the long couch. He still had the pen and pad in one hand. He used the other to show he wanted them to sit on the couch.

"It's time for a little honesty. I had nothing to do with selecting or hiring you guys, and I don't know much about what you've been told or what your qualifications are. I give you orders, and my company pays you, but you don't work for me. All three of you look like you might have been cops at one time, or military, but looks are deceptive. I also don't know how much you know about me."

The three stared at him like so many trained dogs. Their unblinking eyes were focused and attentive, but no more than that.

"It doesn't matter. I have strong reasons to believe that trouble is coming for me soon. It's not going to be something that you or I will be able to prevent, and to keep up my honesty, you won't be of much use in getting me through it. If I do make it through, I'll probably need your help at that time, but not so much until then. Any questions so far?"

The three remained silent.

"I'm in the process of making a list." He held up the pad, where a few lines had been written. "I'd like to have you three pick some things up for me. After you've done that, I want you to take a couple of weeks off. If you're here in the house during that time, it will put you in very serious danger." He looked at each of them in turn, studying their eyes. It was as though he were speaking to men who couldn't hear him or see him.

"I'll be more explicit. People are coming here to kill me. They've already killed three of my former associates living in different states. I don't know yet who the killers are, or what they look like, or even how many. I do know that so far there haven't been any instances of them trying to kill one of my friends and failing. If they find you here, they'll consider killing you a necessary step to get me."

The car assistant raised his hand about six inches.

"A question?"

The man said, "When will the list be ready?"

"Give me fifteen minutes."

The three assistants got up and dispersed, either because he had summoned them from chores they'd been doing and they wanted to finish or to keep him from thinking that they were discussing his revelations where he couldn't hear them.

Summers turned to the notepad and wrote:

6 Glock 17 pistols, 9 mm with two magazines each

3 AR15 rifles with 10-power scopes

500 rounds 5.56 x 45 mm rifle ammunition
300 rounds 9 x 19 mm pistol ammunition
$200,000 in $100 bills

When the assistants returned, Summers handed the car assistant the list. The assistant read through the list and said, "When will you need these items, Mr. Summers?"

"I guess I've needed them for the past two years. I just didn't know it until now. As soon as it's done, you can go someplace safe."

Three days later Brian Summers turned off the long, winding highway onto a wide, flat, dusty space that had been covered with gravel numerous times over the years. It looked as though the gravel wasn't keeping the dust down this summer, and wouldn't help much with the mud next winter either unless more gravel was added.

A steel cattle stile was set into the ground at the boundary between the turnaround space and the ranch road, and above it a wide steel gate was held shut by a thick chain and a heavy combination padlock the size of a man's wallet. Summers waited while the cloud of dust he had kicked up floated over his navy blue BMW and away.

Then he got out of the car and stepped to the padlock, worked the combination he'd been given, and swung the gate open. A flock of quail just beyond the gate ran away from the incursion to disappear into the tall crop of dry weeds to the side. He drove in onto the ranch road and locked the gate again.

The dirt and gravel road went along a sturdy fence with five strands of barbed wire between the steel posts. He could not see exactly where the ranch road went because it climbed to a ridge with a flattened mound on it and then curved around behind the mound.

He began to drive along the road and glanced into his rearview mirror and confirmed what he'd expected: that he was trailing a cloud of dust that stretched a hundred feet and rose into the air about twenty. His arrival would not be a surprise. When his BMW reached the last part of the road and swung up the steep incline to the top of the ridge, the road turned and he found he was almost at the house. He studied it.

The building at first struck him as adobe-inspired, a plain structure with narrow windows on the side facing the highway. As he came closer, they reminded him of the arrow ports of a castle. The walls sloped outward from the flat roof, so they were thicker near the bottom. He noticed two low structures that looked a bit like unfinished water wells—just rings of stone about three feet high— at a distance from the sides of the house.

Summers drove his car slowly up onto the flat area surrounding the house, parked between a van and a pickup truck, and then got out. Ortega was already striding toward him with his right hand held out. They shook hands without speaking. Then Summers pointed toward the house. "It looks a little like where we came from."

Ortega laughed. "I've been working on this place for two years. I decided at that time that I wasn't going to let them put me back in a cage. I bought this ranch, got some guys together, and started building."

"What guys? People you can trust?"

"Relax. They're La Eme, all of them. They know if they talk, the guy who just ate lunch with them will kill them."

Summers took a breath and let it out, and noticed himself becoming Paul Duquesne again. He felt reassured. He had picked Ortega two years ago because Ortega was a respected shot caller in the biggest and most important gang in the prison system. Since the gang had alliances for various purposes with some other powerful gangs, Ortega had been invaluable in getting past the resistance of the prisoners who were in gangs and those who weren't.

"If you trust them, so do I," said Duquesne. "Is Matt here yet?"

"He got in last night in that white pickup with the hard cover on it. It holds a lot of supplies."

"I hear the hint. I brought some things with me too. I brought a new AR15 and two new Glocks for each of us, a lot of ammo, and some cash. I also brought food and water to cover up that stuff in my trunk." He clicked the fob on his key chain and the trunk popped open. Visible were four cases of water and four cases of beer. There were also boxes of canned goods and bags of nuts, dried fruit, flour, sugar, potatoes, and rice.

Ortega said, "Good, Paul. Really good. There's a big water tank up above the house, but if they come, they'll probably cut that off or blow holes in it. The guns and ammo will help a lot if the fight comes this close. I've always kept a few long guns up here in case I need to reach out to tap somebody, but close-up you win by firepower. I watched you all the way from the highway through a rifle scope."

"You could recognize me that far away?"

"You made it up here, didn't you?" He slapped him on the back. "I had the crosshairs on you all the way, and yet here you are, looking good. Let's unload your stuff and take a look at it."

21

Leah Hawkins drove toward the evening sun. Driving across the country was a good way to drop out of sight for a while. Summer afternoons lasted longer than winter ones, and the sun's angle wasn't as low and blinding so early, so this hadn't been a bad driving shift. And driving on the plains that used to be the southern part of the Great Lakes was easy, except when there was road construction.

Leah was an expert driver because of her years as a state police officer and then as a local cop. She had no idea how many days she had spent behind the wheel of a car before she was promoted to homicide detective, but it was at least a few thousand. Even then she had spent long stretches of time in a car, using it as a mobile office while she went from place to place talking to witnesses and technicians, or going to see victims. In homicide the victims were past talking, but she had visited all of them. By now, if she was sitting upright, driving took so little additional effort that being a passenger didn't relax her much.

She was going to have to stop somewhere to sleep soon, and the idea of sleeping in hotels along the highway made her think about Mark. He had been one of those men whose faces assumed a smooth, innocent expression while they slept, like they were children. There were plenty of people, both men and women, who while sleeping looked like they were dead, with jaws slack and mouths—and sometimes eyes—open, their facial muscles devoid of tension so the skin sagged. Mark Ballard's face had looked smooth and happy.

The first time she had slept with Mark Ballard was also the first time she had ever stayed all night with any man, with both of them still lying side by side in the same bed in the morning. Other times when she'd been with men, either she or they would go home after waiting a long enough interval so that it wouldn't seem as though the sex was all that was going on between them, even if it was.

She had tried to keep things that way with Mark too, but he simply wouldn't let her. They'd had exciting, wonderful sex, and they were both relaxed and tired. She had thought of it as feeling like a warm, wet noodle. They were in his hotel room a few miles outside Weldonville, off the highway, because they had not dared meet in Denver, where they both lived and worked in those days. She decided it was best to go, but it was very late—too late to go to her parents' house in Weldonville, and too late to get a room somewhere else without being memorable to anyone who saw her.

She'd tried to get up anyway, but he had held her and made her want to lie there some more. She thought about the fact that it was the first time he'd see her when she didn't have makeup on, and had questionable breath, and wasn't a graceful, tall creature painted in romantic dim light, but an awkward, bony person with big feet and with hair sticking out from her head like straw, and blond eyelashes that made her eyes look like two holes poked in an uncooked pie crust.

What if she snored? Or drooled in her sleep? He was married to Marcia, who was beautiful and small-boned and tiny, like a rare bird. But that night, Mark was falling asleep with, literally, a basketball player. She lay there in his arms fretting about the way she would seem to him until she fell asleep.

She remembered waking up in a panic. The light seemed horribly bright. But at least he wasn't up and walking around. She carefully rolled to the side of the bed and raised her torso so her feet would be planted on the ground. She stepped to the chair where she had left her clothes and purse, and slipped into the bathroom. When she had locked the door, she began to feel safe.

She used the toilet, brushed her teeth, showered quickly, fixed her hair, and applied makeup without yielding to the temptation to put the eye makeup on as thickly as she had in the evening. She opened the door and came out, and realized he was not in the bed. She took a painful indrawn breath. He was gone. No, he wasn't. His suitcase was still there, open on that folding stand.

She heard heavy footsteps outside the door, heard the lock click, and turned to see him coming into the room. He was wearing gym shorts and sneakers and a T-shirt with a dark triangle of sweat on the chest, and there was a thin coating of sweat on his forehead and arms. "Hey, how long have you been up?"

"Not long," she said. Her relief had helped her make her voice sound relaxed and a little amused.

"I woke up early and went for my run. I would have woken you up, but I didn't think you had your running stuff with you. But you're all dressed. If you'll wait a minute, I'll get a shower and take you to breakfast."

"Can't," she said. "I've got to have breakfast with my parents in a little while. If I don't eat a lot, they get worried about me and say I'm not taking care of myself." She went up to him and kissed him.

"I'm sorry. I'm all sweaty and you're so beautiful. I was looking at you while you were asleep and you looked amazing. I almost woke you up, but not for a run."

"I would have swatted you. But the sweat is okay—good, respectable sweat. In fact, it's kind of erotic in a cave-dweller sort of way. But I'm off. Don't forget to call Marcia. She's probably awake already." And Leah was out, walking fast to her car in the morning sunshine.

She had gotten through their first morning, not honestly, but successfully. Soon they had begun sleeping overnight regularly, and she became confident enough to stop hiding what she looked like, because she found that he still loved her, and loved her more as time passed.

Leah tried not to let her sequence of thoughts about Mark Ballard complete itself, but it did, as it always did. She saw him lying beside her in the night of July 19. She heard the first shots and got out of bed and listened, and as she did, she looked back at him. That image had been taken into her memory, unchanging and unmoving, and it was still there.

Later, when she was with the other police officers preparing to make their stand on the west side of Main Street, he showed up, pretending he hadn't been sleeping with her, just a city employee who had heard shots and come to volunteer to help to preserve order. He took a shotgun he had barely known how to use, intending to fight by her and protect her. She had seen the moment when the bullet punched through his head, and left him only a cluster of memories in the heads of two sad women.

She was on the Ohio Turnpike. The map on her phone said there was a service plaza ahead a few miles, so she began to watch for it. A few minutes later, Leah saw the sign and then the sprawling building and vast lots, the gas pumps on the far end, and the long-haul trucks parked in their special area away from the cars, their motors idling. Leah coasted onto the exit drive and parked.

She got out and went to the restroom, and then walked through the arch leading into the food court. She loaded a hamburger, french fries, and a soft drink onto her tray, and added a big cup of coffee with a lid to take with her.

As she sat down to eat, she looked at the big clock on the opposite wall. She had been driving for four hours. She should start looking for a hotel soon. Six hours was a sensible limit. Any more and she might start getting lazy-eyed and stupid. Driving across the country was something to be done with a partner, not alone. It occurred to her that everything she was doing would have been better with a partner. She ate and drank and took her coffee out to the SUV. She arranged everything—coffee cup, jacket, purse, sunglasses—the way she wanted them, started the engine, and eased ahead.

She stopped to refill the gas tank at the station on the far end of the parking lot, and then accelerated up the long entrance lane and launched the SUV onto the turnpike. During her stop the sun had disappeared beyond the horizon. The sky ahead had an orange-red tinge, and the sky she saw in the rearview mirror was already deepening to indigo.

Her large cup of coffee was in the cup holder on the console by her right hand. She thought about the six murders she had committed so far. She had been forced to take Weiss when she had, even though it was not the best time for her. It had taken her some days afterward to realize that it probably had been the best time for her. Weiss was an electronics wizard. Before he would kidnap a girl in a small, open parking lot, he had neutralized the surveillance cameras above the parking lot. She had left his body in the trunk of his own car in his garage, and it might be months, or even years, before he was found. Nobody had been looking anymore except her.

The mess in Buffalo had been terrible. She had gotten Stella Wizshinski, a good woman and a sister cop, murdered in the search for Panko. Nothing could make up for that. She had killed the two men who had killed Stella, but that didn't buy anything for Stella. And now Leah was being protected from apprehension by the arson fire in the print shop. There could be no trace of her prints, DNA, or even any image on any hidden camera that hadn't been burned, and the gun she'd used was the numberless Glock that couldn't be traced.

The murder of Alan Becker had brought a lot of risk, but she'd made sure there wouldn't be recordings from the surveillance cameras in the building. She had covered all the protective domes over the cameras without letting her face be seen by any of them. She had been dressed like a man, and the vest and hooded sweatshirt had covered all the parts of her that might suggest she wasn't one. She'd worn gloves, met nobody coming in or out, and had disguised the number on the license plate on the rear of the van she'd used. Leaving the body in the stairway meant there wouldn't be much contact with it. When the authorities realized that Michael Miller was Alan Becker, they would still not imagine she was the one who had killed him. It was a man who had looked like a workman.

Her biggest form of protection would be her past life. Nobody would see her as a possible suspect unless she got caught in the act. She had been a popular and successful officer in the Colorado Bureau of Investigation, and still had people there who had been sorry to see her go. A couple of them were now high-ranking commanders.

A background investigation would reveal that her salary, expenditures, and savings were all in balance. She'd always made more than she spent, but the surplus would not raise any eyebrows. She had an excellent record of arrests and convictions in Weldonville, having solved and brought to conviction all four homicides that had happened during her time, and done a good job on cases of all kinds. She had always found that a homicide investigator could learn plenty about people by examining credit reports and public records of births, marriages, divorces, inheritances, and name changes. A background report on Leah would have yielded nothing.

When she investigated a suspect, she searched for gossips and detractors. It wouldn't work on her because she didn't attract that kind of attention. When she was young, there had been a certain amount of interest in her. She had been a minor local celebrity since she had gotten tall enough to dunk a basketball in high school games. For a while people had assumed she'd meet some male player at the University of Colorado, marry him, and raise a few very tall children. When that didn't happen, some people just assumed that she was a lesbian who wasn't interested in making any announcements about it. When she became a state cop, hours away from Weldonville in Denver, people forgot about her personal life.

There was some revival of interest later, when Leah returned to Weldonville as a homicide detective. She came back to Weldonville a short time after the new city manager, Mark Ballard, did. People who hung around city hall and the police station learned that Leah had known Ballard and his wife during the time when they'd all lived in Denver. But as far as Leah could tell, the local gossips never took up the story from there.

They could have. Leah's record as a police officer was impeccable. Her personal life was not. She was the girlfriend of the city manager, but the way they had gone about their adultery had never been exciting enough to interest anyone else. She and Ballard slept together at her house about twice a week, nearly always on Monday and Thursday, but the rest of the time they were apart. A few times a year they went off for a couple of weekend days together to some resort where nobody knew them to attend a convention related to Mark Ballard's work. Their cell phone records would have indicated that they didn't even talk to each other every day. There had never been any scandal, and none of the three had said anything to anyone about the others. They were all nice people.

She reached Los Angeles on August 24 and checked into a hotel. There was no question in her mind which man she was going after first. It would have to be the most dangerous one. Matt Bysantski was a violent man, and Paul Duquesne was the one the FBI believed had organized the others and called for a prison break. But they were not charismatic figures who inspired other men. They were people who hired other men.

Martin Ortega was the scary one. He had been one of the leaders —"shot callers" was the common term—for the largest of the Mexican prison gangs. He was a genuine leader. He exhibited all the traits. He had shown physical bravery and ruthlessness many times in fights, shootouts, and killings inside and outside prison, so he was a role model for others. He was cunning and wily in his planning and execution of criminal activities. And he seemed to have spent a lifetime showing loyalty to his superiors and respect to his inferiors, and they returned both. If she didn't get him first, he would have a chance to raise a little army.

She rented a black Mustang and drove to the address in Pacoima that was on the driver's license that said Juan Javier Martinez but carried Ortega's photograph. On the first pass she used her cell phone to make a video of her progress through his neighborhood. Her recording showed which houses had dogs tied in the yard or dog bowls in back, which had toys or bicycles, which had too many cars parked on their lawns or around them to be single-family dwellings, which routes were clear at night and which might be blocked by cars cruising or groups of young men congregating. She searched for police units and police activity. She drove far away and parked, then came back through an hour later, and an hour after that, each time filling in or modifying her earlier observations. She made six trips, stopping only at dawn, when people were getting up to go to work.

She performed reconnaissance runs during the next three days, observing the lives people were living around Ortega's house. After the third day, she had made enough observations. During the time she'd been watching the house, she hadn't seen anyone enter or leave. No curtain was moved. No mail was delivered to the mailbox on the front of the house. And on Wednesday, when all the houses nearby had their black, green, and blue trash bins out at the curb for the trucks to pick up, there were no bins at Ortega's. The house was empty. She would have to go in and see what she could find inside.

She drove to the airport and returned the Mustang she had rented because of the chance that it had become too familiar, and exchanged it for a black Chevrolet Traverse 1LT with a 310-horsepower engine. She had a strong feeling that she might have to leave Ortega's house in a hurry. She used black electrical tape to change some of the numbers on the plates.

She reached the house at 2:30 a.m., parked the car around the corner, and walked the perimeter of the building. It was a small house painted light yellow with a small porch at the front and a broad, dusty yard in the back with one large tree, surrounded by a chain-link fence. She moved from window to window.

When she reached the side window, she stopped. She pushed her small flashlight against the glass, shielded it with her hand, and turned it on.

What she saw inside was a shotgun. He had it rigged as a spring gun. It was an insidious device, but even worse, it could mean that he had left his house because he knew someone was coming for him. The thought hit her so powerfully that she put her back to the wall and stood still, looking outward at the road, the other houses nearby, and the street while she reconsidered this visit.

She saw no sign of anyone, so she began to move again, first around the house, looking in each window as she came to it. There was no sign of electronic wiring or equipment that might be part of an alarm system. That was no surprise to Leah, because summoning patrols and police didn't often appeal to fugitives. Leah selected a small windowpane set into the side door, lifted a loose brick on the walkway, wrapped her jacket around it, and broke the pane. She reached inside and disengaged the deadbolt, slowly turned the knob, then knelt down to the hinge side of the door and pushed it open from the lower corner, where a second spring gun wouldn't be aimed.

She stepped inside with pistol drawn and flashlight sweeping the kitchen. She advanced from room to room quickly, taking one moment to pause at the doorway prepared to fire, and then opening closets, looking under beds, and finally moving to the next room, careful never to leave an unsearched space behind her. She had been right. Nobody was there.

She moved to the living room and examined the spring gun. It was a modern replica of a coach gun—double-barreled and short, with gaudy scrollwork on the steel parts to make it look antique. The shotgun was held fast to a small table by a pair of screw-down woodworking clamps and propped on a bag of sand. The two triggers had monofilament fishing line tied to them and then running to the back wall, where there were eye bolts, and then forward to more eyebolts in the door and the front wall. The way the gun was rigged, one barrel would go off if the front door opened, but the other would go off if someone walked across the dark living room between the door and the gun.

Leah spent the next hour searching the house. She was most interested in finding caches of paper—financial records, mail, bills, or anything else that would reveal a second residence, a car description or license number, the identities and addresses of friends, the numbers of credit accounts. Her search found nothing. Then Leah found a cardboard box pushed to the back of a high shelf in a closet, as though Ortega had forgotten it was there. It occurred to Leah that she probably had found it only because she was taller than Ortega.

In the cardboard box were several oversize paperback books, one of which contained parts breakdowns, model number lists, and schematics for a two-year-old Harley-Davidson motorcycle; the others were catalogs for camping and wilderness equipment and for construction tools and machinery. She picked the catalogs up one by one to shake loose any papers, and then found two manila envelopes lying flat at the bottom of the box.

She shone her flashlight inside them. They held a cache of thumb drives.

She used her phone to photograph the covers of the catalogs, then put the thumb drives from the two envelopes into her jacket pockets and zipped them shut.

She headed for the kitchen, where she had entered the house and could expect to leave it safely. As she stepped into the kitchen, she glanced at the refrigerator. She should take a look at the food in there to see how long Martin Ortega had been gone.

Leah opened the refrigerator, and as she did, two things happened. The bulb above the top shelf of the refrigerator turned the dark room into a lighted one, and a fearsome shape she'd seen and touched only in training sessions, egg-shaped with incised sections that had earned it the nickname "pineapple," tumbled from the spot where it had been propped against the refrigerator door into the empty air in front of her.

Leah saw the grenade fall and hit the kitchen floor, and saw the safety lever that was usually held in place by a pin fly off as the grenade bounced. She knew that when the lever came off, the striker inside hit the cap, and she had three to five seconds before the fuse burned down to the explosive charge.

Leah went to one knee on the floor and snatched the grenade up with one hand while she opened the door of the dishwasher beside her with the other. She tossed the grenade into the lower basket, slammed the door shut so it locked, and then sprang forward and scrambled across the floor toward the dining room like a crab. She made one last effort and launched herself through the doorway just as the fire in the fuse reached the explosive.

The grenade detonated, and the shock hit Leah like a moving wall. The dining room floor seemed to rise to meet her, and in the kitchen, the door of the stainless-steel dishwasher, dented and pierced by shrapnel, flew across the room and stuck in the wallboard. The tiled counter was heaved upward, separating tiles and sloughing them off onto the floor. The cabinets surrounding the dishwasher were blown to splinters, and a spout of water erupted from one of the broken pipes under the sink.

In the dining room, Leah was lying on the wooden floor gasping for breath with her hands still pressed to her ears. Either the belly flop or the concussion had knocked the wind out of her.

The noise had been deafening. She managed to push herself up off the floor and stagger across the kitchen to the back door. She went down the steps as quickly as she could manage, walked with determination until she could balance well enough to run, and made it to her parked car.

Lights were coming on far down the street as people came out to see what had caused the explosion. She got into the car and started it. As she drove the black SUV away from the area, she hoped that whatever was on the thumb drives was worth almost dying for. Then she realized that was too much to ask. Most people died for nothing.

22

For the rest of the night and part of the morning, Leah stayed in bed in her hotel room, sleeping off the effects of her first meeting with a live hand grenade. After the rattling of carts in the hallway woke her a third time, she got up, showered, dressed, and ate, and then returned to her room to see what was on the thumb drives she had taken from Ortega's house.

She plugged one into her laptop and saw a picture gallery of miniatures, six to a row. There were hundreds of them. The drives seemed to be where Ortega kept his personal photographs.

Many of the pictures had been taken at the small single-story yellow house where she had found them. There were pictures of families, both parents heavily tattooed, lovingly holding babies and toddlers. There were about a hundred shots of boys about ten years old engaged in Little League baseball games. The pictures were always a team with blue uniforms against a variety of opponents, most of the games played on a field with fences painted green and then plastered with the ads of sponsors, like in the professional stadiums. In the distant background there was a high earthwork that looked like some ancient monument but was probably related to railroads.

She scanned each of the drives methodically, using a pen to mark each for contents—"LL Baseball," "Friends and Neighbors," etc. As she went on, she began to see things she had not been expecting. There was a picture of Ortega that had to be recent.

In his prison pictures, Martin Ortega had a shaved head with the number 13, representing the letter "M," tattooed on his skull. This picture showed a man with graying hair about three inches long that covered the spot where Ortega's tattoo would have been. He was sitting on a motorcycle in front of his house in Pacoima, with four other men standing around. They all looked Latino, and they had many tattoos, including a couple of full sleeves, but if there was any gang symbolism, it was too difficult for Leah to read.

Leah took a few seconds of staring for her impression to grow from a resemblance to Martin Ortega to an assurance that this was Ortega. She realized she could have walked right up to him and not recognized him in time. Maybe the thumb drive had saved her life.

One photograph showed Ortega in back of his house lying on an oversize hammock in a pair of jeans with a bare chest. Lying on both sides of him were two women with long, silky black hair. One of them was as thin as a model, and the other was curvy and buxom. Both were wearing only bikini bottoms, and had their chests pressed tightly against Ortega's sides to hide from the camera.

She thought maybe these women were the ones who had been staying in the other two bedrooms of Ortega's house. She studied their faces, because if she ever saw one of them, it would mean he was probably nearby. She tapped on another picture to enlarge it. It was Ortega and the women, but this time they were all fully dressed, riding four-wheel off-road vehicles, looking over their shoulders at the camera. They were on a dirt and gravel road and had just gone through an open gate. It was possible to see past the three, up the road. The road veered a bit to the left, and then straightened and ran along a barbed-wire fence up a gradual rise toward the crest of a hill. The hill had a mound on top with what looked like a house.

There were three trees around it that looked as though they had probably been planted for shade some decades ago.

She inserted another thumb drive and saw several rows of pictures that looked like photographs of the same place. She selected one with the same configuration of people. This one was taken from farther outside the property. In this shot it was possible to see a big rural mailbox mounted on a post outside the gate. There was no name on it, but there was the number 24900 stenciled on the box. Standing on the road were four men carrying hunting rifles.

There were five men on motorcycles in one picture. The motorcycles were all facing the camera, so no license plates were visible.

Leah noticed that the shadows of the people on the dirt road always fell to one side, never in front of or behind the people. That meant the dirt road ran north and south, which meant that the highway it joined outside the gate ran east and west.

There was a photograph of Ortega's two girlfriends in the parking lot of a large supermarket. The two women were lifting bags and boxes from two loaded shopping carts and putting them in the back of a pickup truck. She could see big letters along the upper part of the supermarket that said, "SAFEWAY."

But which Safeway store? There were at least a couple thousand of them. There could be a thousand in California alone.

Leah looked at the cars parked around the women's pickup, using her fingers on the screen to expand the photograph. She could see license plates. She began to get excited. Hotel lots were full of cars from other places. Cars parked at supermarkets were mostly local.

Leah read four of them, all California plates.

She used the police code to get onto the Colorado site that provided ownership information for motor vehicles, and requested information on four out-of-state vehicles, all registered in California. The responses took seconds.

The first one was Samuel Waltham, 19 Brock Avenue, Susanville, California. The second was owned by Violet Hughes, Rural Route

34, Johnstonville, California. The third was Robert Mullaney, Janesville, California. The fourth was Doyle Gottfried, Susanville. All of them were in Lassen County.

Leah called up a map on her computer and found Lassen County. It was up near the northeast corner of the state, close to the state lines of both Oregon and Nevada. It seemed like a good place for a fugitive. He could cross the Nevada border in the time it took to get a pizza delivered.

The state lines were a plausible enough reason to hide up there, but she remembered something else. Susanville had a federal prison, and a state one too.

Leah opened Ortega's file to check her memory. Ortega was an alumnus. He had spent four years in the state prison at Susanville. He'd been convicted of grand theft auto and of having drugs for sale. He was twenty years old when he arrived. Maybe he had seen something that would give him an advantage now. The crimes he had committed that first time had not been violent. Maybe they had let him out on work details, and he'd gotten to know the place.

Leah decided to return her SUV to the Los Angeles International Airport rental lot and then get a new car to drive north.

The drive was long. It was 387 miles from Los Angeles to Sacramento, where Leah stopped at a motel for the night. She went online and found a cabin for rent near Honey Lake, off U.S. 395, and rented it over the phone. The realtor who served as rental agent said it was a mile from any other building. She slept, and in the morning she drove the final 197 miles from Sacramento to Susanville.

When she approached Susanville, Leah stopped at the realtor's office. The realtor handed her the keys, a map, and a printed set of instructions with directions to the cabin, and bestowed on Leah a bag of chocolate chip cookies that she had baked.

After Leah had found the cabin and moved in, she explored the roads of Lassen County on her laptop, searching for the ranch in the photographs, with the gravel farm road, the big swinging gate, and the mailbox with the number 24900.

The smaller east-west highways were the state routes 36, 44, 70, and the big one was 299, which ran nearly the width of the state. There was a twist in U.S. 395 that ran east-west for a time north of Reno, Nevada, but that stretch seemed too far away from the small towns of Lassen County to be the place. Leah went on Google and typed in "24900" and the numbers of the routes, and then waited to see what appeared on-screen. Leah tried Highway 70, Highway 44, and then, on Highway 36, she found it. The picture on the screen included the big gate and the beginning of the road going up the hill to the house. But most prominently, she could see the big black mailbox with the number 24900 on it.

23

During the first two days near Susanville Leah spent eight thousand dollars of the city of Weldonville's money on equipment. She found an infrared rifle scope that used body heat to pick out targets in darkness. She bought Level 4 body armor, tested to stop bullets up to and including .30-06. She ordered two sets of black-and-gray camouflage battle dress to go over the armor, with pads on the knees and elbows. She ordered combat boots in the same camouflage. She bought a pack for ammunition, water, and protein bars. She bought camouflage makeup and a marine Ka-Bar fighting knife honed to a razor edge. Finally, she bought a DJI Phantom 4 drone with both thermal-imaging and light-enhancing cameras.

Every night she dressed in full battle gear and prowled the fields and woods near the lake getting accustomed to the gear, the clothing, the packs, and the night-vision scopes. She practiced dropping and freezing to evade searchers, ejecting and replacing ammunition magazines, attaching suppressors to her weapons, finding good cover, attacking and retreating in darkness. Each night when she was finished with her training, she would run a couple of miles, go into Honey Lake for a swim at around 4:30 a.m., and then return to the cabin to sleep.

She used the hours of darkness, slept through most of each day, and gradually became nocturnal. When she wasn't training, she studied the online images and photographs of the target area until she was familiar with every landmark.

After the first week of training, the drone arrived, and Leah began to fly it. At first she flew it only near her cabin in the morning or early evening, learning to steer and getting used to the control mechanisms, seeing and interpreting what the drone's daylight camera saw. She had grown up playing video games and steering mechanized toys, so the concepts were not entirely alien, but the machines she'd used had been crude and clumsy compared with the drone. It took her time to become a good pilot. When she was competent, she began to fly the drone at night, using the light-enhancing camera and then the infrared heat-detecting camera. In a week she was flying it every night, piloting sorties along the perimeter of the lake.

When she had become expert, Leah went out to perform a surveillance mission with the drone. The ranch to the east side of Ortega's plot wasn't a family farm but a big parcel of land that was farmed by a corporation, so there were no people living there. She waited until 3:00 a.m. and parked beside a metal building at the far edge of the ranch to the east of Ortega's, where her car could not be seen. Then she took the drone out of the trunk and launched it.

She began with a run at high altitude using the infrared camera, searching for the body heat of a sentry or guard, but detected none. The engine of one of the vehicles parked on the hill by the house glowed with warmth from some daylight excursion, but there were no human heat signatures. She surveyed the ranch with the regular night-vision-amplified light camera, taking recordings of what the cameras saw. She was as thorough as she could be, making sweeping runs only a hundred feet above the fields and hillside, covering every foot. She stayed higher above and around the house, but managed to circle it several times, hover over it, swing out along the ridge it occupied and the woods on a plateau beyond it, and then land the drone beside her car.

When she returned to the rented cabin, she transferred the recordings to her laptop so she could study them. There were two doors to the house. They both had steel or iron bars on the outer side. As a cop, she knew that it was so a battering ram would be held a few inches from the surface at first and not break through easily. Each door had two squares on its surfaces, which she guessed were steel plates for stopping bullets.

The house itself was not a normal shape. It was like a square in the process of melting, with soft corners and walls that curved outward near the ground. It had a rough surface, like stucco, but Leah had a nasty suspicion. There were two piles of unused rebar in back of the house, and two pretty large cement mixers. The walls might be concrete. She saw two rings of stone about three feet high on both sides of the house, and guessed they could be firing positions.

She had found nothing that looked like an outhouse or a porta-potty in her aerial search. But in an infrared image of the front yard of the house she could see a faint area of lighter yellow running along the ground, which could be the sewer line to a septic tank. The water was cool coming into the house from the tank above the back of the house, warmer leaving the house from the front, and then formed a rectangle of warmer ground a few yards away. There were chemical processes that might be the reason for the warmth above what she thought was the septic tank.

She could see two white tanks in the area near the side of the house. They looked like forty-pound propane tanks for use with barbecue stoves. Maybe that was how they cooked, and maybe even heated the house in cold weather.

A steel tank that held about three thousand gallons was on a rise in back of the house. Running from it was a white PVC pipe with a turn in it leading into the ground in front of it. She couldn't see any power lines running up from the highway to the house, or strung from anywhere. There was also no sign of the kind of service mast that was usually on the front corner of the roof of a house with commercial power. There was a metal shed about thirty feet from the house that might hold a gasoline generator.

She thought about the implications. There didn't seem to be a way to provide power to an alarm system or a set of floodlights, unless they were on a battery system that was charged by running the generator regularly. The infrared camera had picked up no heat at the metal shed.

Each night Leah continued her combat training, her running and her swimming. Twice more she took the drone and drove to Ortega's ranch to do reconnaissance. She hovered the drone close enough to take enhanced light footage of the license plates on the cars parked near the house and then slowly withdrew the drone. She explored the ranches on three sides of the Ortega ranch. She studied the highway that ran past the gate and the mailbox. But most carefully, she used the heat-seeking infrared camera to search for guards or sentries or patrols. She ran the same camera along the upper parts of the house, the three big old oak trees nearby, the fence posts along the gravel access road, and randomly in the nearby fields to detect any faint heat glow of a security camera. She detected nothing.

On the next night Leah was only two nights from the date she had chosen from the start. She was as physically and mentally ready as she was likely to get. She had studied the Ortega ranch and the area around it on several nights. If the men in that house had come expecting to repel an attack, they had long ago become satisfied with their preparations and stopped patrolling. All she could do if she waited was make mistakes and let them see her. The weather service said that in two nights it was supposed to be cloudy with a new moon, so it would be the darkest night she would get for a month.

Over the next two nights she became fully nocturnal. She spent half of each night training and the other half inspecting and preparing every item of her equipment and making sure there was no chance it would fail in stressful conditions. She had been on many police raids in her career, and she knew the time to worry about the smallest details was before leaving home. She didn't want any piece of clothing or gear that pinched or rubbed or made a sound when she walked or made her more visible. She made sure that her firearms were cleaned, oiled, and loaded, and that each magazine was backed up by another loaded magazine. Her electronics all had fresh batteries and spares.

She cleaned the cabin thoroughly, getting rid of any sign that she had ever been there. She washed sheets and towels, vacuumed the cabin, washed the dishes, put the trash in black plastic bags to take with her, wiped every counter, bedpost, and doorknob with antibacterial wipes, and then went over all of them again.

She packed a set of civilian clothes in a black backpack she stored on the floor in the passenger side of the front seat. When she had finished preparing, she closed and locked the door of the cabin and drove away. It was 1:00 a.m.

She drove toward Highway 36, but didn't go past the front gate of 24900. Ortega's entire ranch seemed to have been designed for one particular threat. He appeared to have imagined that what would come for him was a convoy of police or FBI vehicles, which would break through the gate and drive up the long, straight gravel road toward the top of the hill intending to arrest people. That was not what was coming for him. She drove to an intersection with a farm road that met Highway 36 and turned up the road.

Leah pulled off the road onto the farm to the east of Ortega's ranch, where she had piloted on her drone reconnaissance nights. The ranch was much bigger than Ortega's, and the acreage was almost entirely devoted to growing vegetables. She drove up the farm road to the only building, which was a one-and-a-half-story prefabricated metal rectangle, like a big garage.

She took out the drone and launched it. She piloted it upward along the rows of leafy green plants, up the hillside, and then to a higher altitude above the ridge. She made a wide left turn to bring it along the ridge to Ortega's, then guided it in widening circles, looking for body heat. After fifteen minutes, she had found none. She brought the drone back down, put it into a black trash bag, locked it in the car, and began to walk up the hill.

She was carrying her M4 rifle with a night scope attached, her numberless Glock with its silencer screwed on, a supply of loaded magazines for both weapons, and her razor-honed marine Ka-Bar knife. She walked in the rows of vegetables, following the lines straight up the hill to the crest, where there was a dry plateau of uncultivated land occupied by stunted California oaks.

She reached the summit a few hundred yards from the house and turned toward it. The land up there was broken by rock outcroppings and a few steep depressions, so there was little mystery about why it had never been farmed. In many spots the dirt was so thin that it barely covered the bedrock. She slithered under a barbed-wire fence onto Ortega's land, reached the water tank behind the house about ten minutes later, and sat down with her back to the tank.

She studied the house through her night scope and listened. She could hear and feel a gentle wind up here, but that was the only sound. The house was as she had feared. It had a flat roof with a wall that extended above it a little in case someone wanted to use it as a firing position. There were windows, but they were all tall and narrow, like the slit windows in a fort, and they were all closed.

She got to her feet, crouching to stay low, and walked as quietly as possible to the side of the house. She knelt and touched the surface. It was concrete, and this side of it felt cool. It would be impossible to cut or breach in any way. Firing at it would accomplish nothing. She moved around the building, and the only windows she saw were the same—high up and only about four inches wide. The glass was thick, set in steel frames with latches like the ones on basement windows. She kept going around to the front. The door was as it had seemed in the drone's camera—steel rods over steel plates.

She passed the front steps and saw more of the long, narrow windows, all of them closed and latched. As she reached the third side, she still saw nothing that would admit an intruder. Everything was high and narrow and unreachable. She kept moving and turned the corner to the rear of the house.

She saw the two large, white propane tanks at the back of the house. One of them was hooked up to a hot-water heater with a flexible braided half-inch hose. The other was fitted with the same kind of valve and the same kind of hose. The hose went into a conduit made of a length of pipe that had been set into the concrete when it was poured. She looked up and saw that almost eight feet up was a flat, hinged vent cover set into the wall, the kind used in kitchens. There must be a stove and a hood inside, and they must be using propane to fuel the stove.

Leah knelt and turned off the two valves on the tanks. Then she took out the Ka-Bar knife and cut both of the hoses. She pulled out the severed end of the hose leading from the kitchen and set it aside. Then she pushed the remaining length of the hose from the propane tank back through the pipe into the kitchen. She pushed until the hose moved easily into the space, and then she opened the valve on the propane tank.

Next she examined the hot-water heater. Two copper pipes were inserted through other openings built into the concrete wall, one for the lukewarm water supply from the house and another for the heated water flowing back into the house. The copper pipes were a bit smaller than the holes in the wall, and the extra space was packed with rags. She pulled the rags out, cut the hose that went from the propane tank to the hot-water heater, and then stuffed that hose into the opening beside the pipe for the cool water and refilled the extra space with rags. Then she turned on the second propane tank.

As she turned to look in the direction of the big water tank, she saw there were four more forty-pound propane tanks stored under a pair of door-size plywood sheets joined like a peaked roof. She rolled two of them to the place where she'd left the others so they'd be ready.

She crawled away from the house and then walked back up to the water tank, sat down, and held her rifle across her knees, listening for the sound of a door.

At the end of a half hour, Leah went back to the rear of the house, checked the float gauges on the two propane tanks, and saw that they were down to 10 percent. She replaced the two tanks with the full ones she had brought from their storage shelter and turned on the valves. Then she went back to sit beside the water tank, waiting for somebody to move.

24

Paul Duquesne woke. It was dark in the house, but he knew that something was terribly wrong. He tried to sit up in the narrow bed but needed to put his hand on the wall to help himself up. There was pain. He felt as though an ice pick were being pushed into his right temple, an excruciating headache that took up the space behind his eyes. He coughed, and pain came in a sharp throb. He knew that whatever was going on, he must stand up, but he was weak and dizzy. He rose unsteadily, started to topple, but pushed his hand against the wall and held himself there.

His room smelled horrible. Had a skunk somehow gotten caught in this cramped space and sprayed? He tried to see, but the only place a skunk could be was under the bed, and he knew if he crawled down there to look, he might not be able to get up. The next minute, the smell was like rotten eggs.

So much seemed to be happening—to him, to his thoughts. He tried to clear his mind but couldn't focus on anything except pain and discomfort. But after an indeterminate time standing there, he began to recover a bit. He coughed a few times, and that seemed to help. Something awful was going on. Was the horrible smell from a fire—an electrical fire? No, it was a chemical smell, like sulfur dioxide.

He had to wake everyone and then start opening doors and windows. He headed for the doorway, managed to grasp both sides and hold himself there, and then stepped into the hall. He pounded on the first door, not caring whose room it was. "Wake up!" he shouted, but then he had to cough a few times. He knew he had to be louder, so he yelled as loudly as he could, "Come on! Get up! The air is poisoned!" He staggered to the next door and the next, pounded on the doors and shouted, "Help! Help me!"

A door opened, and then another one. The others seemed to be as sickened as he was, but they came into the hallway. He saw that the first one was Ortega. He was carrying a rifle, probably one of the rifles that Duquesne had brought here. The next two had pistols. Duquesne said, "We've got to get air in here." Then he looked around. "Where's—" He couldn't remember the name of the man who was missing. "Bysantski!" he shouted. "Matt! Get up!"

He had noticed that after a time standing, he felt better, and the others seemed to be reviving a little too. The gas, whatever it was, must be heavier than air, lingering thickest near the floor. "Come on. We've got to get outside."

He staggered toward the front door.

"Wait!" shouted Ortega. He pushed Duquesne aside and stepped to one of the narrow windows that looked like gun ports, lifted the latch, and pulled the window inward.

"What are you doing?" It was Bysantski's voice. Had he been up all along?

Ortega had his eye to the window.

"That's not enough air. We've got to go out," said Bysantski.

Ortega ignored him. He stepped back a pace so the rifle muzzle wouldn't protrude out the window. "I'm going to fire off a few rounds. If they're out there, they'll fire back. If they don't, we'll know it's safe."

In the very dim light Paul Duquesne saw Ortega's finger move into the trigger guard and begin to pull back. "Don't!"

The round fired and the muzzle flash ignited the propane gas that had filled the concrete house.

From beside the water tank, Leah saw all the narrow glass windows blown outward at once. Cracks appeared in the concrete walls, but they were so heavily built that most of the force of the blast burst upward through the roof. Wooden beams jutted up over the walls, and terra-cotta roof tiles shattered and flew everywhere. The plywood sheets beneath the tile layer were blown apart, and flames from the inside billowed upward into the night sky.

After about ten seconds, the rounds of ammunition hoarded in the house began to cook off and fire in all directions, most of them pounding against the concrete walls and caroming everywhere until their energy was expended.

Leah dropped to her stomach and aimed her rifle at the back door. The door was shut. She waited for it to open. She waited a full minute, then another, then got up and backed away.

When Leah was a distance from the house and there was still no sign of anyone leaving the house, she turned and ran up onto the plateau. As she ran along the crest of the hill, the frequency of the rifle and pistol rounds going off in the house increased. A few times, what were probably thirty-round rifle magazines went off in bursts, so the sound was like a pitched battle being fought with automatic weapons. Leah kept running hard for nearly ten minutes without slowing, trying not to fall or turn an ankle in the dark.

Just after she had gone between the strands of barbed wire onto the next ranch, she heard the first of the helicopters. There was the deep growl of the engines and the *chop-chop-chop* of the rotors from far off, but then the sounds grew louder.

She felt tempted to hide among the oak trees, but she knew from a career of police pursuits that hiding from a helicopter among the trees was a foolish idea. She kept running. The only way to beat the choppers was to be where they weren't looking. For a time, the attention of the helicopter pilot would be fully engaged by the burning house and the explosions, and this period was her only opportunity. Once the helicopter started moving over the larger area that included her, she was lost.

She turned right and dashed downhill between the rows of vegetables. As she descended, she built up to a speed that she knew was dangerous, but she had to take the chance. She was determined that she was not going to defend herself by firing her rifle at a police officer.

Her steps came down on the soft-tilled and irrigated soil, so she was able to control the shocks. If she kept herself between the rows, she could probably avoid getting tangled in the plants and tripping. Her long legs were an advantage, because she could take giant steps on the downgrade and not let her torso get ahead of her feet, causing her to tumble. She didn't waste time looking over her shoulder for the helicopter, because nothing she was going to learn would be worth the cost of slowing down.

In another minute she was on level ground, and the big garage-like storage building was just ahead. She resisted the temptation to let her pace diminish because she was near the end. Instead she concentrated on sprinting, landing on her toes, and digging in on each step.

She reached the car, slung her backpack off her shoulder into the passenger seat, and shoved her rifle in beside it. She started the car and drove ahead with the headlights off. In a moment she reached Highway 36, turned onto it, and drove to the east, away from Ortega's ranch with her lights still off. No other cars were on this stretch of the highway at this hour, so she straddled the centerline and concentrated on keeping the SUV on the pavement. She had gone along for about ten minutes before she switched on the headlights.

She turned onto Interstate 385, and when she reached Honey Lake, she pulled up to the cabin she had rented and changed her clothes in the car. She had selected a summer dress and some comfortable flat shoes, which was the least warlike costume she had with her. She bundled up her incriminating camouflage clothes and stuffed them in another trash bag. She unloaded her weapons and placed them with their ammunition behind the back seat under the carpeted layer that covered the spare tire.

She drove on, staring out to the limit of the high-beam headlights ahead of her and into the darkness beyond. When she reached the realty office in Susanville, she pushed through the mail slot an envelope containing a thank-you note and the key to the cabin. She drove to Reno on Route 395. She made it as far as Elko before she threw away the trash bags from Honey Lake, the camouflage uniform, and the boots. She was still on a nocturnal schedule, so she drove on through the dark hours. She kept going into the dawn and through the day.

When she stopped the next evening in Salt Lake City, she sat on the bed in her hotel room and used her laptop to read an email sent by Sergeant Art Sprague in Weldonville, Colorado.

"One hour ago, the Weldonville Police Department got an FBI notification that the bodies of five men were identified in a fire outside Susanville, California. They were Jesus Castillo, Manuel Soto, Martin Ortega, Matthew Bysantski, and Paul Duquesne."

Leah turned off the computer, lay back on the bed, and stared up at the ceiling. She had gotten Weiss in Florida, Panko in Buffalo, Becker in New York, and now Ortega, Bysantski, and Duquesne all at once in Susanville. She had gotten six of the twelve, plus a few of their friends and relatives. She had no more leads to follow.

Three days later, Leah Hawkins drove the rented SUV up to the parking lot door of the Weldonville Public Safety Building and parked. She went inside and found Sergeant Art Sprague in the front office of the Police Department behind the counter. "Leah!" he said. "Welcome home."

She said, "Thanks, Art. Can you unlock the safe room so I can unload some stuff into it? I've got a car out there in back."

"I'd be happy to," he said. He followed her out to the SUV and helped her carry her rifle, the smaller hard-sided case containing pistols, and the packs of loaded magazines in the back door and into the safe room. She had disassembled the drone so it would fit into its carrying case with its controls, so it was just another box with a handle. There was another carrying case full of surveillance cameras and transmitters.

When everything was inside the room, they set each firearm on the work table in the center of the room.

Art picked up a pistol and sniffed it. "I'll get Danny to start cleaning these, and the rifle too. What do you want me to do with the electronics and stuff?"

"Better leave them alone," said Leah. "They're all boxed, and that padding keeps them safer."

"You home for good?"

"Probably just for a while. I need to do some homework."

"Just let me know if you need help."

"I will," she said. "Thanks." She looked at the weapons on the table. "Oh, yeah. Tell Danny or anybody else you have cleaning guns to wear surgical gloves and not to forget to wipe all the surfaces with a cloth after they're oiled. Make sure he checks the chambers before he gets started."

"Of course. I'll check them myself."

"Thanks, Art. I drove all night last night, so I'm going home for some sleep. I'll be in officially tomorrow morning."

*   *   *

Charles Duquesne's cab driver took him from Los Angeles International Airport to the 467 LLC office on Wilshire Boulevard. A young man in a suit, clearly one of the 467 LLC employees, was already in the doorway when the vehicle pulled up at the curb. The man opened the rear door of the car to let Charlie out, and then shut it and hurried to open the door of the building.

"Good afternoon, sir," the man said. "I'm Dale Winters."

Charlie smiled. "Hi, Dale," he said. "Nice to meet you." Charlie was comfortable with who he was and how he fit into the universe. He was exactly like all the friends he'd known growing up, the boys from old, wealthy families who went to the same few prep schools in New England and then met each other again in the same few colleges. Now they were older, and had assumed adult roles in their families, but they were not much changed from the hearty, smiling boys they had been at school. Charlie had been taught that he was a superior being, as a thoroughbred horse was superior. His superiority didn't convey any more responsibility than a horse's did. His smile was not at all the sign of an emotion or a mood. It was a reward to be bestowed on people who were of use.

He followed Dale Winters past a guard at a desk, who waved them on without resorting to the sign-in sheet, and into the elevator. The door opened on the fourth floor, and he followed Winters into the 467 suite. He had memorized his guide's name as effortlessly as he memorized the names of other inferiors he met. It would still be present in the front of his brain until he left Los Angeles, and then it would dissolve.

They moved into the reception area, but there was no receptionist. Everyone here, male or female, was a lawyer or an accountant, or both. There were no clients or customers to visit the office, so there was no one to greet them and no waiting room for them, only a high gray counter like a bulwark facing the doorway.

The two men walked past the barrier and into the office of Brian Summers. There was nobody behind the desk, and nobody was surprised, because the death of Summers was the reason for this occasion.

A moment later an older man stepped in and held out his hand. "Mr. Duquesne? I'm Tyler Walsh. We've got the papers prepared for you. Would you like to look at them here in Mr. Summers's office or in the conference room?"

Charlie said, "Out of respect for old 'Brian,' I think I prefer the conference room."

"And what can I bring you while you're at it—coffee, a soft drink, water, sparkling or flat?"

"Coffee, cream no sugar, Tyler," Charlie said. "Are you the attorney who worked on the papers?"

"I'm one of them, sir."

"Then maybe Dale can get the coffee. Would you mind, Dale?"

"I'm happy to, sir," said Dale. He moved toward the door with alacrity. Charlie could tell that, as he had expected, he had made a convert of Dale, who was gratified that a member of the Duquesne family had remembered his name for three or four minutes.

The two older men entered the conference room. Charlie said, "I hope that wasn't out of line, and Dale is still young enough to fetch coffee."

"Of course, sir."

"I envy him that," said Charlie. "I can remember the day came when I had been working for a year or two at Duquesne Frères in New York, when I came in and there was a message waiting for me from Nancy Hemphill. She was my uncle Mark's chief assistant, an ageless woman made of stainless steel. She was almost supernaturally perceptive and rightly feared. The note said she wanted to see me first thing. 'First thing' was underlined. I went in and found her at her desk. The surface held no papers and not a mote of dust, as usual. She said, 'Good. You're here.' I waited. She said,

'It's time to tell you that you are too old to fuck the women at the office. That ends when you're no longer the one to bring them coffee. When you get to be one of the coffee recipients, you're a boss and it's harassment.'

"I said, 'Does that mean I'm getting promoted?' She said, 'Yes. I'm sure you'll be miserable for a time, but it's for the best.' As always, she was right."

Tyler Walsh laughed with exactly the right brief, knowing chuckle. Reacting to what the great and powerful said required a finely calibrated sense of proportion.

Charlie sat down at the head of the conference table and waited while Mr. Walsh laid sets of printed papers in front of him.

"This one says your company, Aegil, agrees to purchase the 467 LLC for seven thousand shares of Aegil stock. These shares would become assets of the 467 LLC, which, as soon as the transaction is complete, will be wholly owned by Aegil."

Charlie signed the paper and waited for the next.

"This is to register the transfer, which makes Aegil the owner of this building."

The next one appeared from the file. "This one clears the bank accounts of 467 LLC and deposits them in a new account owned by Aegil."

Charlie signed them both.

"As you know, there's a house here in Los Angeles."

"Yes," said Charlie.

"Here you have two options. Since we didn't know your preference, we produced papers for both. This one puts the house up for sale, with the proceeds going back to the 467 LLC. That would, of course, make them an asset of Aegil."

"And the other?"

"This contract simply transfers ownership of the home to Aegil and leaves it as a physical asset."

"What's your advice?"

"We're mixed, sir. The house last sold for a bargain price of three million two hundred thousand two years ago. Houses in this area have appreciated at seven percent a year for over twenty-five years, and lately the process is accelerating. But there would be the continuing expenses for insurance, maintenance, cleaning, gardening, pool service, water and power, and security, all amounting to a substantial cost. Property taxes are limited to about one and a half percent in California, but at three million, that's still forty-five thousand a year. And of course, the intangibles and unknowables might make keeping the property unwise."

"Examples?"

"Mr. Summers was in contact with some people who were worrisome. Before he passed away, he made and received phone calls from some of them, including two of the men who were with him at his death. Before that, he was a regular client of female escorts, who were driven to his house. This raises the possibility that other people, from drug suppliers to friends of these women, might—"

"I get the idea," Charlie said. "I'm going to take both papers with me. I'll go and look at the house, and then I'll send you the order we want executed."

"Yes, sir. I'll get some pre-addressed envelopes to go with them."

"And these are the last papers?"

"Yes."

"You know that I represent all the heirs of Brian Summers, don't you?"

"Of course."

"And there are no other assets?"

"No, sir. Actually, you're just claiming the assets of a company that never had an independent existence. You just took possession as though in an uncontested repossession."

"Right. Good work, Tyler. And please give my compliments to the other attorneys. You worked quickly. Can you have somebody drive me to the house and show me around? I'd like to catch a plane out early tomorrow morning. You know how it is. If you're not out of Los Angeles early, then by the time you reach New York, the whole day is gone."

As Charlie walked back out to the office, Dale arrived with his coffee, so Charlie sipped it as he went to inspect his cousin's space. He made sure he went through his cousin Paul's desk and his cabinets thoroughly enough. There was no problem, because he found no papers at all, let alone anything with the Duquesne family name on it. He knew that searching the house would take a bit longer. As soon as he was sure there was nothing that would further embarrass the family in that house, he would authorize its immediate sale. He should easily make the 7:00 a.m. flight.

25

The odd deaths of Martin Ortega, Matthew Bysantski, and Paul Duquesne were a big news story for a day and a half, until stranger and fresher stories replaced that one. The extra half-day was entirely due to the inclusion of Paul Duquesne, the outlaw son of a family that was well established before the colonies of New Jersey, Pennsylvania, or Georgia were founded.

The police in Northern California knew that whatever they revealed about the case might be sensitive to a powerful family, and so they couldn't release enough to stimulate the appetite of the public for grim details. The story also had built into it an aspect that contributed to its short life span. Criminals tended to band together, and they tended to have enemies who were also criminals, and it was not uncommon for one set of criminals to kill another. What killed stories was ordinariness.

But this time there were segments of the population who shared a professional interest in the story. As soon as the first day, many emails, text messages, and telephone calls were exchanged, reaching parts of the country far from California.

The most and earliest were from law enforcement officials to other law enforcement officials. Many were forwarded copies of official reports. "FYI" or "Seen this?" were ways the senders conveyed their satisfaction. It seemed to be the fulfillment of a law of nature, and a restoration of balance. Crimes weren't always punished, but criminals always ended.

Other people took the news differently. Six of them spoke on that day when Leah Hawkins slept in her small house on Calloway Street in Weldonville and two police officers cleaned and stored the guns that had been used in the murders of the six escapees from Weldonville prison.

The remaining six had all been living for two years under the names that Regina Varga had invented for them, and which were embossed on the driver's licenses, credit cards, and other identification they carried. The first call they received came from her, telling them about the series of killings that had gone on during the previous few weeks in Florida, Buffalo, and New York City. The Susanville, California, killings had to be part of the series.

The first call she made was to Timothy McKinney. He listened to the warning and afterward remained silent.

"Tim, are you still there?"

"Yeah. It's a strange feeling. It's hard to think of those guys as dead."

"Okay," she said, a bit of the frustration she felt beginning to be audible in her voice. She had heard this before from clients. "Now you know what I know. You're probably in trouble. If I were you, I'd do something about it. But it's up to you. I'm going out of this business, at least for a while, so I may be hard to reach."

"You're telling me you won't help us again if we need to disappear?"

"A month ago I went to four funerals. My brothers are dead. Our shop was burned. The machines we used are destroyed. The technology changes so fast, I don't even know what I'd buy to replace them. I have to find out what the next thing is and get some training. The one thing I can do for people right now is passports."

"How can you do that if you can't make a driver's license anymore?"

"I can do it. This is very difficult, but it works. It takes great artistry, things nobody else but me can do. If you want one, I'll do it." What she did was to begin with a genuine expired passport. Most of the artistry she was referring to was done on the old passport sent in with an application for renewal. She would show a change of address, alter the name, and sometimes she would tamper with and replace the original picture so that it looked like a younger version of the client and match the new photographs. Then she would submit the application, including the old passport she had transformed.

"How much is it?"

"Twenty-five."

"Hundred?"

"Thousand. It's a federal crime. It's probably twenty-five years in prison—a lousy thousand dollars a year. And what you get is a real passport, good for ten years, not a street counterfeit. And once you've got the new one, you can renew it in ten years yourself. It's real."

"That's a good offer, but maybe not right now. How long does it take to do?"

"It takes as long as it takes. You're dealing with delicate work, and with the U.S. government. If you might need one, don't wait."

Regina Varga sold four passports that day. Since the originals were ones she picked up in bulk from people who resold papers and identification from estate sales, she paid an average of $10 for them, and $145 plus postage for a renewal application. But she was not lying about the forgery work. It was difficult and risky.

The six men called each other and arranged to meet in the best place any of them had. The best was an out-of-the-way spot in northwest Arkansas, not far from the Missouri border. The place was called Ararat, and it was the world headquarters of the Swift Sword of the Savior, USA.

Their host was Lee Wolf. Paul Duquesne had chosen him for transfer to Weldonville prison to be one of the organizers of the July 19 breakout because Wolf was a leader of a coalition of white supremacist prison organizations. He had been convicted of the federal crimes of manufacture of explosives, arson, and conspiracy to commit murder. He had also been charged with simple murder, but the U.S. attorney had dropped that one because it wasn't clear that he had pulled the trigger, and a weak charge might taint the other charges. The sentences for what they could prove would make him over 150 years old before his release date.

Lee Wolf was not especially unhappy about the deaths of the five men who had been in the concrete house in California. He had been a rival and an enemy of Martin Ortega's, because he didn't like Hispanic people of any sort, but particularly not Mexican prison gangs. At Weldonville, both men had seen the practicality of a temporary cessation of hostilities until after July 19. This had ensured a majority of violent prison organizations would participate.

Lee Wolf had been living in the new compound of the Swift Sword congregation at Ararat for the two years since the prison break. The original compound had been in Oklahoma, but the explosions, fires, and other activities that had ended in the conviction of Lee Wolf and a few others had prompted the survivors to disband and then reappear in the Ozarks, where there were lakes, mountains, forests, and a number of old towns where they could send foragers to buy supplies without attracting too much attention.

At Ararat, Lee Wolf was often called Pastor Lee, or sometimes just the Pastor. When he described the compound at Ararat and his place in it to his fellow escapees, the others all agreed to travel there to talk. One by one, the other five arrived by car, all of their license plates from other states. They were Timothy

McKinney, Edison Leonard, Joseph Lambert, Lonny Mann, and James Holliman.

After they had been installed in a building that was used for storage but had been outfitted with bunks, they went to a smaller, simple wooden building and sat around Lee Wolf's table. They talked about how good it had been to have two years of freedom. They all implied that they were thriving but didn't say enough about their new operations to make them vulnerable. None of them forgot that the other five were, after all, some of the most dishonest and vicious men they had ever met.

The one who opened the serious part of the conversation was Ed Leonard. "With the exception of Lee, we've each come a very long way to get here. We wouldn't have come if we didn't believe what Reggie Varga was saying. So what do you think is going on?"

"I think they're hired killers," Tim McKinney said. "Specialists." He was tall and broad-shouldered, and had kept himself in fighting shape. He had been brought up on a farm and joined the military young. He had been either a Navy Seal or an Army Special Forces operator, depending on whom he was talking to, but none of these men demanded strict truth, because they had seen him kill. How he had learned didn't matter.

Lonny Mann, who looked as though he had evolved to compete with McKinney for the same spot in the universe, said, "Hired? Who would hire anybody to do what the FBI would do for nothing?"

Ed Leonard said, "I think the FBI would have arrested those guys, or at least tried to, before they killed anybody. They arrested me, and I'm sure every last one of them hated me and would have loved to shoot."

"I think you're right," said Holliman. "When I heard about it, I went online for a couple of days reading everything I could find about it. These were all killings. Executions. Nobody was trying to bring any of them to a court. Somebody bought himself some hits."

"There you go," said Lambert. "I read up on it too. This wasn't even a dead-or-alive thing, like bounty hunters. It was just dead. When they got Ortega and Bysantski and Duquesne, they piped propane gas into the house and blew them up. Cops might love to do that, but they can't."

The men all sat in silence for a moment while the thought settled on them like a weight. Then Holliman said, "They got six guys already, six guys who never had anything to do with each other except when we did the breakout from Weldonville. These people managed to find all six, one of them in Florida, one in Buffalo, one in New York, and the others in Northern California." He poked the table with his index finger. "It's only a matter of time before they find the rest of us."

"There are a lot of hired killers in the world," said Lee Wolf. "I've done a bit of that kind of work myself, and I'm sure some of you have too. And I think that aspect of things deserves a closer look."

"What part?" asked Holliman.

"It's a business deal. First, a person has to decide he wants somebody dead. Then he realizes he doesn't want to try to do it himself. He finds a guy, or in this case, probably a squad, to do the hit and tries to make a deal. The hit squad hears who they're supposed to kill and how much the customer will pay for the job. They make counteroffers and agree on a price, a number of dollars. The hit squad isn't after the target because they hate him, but to get that money. It's business."

"Right," said McKinney.

"But the hit squad won't take the job unless they're positive they can do it without getting shot or caught themselves."

"Right again," said Leonard.

"And in this case, the hit squad has already killed six out of the twelve of us. So, they're probably right—they can kill all of us."

"That's a worry," Joe Lambert said.

Lee Wolf went on. "So, the best thing for us is to assume that waiting for them to come and kill each of us isn't a great idea." He looked around and saw the others nodding. "Nor is going out after them."

"What?" Holliman was shocked. "What *is* a good idea then?"

"Going after the customer who hired them. That's the enemy, our real problem. Not which group of killers got hired, but the person doing the hiring. The killers don't give the remotest shit about us. They won't kill us for nothing. If they don't think they'll get paid, they won't do it at all. We have to go after the employer."

"But we don't know who that is," said McKinney.

"Oh, yeah," Wolf said. "I think we do."

"Who?"

"Let's think about it. What did the twelve of us do? We killed about twenty guards, all of them locals from Weldonville. We took their clothes and their cars and drove into town. We raised as much hell as we could there—stealing, raping, killing. We caused as much harm and confusion as we could, so no cops in town or coming to town would know where to go first or what to do. Then we all got out of there in time to be gone before the inmates on foot could reach the place. They didn't have any choice. They had to steal and cause trouble, because they didn't have cars, or civilian clothes, or money, or food, or even water. A lot of people got killed, including some of them."

"So, you think it's somebody in Weldonville?"

"When I hear somebody wants to kill me, I think back on my life. I've got people all over the country who would love to see me dead. I'm sure you do too. But if I think about who would be willing to pay a first-rate hit squad to get all twelve of us, there's only those folks in Weldonville, Colorado—those widows, orphans, and childless parents we made that way. And the fact that they hired killers to get us is their recognition that they can't do it themselves.

We have nothing to fear from them. We know we can hurt them, kill them if we want. We've done it before."

Lonny Mann said, "That makes sense."

"I'll go for it," McKinney said. "It's better than sitting in my house flinching every time I hear a sound in the yard or see a car go by too slow."

Lambert said, "If we do it, we can't go in and half-ass it. We've got to ruin what's left of the place. We need to show them that hiring killers won't protect them, because we know who's behind it."

"We've got to make them too scared and defeated to do anything again," said Holliman. "I'm in."

"Of course you are," Lee Wolf said. "We all are. There's no place else to be."

"What's next?" Leonard asked.

"We pack some gear and leave in the morning. But first, I've got a sermon to preach."

The sun was moving westward but was still over the tops of the big trees on the west side of the settlement when the dinners were barbecued on a dozen grills made of oil drums cut lengthwise and installed near the center of the broad clearing away from the cottages and common buildings. The meat dripped onto the charcoal and sizzled and smoked. When the smell of it was strong, the people got in line, took their dishes and cutlery from the long table set up for it, took potato salad, macaroni salad, coleslaw, and beef, and went off to the picnic tables to eat.

There were not only men, but couples with children and a number of single women, people who lived here because something about the philosophy of hatred and envy and fear that was taught here sounded like the truth to them. Lee Wolf led his five guests to one of the tables and ate with them, but then he got up and went from table to table, chatting, smiling, and acknowledging his people like the mayor of a small town.

Before the sun set, people gathered their dishes and implements and took them to one of the steel drums that had been cut in half to make a tub. It was over a fire and it was full of soapy water. The other half of the steel drum was full of clear water being heated up for rinsing the dishes after they'd been washed. When the process was complete, the dishes and silverware would be returned to the table to air-dry.

As night fell, the people of the Swift Sword of the Savior went to the large canvas tent in the middle of the grounds. The tent had rows of folding chairs facing a podium and lectern. A few men lowered the sides, and people filed in through the openings at each end, pushing the mosquito netting aside like a curtain and letting it close again behind them. When the members were inside, Pastor Lee Wolf appeared on the podium. He had no papers or book, just leaned his elbow on the lectern and waited.

He had a strong voice, and so there was no need for a microphone. "Evening, folks," he called out.

As people stopped chatting and looked up at him, the silence grew profound. "Today I've been thinking a lot about us," he said. "You and I are here in this place for a common purpose. We got here in different ways, on different paths, and this is by no means our final destination. We have spent a couple of years here learning about the world and our places in it. One day each of us will look around and say, 'I've learned about all I can in this place,' or maybe, 'I'd like to stay and keep learning, but I can't. I'm being called elsewhere.' And we'll know it's time to move on, so we will.

"For this time, we've taken ourselves out of the chaotic, pointless, competitive, stupid society we were born into, mostly because it had become impure and corrupted by newcomers and inferiors and their helpers and apologists. We had enough of the fake political system and the rule of degenerates and hypocrites. So we kicked ourselves out. We became outcasts.

"In order to do that, we've had to learn to protect ourselves and each other. We learned to fight, to cut a throat, to shoot. We learned that when they expect you to *give in* is the time to *dig in*. We've also learned that sometimes the way to win is to make them think you're retreating. We learned to disperse and disappear, to become indistinguishable from our surroundings, to live in the enormous forests of this continent or to be in plain sight in the most crowded cities, and then come together again when it's safe.

"That brings us to now. Tonight, we have five guests." He pointed at the five, who were sitting in a row at the back of the tent. "They came to see me, and they brought with them a problem. It's my problem too, so the six of us are going off to solve it together."

He looked around him at his audience. Most were on the folding chairs, and others stood around the walls of the tent, their arms folded in front of them. Many of them wore pistols in holsters. "I'll thank you for not worrying, or saying that you hope what I'm doing isn't dangerous. Whenever I go out in the world, whether it involves violence or not isn't up to me. It's up to them. I'm seldom looking for trouble these days. The time isn't right yet. But I'm always ready for it.

"If you study this planet we live on as I have, you know that violence is pretty routine. Killing is as natural as eating. Everybody is a killer. Do you have any idea who died making your clothes or shoes or cell phone, or even what country they lived in? Do you know who got shot off the land where the gas in the tank of your car came from? No, you don't, and you don't care. I don't either. That beef we had for dinner tonight sure was good, wasn't it? Think about all the animals that die so I can eat meat every day. I don't eat as much meat as I used to—no more than two or three steers a year, and a few pigs, but they've got fat and cholesterol, and I want to live forever. So I've added in about a hundred chickens a year, and about a hundred fish. Even if I don't shoot it, hook it, or cut its throat, I still kill it. My life requires the taking of all those other lives. If we didn't eat meat, you know how much hay or something we'd need each day for the same nutrition? About a bushel or so. But we can't, because we're not creatures that can process it. We're creatures who kill, because we thrive on the flesh and on the killing too.

"Think about your life, ladies and gentlemen. The first thing you learned as a baby was not to get shit on yourself, and the second was that the planet is populated by things that mean you harm. Most of the ones you have to worry about don't weigh three tons and charge you at fifty miles an hour. They look just like you. We came here for a simple bit of education that your mama wasn't able to give you. It's learning how to kill those bastards before they kill you.

"But make no mistake. I am a religious man, and I believe in Jesus. It takes a lot of courage to decide it's better to be the one who dies instead of the one who kills. If you're that sort of person, you'll get from me deep respect and a nice funeral. But I'm not that sort myself.

"Now, these gentlemen and I are about to leave you for a while. Some of us, for one reason or another, may not ever be back here. So tonight we're giving you our final regards, just in case. We'll be leaving at first light to go take care of our business. While we're gone, the fate of the rest of you will be in your own hands. The truth is, it always was, and you've done very well for the past few years, both in Oklahoma and here. Continue to be vigilant. I don't think that anybody the six of us might offend or frighten will be able to trace us back here and blame you, but be prepared for it anyway. That's the end of my little talk. Good night, friends. I hope I see you soon."

The next morning, when the sky was just light enough to begin imparting color to the world and the first chirping of birds in the trees began, two engines turned over and started, and two vehicles advanced out of the flat compound and moved onto the narrow dirt road through the woods. The highway was just over three miles away, and following its winding, slow descent out of the hills would take time, but it was serviceable, and the destination was set and clear. They had all been there before.

26

Leah Hawkins woke as the sunlight began finding its way into her room through the very narrow spaces between the slats of her shutters. The stimuli that had broken through into her sleep were the sounds of the familiar birds in the city of Weldonville—first the cooing of the mourning doves and then the warbling of mockingbirds. When the squawking of the jays and magpies began, a person had to admit it was morning.

When she moved, she felt the smooth, firm surface of the California king mattress she had bought five years ago for a sale price that was still too high, but which had been a good investment. She and Mark Ballard had both been tall and long-limbed, so the extra space had been good. And Leah had never spent much money on anything, so she could afford the luxury.

She stretched on the bed to limber up her back, and then swung her legs off the bed to the floor and walked to the adjoining bathroom. As her eyes got used to the light, she stared hard at everything. She had hired Mrs. Creeden from across the street to keep an eye on the house while she was gone, to clean it once a week, water the indoor plants, and change a few things arbitrarily when she did—pull a shade up or down, move a plant to a different window.

It had given Mrs. Creeden a bit of extra cash, and kept Leah from worrying. As she looked around, she realized there was no dust. When Leah had lived here, there were places where dust accumulated, but no more. Things had undoubtedly been very clean after the first week's visit. Since then they had been polished. Before she left again, she would have to tell Mrs. Creeden that she could relax her standards a bit.

Leah showered. She had brought a couple of detective suits on the hunt for the killers. She had worn them only a couple of times, but they had been packed and unpacked a lot, so they were going to the dry cleaner. She looked at the supply in her closet. There were black suits, dark gray, navy blue, and light gray, all pressed and in cleaners' bags. She picked black this time, because it looked enough like a Weldonville police uniform to fool the eye from a distance, and she wanted her time here to look professional. Two people knew what she had been doing while she was away. Most didn't, and there was also a chance that strangers might visit who expected things to be the same.

She put her badge and cuffs on her belt, and her Glock in its holster, where it would be hidden by her coat. She stepped into the closet so she could see herself from two sides in the full-length mirrors.

She put on her polished black cop shoes and went into the kitchen, made instant coffee, and heated a frozen egg-and-bagel object in the microwave. She had not yet turned in the rental car, so she drove it to the police lot at the Public Safety Building. She would have somebody follow her to surrender it at the lot in Denver later.

Because she was over an hour early for the day shift, she got out and walked around the building to the front entrance. There was a new sight, a plaque in bronze and black about the size of a door.

The sense of familiarity that had been like a gentle current moving her along went away. The plaque had been delivered at least a year after it had been ordered and was installed while she was gone. The top of the metal surface had big letters and numbers that said only "JULY 19" and the year.

Below it in smaller letters were a few lines about the mass escape from the federal penitentiary at Weldonville. Under that was a heading that said, "FEDERAL CORRECTIONS OFFICERS WHO GAVE THEIR LIVES." There were forty-two of them, some of them familiar —the warden, Gene Humphry, Paul Scott, Will McGovern, Bill Halvorsen's brother Nick. She noticed Ciccio, Decker, Yashinsky, Tiedemann, Polk, Pelletier, Costa.

There was a column headed "WELDONVILLE OFFICERS WHO GAVE THEIR LIVES." It was led by Joseph Roberts, the chief of police, and then, curiously, Mark Ballard, city manager, and then the sergeant and seven patrolmen killed in the battle of Main Street. The cops had been like members of her family. Willenz and Gutierrez, the two she'd driven to the fight; Diane Krantz and Kylee Fortin, the two women cops she had helped train; Dan Kazmerdjian, Dick Turner, Tom Bond. Then came a much longer list titled "CITIZENS OF WELDONVILLE." Leah's eyes ran down the columns, as though weighted by gravity. She knew the names so well that she wasn't reading, just scanning for familiar people in a crowd.

She saw Katherine Long, Katy Long, and James Long, the family of that man from New York who had volunteered to go after the killers. She found Marjorie Clay's parents, and Kristen Green's father and her sister Stephanie, a McClellan who was Ray's cousin that he'd barely known. Leah's best school friend Kathy Harris was there, the other tall girl in her class. She saw the names of people she'd known who had been as old as in their eighties and ones younger than ten. There were some she had deeply admired and others she had arrested. She looked away.

She was at the top of the steps, and kept walking, relieved to get past the long list of names. She stepped into the building through the double glass doors and saw Fred Burmeyer, one of the cops who had survived the fight on Main.

"Hello, Chief," he said.

Leah said, "The chief's out there on the plaque."

"Yep, and we miss him, but somebody's got to do it, and we're glad we had you to step in."

"Thanks, Fred. How have you been?"

"Not too bad. We're mostly writing tickets, keeping people friendly and the drunks out of the road."

"Good," she said. "That's what the town hired us for. Be safe."

She walked into the front entrance to the police station, past the counter where the general public was served, and into the office bay. Art Sprague, the top sergeant, sat at his desk outside the glass wall of her office. She unlocked the office door and said, "Morning, Art. Come on in."

When he came in, she said, "You could have used the chief's office while I was gone."

Art shrugged. "Thanks, Leah. But moving into somebody else's space while they're gone is just an extra job. In fact it's two. You have to move out again too. And now and then we'll get a visit from a state cop or one of the feds from the prison. If they see you're not in your office, you're just out. If they see somebody else in your office, then you're gone."

"Got it. Thanks, Art. Men sure are devious and manipulative." She sat down behind the desk. "Now, is there anything I can do to take some of the weight of the work off while I'm here?"

"Not much. We're breaking up domestic squabbles and confiscating illegal fireworks. The few regular reports that go to the state or the court are sitting in your in-box waiting for your signature. That's about it."

She glanced at the stack of folders in the basket at the corner of her desk. "I can take care of those this morning. If you have time, can you collect everything about July 19 that has come in from the FBI or the state police since I left?"

"Sure," he said. "It's all together. I'll bring it in a few minutes."

"Thanks, Art," she said. She lifted the stack of forms and reports and set them in the center of the desk, selected a pen from the center drawer, and went to work.

She read reports and signed them, read the forms and initialed them, and gradually worked her way down to the empty blotter. When she looked up, it was already one-thirty. She collected the papers that had to be filed and put them in their proper places; prepared the reports for mailing to government offices and put them in envelopes, stamped them with the city's postage meter, and set them on the counter for the mailman's three o'clock pickup.

When she finished, it was two, and Art returned from lunch. When he did, he found Leah's note: "Good work, Art." Leah was out walking toward Bremmer's restaurant.

The summer was more than half over, and the trees were thick with big green leaves. She had spent so many of her seasons here that she was already thinking about how broad and colorful they would be in October. But summer was at its best, and it reminded her of the summers when she was a girl, the hot afternoons stretching on so there was time to play nine innings of baseball and then go swimming and then play chase, her neighborhood's version of hide-and-seek, until after dark.

The chase games often had more than twenty kids playing. The ones captured had to become members of the mob of chasers, so the odds against the runner grew worse and worse. Leah's disadvantage had been her height, so hiding places were not the answer for her. She had to keep moving, anticipating the patrol routes of the chasers and the spots where they would look for her. Leah's time would come later in the game, when most people were already caught, and the light was becoming dim. She would lure as many of the chasers as far away as she could from the tall tree they used for home base, and then use her long, rapid strides to outdistance them and beat them to the tree. She remembered slapping the bark and yelling, "Home free!" It had seemed natural, but as she thought about it now, she wondered where that expression had come from.

She walked to the front of Bremmer's and then inside. Annie Bremmer's eyes widened and then recovered, and she hugged Leah. "You're back," she whispered.

"Just for a while," Leah whispered back.

Annie led her to the booth where they had sat together sometimes with their middle school friends, while Annie's father brought them identical dinners with cola and ginger ale in wineglasses.

This afternoon Leah had a tuna salad and a cup of coffee. Annie sat with her for a few minutes, which Leah spent asking about the rare vacation Annie had taken with her husband, Dave, and the two children. It sounded nice to Leah. At three o'clock, Leah walked back to her office in the Public Safety Building. This time she went in the back way.

She spent the rest of the afternoon reading the information that had been shared by law enforcement agencies during her absence. As she had feared, the bulk of the information was about what Leah had done. She was pleased to see that the FBI and the local cops thought of each of the killings as a local crime, unrelated to the deaths of other former prisoners from Weldonville who had died in other parts of the country that summer. A high percentage of the men who died violent deaths each year had been in prison at some point, and federal prisons alone held about 184,000 prisoners at a time. The average federal inmate was white, about thirty-six years old—roughly what the twelve had been—so the reports of their deaths hadn't stood out at first.

She noticed a disappointing trend too. The FBI information had dwindled. As soon as the shooting had stopped on July 20 two years ago and order had been restored, the FBI had begun to assert its jurisdiction. Weldonville Penitentiary was a federal facility. The murdered guards and support staff had been federal employees. Escape was a federal crime. Anyone who had not been caught in the first twenty-four hours had probably crossed a state line or two.

Leah had asked for the favor of exceptional information sharing. She had pointed out that the crimes committed in the city limits of Weldonville—murder, rape, arson, grand larceny, auto theft, weapons charges—were also violations of Colorado laws. At the time of this discussion Leah had been standing on Main Street, where there had been a decisive and ferocious battle that no federal officer had even arrived in time to witness. Bodies were still being removed from the corner of Main and Constitution because there were too few ambulances to reinforce the single coroner's van, and bodies had to be transported to other towns to await autopsies.

The agreement had been largely unspoken. The terms had seemed to be that Leah and city officials would not point out on national television that if a federal prison failed, the local citizens and their police were on their own. In return, the FBI would be uncharacteristically open and cooperative with the Weldonville officials. They would provide prompt updates on whatever they learned about the escaped inmates. At the time, nobody had known that there would be a federal grant to Weldonville to rebuild its public safety program. The FBI may not have suggested it, but they certainly hadn't blocked it either.

The first year had brought a flood of information that had come from criminal investigations, trials, prisoner records, and the crime scene reports from the Weldonville prison break. They were massive and detailed, including DNA profiles, fingerprints, and photographs. But now that the second year had passed, there was very little new information about any of the men. What Leah was reading was mainly about the six men she had killed, and most of the information was misinterpreted.

Weiss's body might not be found for years. His mother's garage was now a kind of family tomb he shared with her. Victor Panko had been only one of five victims who had died violently in Buffalo in one night, four of them relatives. Their workshop had been burned in an arson fire, and contained barely identifiable machines for making IDs and credit cards, so the local police suspected that some crew involved in immigration fraud or human trafficking had turned on the family. Alan Becker's death in New York City looked a lot like an organized crime hit, but nobody had found any evidence, or even rumor, that he'd had any dealings with organized criminals. The three men killed in California had died on a ranch owned by Martin Ortega under a false name, and they had died with two other members of Ortega's prison gang. What Bysantski and Duquesne had been doing at the stronghold of a Mexican gang at the time was unknown. A hoard of weapons had been in the house, and the huge supply of ammunition that had cooked off in the fire had made it impossible for firefighters to enter until everything combustible had been consumed. Nobody had any theories about foul play, and most thought it might have been an accident caused by misuse of propane intended for cooking and heating.

The findings on the deaths led nowhere and implicated no suspects, which made Leah feel relieved. She reread the information that was included on the remaining six fugitives, but she found little that she hadn't known already. Lee Wolf, Timothy McKinney, Edison Leonard, Joseph Lambert, James Holliman, and Lonny Mann were assumed to be alive, simply because there was no information to the contrary.

Lee Wolf's group, the Swift Sword of the Savior, had apparently disbanded after Wolf and a few others had been convicted of, among other crimes, bombing and burning a predominantly African American church, a synagogue, and a school in Oklahoma. But recently there had been some posts and recordings on the dark web by people hinting that they were members. There had been no mention of Wolf.

Timothy McKinney might have been seen in Idaho the previous summer. A hiker backpacking in the mountains had taken a few photographs of people at a rest spot near a spring. One man objected, snatched the camera, and opened it to expose the film before throwing it on the ground. He didn't notice that the man's girlfriend was recording the event with her cell phone. A woman in the park police office thought he looked a bit like Timothy McKinney. So did the FBI and its facial-recognition software, but he had not been seen again.

There were similar tips on Mann and Holliman, but none of them struck Leah as promising, and the FBI was apparently waiting for further leads.

That afternoon, Leah called the mayor to tell him she was in town. He said, "That's great, Leah. Do you think you could come to a closed-door session of the city council on Wednesday night? It would help keep the council happy if you could tell them something soothing about your sabbatical. Phil and I would also like to hear anything you can tell us about how things are actually going."

"I'll be there," she said.

"What time?"

"Whatever time you hold it."

"We like to do these things at eight. That way everybody has time to get something to eat before we start. I've found it makes them less peckish. More business gets done with fewer questions and arguments."

"I'm for that," she said. "I'll see you at eight on Wednesday."

"Good."

Leah went to bed early that night. It was because she wanted to get used to the mountain standard time, since she might be in Weldonville for a while. She had also spent some of the previous night thinking about revenge and the taking of lives.

Leah Hawkins was not a religious person. Among the big old buildings surrounding the city park were Weldonville's half dozen churches. The church she had walked out of one Sunday morning and seldom visited again was the Presbyterian one. It had happened the summer when she was about to turn thirteen. As she had gone down the sidewalk that Sunday morning, she had suddenly understood that if there was a God, He would look down on her next Sunday with the same love if she was in her family's pew or swimming at the lake.

Lately she had noticed a subtle and unwelcome change. She had begun to feel a memory of her buried religious life. If childhood piety was like having chicken pox, its resurgence was like shingles—the itching had come back decades later as pain. She caught herself many nights silently mouthing the words "Thank you," leaving out what she was thankful for, which was "today," the one she'd just had. Sometimes she would catch herself asking, "Please take care of" somebody.

Lately she had caught herself forming the words "Please forgive." She would stop in the middle if she could do it in time. The rule for forgiveness between man and God, as she had grown up understanding it, was that you couldn't be forgiven if you didn't sincerely regret what you'd done and intend to quit doing it. She was not interested in repenting. She wouldn't have begun killing people if she hadn't considered it carefully and decided she should go out and get them. Her crimes were not accidents or mistakes. Anyway, the version of Christianity she knew was not the kind in which anybody was willing to waste his time listening to your regrets, least of all God. And innocence wasn't something that could be restored.

She fell asleep with these thoughts in mind, and when she woke, the dream she interrupted had something to do with Mark Ballard. She made no effort to bring it back to explore the details.

Leah got up, walked to the station early, and went to work reading all the information she could find on the six men who were still at large. She hated to think that they were all still out in the world somewhere, alive and free, because they had wasted the lives of nearly a hundred people who had lived within a short walk from where she sat.

27

On Wednesday evening at six-thirty Leah got up from her desk in the Public Safety Building and walked to Steele's Stand near the Tivoli Theater. When she was a teenager, the only foods the place sold were hamburgers, hot dogs, french fries, and onion rings. The drinks were soft drinks and milkshakes, the kind that were thin enough to sip through a straw.

Steele's was still called Steele's, but the last Steele, Shirley, had been killed on July 19. The menu now included burritos, tacos, kimchi, three salads, ramen, and breakfast meals that were served from 6:00 a.m. until 11:00 a.m. A person like Leah, who had spent a beautiful summer day in an office or a school, could still sit at one of the outdoor tables under shade trees, and that was where Leah chose to be.

She savored her unhealthy food and then walked back toward her office to pick up the files she wanted to bring to the council meeting at city hall.

Joe Lambert was driving the lead car when the six convicts reached Weldonville. The afternoon sun was sinking behind a slight rise in the land now, but the sky was still bright above it to the west. He said, "I don't think coming in this early is a good idea. Even if we don't come across somebody who saw us two years ago, somebody who sees us now will remember us later."

Tim McKinney said, "I thought that was what we wanted, what we drove all this way for. We want them all to remember us for the rest of their lives."

"Yeah, well, I'd like to be able to drive away from here tomorrow and forget them for the rest of mine."

Jim Holliman laughed. "If you feel that way, do your best to put the fear in them tonight."

"It's just that coming back here before dark is pressing our luck."

There was a buzz, and McKinney answered his phone. "Yeah?"

It was Lee Wolf. "Hi, Timothy. Ask your friend Joseph to pull around the park and go past the police station and city hall, will you?"

McKinney said, "Pull around that park and go by the police station and city hall."

Lambert said, "Could we be any more overconfident?"

Lee Wolf said, "Put me on speaker." McKinney did and held the phone in his lap, and Wolf seemed to hear the difference. He said, "We're just taking precautions, doing our due diligence. Keep it slow, Joe. I want to see everything."

The two cars went past the Public Safety Building, and Wolf said, "Well, that looks reassuring. There are four, no, five cars in the police parking lot at this moment. It's seven-thirty and the whole police force is taking the night off."

The cars drove along the street for two blocks and passed city hall. Three people were standing on the front steps by the open doors. There was a woman in her sixties with short, curly hair wearing a black dress with a pattern of big white flowers and carrying an armload of papers fastened in identical-looking navy blue folders; a middle-aged man wearing a short-sleeved shirt in a faint-blue plaid and khaki pants; and beside him, a fat uniformed policeman who looked about the age of the woman.

The hallway beyond them was brightly lit, and the old marble floor shone with fresh buffing. At the end of the hall was an open door to a lighted meeting room in which a few other people were visible. The cars swept past city hall, and the view was behind them, but they passed another pair of men walking toward the old stone building.

"There seems to be something going on in city hall tonight," Lonny Mann said.

"Yes, there does," said Lee Wolf. "Keep going out to the highway and turn south away from the prison. Then stop at that turnoff we passed on the way in. We'll talk."

Leah closed her office door at the station in the Public Safety Building but didn't lock the door in case one of the night shift officers needed something out of it. She walked past the front counter and called out to Danny, who was stationed there tonight to deal with the public, "The boss is going to a council meeting. You can tell the girls to bring in the liquor and get the party started."

"Yes, ma'am," said Danny. "I'll do that."

Then she was out the door. The sun was lower now, but the rays were still bright and strong. Leah had to protect her eyes from the glare. She walked along the street carrying the six files she had picked out. Her long legs brought her to city hall, where she took the steps two at a time and went inside.

Tim Munson, the old police sergeant whose actual job during business hours was courthouse bailiff, was on duty for the special council meeting. "Evening, Leah," he said.

"Hi, Tim. Nice to see you again. Everybody in there?"

"I think so," he said. "They're all anxious to see you."

"Better not keep them waiting." She unbuckled the belt carrying her badge, pistol, handcuffs, and pepper spray, and handed it to him. Then she gave him her phone and stepped through the arch of the metal detector.

The sergeant opened the gun safe and put her belongings inside, as the nearly 150-year tradition of Weldonville demanded. Firearms had never been allowed in the city council chamber. Phones hadn't been prohibited until about two years after they'd been invented and begun going off everywhere.

As she stepped through the doorway into the council chamber, Linda Harris seemed to spring at her, throwing her arms around her in a tight embrace. "Leah, I'm so glad to see you."

"It's good to see you too, Linda." Leah was a head taller, and could see over her. When Leah was playing sports in high school with Kathy Harris, Linda had been the mother who volunteered for everything, brought snacks and drinks, and supplied rides to distant tournaments in the off-season. At the time, Leah had wondered how such a short woman had produced Kathy, who had been as tall as Leah. The absent father must have been something.

Mayor Donaldson was next. He shook her hand with great formality and said, "Lieutenant, thank you for coming."

"Mr. Mayor," she said.

After him came the others—City Attorney Phil Haymes, Nora Fields, David Hall, City Comptroller Nell Hoagland, and the insurance broker Mark Stein, arriving last with his suit coat on but his tie loosened. Mayor Donaldson closed the council chamber door, walked to the conference table, and sat at the end. One by one, the others took their seats.

"The meeting is called to order," he said. "Who has questions for Lieutenant Hawkins?"

Phil Haymes said, "Leah, we're interested in a general outline of what's happened since we saw you last. Just tell us what you can. There won't be any notes or recordings. I've already written the draft of the minutes of the meeting, and they'll contain no information about personnel matters."

Leah took a deep breath. "As you know, I left town a couple of months ago to learn new police techniques and organizational skills. But since then, some information has been forwarded to the police department by the FBI that the council would like to know, and the mayor thought it would be worthwhile to come and report on it."

"Wonderful." said Nell Hoagland. "We can't wait."

Leah said, "There's been some progress."

"Amazing," said Nora Fields. "Two years and two months after the nineteenth."

Leah shrugged. "You can never tell when an old case will suddenly come alive again."

"I'll say," said Mayor Donaldson. "They got five so far, by my count."

"Six, actually," said Leah. "The ones who have been accounted for were Becker, Panko, Ortega, Bysantski, Duquesne, and Weiss."

"I missed one," said Donaldson. "I didn't see anything in print about Weiss."

"Mr. Weiss's death has not been announced publicly yet."

"Oh," said Nell Hoagland. "*Oh.*"

Leah went on. "That leaves six who haven't been found." She opened her file and took out a stack of photographs. "You can pass these around. They're labeled on the backs. They are Timothy McKinney, Joseph Lambert, James Holliman, Edison Leonard, Lonny Mann, and Lee Wolf. One of the reasons I came back to Weldonville at this point was to see what else the FBI and other agencies might have learned, what they've tried, where they've looked, who they've talked to, and so on. It's a lot less convenient to try to keep up with these things from the road. But they may find a connection between any of these men and the living criminals who haven't turned up yet."

"We're glad to see you home," said Linda Harris. "Even if it's for research."

"Thank you," said Leah. "And I should mention that I've been learning a lot while I've been away. I'll have some recommendations when I'm back for good."

Nell Hoagland said, "I would like to add that so far you've been quite easy on the budget."

"The kind of work I've been doing is mostly traveling from one jurisdiction to another, and then doing a lot of looking and listening. It doesn't usually cost much."

Phil Haymes changed the subject. "This could be our last report until your training and study project is complete. Isn't that right?"

Leah looked around. "You're all more experienced at government than I am, but isn't that the way it works? The more reports, the worse things are going and the longer they'll take."

Mayor Donaldson chuckled. "Ain't that the truth."

Haymes said, "No argument there. But what I meant was, if anybody has questions for the lieutenant, this would be a great time for them. Once this meeting is over, it would not be appropriate to approach Lieutenant Hawkins independently to ask for reports. When she's finished, there will probably be a report with her suggestions."

David Hall, who seldom spoke but usually communicated his opinions during meetings with nods and frowns and sighs, said, "Good enough."

Mayor Donaldson said, "And of course if there's anything any of us can do, we'll do it. As we told you at our last meeting with you, I'm staying in office and in the city at least until you're done, and so are several other people, including Mr. Haymes."

Nora Fields said, "I have a question. If it's out of order, just say so, but I have to wonder. The authorities have managed to bring half of the twelve to justice. Does anyone else feel the same relief I do? I mean, half are accounted for. The other six must know that. Won't they be living in fear for the rest of their lives, too scared to do anything to harm our town again, or to harm anyone else?"

Leah said, "It's a good question, and I've spent some time thinking about it. My opinion is that it wouldn't work that way. We know who the other six men are. They've all been convicted of doing terrible things for money when they were young and poor, and more terrible things after they'd gotten rich, and more when they were broke again. They all killed people four miles from here to escape from prison, and killed more people here in town after they were free and could have just driven past the exit and stayed on the highway to the interstate. I don't think any of them is someone who is likely to change now. Just like you, I feel better since we got the news, but I won't feel sure it's over until we hear they're all in jail or dead."

There was a sudden shout from the hallway outside the door, and then more shouts, men's voices roaring in anger, and then three loud bangs that could only be gunfire. The shots echoed off the high ceilings and marble floor, and out of the echo came the sound of running feet.

Leah was up and at the door, her right hand automatically reaching for her pistol, but not finding it. She opened the door a crack and looked out, and what she saw was terrible. Sergeant Munson was down beside the metal detector, not moving, and she could see blood pooling around him. The rest of the scene was filled with motion, a half dozen men in dark clothes and ski masks sprinting up the hall toward the chamber.

She slammed the door, turned the lock, and called to the others, "Take cover behind the desks in the chamber." She pointed at the semicircle of wooden desks marked with placards carrying their names used for public meetings. She pushed Nora Fields and Nell Hoagland in the right direction.

There was a loud thud as something heavy hit the locked door. It seemed to be the sound of one or two men hurling their shoulders against it. The old oak door didn't budge.

Leah shouted, "Get down!" at the people who were still standing by the desks, and ducked down herself. As she did, she snatched the letter opener from the mayor's desk set.

The second she was down, there were loud bangs as the men in the hall fired rifle rounds through the door, splintering the wood by the door lock. The shots hit the marble floor and ricocheted upward into the walls of the chamber.

There was a loud thump, and this time the door flew open and banged against the wall beside it. Two men charged in after it and stopped on either side of the door with shouldered rifles. The next three appeared and took up positions ten feet farther in, scanning for targets.

The last man stopped in the doorway, and then stepped out again, looked back the way he'd come, and posted himself there as a lookout.

One of the two men by the door stepped forward into the council chamber and stood in front of the semicircle of desks. He held his rifle upward in one hand and fired two rounds, a deafening sound in the small space. He yelled, "I want to see you and count you. If I do that, you're alive. Anybody who doesn't stand up and come forward on the first call is dead. Do you understand?"

Leah stood up first to show the others it was the only choice. Tentatively, one by one, the others stood up.

The man had an accent. Lee Wolf and Lonny Mann were both from the South, so she was sure this was one of them. "There. Very good," the man said. "Are you the village council or the school board, or what?"

Mayor Donaldson said, "I'm the mayor, and these people are the city council. Weldonville was a city when it was incorporated in 1873." He pointed over his shoulder at the city seal mounted on the wall over his desk. Below the picture of the buffalo and the antelope in the long grass, it plainly said, "1873."

The man called out, "Did you hear that, gentlemen? The city council and the mayor himself. The Lord seems to have guided us to the right place at His chosen time." There was no doubt now. He was Lee Wolf.

"Who are you?" Nell Hoagland asked. "And what do you want here?"

"I guess you could say we're here because you didn't leave well enough alone. It's been over two years since the Weldonville prison break. You hired some people, a death squad, to go out and find the twelve men who planned the escape and managed to keep the freedom they had earned. You hired some pretty good hunters. They killed six of us before the rest of us ever heard about it. I hope it cost you a whole lot of money."

"You're the missing prisoners?" Dave Hall asked.

"No, we're the missing free men. The prisoners aren't missing. They're all still behind those prison walls because they didn't have the guts to walk out an open door."

Phil Haymes said, "What do you want?"

"We want what we've got. You. We're going to use you to show people what a mistake you all made by hiring a bunch of killers. We're here to punish you so what's left of your town will remember."

Haymes said, "If you're from that prison break, then you have nothing more to gain here. You're out already. You can't do better than that."

One of the masked men swung his rifle so the butt pounded against Haymes's head and knocked him to the floor. "Shut up." Leah guessed from the man's size and the light-colored eyelashes she could see in the eyeholes of his mask that he was Tim McKinney.

Lee Wolf said, "Now, people. You're not getting the point of our visit. We're not here to have a two-sided evaluation of what we do. The point is to show people around here that trying to harm us is futile, because the only ones who are going to get revenge are the six of us. Not you or your town."

"Revenge for what?" Mark Stein asked.

"Now that, unlike the others, is a good question. You, or your city, or some do-gooder around here who felt sorry for you, decided to put a contract out on the twelve men who escaped two years ago. So far six of us have been—I hate to use a crude term for it—butchered. Our revenge is for killing those six. We're also making sure nobody sends anyone after us again. If they do, we can always come back and make you hurt and hurt."

He strutted along the arc of desks, staring hard at each of the council members as he passed. Leah had been studying him and the other five men quietly, carefully, without moving or catching anyone's attention. She stood with her knees bent and shoulders hunched to give the impression that she was shorter and weaker than she was.

"We never did any of the things you say," Nell Hoagland said. "And what do you expect to accomplish here?"

"Well, I heard that one of the attacks your boys made ended with burning down a workshop with two men in it. Whether they were still alive or not isn't clear, but they weren't alive after that. The second thing that comes to mind was filling a house where people were sleeping with propane, so there would be a fiery explosion. So, when I think about what would make us feel better, how could it not involve fire?"

28

The six convicts conferred among themselves for a few seconds. Two of them left the room and went in different directions, probably to see if the noise had brought out any unwelcome people. Leah didn't have much hope that any shots had been heard. The old building was local stone and masonry built over tree-trunk-beam frames, with planks planed two inches thick. The interior layers were wood, lath, and plaster, and the roof was slate. The inner finish was all marble floors and oak woodwork. The buildings on all sides were municipal or commercial, and not occupied at night. Very soon both men trotted back into the room looking confident.

Leah was aware that the other captives all occasionally glanced in her direction, or tried to appear to stare into space while keeping her in the periphery of their vision. She kept her mind off them and on the six captors, and thought about the opportunity to do something. She had been in this building many times in the past few years, usually for trials in the courtroom near the back of the building. She was hoping the members of the council would know much more about the building than she did.

She was watchful, making calculations. She was six feet two inches tall, so her reach was probably about three feet with either arm, but if she stretched or half-turned and bent toward an object, it might be four feet, or even five. She knew she could deliver a punch that way or grasp something in a half second or so. If she stood on the balls of her feet and pushed off, she could add nearly another foot. She had been a natural athlete who had trained hard and worked at it, and after she became a cop, she had stayed in shape. Even after she was promoted from the street to a desk, she kept at it because she liked gyms better than hospitals and health better than weakness. But the odds against her were terrible.

Lee Wolf didn't want to let the hostages calm down or do any thinking, so he kept on talking. "What we need at this point is gasoline, gentlemen. There's no need to keep these good people marinating in their own sweat any longer. That means we've got to get the five-gallon cans we bought on the way here, and the siphon. There are cars out in the back parking lot, and these people won't be driving home tonight, so they should be able to spare the gas. Joe and Jim and I will stay here and have a talk with the council while the rest of you bring what we need."

Leah noted that the others simply set off without comment. These were dangerous, angry, vicious men at best. Some had been described in the files as psychotic, yet they all seemed to have agreed in advance to let Lee Wolf be their leader and spokesman. She had hoped that when the six of them were together, there might be dissention, even old irritations that might flare up, but her hope that it would happen soon enough vanished. For now they were in perfect agreement.

With the vanishing of that hope came a new one. There had been six in the building, and because they were being agreeable, there were now only three. She studied the men left in the room. All three were of average size, slightly shorter than she was. She was relieved that McKinney had been one of the three to leave, because grappling with him would be impossible. He could over-power her instantly.

She kept looking, and watched Joe Lambert walk slowly along the arc of desks. After three steps he abruptly spun to look behind him at the people he had just passed, bringing the barrel of his rifle around with him as though he might shoot them if he caught them moving. He paused there, glaring as though he could read their minds.

Leah had played thousands of games, and she had a feel for other players' movements, fakes, and feints. When Lambert resumed his walk, she knew that he was going to look again, just like a pitcher holding a runner on first base. She knew that this time he would take fewer steps before he did the surprise spin, probably two steps. She held the other captors in her vision for a second. Lee Wolf was looking toward the back of the audience section of the room, where an unobtrusive door seemed to interest him. James Holliman was sitting on the conference table with his left hand holding his rifle straight up, the butt resting on the table top. She returned her eyes to Joe Lambert. One step, two steps, and there was the turn.

As he pivoted toward the captives behind the arc of desks, Leah launched herself over the mayor's desk behind him, her long arms snaking around him and squeezing him in a rough embrace. Her left arm hooked around his neck, and the right brought the letter opener around to stab it into Lambert's chest. She felt the point pierce his shirt, but it stopped there because there was something under it. His torso hadn't had the squared look of body armor, but something impermeable was under the cloth.

Jim Holliman fired a wild shot into the ceiling with his left hand, and while the shot only dislodged plaster dust onto his head and the floor, it seemed to energize Joe Lambert. He dashed forward away from the desks, dragging Leah behind him over the top of the desk. She still had the letter opener clutched in her fist, so she plunged the pointed blade into the side of his neck.

Holliman's next shots hit one of the desks and the wall above it, but Lambert was on his hands and knees, struggling to raise himself to his feet with Leah on his back. She grasped his rifle, but his hands were too strong for her to wrench it away. Leah managed to reach the trigger guard and fire a shot in the general direction of Lee Wolf, who dove to the end of one row of built-in wooden seats and out of Leah's view.

Lambert's breaths were making a terrible rasping noise as he tried to suck in air past the blade in his throat. He rolled to use the weight of his body to keep Leah's hands away from the trigger, but she fired off three more shots that went to Holliman's part of the room before Lambert's shoulder pressed her wrist to the floor and she couldn't reach the trigger.

Her body seemed to know what the only possible move was. While Lambert was down, Wolf was lying between seats, and Holliman had dropped to the floor beyond the conference table, she withdrew her hand, leapt up, and charged. Her life depended on reaching Holliman before he could train his rifle on her and fire. She dashed toward him, her long legs taking yards at a stride. Holliman clutched the foregrip of the rifle, fumbled with the receiver to get his finger into the trigger guard, and raised the barrel. Leah's time was gone.

She grasped the edge of the conference table as she reached it, and pulled it upward as hard as she could. The table tipped, the near side rising and the far side falling down hard between her and Holliman.

He fired four rounds through the tabletop, but she was moving fast, and he couldn't actually see her because of the table, and he couldn't adjust his aim any faster than he did. He kept firing even after she was past him, his shots pounding into the walls on the other side of the council chamber.

Now there were other shots coming from the direction where Lee Wolf lay, but none of them hit flesh. As Leah dashed toward the door, she sensed another body close to her right side, running with her. Once she was through the door, she turned her head and saw Phil Haymes beside her.

She said, "Lock the back door. Buy us time."

He turned and ran along the hall toward the back door.

Leah knew that her destination had to be different. She ran toward the front of the building, where Sergeant Tim Munson lay dead. She knelt in the blood by his body and worked the handle to open the gun safe, but it wouldn't budge. The city tradition of keeping guns out of the council chamber was going to kill them all.

She heard the sound of glass breaking near the back of the building and looked in that direction. But the back door was solid, without glass to break, so she had no idea what the noise was. It didn't matter. Nothing mattered but what was happening here. She ran her hand along Munson's belt to the holster where his sidearm had been, but the holster was empty. They had taken the gun off his body when they'd come into the building.

She heard heavy footsteps coming from the direction of the council chamber, but she couldn't stop to look, because she had one more hope. Munson had been a street cop in Denver for nearly his whole career. Those guys carried backup weapons. She reached for Munson's ankles and encircled them with her hands, but there was no ankle holster.

Maybe a knife, she thought, one of those big ones like she used to carry as a state cop to slice through a seat belt to free somebody from a car wreck. She reached into Munson's left-side thigh-level pocket and felt the grips of the backup gun. It was a compact .380 automatic. *Thank you, thank you,* she thought as she took it, pulled the slide, and whirled her body into a sitting position with her knees up, facing the sound of footsteps.

James Holliman was running hard toward her. She rested her right elbow on her right knee with the gun in both hands and fired. A hole like a big pockmark appeared in the middle of Holliman's forehead. He seemed to take a full step forward, but his other foot did not come up to take his weight, and he fell facedown, slid to a stop, and lay still.

Leah got to her feet, snatched up the rifle he had dropped, and ran toward the door to the council chamber. Lambert was lying on the floor on his belly. As he turned toward her, she shot him with Tim Munson's pistol and then stepped into the chamber with the rifle at her shoulder, looking for Lee Wolf.

"Where is the other one?" she called out.

Donaldson said, "He ducked out the fire exit to the street."

She turned and ran along the hall toward the rear entrance to the building. As she ran, she could see that Phil Haymes had locked the bolt on the big bronze back door. He was standing beside it, holding the long-handled fire ax he'd taken from the glass case in the hallway by the mayor's office, where there was also an old reel of flat canvas fire hose. There was a loud sound of something hitting the door. It shook and showed a bit of warping, but it held.

As Leah approached, the door was hit again and opened. She could see that the men outside had hotwired a car in the lot and driven it against the door. The first one to slide in over the hood of the car was Tim McKinney.

Phil Haymes swung the ax with a level swing, and the blade caught McKinney just below the Adam's apple. He was knocked backward, and then went to his knees, both hands clutching his neck. Leah could see there was blood. She fired Sergeant Tim Munson's pistol once into his forehead, and he fell.

She edged past him to see outside, but the others were gone. She heard the scream of sirens coming from the direction of the Public Safety Building. "Take this." She handed Phil Haymes the rifle. She ran back to the council chamber and stopped in front of the council members.

"What about the other three?" Dave Hall asked.

"I just heard sirens. We only had four men on duty tonight. Either they'll catch the others, or they won't."

29

The four police officers who had been dispatched to pursue the three fleeing men had not found them. No description of the two cars was passed on to other law enforcement agencies.

Leah did not finish her supervision of the aftermath until 6:00 a.m. The coroner's men removed the three escapees' bodies and the body of Sergeant Tim Munson from city hall. A pickup fire crew helped mop the blood from the marble floors, scrubbed the spatter from several walls, spackled bullet holes, sanded them, and repainted or revarnished the surfaces. The rear door of the building had to be boarded up temporarily.

Mayor Donaldson told the cleanup crews that the six escapees had come to seek revenge for the deaths of prisoners during the battle of Main Street two years ago and that Sergeant Munson had shot three of them before succumbing to his wounds. The role of Lieutenant Hawkins in the fighting was barely mentioned.

The groundskeepers at Mount Olivet Cemetery dug a deeper grave than usual with a backhoe and buried the bodies of Timothy McKinney, James Holliman, and Joseph Lambert in a stack and placed a bronze plaque over it with the name PAULA FOSSELMAN, 1871–1939. The plaque had been hanging in the cemetery's garage as a souvenir. It was once used as a sample to sell grave markers by a long-defunct company in Ohio that used to sell mail-order work to communities in the West.

For two weeks Leah and the police force remained on alert, watching for signs that the three escapees might make a second attempt on some part of Weldonville. Observers from the fire department were placed near the major roads into the city.

Near the end of that time, Leah composed a letter to be held in the personnel file of Sergeant Tim Munson in case any unknown relatives ever turned up. It gave him credit for the shooting of the three escaped convicts who attacked city hall. It also gave the true location of the criminals' bodies in case it was necessary to verify that they'd been shot in their heads by Munson's .380 backup weapon after he had been gravely wounded. His .380 pistol was placed in the safe room of the Public Safety Building as evidence.

A few days later Leah was on a flight from Denver to Little Rock, Arkansas. She had left late at night, so she'd bought a sandwich to take on the plane, eaten it while waiting for her boarding group to be called, and then fallen asleep during the flight. She woke when the air pressure changed as the plane descended for landing.

Leah spent a night and a day in Little Rock in room 502 at the Capital Hotel on Markham Street studying and getting ready. The upper floors offered a nonscenic view, and were not especially luxurious, so she had predicted they would be quiet and not have much casual traffic.

She had reviewed the emails from the FBI while she was in Weldonville. The reason she had chosen Little Rock was an intelligence report that said they'd been picking up podcasts on the dark web that claimed to be from the Swift Sword of the Savior, which seemed to be making some kind of comeback. The FBI was not sure if the attribution was true, but there had been a suggestion based on a comparison of ideas, expressions, vocabulary, and so on, that they might be. The FBI didn't have a location, because, like a lot of things on the dark web, it was coming from several hosts in places like Moldova. They believed that the original signal could be coming from northern Arkansas or southern Missouri, in Ozark country, because a number of the original members were from that region.

Leah kept thinking about the men who had just raided Weldonville. They had arrived expecting to meet no resistance. It was a sneak attack, and they were heavily armed, going against a bunch of civilians, but it hadn't worked out well for them. The three who had not been killed had to run away to avoid getting caught.

There was no easy way to know where they had headed after that. Maybe Lonny Mann had been taking cooking classes in Paris and had room in his atelier apartment for guests, or Edison Leonard had been living in a Nevada brothel and invited his two friends home with him. But within the next week or two, those three were going to want to feel safe. No matter where they were, no matter how sad or angry or reckless they were about their dead companions, their only priority was going to be their own well-being. They would head to the safest place they had among them. And she believed that the place they'd feel safest was with Lee Wolf and the rest of the sick, racist psychotics hiding in the woods somewhere preparing for the end of the world. They wouldn't be in a place where there were a lot of tourists, because armed groups didn't do well in crowds, or in a place where there were a lot of people of different races, because they hated everybody who wasn't just like them.

Leah had been reviewing the files from the period when Lee Wolf had been arrested. In Oklahoma, there were around a hundred who lived on the compound and about twice that many occasional members who came for meetings now and then. If they had moved all the way out to some remote place, their strength was probably half that. She predicted there would be fifty around Lee Wolf and a hundred somewhere on the periphery.

Leah knew what to look for. Fifty people would need a lot of food, water, gasoline, and whatever else other people used. Somebody would have to drive into a town now and then to buy that stuff.

30

Lee Wolf had taken the car that Joe Lambert had brought with him from Oregon and then driven to Weldonville. Wolf had left his car in Arkansas in the Swift Sword settlement. It wasn't registered to him, but to a fictitious woman named Maura Banks. The group had always been very generous about making sure Pastor Lee was supplied with the things he needed to get along—food, clothing, shelter, and a car were about all anybody needed, and he had them. All members of the group who were able to work at paying jobs did so, but of course, Lee Wolf couldn't. He was a federal fugitive. A paycheck with his name and social security number on it might as well be radioactive. It would kill him quicker than cancer.

Wednesday night, when Lee Wolf had been in the council chamber in Weldonville and had heard the unmistakable sounds of a two-sided gunfight going on out in the hallway, he had looked at the floor and seen Joe Lambert for a second, trying to crawl with what looked like a dagger in his throat. Wolf and Lambert were the only former prisoners in the room. He knelt beside Lambert, his eyes flicking to the hostages and back to Lambert. He reached into Lambert's pocket and took his car keys. He murmured, "You're not going to be able to drive, Joe. Don't worry, I'll get you out of here."

He stood and glared at the hostages. Should he try to shoot them all? No, that would just make him the emergency and direct the hostile gunfire toward himself. He looked at Lambert again. Should he try to lift him and drag him out? That would leave the hostages alone. But what could Lambert do against them anyway? The questions came in rapid succession, but there were no answers. Wolf couldn't let himself be paralyzed by indecision. He had to move. He stepped to the door in the back of the council chamber. He could see now that it had the chipped and faded word "FIRE" painted on the wood. He turned the knob and, as though in a dream, it opened. He expected to see another shiny floor, or at least a wall, but the door led directly outside.

He reassured himself that he had not been running away. It was all that noise, the horror of seeing Lambert grotesquely wounded and crawling on the floor, the smell of gunfire. Outside it was cool and dark, the air was fresh, and the noises were far away and muted. It was as though Wolf had opened the door and fallen out.

When he found himself out there, the fire door was already closing. There was no doorknob on the outside, so he couldn't have gone back in if he had wanted to. He thought of the next best move, which was to run around to the front of the building and kill the woman from behind to protect the others. When he told the others about it, he said he had gone around and found it locked, but actually he hadn't been able to make his feet move in that direction. He said the front doors were locked from the inside, that maybe the old cop had done it before he died, or maybe the big blond woman. Either way, he told them, there was no getting in that entrance.

He told them of running around the rest of the building to find another open door, or even a window he could break to get in behind the woman, but he hadn't done that. Actually, all he had done was run to Joe Lambert's car parked down the street, open it with the key he had taken from Lambert, get inside, start the engine, and keep his head low while he looked and listened.

He waited, but the next thing he saw that he could interpret was the other car that the group had driven from Arkansas. It pulled out of the parking lot behind city hall and took off fast. He could see only two men in it, but he had decided to assume that the other three must be accounted for, meaning not his problem. At that point all he could think to do was to follow the car that was getting away.

Later Lee Wolf had to admit modestly that he was proud to have been the last man to leave the city of Weldonville that night. He had stayed the longest, "stood my ground the longest," as he described it, and then hung back to ensure the others wouldn't be overtaken, or even pursued.

When Edison Leonard called him on the cell phone and told him that Holliman had been shot in the head and McKinney had been hit in the neck with an ax and Lambert had never been able to crawl out of the council chamber, he had wept. He had pulled himself together after a few seconds and told his own story and wept again, more heroically. The more he told the others about his part in the battle, the more certainty he felt about the details, particularly the reasons for each of his actions.

He also found it necessary to mention that he had not only heard the sirens coming toward city hall as they had, but he had also stayed long enough to see the SWAT team running along the back street toward the building. Leonard and Mann should never doubt that they had done the right thing in getting out, because what they had not seen coming had been worse than what they had seen. The truth was that the SWAT team originated in Lee Wolf's head after they'd all left town, and the sirens had been the sounds of two police officers in two cars making all the noise they could because nobody else was coming.

The three surviving escapees drove hard for the first three hours, and that brought them onto the flatlands of Kansas on Interstate 70. They stopped for a break after that, but not together. If the pursuers in Colorado knew anything about them, it was that they'd come and gone in two cars, so on the way out, they made their single stop for gas, a restroom break, and breakfast in different towns, and not on the interstate highway, where everything was likely to be recorded by surveillance cameras.

Nearly twelve hours and six hundred miles of driving brought them as far as Kansas City, Missouri. Lee Wolf didn't mind being the one who was alone in a car and had to do all the driving himself. He had confidence that in any foreseeable situation, he was more likely to survive than Lonny Mann or Edison Leonard. It wasn't something he would have said aloud, but he was sure of it.

He didn't call them on the burner cell phones again until he was on U.S. 24 and leaving Kansas City. He reminded them of the directions to where they were going and made sure that Leonard could recite them into the phone. He also told them that when they reached the end of the open highway part of the trip, they should pull over and wait for him to catch up.

He said, "We members of the Swift Sword of the Savior are a bunch of violent lunatics, and if that's what you are, you keep track of every bit of news you can get. If they've heard about what happened in Colorado, they might assume the next people coming up that road toward them will be cops of one sort or another. The safest way is to go up with me."

"Where is the boundary line?" asked Leonard. "Where's the place where they might start to get nervous?"

"It all depends," said Wolf. "These are free men, and free men think for themselves. If they recognize you, there won't be a problem. But if they don't, it's best to stick close to me."

Late that afternoon, Lee Wolf came upon the other car parked a mile from the start of the road leading up into the hills. He had made a lengthy stop in the last town to do some shopping, so they had been waiting for some time. He rolled down his window. "If you've got any guns in the car with you, put them in the trunk now."

"We already did."

"Good. Then follow me." He drove past them and up the smaller road. The next half hour was spent listening to the high whine of the gears as the cars climbed. The road wound and half-twisted to find the vulnerabilities of the land, the places where pavement could be laid over rock, the spots where a steep incline was made easier by using rocks and concrete to extend its length. Some stretches rose until there seemed to be no more road, but when the car got there, a hairpin turn sent them upward in the other direction.

Near the top of the hill, the road straightened and even widened a little, and there was a gravel jog off to the right into the trees. The two cars took it and kept going for about a mile until it opened into the grassy meadow with the buildings on it. Lee Wolf set the speed. It was a pace he had chosen to be respectful. It respected people's concern for any children who might be playing there, or anyone who might be annoyed by cars kicking up dust, or the ones who were always on the lookout for hostile intruders and didn't like having to look up from whatever work they were doing to make sure a gun was in reach.

As the two cars slowly moved across the meadow, people came out to smile and wave at Lee Wolf. He drove to the front of the plain clapboard structure where he lived and waited until the other car pulled in beside him. Edison Leonard and Lonny Mann got out of their car, and he said, "You can go right in if you want. I stopped for some groceries on the way, and I've got to get them to the kitchen."

He backed up about twenty yards to the big cookhouse, opened his trunk, got out of the car, and began to unload. People who had stopped what they'd been doing to see him gathered to help. He had several five-gallon bottles of drinking water, two cases of egg cartons, bags of rice, sugar, flour, salt, and baking powder. He had two crates of fresh meat—beef, chicken, pork, sausages, turkey—all packed in ice. His biggest investment had been in canned goods. There were two dozen canned hams, flats of canned chili, soups, beans, vegetables, fruits, and tomato sauce. He had cases of beer and soft drinks, and a dozen bottles of scotch and a dozen of vodka.

As people helped unload, they talked. "So, you're back," said a man named Bob Carpenter. "You okay?"

"We had kind of a rough time," said Lee. "We lost three good men. I brought the other two back with me. But I thought it would cheer us up to stop and pick up some supplies on the way home."

The canned, bottled, and preserved food went on the shelves in the big pantry of the cookhouse, but the perishables had to be refrigerated. The camp's icehouse was only a few yards away, built from a set of nineteenth-century plans reprinted in a survival-ist manual. It was a brick structure, mostly underground, lined in zinc and cork with sawdust around the sides. The group had harvested big squares of ice from a shallow lake nearby during the winter, replenished now and then during trips to town. The icehouse was also equipped with a refrigeration unit that could be powered by a gasoline generator, but so far it had never been used.

Lee Wolf had been confident that when people helped unload and saw what he had brought to contribute, their reaction would be good, and it was. He had been careful to include things that the end-of-the-worlders would consider practical, and also things that would brighten the outlook of the non-fanatics who drank and gave their kids candy.

One of them said, "You had three die. Nobody just got wounded?"

"They all did," said Wolf. "They kept fighting until they got a fatal hit. I left here with them because they were men I respected. I respect them more now that I saw them die."

"We've been watching the news online, but so far we haven't seen anything about it."

Lee Wolf looked at the man in surprise. "Now that is strange. We actually took over city hall in Weldonville, Colorado, for a while. I would have thought that the feds would be so proud of defeating six men with only a couple hundred agents that they'd put it on every screen twenty-four hours a day."

A man named Andy Potts said, "They might be reenacting it for public consumption before they release it. They've been doing that since the sixties."

"Could be," said Wolf. He never disagreed with Andy, who was always looking for a chance to convince people that the news releases about the government were the secret disinformation projects of Hollywood Jews.

Wolf went back to his cottage, where Edison Leonard and Lonny Mann were eating hamburgers at his kitchen table, which was covered with bags and wrappers. Leonard said, "Want a burger?"

"Maybe," Wolf said. He sat down and felt the bag, which was still a bit above room temperature. "How old are they?"

"We bought them just before we met up with you. Maybe forty-five minutes."

He opened one and began to eat. "Thank you."

Mann said, "We saw you bought a bunch of stuff too. What was all that?"

"Mostly stuff for the whole congregation. It's important to contribute, and it saves somebody a trip to town and showing his face another day. Have you thought about what's next for you?"

"Not me," said Lonny Mann. "Not much, anyway."

"Me neither," Edison Leonard said. "I've been thinking I'll go back to Michigan for a while, and get in touch with Reggie Varga. If she can get me fresh ID and a real passport, things might work out for me yet."

Wolf said, "You might want to give it a little time before you make a move."

"I thought this place was safe," Leonard said. "No police know about it yet, and all that."

"All true," Wolf said. "It's safe. The last place we were was Oklahoma five years ago. We all went our separate ways, and now we're back together. We're in a quiet regrouping and rebuilding phase now. This land was owned by the uncle of one of our members. We pooled our money and bought a plot right in the middle of a lot of land he owns, so there won't be any neighbors for a very long time."

"Then maybe we should stay for a while."

"I think that's the safest," said Wolf.

"How long should we stay?" Leonard asked.

"I can't tell what the people in Weldonville know about us. They could have surveillance footage of our cars coming into town or leaving. If they do, they might be able to pick us out on the recordings from Interstate 70 or U.S. 24. That would bring them pretty close—to Kansas City."

"Do you think they have it?"

"I don't know. But it never hurts to be careful. We can't trade in those two cars or report anything about them to any DMV or insurance company. Eventually they'll have to be chopped or driven off a cliff in a remote place."

"I suppose you're right," said Lonny Mann. "Leaving here is going to be a lot of trouble."

"And it's not a good idea to rush it," said Leonard.

Lee Wolf sighed. "If you'll be here a while, then you'll want to make yourselves indispensable members of society."

"What does that mean?"

"I don't know what your financial situation is after only two years out of prison, but if you have money, share some of it as soon as possible—buy supplies, ammo, and so on. When there's work to be done, be first in line to help."

"Anything else?"

"Watch them closely. If they think you're not helping and food gets scarce, you'll have about one more day here. If you do something they don't like, you'll have less."

31

Leah drove from town to town throughout the Ozark region, exploring. There was Bentonville, Arkansas, a built-up, sophisticated place because it was where Walmart had its headquarters, and money had a way of overflowing into its surroundings. There was Eureka Springs, which was partly like a museum, with its two nineteenth-century hotels and steep streets, and partly like an art colony. She visited Fayetteville and the University of Arkansas, Huntsville, Rogers, Siloam Springs, and Springdale.

The Ouachita Mountains had some high, rough country, and so did the Boston Mountains. She kept passing signs commemorating Civil War battles where up to three thousand men were killed over territory that must have seemed as remote and wild as Amazonia to some of them.

Lake of the Ozarks turned out to be a huge expanse of water full of giant cruisers, speedboats, Jet Skis, and drunken partiers. The minute Leah saw it, she was sure nobody would hide there.

She stopped in many small towns and wandered around. If there was a large gun store, she went there to look and listen, hoping to find people who were trying to make large purchases of ammunition or multiple identical firearms. She didn't find any who made her suspicious enough to follow. She also spent time at food markets watching for people buying enough food for a few dozen people. She saw none of those either.

It occurred to Leah that if a fanatical group based in Oklahoma disbanded and had come back together to start up again in Missouri or Arkansas, they would have needed to find jobs. She might be able to use this information by making a list of the employers who hired large numbers of new arrivals without requiring degrees or credentials, and then watching the doors at shift changes.

Leah wasn't looking just for the members of the Swift Sword of the Savior. She also had to look for people who were looking for the Swift Sword of the Savior. She didn't want to find the group right as an army of federal investigators arrived.

While Leah was interested in the domestic terrorists, she had to be sure not to miss any federal agents. Either group would be carrying concealed weapons on their bodies and probably long guns in their vehicles. Seeing a suspicious bulge might be less than conclusive in this region because Arkansas was a "shall issue" state, where getting a concealed-weapon permit meant asking for one, and Missouri, a short drive to the north, didn't require any permit.

Leah had spent her working life around law enforcement people of all kinds. She had some confidence that she could pick out a federal agent. She favored looking at shoes and watches. Usually if the person, male or female, was a federal officer, he would wear shoes with rubber soles and sturdy leather uppers, often with roomy box-toes reminiscent of combat boots. The agents also disproportionately favored watches with thin cases, dark faces with large numbers, a sweep second hand, and a fabric band. The women didn't wear shorts or skirts unless every single other woman was wearing them, and no tank tops. They never wore dangling earrings or hoops.

In their photographs, the male members of the Swift Sword of the Savior looked a lot like farmers or tradesmen. They wore blue jeans, baseball caps, T-shirts with long-sleeve shirts over them, and usually some kind of work boot. Leah had seen a number of photographs of Lee Wolf and the accomplices arrested for helping him with the bombings, arsons, and murders—both surveillance shots and mug shots. The photographs had not included any women.

She had decided that the women wouldn't be wearing overly conservative, modest clothes. If a woman was up to no good, she would want to look like the majority. Leah also didn't believe that the motivation for any group that would include Lee Wolf could be religion. Their record of arson and murder proved it wasn't Jesus because they thought like Jesus; it was Jesus because saying the group was Christian meant "You'd better look just like me."

Leah Hawkins watched and listened in six towns on the average day, mostly near the border between Arkansas and Missouri, but nothing led her closer to the place where the three killers were hiding.

At night Leah sat in her hotel with her laptop on, trying to find her way onto the site that was being used by the Swift Sword of the Savior. Each night she gave it another try. She had gotten into the dark web through Tor and tried finding the site by typing in the group's name, all the subjects she could remember that white militias liked to talk about, various names for the region, and even scrambled letters made from the name of the group. Nothing worked. Finally, as she became more impatient, she looked at the date on her computer.

She typed "September 30," and then scrolled through long lists of posts, sites, updates on things she had no time to identify, and then stopped. She clicked on something that said, "Today's Subversive Thought," posted August 21.

There was a male voice. "It's getting to be the tail end of summer, and you know what that means. It's the time of year when most of the country's kids go back to school. I understand that in some places like California, a lot of them have started already.

The whole idea is to get another great big dose of propaganda to socialize the kids."

"Is that you?" Leah whispered. "It sounds like you." Only a few weeks ago she had spent a nightmarish evening listening to his voice.

"They learn to love their neighbor, regardless of which sex he is, and do unto others, and share. I guess you could see that as all one lesson."

Yes, it was definitely Lee Wolf.

"And then they learn a lot of probably useless stuff," the voice said. "They study languages. When I was a kid, they used to make you learn French. They called it the language of culture, which is still important to a lot of rich people. Their idea of culture is ordering fancy food in French restaurants. None of them ever got good enough to carry on a real conversation, and who actually needs to talk to French people anyway? That's kind of tapered off. Now it's Spanish. They're taking over this country, so we may as well speak our new language.

"The plain truth is that if anybody in power had a brain, they wouldn't force children to go sit indoors and be indoctrinated with the boatload of stupid and self-punishing propaganda that was made up by all the spinsters, female and male, who never learned to be strong, quick, or brave, and think those qualities don't exist or don't matter anymore.

"They'd be better off letting the kids run wild until the beginning of hunting season. Where we live, bobcat season opens on September 1 and lasts until the end of February. I don't know if whoever is listening has been up close to a bobcat. Probably even if you were, you don't know it. They're very hard to find. But if you get one of those boys cornered and wounded, then you've got a reason to think. He's not as big as a man, but the reason he doesn't have to be bigger is because all he consists of is claws and teeth and a pair of pointy ears. A young person who is skilled enough to bag a bobcat is wasting his time in any grade below the tenth. And if you have one of those prodigies who is ready for postgraduate study, there's also a bow-hunting season for bear. It starts a bit later, on September 23, and only lasts until November 30.

"If you want to teach a teenager that life doesn't give you seven or eight do-overs and one-more-chances, have him go out to kill a bear with a bow and arrow. A bear is a big animal, and he's not that hard to hit, especially when he gets up on his hind legs and waddles toward you. But he only does that when he's too close to run away from. So he's easy to hit, but hard to kill. You have to draw the bow back pretty far to get the power, and then keep your head and hit him in a vital spot. At that point, if he's not dead, you are."

Leah listened to minute after minute of the diatribe until he finished. It went on for some time. When Lee Wolf concluded, she glanced at a note she'd written down and then started typing into the laptop. The bobcat hunting season was September 1 in the state of Arkansas. In Missouri it wasn't until November 15. The Swift Sword of the Savior was in Arkansas.

At the Ararat community, Lonny Mann and Edison Leonard were helping clear a new plot for a vegetable garden. The process required hard labor. A line of men with machetes waded into a large, rectangular plot, which had been marked by rags tied to a branch on each corner, and hacked down and carried off a thick layer of weeds and brush. Men with axes, chain saws, and spades followed them. They cut the trunks of trees, saplings, and bushes, dug down and severed roots and pulled the stumps, and carried them off the plot. Behind them came Ed Leonard, Lonny Mann, and other men with mattocks and hoes to break up the sod to expose the soil. As they worked, they found and dug out rocks and carried them to the perimeter.

Lee Wolf's advice had not been wasted on either of them. There was no way to know what the ramifications of the disastrous raid on Weldonville might be. Violent acts could leave dozens of trails to the person who had done them. And in this particular situation, the authorities already knew their names and had their fingerprints, DNA, and photographs.

Wolf was out working in the patch too. The group had grown some vegetables in the spring and early summer, but now they were making a bigger effort. Second plantings of beets, kale, carrots, lettuce, peas, squash, and spinach could all be harvested late in November most years, and this large plot could make a big difference. Whatever they grew, they wouldn't have to buy.

Wolf made a big show of being one of the first to begin work and the last to stop to rest. He had no shirt on, but wore a bandanna around his head to keep the sweat out of his eyes. Lonny Mann and Edison Leonard did the same to give the impression of hard labor. They knew that what caused the need for more food was more people, so they needed to be counted in this project.

It occurred to Edison Leonard that what had got him into trouble in the first place was not wanting to spend his days sweating in a field like this. But here he was, twenty years down the line, doing the same work he had stolen and killed to avoid. It was kind of funny, and he chuckled as he swung his mattock to claw up a clump of weedy earth, then pried it out effectively. He decided that he and Lee and Lonny were about the best laborers in the crew, because they had all spent years in prison, where there was a lot of time to fill, and they had all built muscle by lifting weights and doing pull-ups and push-ups.

"What are you laughing at?"

He turned his head in surprise, because it was a female voice. The woman was in her early thirties, and she wore a T-shirt, a long and loose skirt, and a wide straw hat. She was carrying a pair of plastic buckets that contained water and a couple of ladles and tin cups.

"I was just thinking about how many surprises there are in life," he said. "I went to school to be an engineer, and a few things happened, and here I am." He grinned at her. "Not all surprises are that kind though. Some are the 'prize' in 'surprise.'"

"All I'm offering you is water, hon." Her smile was bright, pretty, and knowing. She fished a blue-speckled metal cup out of the water, gave it to him full, and locked eyes with him as he drank it down.

He finished and handed it back to her, and she dropped it back in the bucket. "That was great, thank you," he said. "But is that sanitary?"

She shrugged and smiled. "Probably not. But I've noticed none of the very best things are."

He said, "You're right about that. Thank you again, ma'am." He turned to look at the next yard of turf ahead.

"Charlotte."

"Hmm?" He turned to her.

"My name is Charlotte."

"A beautiful name for a beautiful person. Not a bad city either."

"See you." She bent at the knees to pick up the pair of buckets. She had wrapped the handles with a pair of dishcloths to keep them from hurting her hands, so she adjusted them, stood, and moved on to the next man, who was one of the locals. She gave him the same cup.

The sun was hot, and the work was hard and repetitive. Just being able to straighten his back and pause for a minute or two had been a pleasure.

He worked steadily, pulling up more grass and brush to bare the soil, trying to make as much progress as he could. Whenever his mattock hit rock, he would pry the stone up if he could and set it at the edge of the plot. A bit later he came to a patch where there must have been a lot of shrubs and saplings. One of the men with the chain saws had come through to get rid of the standing wood, but did little with the roots. Ed stuck the pick side of the mattock under each of the roots, leaned back on the handle, and pried up the root, then tossed it aside with the rocks.

Lonny Mann was slacking. Leonard could tell. He was probably tired, or maybe just bored from the work. His movements were exaggerated. When he picked up something he'd extracted from the garden plot, he would stagger with it to the edge as though it weighed hundreds of pounds, sometimes grunting with the supposed effort.

Leonard resented it. Mann was endangering him too. The hard labor was intended to bring them closer to the members of the community, a show that the two guests were willing to make a sincere effort to fit in and contribute to the welfare of all. Leonard had been working in all sincerity from the moment he'd been awakened in the morning until now. What was now? About two-thirty, judging from the height and ferocity of the sun. Eight to noon was four hours, which made it six and a half hours he'd been at it today. He had assumed Mann was doing the same until now.

Leonard forced himself to keep his eyes off Mann while he worked. When people saw someone looking, they looked in the same direction. When he had worn himself out with the mattock and reached the edge of the cleared ground with the other men in the line with him, he stood and leaned on the handle for a moment. One of the others near him said, "Boy, I'm glad to get to the end of that row."

"Me too," Leonard said. "It's a lot of work, but when the vegetables grow in, it will be worth it."

When Lonny Mann came up to join them a few minutes later, Ed Leonard moved off to return his mattock to the tool shed and trade it for a long-handled pry bar. He returned to the foot of the vegetable plot and began to pry up rocks he hadn't been able to budge with his mattock. He was determined to keep himself from being grouped with Lonny Mann as a faker and half-hearted worker.

A short time later, he heard the woman's voice. "Hey, farm boy. You thirsty again?"

Charlotte was close to his shoulder with her buckets. She set them down and handed him the blue cup again. "Thank you," he said. "This really helps."

He looked at her, but saw that she wasn't looking at him anymore. Her eyes were focused on something far off. She looked away from that direction and said, "Don't wait for somebody to come to you. Drink whenever you can. If you faint out here, they'll never let you forget it."

"I'll remember that."

She took the cup back, tossed it in her bucket, and moved on to another thirsty worker.

There were men returning from other places now, probably from jobs in the surrounding towns, or from supply trips. Many of them picked up tools and stepped onto the ground that was being cleared for cultivation. Within about a half hour, the original crew that had begun in early morning was nearly replaced. Chain saws whined again, and men and women with hoes and mattocks followed them in lines on the field. Eventually a large man Ed didn't know came up to him and said, "Why don't you let me take over for a while?"

The man seemed friendly, and didn't seem to expect a refusal, so Leonard let him go to work. The man was strong and fresh, so he made good progress in removing rocks.

Ed walked up the hill to the pond where people swam, immersed himself in the cold spring water, lay on the bank for a few minutes resting, and then walked down to the storehouse, where he had been living with Lonny Mann. As he put on some clean clothes, he heard voices.

He moved slightly closer to the center of the storehouse and saw a scene that seemed tense. Lonny Mann was sitting on his bunk with his arms folded, staring at Lee Wolf with a sullen expression. Wolf said, "I'm only trying to help you. If they think you're faking the work, they'll wonder what else you might be faking. You have to realize that these people are tender anyway. For their adult lives, they've been told that the way they think is so old-fashioned, it's stupid. The jobs they know how to do are practically obsolete. If a machine isn't already doing them, it's because the machine is too valuable to use that way. They can't live on the money they make. They feel like their country has been taken from them and given to other people. They were lost and scared and mad to begin with, and since I've been with them, the government locked a bunch of them up with me. I'm out, but the others are still in cages in different parts of the country. Just don't play with these people."

Ed Leonard felt a slight, barely perceptible sense of satisfaction. He let it carry him out the door, then to dinner at the picnic tables in the middle of the common green, and through the nightly meeting, and then well into the next morning of work. What carried him through the rest of the day's work was that the woman named Charlotte visited him three times in the field, and introduced him to two other women on the water crew. As they left, she told him that they had seen how hard he worked and had asked about him. That carried him through another day of work, and he knew he was working even harder because of what they'd said. He wondered if they were laughing at him for it, but he decided that motivation was a gift, even if it wasn't intended that way.

32

Narrowing down the places where the Swift Sword of the Savior might have settled was a slow process for Leah. She kept making the circuit of small Arkansas Ozark towns. She went to Laundromats and coffee shops and hair stylists and post offices and churches to read the announcements and invitations on the bulletin boards, hoping for a meeting or a picnic or a potluck open to new members.

She didn't expect the group to use their name. She expected instead that there would be hints. Maybe there would be a white cross in a red circle, maybe a blood drop in a diamond shape, or a Confederate flag. If there was text, it might overuse the word "Christian," or it might use less ambiguous words like "Aryan" or "Nordic" or even just plain "white." It was also possible the messages would not be overt, because the hosts would wait to deliver them orally at the event.

Every time Leah saw a pile of small pamphlets printed on newsprint, she took one. Even if all it contained were ads for post-hole diggers and weed whackers, there might be useful leads. Even the name and address of the printer could help.

She made use of every visit to a town to learn something. She didn't just walk through a café; she sat down and ordered food and eavesdropped on the other customers while she waited for it, ate it, and paid for it.

Whenever she was on a long drive, she would listen to the podcasts of the man who sounded like Lee Wolf. She was alert for anything he said that might refer to a place. When she stopped in a hotel anywhere, she would listen. When no new podcast was available, she would search the Internet for information about people connected with Edison Leonard or Lonny Mann or Lee Wolf.

The days passed in quiet research and observation, but there weren't any breakthroughs. She knew that this region was the most likely one for the three men to be hiding. There were mountains, thick woods, rivers, and lakes. But there was possibly one place where they were hiding, and a vast number of places where they weren't. There were many thousands of visitors in the summer driving cars bearing out-of-state plates, and there were people who didn't seem to be doing much, not because they were criminals or federal agents, but because they were on vacation. There were people who looked like right-wing militia members who turned out to be painters and sculptors represented by galleries in New York and Los Angeles. People she followed drove to Bentonville to pitch some product to the Walmart executives for inclusion in stores.

After three weeks, Leah asked Art Sprague at the Weldonville police station to mail her the drone she'd used in California. When it arrived, she began waiting near highways in the early morning watching for cars to come down the roads from the mountains to drive toward the towns. When she spotted a likely road, she would send the drone up to backtrack the roads to higher altitudes and search the forested land for settlements. At the end of the fourth week, she had eliminated hundreds of places, but she was aware that thousands remained.

* * *

Ed Leonard lasted through the clearing of the garden plot. The work of removing rocks and stumps was backbreaking, but then it was over. Other crews began to run a rototiller up and down the length of the field, and if any undiscovered rocks turned up, he didn't hear of it. The next phase was to build a pipeline from the bed of one of the lakes high above the community down to the large farm plot.

Laying the pipe required that a crew of men dig a narrow trench from the edge of the lake along the wooded slope all the way down to the garden. The intake was suspended a few feet above the bottom of the lake to avoid blockages, and ten feet below the surface in summer to prevent having the intake protrude above the water line. The downward tilt of the irrigation pipe from the lake was pronounced, but shut-off valves at several spots along the route would control the velocity of the flow. The downward tilt would also facilitate the draining of the pipes in winter to prevent them from freezing and bursting.

At break time each day, Ed would walk down to the vegetable plot and watch the work. A team composed mostly of women and children worked to plant the winter seeds, and another male labor crew was laying more PVC pipe that would feed sprinkler heads to water the crops during dry weeks. He would always find a seat where he could see Charlotte work.

She was bent over with a trowel and a bag of seeds, making a hole and then putting three or so in it, stepping on it to bury them, and then bending for the next hole. He couldn't help noticing that as she worked and sweated, the thin cotton cloth of her skirt and blouse tended to cling to her. She would go on working, pretending to be unaware that he was watching. When someone else would call, "Time," she would straighten, appear to notice him, and smile before she walked off with the other women of her crew for their break.

He always took that as the sign that he should go back to his own work on the pipeline. One afternoon, as he was coming back down the hill on a wooded trail at the end of the workday, he rounded a curve and saw her sitting on a log. He stopped and stared at her for a moment, not sure what she was doing there.

"Come on, Ed," she said. "Are you suddenly afraid of me after staring at me all those times? Was that what you were thinking? 'She's scary?'"

He walked the rest of the way to the turn where she sat. "No, I guess it wasn't." She stood up a foot or so from him and looked into his eyes.

She said, "I know some things about you, but you know very little about me."

"That's true."

"First thing is, I'm married. My husband's name is Bob Carpenter." She held her hand out, grasped his, and gave it a shake. "Charlotte Carpenter. Pleased to meet you."

"I didn't know," he said. "I'm really sorry for that."

She inched closer, smiling. "I didn't mean to ruin your whole day. I just needed you to know. The first day I met you, he came home early from town, but I saw him before he saw me with you, so I could move on."

Ed said, "I think that you just did ruin my whole day."

She took his right hand again, and he thought that she would shake it again and say, "Now go away and leave me alone." She didn't. She placed his hand on her left breast.

He leaned closer and kissed her, very gently at first, and then more deeply and passionately, both hands beginning to move, to feel the shape of her body. She pushed him and stepped back.

"Cut it out now. I don't want you to get me all hot and bothered right now. I would like to fool around with you, but I don't want to get caught and hurt Bob's feelings, and I certainly don't want to get him mad at me. So you'll have to be patient and let me handle how it happens, and when it happens." She stepped back. "I just wanted you to know I wasn't just flirting, and I wanted to be close up with you for a minute and see if I still wanted to."

"Do you?"

"I just said that I did. Do you?"

"Of course."

"Then we will. But you've got to stop staring at me like you do. And don't act like you never saw me before either. Treat me like you treat everybody."

"I will."

"All right then." She turned away and took another branch of the path that went off to the right. He went to the left, and took his time getting down to the big clearing where the buildings were so they wouldn't arrive at the same time.

For the next few days Ed kept at the project he was working on. He saw Charlotte only a couple of times and even then from a distance. She did more digging and planting at the big vegetable garden with about thirty other people. He saw her once bringing drinking water in buckets to share with the crew of planters. He saw her another time at the lake where people swam, keeping an eye on a dozen children from the age of about twelve down to the size she had to carry while she held another by the hand. He moved on as quickly as he could without looking at her again.

Two nights later he was at the dinner serving line holding a plate and silverware. He accepted a good-looking piece of beef from Adam Hayes, who had the unofficial title of "grill master." He felt pleased about the beef, because Hayes had been known to give people he didn't like or respect inferior cuts. He thanked him and went on to the table of casseroles and bread and salads, and let the women there put a couple of spoonfuls on his plate. He said, "Thank you, ma'am," and moved on.

Then, from somewhere behind him, he heard Charlotte's voice. "Don't turn around. Look to your left. That's my house, with the wooden bluebird nailed to the door." He looked that way and identified the bird.

"Be at the back window at eleven thirty-seven."

He didn't look behind him, just moved to the next station, which had cups of water. He took one and went to sit with Lee Wolf, the first one at a picnic table.

Wolf looked up and said, "Hey, Ed. I've been meaning to tell you what a fine job you've been doing. Good for you."

"Thanks, Lee," he said. "Folks have been nice." It occurred to him that he had never in his life referred to a group of people as "folks." He'd been born in Worcester, Massachusetts. But the Swift Sword people's way of talking was as contagious as prison talk.

After dinner and the evening meeting he went back to the storage building where he and Lonny Mann slept. They had divided the place in half after the other three were killed, because sleeping in close quarters was like prison, and space was a luxury. Each man had a bunk with a blanket and pillow, placed near the door at one end of the rectangular building so he could go out his own door to the nearest outhouse. Ed lay still in his bunk and listened to Lonny Mann's breathing.

He waited while it slowed down, and then while it turned into a snore. He used some of the time after that rolling his blanket into a torso, stuffing it into a T-shirt and jeans, and then covering it with a spare blanket. At 11:30 p.m. he went out and around the back of the storage building and into the woods.

Ed made a wide circle around the meadow where the community houses stood and emerged from the woods behind Charlotte Carpenter's house at 11:37.

The rear window was four panes fitted like double doors with hinges and a latch. He was sure that was because the group hadn't had skilled carpenters who could have installed sliding windows with sash weights. This kind of window was quieter, so he was glad. The window swung open inward and he followed it, climbing over the sill into a dark room. All he could tell about the space was that it was small and square, not a bedroom, but something else.

The window swung shut, and a graceful hand latched it again. She stepped into him. Her body pressed against his, and his arms automatically encircled her. She was naked.

She said, "Don't be shy, hon. Take them off. I've been looking forward to this."

He stepped out of his jeans and shorts, tugged his T-shirt up over his head, and realized she was helping him get it off. They seemed to melt together, and in a moment they were crouching on a soft surface that was not a bed, but a mattress that had a plastic surface and a few inches of foam rubber like the narrow mattress of a piece of lawn furniture. There were also some throw pillows. He gave the mattress no thought because by then his attention was fully engaged with her, his hands moving to caress her, exploring her body and letting her touch his. The process was hurried and eager, and the excitement grew, until in a short time they were making love. That was the term that came to him. They were quick and wild, even feverish in the small, dark room. There was a voracity that seemed to come from the forbidden nature of their new relationship, which was partly an agreement to do what they were not supposed to do. The transgression made them elated and burned away all the barriers and caution and even gentleness. They had granted themselves the right to take and take.

When they at last had to stop and lay side by side for a moment, he whispered, "Is this safe?"

"Do you mean is my husband home, or do I take the pill? He's away tonight, and I do."

"Good." He lay still for a moment. "Of course, worrying about those two questions helped me last longer."

She giggled. "You'll just have to go back to thinking about baseball to control yourself, like other men."

"It's our national game."

She put one leg over him and raised herself up to straddle him. "No, this is our national game." She leaned forward and kissed his lips, a long, lingering, wet kiss. He felt her nipples just barely touch his chest, and her hips began to move, her pelvis grinding slowly against him, reawakening his feelings for her.

He adjusted his position on the mattress slightly, and she gave a sigh that trailed off into a moan. "Second inning," she said.

The lovemaking went on for about two and a half hours before they lay still and stayed there, both covered with sweat and panting. When Charlotte's breathing returned to normal, she said, "What time is it?"

He sat up, held his watch to the window, and moved the curtain an inch. "About two. But if that's what you're thinking, it's time for me to go."

"That's true," she said. "We both have to get up in three or four hours and put in a day of work, or people will wonder why we're both tired."

"Will they?"

"You bet." She took his face in her hands and kissed him. "Don't let me down on that, because I just had a really great time, and I won't be able to invite you again if I can't rely on your judgment."

He kissed her back. "I'll see you at six." Then he said, "No, better not. But I'll be up then doing some kind of work where people can see me."

"There you go," she said. "I knew you weren't stupid."

He dressed quickly, and they both stood on the mattress. "What is this, anyway? Your bed?"

"No," she said. "I have a regular bed in the bedroom that I share with my husband. This is just a pad from a lawn chair. It means I don't have to change the sheets and blankets before he comes home."

"Does eleven thirty-seven have some meaning?"

"The opposite. No meaning. People who are meeting in secret usually meet on the hour or half hour."

"Very practical," he said. "I hope you get in touch with me soon. I'll be thinking about you."

"Don't," she said. "Let me do the thinking."

He went out the back window and heard the slow, soft sound of it closing and then the latch turning to lock it. He made his way around the margin of trees and brush to the building he shared with Lonny Mann. He set his alarm and went to sleep.

33

Leah worked each day from early morning until late at night. She could not be as open and visible in towns as she would have liked, because during the raid on Weldonville city hall, all three fugitives had seen her. She tried to do much of her searching for them by car, driving up and down the streets near bars and restaurants, parking in the lots of supermarkets, and watching the checkout lines through the big front windows.

Every evening Leah explored night spots, usually restaurants, diners, and quiet places where there was a chance to overhear conversations. She also went to a number of fast-food and take-out places, because the Swift Sword people were probably not rich. After it was too late to order food, she would go to bars. She knew that some members of a religious group probably wouldn't be drinkers, but some might be, and she also knew that she might hear more from people who weren't members than from people who were. People gossiped about new neighbors and strangers who had secrets, not about themselves.

One night she was sitting in a gravel parking lot casing a bar that was housed in a giant converted barn with a neon sign that said, WALLY'S SKY CLUB. She supposed the name had to do with the fact that it was at the top of a mountain. As she watched, four couples walked from the dimly lit gravel parking lot into the barn-like wooden structure. Leah considered that a good omen, because the more pairs and single women were in a bar, the less likely the men had nothing to do but fight. She heard the sound of a violin being tuned, a burst of applause, and then a live country band began to play. The door opened and stayed open as the couples streamed inside, and Leah watched men and women in jeans, cowboy hats, and boots form themselves into ranks and begin doing a line dance.

Leah stayed outside. A tall woman like her coming in alone attracted a certain amount of notice, and the right amount of notice tonight was none. The new couples formed their own row in the back and did a boot scoot with the others. After a few minutes, the band didn't stop, but just moved on into a new song, and the crowd started an electric slide. Leah spotted a pretty woman with long black hair wearing a crushed straw cowboy hat, a white lace top, and skin-tight jeans who seemed to be acting as the dance leader. Whatever she was doing, the rest of the people did too. It occurred to Leah that maybe she was paid by the bar or the band. When the song ended, the woman went off for a drink, so the crowd began to dance on their own, most of them doing a two-step, cruising around the floor on random courses.

She scanned the faces of the men she could see through the open door, but none of them looked like the men she was hunting for. She turned her attention to people coming and going in the parking lot. Wolf, Mann, and Leonard might not be dancers, and they probably wouldn't dare go out to pick up strange women this soon after the raid on Weldonville, but they probably didn't mind having a drink. She sat through the band's second set, and then saw some of the patrons going outside.

Some of them had come out to cool off, as though Wally's air-conditioning wasn't sufficiently powerful to make up for the dancing. Some lit cigarettes, and she could see the tiny orange tips and then the strands of smoke curling and folding in on themselves and rising to catch the light from fixtures mounted above the barn door.

She watched one couple separate themselves from the others. The woman, who had long, dark hair, lifted it off the back of her neck to let the air cool her. She followed her escort away from the building and then stopped under one of the lamps mounted on a pole in the lot. The man was big and tall, with a short, thick beard with a little gray in it, but the woman was the one who caught Leah's attention.

She was wearing a bright yellow T-shirt with black printing on it. There was a picture of a broadsword with the hilt up and the blade down, so it looked like a cross. And above the handle were the three letters "sss."

Leah slumped low in the driver's seat of her rental car and let her eyes follow them. The man opened the driver's side of a red pickup truck and got in, and the woman headed for the passenger side and climbed in after him.

Leah waited to hear the man start the pickup before she turned the key on her rental car.

34

Bob Carpenter drove the red pickup out of the parking lot behind Wally's Sky Club. As he accelerated, the rear tires threw a volley of pea-size gravel into the air, where it bounced off the cars in the last row.

Charlotte said, "Jesus, Bob. You're driving way too fast."

"I've got the truck under control. I drive it every day of my life, so it's like part of my body. Don't tell me you're scared."

"Yeah, I'm scared. You're under the influence, for one thing. You've got control in the parking lot of a bar lit up like Christmas, but we're driving onto a dark road through thick woods. What happens when that twelve-point buck leaps into the road? Deer don't hang around at bars, but a hundred yards down the road we could be dead. It happens all the time on these mountain roads."

"If it's a twelve-point buck, I'll pistol-shoot him and make him into a trophy. You can hang our socks on his antlers to dry."

Charlotte put her hand on his thigh. "Slow down for me, Bobby."

He took his foot off the gas pedal, but he also took his eyes off the dark road and looked at her instead. "There. Is that slow enough?"

"It's a start," she said. "Just pay attention to the road. I don't want to spend the night in a jail or a hospital, or move into a cemetery tomorrow."

He drove on for a time, but she could tell he wasn't keeping the car straight or steady. He was drifting and then correcting. She watched his eyes closely and kept glancing at the speedometer to be sure he didn't keep the needle creeping up. He was a man who could be a lot of fun when he was out drinking, but sometimes later, after the drinking was over, he could get cranky and mean. She wanted to keep on his good side so that didn't happen tonight.

She felt a bit uneasy about things right now. He had been out with Dave Sherman on a handyman job for four days, building a corral and a shed-size barn for a woman in Fayetteville whose daughter had a horse. That was when she had invited Ed Leonard to visit her. It was a matter of importance to her to keep Bob feeling warm and confident about her.

He could be suspicious, and she didn't always have to make a mistake to make him that way. When he acted jealous, she often sensed that it was because while he had been away on a job, he had slept with another woman and projected his guilt on Charlotte. If he was doing it, maybe she was too.

He had been with Dave Sherman this time, and that was a sign. Dave Sherman was a good-looking single man with no rules to follow. He was sometimes gone for a short job—a delivery or a shopping trip—for five or six days. She had never seen any advantage in spying on her husband when he was off with Dave Sherman. What would she get for catching him? But she thought Bob's straying at those times was pretty likely. And he did seem to be blaming her for whatever had happened.

Charlotte was determined to keep everything easy and calm tonight, so she said nothing when she saw he was speeding up.

He said, "Wow, that's irritating."

"What is?"

"The headlights of that car back there."

She turned in her seat and looked out the rear window over the truck bed. There was a pair of headlights back there. They didn't seem overly bright, but they were there. "I see them," she said. "They're pretty far back."

He began to speed up some more. "I didn't mean the glare. But I don't want to have them follow us home. We're only a couple of miles out from Ararat."

She smiled. "You want me to drive while you get out your tool-box and throw roofing nails on the road?"

"No. I'll pull onto the uphill road and stop a ways up to wait for them to round the bend, then stop them to ask what they're up to."

It was a terrible idea, but she knew there would be no way to dissuade him now that he had an idea and felt it was a good one.

She remained silent and watched the other car, which stayed back so it was only a pair of headlights. She hoped it would make a turn somewhere soon.

The lights stayed behind them for the next two miles until he went upward toward the place where the mountain road began. Bob drove up, his speed higher than it should be, bouncing and turning on the uneven, inclined pavement. A couple of times Bob took a turn too tightly, and she heard weeds and sticks scraping the side of the truck. He went up about three hundred yards and then stopped. He jumped down from the cab, went to the locked toolbox, opened it, and took out an AR15 rifle.

From far behind them, Leah could see that the pickup's headlights were now stationary, tilted uphill. They looked like a funnel of light shining upward to illuminate the upper branches of the trees. Then they went out. The pickup had stopped.

Leah drove along the highway toward the entrance to the uphill road, but then stayed on the highway instead of turning upward.

She drove on for a few minutes, until she was sure the red pickup truck hadn't turned around and come back down to follow her. She made a turn at the next opportunity and took a slightly longer route toward the hotel where she was staying the night.

Up the mountain road, Bob and Charlotte Carpenter were in the open flat bed of the pickup. She sat with her back leaning against the cab and her arms folded, while Bob crouched, his rifle at his shoulder and resting on the built-in toolbox, aiming the weapon at the center of the narrow road.

As the minutes passed, Charlotte felt more and more firmly convinced that the second car had not been following them. Why would anybody do that anyway? To rob them? Any conscious adult human being who got one look at Bob Carpenter would know he was not the man they wanted to pick on. He was big and formidable physically, and everything about him said he was probably armed. She hoped he wasn't going to get paranoid every time he got drunk.

She didn't mind this time, really. They had gotten out for an evening away from Ararat. She loved dancing, and there had been a good country band. It was also nice to be reminded that she was still a pretty woman. Even though she was past the bride stage, she had drawn a fair number of appreciative looks from men tonight. If she had been alone, they would have bought her plenty of drinks and competed for her attention.

She sat there for a long time. After a while, she heard Bob's breathing start to rasp and then make an occasional snort. She got up and hugged him, her cheek touching his.

In her sweetest voice she said, "Come on, Bobby. You dozed off for a minute." She had her free hand on the rifle's barrel, and as Bob raised his head she slid the gun out of his loose grasp. She released the magazine and opened the chamber to take out the round, and then set the rifle and magazine back in the toolbox. As he made his way to the tailgate, she stepped to the side and jumped so she could get to the driver's seat first.

"I'll drive," she said. "You can relax the rest of the way home."

35

When Bob Carpenter woke up the next day, he reached across the bed for Charlotte and found that his hand just kept going across the flat sheet. He patted the spot where she usually was and then opened his eyes. The sun was high already, but it was coming in the wrong side of the house. It took him a second to sort that out—and realize that it was after noon.

He sat up and said aloud, "Charlotte?" The house was too small to make it necessary to raise his voice much, and his head was hurting and felt as though it had swelled in his sleep. His mouth was dry, so it was not pleasant to talk either. He got up and walked to the next room. They used it as a half-kitchen because it was where the counters and cupboards were. Charlotte mixed and stirred things here, but most of the heating was done at the community kitchen or the big grills outside. He often saw Charlotte here reading or listening to the radio or sewing, but not today.

He picked up his watch from the counter. It was 2:13 p.m. He had slept away most of the day. She had probably been up since 6:00 or 7:00 a.m. and gone out to be in some work detail with her friends. Today he felt discouraged about things. He took a dismal inventory. He felt practically sick today from drinking, and his wife had not exhibited any interest or even much tolerance for his impulse to have sex with her last night. He had committed both of them to the Swift Sword of the Savior two years after they'd been married, which was now almost eight years ago, and all he'd gotten out of it was a marginal life in the woods. The great change in society that he and Charlotte had signed on to promote didn't seem to have happened, except in the fantastical speeches of people who worked in politics. There was no sign that Jesus was in a mood to do anything much to make any of that real. As for the regular people, they got nothing out of anything. They were only expected to give up more and more and repeat slogans.

From year to year, Charlotte had shown less interest in any of it. The whole revolution had disappeared from her talk a long time ago. She had always been mostly interested in the religious part of it anyway, but even that had faded. She was still just as busy and active as ever, but she was engaged in things that weren't going to bring on a new society or kill any liberals or anything. She was always planting beans, baking bread, or sewing quilts from worn-out clothes with her friends. They were like a bunch of high school girls, spending their time chattering and gossiping or babysitting each other's kids.

She used to want kids of her own, but she never asked him to give her children anymore. She had always said it was part of the long-term fight to keep growing the numbers of righteous white-skinned people. Now she seemed to have lost interest.

He took off his T-shirt and put on a pair of shorts and walked up the hill to the upper lake for a bath. When he got there and stepped out of his boots, he put his feet down gingerly, trying to keep the stones from stabbing his soles. The water felt icy, but as soon as he could, he sat down in the water and raised his feet so he could float a little. He lay back and pushed off the bottom with his hands to drift into deeper water.

He heard a familiar voice. "Bob!" it said. "Hey, Bob!" He turned and saw Lee Wolf on the shore. When their eyes met, Wolf said, "Taking a break from the morning's work, huh?"

He didn't want to answer that, so he called, "Hey, Lee. What are you up to?"

"Come on out. I want to talk to you."

Bob felt reluctant about it. Getting into the lake had been a lot of work, and it had been painful. But he stood, tried tiptoeing over the stones, and was aware that he looked silly and weak trying not to show the pain and chill. When he got to the shore, he stepped into his boots.

"Let's walk," said Wolf.

Carpenter went with him, clomping along the downward trail with his boots untied.

"You're one of the stalwarts," Wolf said. "One of the elders of the church. You and Charlotte have always been people the rest of us count on. The penalty for that is that when we're in need, you get called on more often than most people."

Bob Carpenter was dreading the next thing. Was Lee Wolf about to berate him for sleeping all day? "Is there a problem?"

"Right now we're developing one. I hope it's temporary. Not enough money has been coming in this summer. We have been doing some heavy building to improve things, and in the long run something like a new field of crops will help us be self-sufficient. But it costs money to buy tools, seed, fertilizer, water pipes, pumps, and so on."

"Well, if it's the money from the little work trip Dave Sherman and I just took, that money belongs to the community. I'll bring it to you as soon as I get dressed."

"Keep it for now, Bob. I think we may need to spend some on the plan we're working on. You and I and two others—probably Dave Sherman and possibly Lonny Mann—will be going out to raise some real money."

"How?"

"I haven't wanted to do this, and I've resisted it for years, and I've been praying on it. But I think that, for once, we have to do it the direct way, just once, to get us through the next year. We've got to rob a bank."

"When?"

Wolf threw his arms around Bob and patted his back, hard, then released him. "That's what I mean about you. Some people might hem and haw or argue about it. You just say, 'When?'" He paused. "I think the time to begin is right away—maybe a couple of days."

"Where is there a bank we can rob?"

"I'm guessing Louisiana. We can make it look like we came and went from Texas, and come back here to Arkansas and lay low. But we'll have to do some shopping to pick the right bank. We need to get started on it."

The next night, the evening meeting was a bit dull. One after another the leaders, or at least influential members, of various work crews gave progress reports about their projects. The winter vegetables had been planted in the vast new garden, the irrigation system construction was complete and had been run for two days to get the growth period of the new crops started. A separate crew of weeders would begin making regular passes over the ground in a week. The windmill electricity project was still under study because of the high cost of the machines required. Besides the financing problem, there was also a question of how much additional visibility would be caused by mounting a windmill in a high place.

Lee Wolf was at the meeting, but he didn't say much or seem to be anything more than one of the members of the community. While one of the reports was delivered, he would nod in approval at everything and then clap his hands like everyone else.

As Ed Leonard watched Wolf, he developed a greater respect for his talent for leadership. That night he saw that Wolf was underscoring his humility and the purity of his motives. He behaved as though the accomplishments all belonged to the laborers and their crew chiefs. He didn't act as their leader complimenting them. Instead he knew when to listen and shut up. Four leaders gave reports during that meeting, and every one of them left the tent that night thinking that Lee Wolf was pure benevolence and wisdom, and was a personal supporter of theirs. When the meeting was over, he watched Wolf shake hands with each of the four and thank them simply and quietly, but with a big, generous smile.

Edison Leonard started to leave along with Lonny Mann, but Wolf spotted them and trotted after them. As he walked with them toward the storage building, he said, "How are you guys doing these days? Catch me up."

Ed said, "I'm doing fine. I think I'm slowly making some friends. I'm not in any hurry to go back out to the world again."

Wolf patted his back. "That's what I've been hearing, and when I've seen you, it seemed you were happy." He turned. "How about you, Lonny?"

"I don't know," said Mann. "I'm getting by. I figure that as long as the time keeps passing, I'm getting safer."

"We all are," Wolf said. "Just hang in as well as you can, smile at people, and speak when spoken to. There will be people who appreciate it and come to like you for your quiet ways. Just make sure you keep contributing. They're sharing with us, and so we have to share too—money, work, ideas."

"I will," said Lonny.

They reached the storage building and went inside. Wolf said, "I don't want to forget to tell you what I'm up to."

"What is it?" asked Ed. "What's going on?"

"I'm going to take a few guys out and get us some money. It's going to be quick and efficient in execution, but first we've got to pick out what we can hit."

"What do you mean? Is this a robbery?"

"Sure is," Lee Wolf said. "Ararat needs money. I want you to know that by not taking either of you, it's not to say I don't trust you, or you're not the best men I could take. You are. But there are other considerations. One is that you and I have an extra problem hanging over our heads. A fingerprint of ours left in the bank would launch a manhunt, even if we did nothing. But also, these men I've picked are part of the community. They have loyalty not just to me, but to each other, and that is essential. Besides, if this place is to survive, I've got to get the key men dedicated to it in a deeper way. I need them committed. When you've broken a few laws and taken some real risks, it's got a hold on you, and you don't ask if it's worth sacrificing for anymore. You already did some of the sacrificing, so it must be."

He looked at them with regret. "This time it won't be you, but this will pay off for all of us in the long run."

Edison Leonard said, "It's fine, Lee. I appreciate your coming to explain it. I won't worry about it, just wish you luck."

Lonny Mann sat for a moment with his brows knitted and his lips pursed. "I don't care. After that visit to Weldonville, I'd just as soon stay here."

Wolf stared at him for a second and then shrugged. "Well, I'll see you guys around."

When Wolf left, Mann said to Leonard, "What? You want to start robbing banks too? Be my guest."

"No, not really. But I think I would like to spend the next year or so in a remote place like this surrounded by men who think of me as a close friend of theirs. It'll throw off the police and FBI, and it will also give the people Weldonville hired to kill us time to give up and move on."

Mann shrugged. "I have no desire to spend years dirt farming and working odd jobs in and out of these shitty little towns."

"Not forever, no," said Leonard. But for now it's not so bad. People have been willing to share with us and accept us, even though we add to their risks."

Mann stood up. "I'm going to bed. But before I do, I should warn you. Wolf isn't trying to get this little heaven-on-earth out of a financial bind. He's rebuilding his army of suckers to make him rich. Good night." He walked to the other end of the building and turned off the light.

Leah Hawkins spent time studying the aerial maps of the land from the highway intersection where Wally's Sky Club stood and the beginning of the narrow uphill road where she had followed the red pickup truck.

Leah wanted to hunt down the woman with the yellow T-shirt. She had seen her face for only about ten seconds, but she thought she would recognize it if she saw it again. She knew that driving up that road was not a good idea, and she wasn't ready to try walking up there before she knew more about what she would find and how far the walk would be. Meanwhile she would be looking for other T-shirts with the same picture on them.

She went to Wally's Sky Bar several times, searching for the woman or the T-shirt, whichever turned up first. There wasn't any dancing on weeknights, so she ordered food and stayed for a couple of drinks, but the place never filled up, and the woman didn't return.

She changed rental cars and then set up a surveillance on a paved spot about a half mile from the entrance to the uphill road where the red pickup had gone. She bought a spotter's scope and aimed it at the place where the smaller road met the highway.

In the early morning beginning at five o'clock before the sun came up, a few cars came down the road to the highway and kept going. Leah photographed each one at the point where it reached the last turn and had to slow down and stop to watch for highway traffic. They seemed to be carpools, because each car had three to five people in it. It looked like a bunch of commuters lived up that road.

The next day was the same, and the next. On the fourth day she came back from her hotel with a few transponders for attaching to cars so she could use a computer to see where they went.

She watched through her rear window as a car full of men emerged from the mountain road. It was too many people to be anything but a carpool with multiple stops, so she let it disappear down the highway. Then there was a truck containing two women, but they both appeared to notice Leah's car. The third vehicle was a silver Toyota Corolla with three women in it, and it was going slowly down the mountain road to the highway.

She rested the scope on the seatback beside the right headrest and focused on the next vehicle. There seemed to be three men in a gray car. No, four men. The hood ornament on the front looked like the Subaru medallion with the stars. The vehicle was about the size of a Crosstrek or a Forester. Her breath caught in her throat. The man in the passenger seat looked like Lee Wolf.

She set the scope on the passenger seat, pulled out the Glock with no serial numbers, and pulled the slide back to let the first round into the chamber. Then she put on her baseball cap to cover her hair and her sunglasses on, and waited.

The car was coming up fast. She lowered the windows on both sides of the car, sat back, and held her pistol in both hands. If the women who had seen her earlier had warned them by phone, they might very well stop to investigate. She wanted to start her engine, but that would turn the taillights on, so she didn't.

She leaned back in her seat and watched the car in her side mirror coming toward her. The man she had thought looked like Lee Wolf was sitting in the right-hand seat, and she was in the left. She kept her eyes on that space. He would come within about ten feet of her face in three seconds . . . two . . . one.

As the other car arrived and flashed past, she kept her eyes on the mirror to her left. He was Lee Wolf. But in another second the car was a hundred feet past, and then far ahead of her and gaining ground. As she started her engine, she glanced at the gas gauge to be sure it still read full. This could be a long ride.

36

Charlotte Carpenter passed by Ed Leonard at the edge of the vegetable garden that morning about an hour after the men left for Louisiana. She said only, "Eleven seventeen?" and he said, "Sure." Then the long, hot day passed, and the evening brought cooler breezes.

When it was 11:17, she opened the back window of her house, but she didn't look outside. She knew that Edison Leonard would be there. He climbed in over the sill. Before she shut the window, she let him see the nightie she was wearing. It was silky and clingy with string straps and a hem that came right up within one inch of the level where it would have shown everything.

He seemed to like the cool, smooth feel of the fabric. He didn't just lift it off as she had pictured. He reached up under it to place the palm of his hand on her belly and then moved it to her backside and then everywhere, as she kissed him, excited by it and eager already. She was remembering the first time and thinking about what he had done then and what he might do this time. She had thought about him for days, and every time she caught him looking at her again with that longing and intensity, she had felt the fluttering in her stomach. She had given him a stern, cold look to make him stop, but she had wanted to put her arms around him and whisper to him to save it all up for now.

He seemed to have done that. He was touching her skin, moving in swirls on her back and belly and then every forbidden place, and she loved it. She felt appreciated and treasured and understood and claimed and possessed. She knelt on the mattress in front of him, undid his belt, and undressed him, lingering to touch and kiss and hold.

And then he pulled the garment up over her head and off, and knelt down with her. He did all the things that she had wished he would think of doing, not in the kind of hurry he had been in the first night. He took his time so that when each move came, she was eager and then grateful. She savored every feeling until it ended. She lay back and he lay beside her, both of them catching their breath.

She said, "We don't have to worry tonight. Bobby isn't going to come home. He went with Lee Wolf and Dave Sherman and Tony Wagner to do some work out of state. He'll call me as soon as they head home."

"Good," said Ed. He knew they had gone in the morning and what they were planning, but he could not see how talking more about her husband would help him.

She seemed to read his mind. "You don't like my mentioning him, do you?"

"I'd rather think about you."

"Don't you love the feeling that you're naked with another man's naked wife? Doesn't that feeling that you're doing something forbidden turn you on a little? That she's yours when you want to take her, that she'll do this for you? And this? That you can take her over and over, and—"

He moved swiftly over her and she stopped talking, or stopped using words. The night passed without either of them noticing the hour. Each time they stopped, something happened that made them turn to each other again. Then they heard the tweets of small birds, high in the trees, and then the first warbles.

"Get up, lover," she said. "You've got to get out of here now."

He tugged on his clothes while she opened the window for him, and then he was out and slipping into the woods at the edge of the clearing. He did not linger this time, didn't look at his watch or pause to listen for footsteps.

When he got to the storage building, he paused at the edge of the woods for a moment to be sure the way was safe. Across the green a hundred yards away he saw a light come on in a window. He moved quickly to his door and grasped the knob.

It wouldn't turn. He crouched on the steps, put pressure on it, then examined the space he'd created to see if the crack was wide enough so he could jimmy the lock with his pocketknife.

Suddenly the door swung open, and Lonny Mann was standing above him in the doorway, grinning. "Hi, Ed."

"Let me in." Ed ducked low and barreled in under Lonny's arm, as Lonny tried to lower it to hold him out. Ed closed the door behind him and set the lock. "That wasn't funny," he said.

"I think it was," Lonny said. "I'll bet it's the first time I've laughed since that trip to Weldonville—you looking all wide-eyed and scared, like you got caught stealing something from somebody while he was away."

Leonard was silent for a moment, thinking carefully about the consequences of the various things he could say. Finally he said, "I guess it's time to get up anyway, so I will. You can go back to sleep for a while if you want."

"I'd rather stay up while you tell me all about it."

"I don't know what you're talking about. I just got up to go to the outhouse. I thought I heard something, so I waited around a little to see if somebody was here who didn't belong. But I didn't see anybody. I thought I must have locked the door by accident."

"Nope," said Lonny Mann. "That was me. I locked it. Tell me about you and Charlotte."

"There is no me and Charlotte."

"Good," said Lonny. "I'm relieved to hear that. It leaves the way clear for me."

Leah had been following the Subaru since morning. They were heading south on Route 71 again, after taking detours that lasted most of the day. When she looked at the map on her phone, she thought they could be heading for Shreveport, Louisiana.

The ideal strategy for her would be to get a transponder onto their car. She had adapted the plan for the Subaru, but so far, when the Subaru had stopped, they'd never all left the car at once.

All she could do was keep following, keep watching, and keep using the methods she had learned for tailing suspects without getting noticed. She would change lanes when they went around a curve so they wouldn't see her doing it, change the look of her head-lights in rural areas by falling far back and turning on the brights for a while, hide behind a truck for as long as she could stay with it, or join a pack of cars and stay in the middle long enough for the driver ahead to lose track of what vehicles were behind him. She had even pulled over on a deserted stretch to get out to pee and then drove hard until she saw them ahead again.

She didn't understand the trip or the way the four men were making it, but she was sure that the face she had seen belonged to Lee Wolf. She would follow him for as long as it took.

The next day was difficult for Ed Leonard. He had denied having a relationship with Charlotte Carpenter, but there was no way in the world that Lonny Mann had believed him. Leonard had barely slept because he had left Charlotte's house just before dawn, so he felt as though his brain were drugged and couldn't stay alert. He worked hard all day in the summer heat and humidity, digging a trench for a second pipe leading from the upper lake to a lower-level reservoir that he had suggested. The idea was to have a wide and deep cistern underground made of bricks and concrete, for the times when drinking and bathing water was scarce.

The shovel work made his back stiffen and his arms feel limp and strained. Whenever he had a chance to stop, he tried to spot Charlotte and warn her about Lonny Mann, but he never saw her.

At the end of the day, he washed at the upper lake with the other men working there, came down and changed in the storage building, and went to the area near the central kitchen for dinner. He exchanged friendly conversation with the family sitting at the same picnic table while eating dinner, had a drink of whiskey to relax his sore muscles, and then went back to the storage building.

In the morning he felt better because of the extra sleep. He went up the hill to work. He stayed at it all day, trying to help his image, to stay away from Lonny Mann, and to hope Mann got over the idea that he had a relationship with Charlotte.

Late in the day, as he was getting ready to quit work, he saw her. She was in the woods, walking the perimeter of the lake. He stepped into the path and waited for her to reach him.

When she arrived, she looked upset. She gave him no greeting, just said, "Last night I got a visit from Lonny Mann. He came to my front door."

"Oh, no. I'm sorry," Ed said. "He asked me about you and I denied it. What did he say to you?"

"That he figured it out and you admitted it. Then you told him all about it. He said that you wanted me to sleep with him too. He said you told him you wouldn't be jealous. He told me that you were close in prison and shared everything. I told him there was nothing between you and me. He laughed at that and told me that if I didn't do it, he'd tell my husband. He said I already have two men, why not three."

"None of that's true. I'm sorry he said that."

"I told him that all I had to do was scream 'rape,' and there would be a dozen armed men bursting through the door to kill him."

"It worked?"

"He left. And that's what I'm going to do now. I thought you had a right to know. I'm going to stop meeting you for a while and see if he gives up." She stepped onto another branch of the path, and she was gone. In a moment he heard other female voices, and then hers.

He really would hate to lose his nights with her, but now that Lonnie Mann had made an overt move to butt in, the whole perfect relationship was about to end anyway. Mann was dangerous, and he would not give up. It occurred to Ed that usually the man who survived in these disputes was the one who did the most unexpected thing first.

His most unexpected move would be to kill Charlotte and frame Lonnie Mann for it. On work details Mann often carried a distinctive long-bladed hunting knife, and Ed had heard some of the men on the work crews mention it. Ed had killed a few women in the past, and Mann's knife would be good for that. If he took her by surprise, it would be very quick and quiet. But as he considered the idea, he thought of problems. Using the knife on her wouldn't be enough to frame Mann. The knife would have to be found in her or beside her, and why would Mann kill her and leave his knife? Ed could kill her and then leave the knife bloody in its sheath, but that meant he'd have to somehow get the local men to look at it for blood. No matter what plan he thought of, he would always be the one who said Mann had done it, and that would make people suspicious of him. His mind moved on to other strategies.

Late that night, Edison Leonard lay on his bed in the storage building. From time to time he would fall into a light, anxious sleep, but any sound or the absence of sound would bring him back to full consciousness. There was an owl's hoot, and later for a time there was a faint breeze that rustled the leaves of the surrounding trees. For a long time he lay listening to Lonny Mann's breathing.

This night felt like the nights he had spent in the federal prison at Victorville years ago. He had been on one side of a vendetta between two cliques, his and another, who had been fighting over ownership of certain desirable parts of the exercise yard. The issue wasn't important. It was just all they had to fight about. During the worst of it, they had tried to get opponents hurt and into the infirmary so they could be reached during the night.

Ed had developed a fear that Lonny Mann might want to kill him in his sleep. A person who was not a wholehearted friend was a potential enemy. Ed had already resented Lonny for not working hard and risking Ed's reputation along with his own. He was sure Lonny had detected the resentment. And now Ed had lied to Lonny about having sex with Charlotte. They had both been out of prison for two years already, but the crazy old claustrophobic calculations were still in Ed's mind. Why not in Lonny's? The old aggression and intimidation of prison weren't that easy to shake off. Lonny might be capable of killing Ed so he would have no rival with Charlotte and so she would be frightened enough to submit.

Ed Leonard listened to the breathing coming from the other end of the storage building. He tried to tell whether the long, slow breaths were genuine sleep or Lonny Mann skillfully pretending he was asleep. Fake sleep was a two-part attack on his defenses, designed to fool him into feeling safe and to actually make him sleepy.

Lonny was someone he would never have wanted to be with in this situation. Lonny had been sentenced to life at least twice, once for killing an inmate in prison. He had also bragged in Ed's presence about his dealings with women before incarceration. He talked about things he had done to women and the things he was planning to do in Weldonville when the breakout came. Enslaving a beautiful woman like Charlotte might be too much for Lonny to resist.

Ed couldn't be sure Lonny had turned on him, but he had thought about Lonny so hard that it would have seemed foolish not to take precautions for the night.

He had gone to his car at the edge of the woods and taken some items from it in the dark. He had taken the rubber floor mats from the car and some duct tape. Once the lights in the storage building were out, he had wrapped the two smaller rear mats around his forearms and taped them there. He had wrapped the longer, wider mat from the passenger seat around his midsection and taped it around and around to hold it. He had taken the tire iron from the trunk and a razor-sharp knife from the toolbox. He held the two weapons in his hands in the proper positions, with the tire iron on the right and the knife on the left.

For a moment he considered replacing the knife with his pistol, but a gunshot would make enough noise to bring everyone running, and he was fairly sure they would kill both him and Lonny in the dark. It was less risky for them than waiting for hours to sort things out in daylight. They didn't owe him a trial, and they certainly didn't owe Lonny anything.

He lay awake for a long time and then dozed. At just after 3:00 a.m. he heard the old sounds stop and new sounds start. Lonny had stopped his slow, rhythmic breathing. There was no sound of breathing at all.

Ed must have rolled over in his sleep. He was facing the wall and the door instead of facing Lonny's end of the room. He regretted it, but if he stirred now, he could be lost.

He heard a whispery sound as a shoe moved a bit on the concrete floor. He decided it was Lonny Mann's work boot. The sound was just a dry whisper of the hard rubber sole over the concrete. Leonard was sure it meant that Mann hadn't wiped his feet on the mat when he'd come in, and the dust was making the shoe lose a little of its traction.

He grasped his knife with his left hand and the end of the tire iron with his right, without moving anything but his fingers under the covers.

There was the whispery sound, another, and another, moving more rapidly now. And then Ed felt the punch of the knife blade. It hit his back behind his heart between the fourth and fifth ribs, but that was where the rubber mat was wrapped thickest around him. The blade punctured the outer layer of rubber, but it was a blow, a stab not deep enough to slide into him. He rolled fast toward his assailant and swung the tire iron at him.

Lonny Mann jumped backward and evaded the swing, but as soon as the lug end of the iron swept past his face, he attacked again, advancing two steps, slashing wildly at Leonard with the long-bladed hunting knife.

Leonard raised both arms, taking the slashes on the floor mats taped around his forearms. He rolled off the bed away from Mann, who tried to pursue his advantage by leaping up onto the bed and running across it at him.

Leonard swung the tire iron low this time and caught Mann on the side of the left knee. He heard a howl that rose as Mann dropped to the bed. He swung again, this time at Mann's right arm, and caught him just at the wrist. Mann's knife fell to the floor.

Leonard saw Mann's left hand move to his waistband. Leonard hit the left hand with the tire iron and then stabbed his own knife into the space below Mann's rib cage. He ran the knife upward under the ribs and completed the maneuver inmates called "running the gears," moving the handle in an H-shape like a person shifting the standard transmission of a car. Then he moved Lonny Mann's damaged left hand and took the gun from his belt. He didn't have to examine him further to know that Mann was dead.

He stood in the dark room pulling the duct tape off the floor mats he'd wrapped around him and dropping them on the floor. The rubber mats suddenly seemed smothering and tight, and he could barely get them off fast enough. He opened the door on his end of the building and walked to the other end to do the same, and felt the cool air move through freely, lifting the heat from his sweat-soaked body.

The open doors admitted some light from the moon and stars, and that helped him focus his thoughts. He had to do something to make all this blood and Lonny Mann's body look like a case of self-defense and not murder. He didn't know the people in the community well enough to be sure what their first reaction would be, and Lee Wolf was away, so there was no way to ask him what to do.

Then he knew. He had his car, if only it still started. If it didn't, he could take a battery from another car and return it later. He could load Mann's body into the car trunk with the weapons and blood-stained sheets and so on, drive it somewhere in the mountains, and bury it. He would need help cleaning up the storage building, but he knew exactly whom to ask.

He trotted across the open meadow. He was not able to spare the time to walk around the community's perimeter tonight. He was aware that he must be covered with Lonny Mann's blood and looking terrible, but he needed to use every second of time and hope that nobody woke up and saw him.

He ran straight for the house with the bluebird cutout nailed to the door. When he reached it, he kept going around to the rear window. He stopped there and tapped on the glass. There was no response.

He knocked again, this time a little harder. It occurred to him that she didn't sleep in the little room with the mattress. That was just a room for supplies and things, part pantry and part closet. She and her husband had a bedroom. He walked around the building and knocked on another window with curtains blocking the view.

Then he went to another and did the same. He made it around the building to the back window she had opened for him other nights. He rapped harder on the glass, and a moment later he heard small, light feet moving toward him.

The window swung inward as before, and he saw her. She was wearing gym shorts and a T-shirt as pajamas tonight. She took a deep breath as she saw him and jumped back.

"Wait, it's me," he said in a breathy whisper. "It's Ed."

"Oh my God," she said. "You're covered with blood. Why are you covered with blood?"

"It was Lonny. He came after me in the middle of the night, and I had to kill him."

"And you came to my house like this? At first light people can follow your bloody footsteps straight to my back window."

"Look, I really need your help. We have to get rid of the body, clean up the mess, maybe pour water on the footprints—"

"Wait here. I'll be right out." She disappeared from the window into the darkness of the interior. After a surprisingly short time she returned. While he watched, she threw her head back and let out a loud, piercing scream.

She lifted her right arm and he saw the .45 pistol. She fired, and Edison Leonard felt the hot, terrible pain of the bullet in his lower torso, and it left him on his back in the fragrant grass.

She said, "This can't be two men fighting over me, hon. It's got to be one escaped convict killed the other and went berserk." She took the pistol in both hands and fired the second round through his head. Then she threw her head back and screamed again.

37

In daylight, as Leah drove, she checked her phone for emails. She scrolled through some lines that were the garbage that every electronic device seemed to pick up automatically, and then saw the identifier ASprague@WeldonvillePD and the subject "Forward from FBI."

"Internal communication, not for dissemination," the heading said. "At 0900 September 5 two deceased males were found in a wooded area 75 yards from Highway 44 in Mark Twain National Forest, near Fort Leonard Wood, Missouri. Both men died violently, apparently from knife and gunshot wounds. The men have been identified by fingerprint evidence as prisoners who escaped two years ago from the federal penitentiary at Weldonville, Colorado. Their names are Edison Leonard, age 37, and Lonny Mann, age 41."

She read the email again as she drove. She couldn't quite take in the details, or be sure of them after a few seconds. She had no doubt that somebody had killed them in Arkansas, where they had been hiding, and dumped the bodies up in Missouri. The most obvious suspect was Lee Wolf, simply because he was probably the nearest murderer, but unless he had killed them three days ago, he wasn't around to do it. She had been following him for two days.

If they'd been staying in a compound in the woods with the pack of armed fanatics Lee Wolf had reassembled in Arkansas, maybe they had just pissed some of them off. Or maybe they had been out in Missouri on some kind of errand, and they had offended somebody there. They had been belligerent and violent. Maybe they had just bumped into some of the wrong men to bully. Their bodies were dumped near an army base. They could have found thousands of men there that it wouldn't be wise to start up with. She knew that she wasn't going to understand this until the rest of the investigation was done, if ever. She put away the phone and kept her eyes on the road ahead.

A half hour later, the Subaru pulled off the highway at Shreveport. The car glided across the next intersection and into a Mobil station. One of the men got out and started a gas pump, then put the nozzle in the gas tank. The other three were on the way to the restrooms on the far side of the building. Lee Wolf was one of the three, so Leah knew she had no chance to pick him off.

Leah turned off the highway and into the rival gas station across the road and pulled up at a pump. Her rifle was in the back of the car under the floor with the spare tire. She could get her hands on it, but she was surrounded by people getting gas, buying snacks, and coming to and from the restrooms. Both gas stations had surveillance cameras.

Leah had to be closer. She pulled forward past the pumps and drove across the road to the station where the Subaru was stopped. She got out, swiped her card on the gas pump, stuck the nozzle in her gas tank to fill it, and walked.

She walked past the car, crouched as though she had dropped something, stuck a transponder onto the bare metal gas tank, and felt the magnet stick. She pretended to pick something up and put it into her pocket, stood, and headed for the ladies' room, going the opposite way around the building from the way the men had gone.

While Leah was in the ladies' room, she turned to the tracking app on her phone. She saw the red dot that symbolized the transponder she'd put on the Subaru. As she watched, the red dot moved slightly, and then stopped, as though the driver was waiting for an opening in the traffic or the signal to change, and then pulled out.

The dot returned to the interstate highway and up the eastbound side.

When she returned to her car, the tank was full and the pump had clicked off. She put the nozzle back on the pump, got into the driver's seat, and went after the Subaru. She hoped that they were going to stop and sleep somewhere, because she was having terrible trouble staying awake.

It had been a hellish trip for her. The Subaru had taken numerous side trips through dozens of small towns, driving slowly like tourists sometimes, and taking long detours through business districts. The Subaru doubled back a few times, so Leah had been afraid they might have spotted her. They had changed drivers a few times, but Leah couldn't.

Now that she was able to follow them with her phone, she didn't have to be close enough to see them, but she couldn't let them get so far ahead that she lost their signal. She would go fast until she caught up, and then she'd drop back and be invisible. Leah caught up enough within the next ten minutes, saw the Subaru, slowed a bit so she couldn't be seen, and then relied on the transponder's signal.

She followed the Subaru from a distance. It was moving toward the Shreveport airport. The signs appeared more frequently. Finally, there was one that said, "RENTAL CAR RETURN." The Subaru took it.

"Oh crap," she said. It was puzzling that they were here at all. It was a destination they could have reached on the first day. Now were they going to fly somewhere?

She followed the Subaru until it swung into the lot for one of the rental car agencies. She pulled into a striped space near the entrance, jumped out, and dodged up the nearest aisle of parked cars.

As she was walking across the concrete floor of the rental structure, she could see that one man was going to fetch a car and the other three men were waiting by the rental kiosk with their luggage. One of the three was Lee Wolf. She sped up and gave them a wide berth, moving to intercept the one going for the car.

She was rapidly closing the distance between her and the man. The man heard her footsteps, then nearly tripped as he turned his head over his shoulder to look at her. She came closer, smiling warmly, all teeth. "Can I help you find your car, sir? Here, let me see your key tag."

He let her take the key with the plastic tag on it. "Row R, Number 18. "Right this way."

She led him to a gray Chevrolet Malibu, handed him the keys, and turned to go. As he opened the door and sat in the driver's seat, she used that moment to bend down as though checking the odometer. She put another transponder under the rocker panel of the car, bobbed up, and left. In a moment she was in her own rental car, driving forward to skirt the various entrances to the rental returns and continuing on and out.

Lee Wolf was driving. He was always careful to take a turn at whatever chores other people were expected to do. If it seemed wise to have one person go into a diner and buy four sandwiches while the others stayed out of sight, then the first to offer to fetch the sandwiches was Lee Wolf.

He drove along Interstate 20 shopping for the right kind of town. Shreveport had been too big, too urban, and too busy. Alexandria was too close to Shreveport, as were Bossier and Haughton. Sibley and Vienna were a bit too small. He liked West Monroe and Monroe for this kind of robbery, but he kept going past them, examining a few other towns for most of the day, before he returned to West Monroe.

He turned off the interstate and onto the bridge over the Ouachita River. This was a wide, navigable river, and the bridge was a long, low span rising to a swing bridge at the center made of steel grating with a superstructure of steel girders. After that the bridge continued as a long, low span of pavement into what Wolf thought of as Monroe proper.

He had come through the town years ago, and it was almost as he remembered it. The city was not ugly, but not beautiful either. It was more poor than rich, but it had a few good-size office buildings. There was a University of Louisiana campus, but Wolf never sought it out. As he told the others, "We're not here for their diplomas. Their money will be enough." The police station was on Grand Street, so he made a mental note to keep Grand Street at a distance. When they had been through town several different ways, he stopped outside town on a lonely road.

"What do you think?" he said.

"What do you mean?" asked Dave Sherman.

"That was it," Wolf said. "We've been there."

Bob Carpenter tried to help the conversation along, to preserve the good mood. "I thought the idea was to get a pile of money. This place doesn't look like they've got much of it."

Tony Wagner said, "I did see a couple of banks, but they didn't look like much."

Wolf said gently, "I'm sorry, guys. I haven't been very clear about this, and that's not fair. Remember who we are. We're a subcommittee working for the Community of Ararat, provisional capital of the Swift Sword of the Savior, USA. We are out to get enough money to tide the community over this fall and winter, with the confidence that in the spring our needs will be met with an influx of normal funds and a growth in our food supply. We are not capitalists—we are groundbreakers for a Christian civilization. Remember what the Lord's Prayer says? 'Give us this day our daily bread.' Not a continuous feast, or a chauffeured Rolls-Royce to take us to all the three-star French restaurants. We're not asking the Lord for more than we need for *this day*, nor are we taking bread out of the mouths of others. We're going to rob a bank. All the money is insured by the federal government. We're just bleeding the beast."

Dave Sherman said, "But wouldn't it make sense to go for a big bank, where there's more money?"

"Not really," said Lee Wolf. "If you study a big bank in the center of Manhattan, it has a whole lot of net worth. At any moment they have billions of dollars in deposit accounts, collateral on loans they've made, stock and bond investments, contracts for precious metals. In some of those banks it's tens of billions, and some probably hundreds of billions. But it's not where you can put your hand on it. Some of it is ownership of land, or office buildings and skyscrapers, and some is just numbers on a balance sheet that's not even physical. It's on a computer server somewhere, and it's on the move. It can disappear from there to a bank in Zurich or Hong Kong in a thousandth of a second, and something else will appear there. Or not even there, but in the home office in Brussels, London, or Tokyo. The point is, none of it is worth anything to us because we can't put it in a bag and carry it home. All we want is about four laundry bags full of cash. And where does that come from?"

"Beats me," said Tony Wagner. "Never seen a bank without some."

"All banks do have some," Wolf said. "They have enough for the immediate needs of their customers. A giant bank in New York won't need a lot of cash most days—just enough to stock the cash registers of the stores and restaurants for a few blocks around. They don't need enough for all of Manhattan, because there are four or five other banks in the next couple of blocks. They don't use much cash. They don't do lending, investing, transferring, or anything in cash. In big cities even the prostitutes take credit cards. Nobody needs cash, so they don't keep much around."

"So you're saying—"

"I'm saying a bank in Monroe or West Monroe, Louisiana, probably needs to keep around about as much cash as a bank in Manhattan. There are still construction companies in these little towns that buy wood from some guy's land, where he runs a sawmill to cut and plane it. He probably makes his payroll in cash too, so he doesn't have to fill out forty pages of forms when he hires an extra man for a week's work. If he's rich enough to have help at home, he pays them in cash. This is a land of truck farmers, shopkeepers, owners of small restaurants and repair shops, and tradesmen. If you buy a car secondhand, it's probably from the guy who drove it first, and he's not going to take a check unless he knows you. Maybe not even then."

Bob Carpenter smiled. "You're saying these small banks in small towns are as good as anywhere."

"For what we want they are," Wolf said. "What we want is four bags of cash money, and it doesn't have to be hundreds. Small bills are less money, but they're safer for people like us to spend. And besides that, if we steal it here, what we're up against isn't the police department of the city of New Orleans. We're up against whoever drew patrol duty in West Monroe today."

At 5:45 p.m. two men entered the Monroe Manufacturers' Bank. The clerks and assistants from the small businesses nearby had come in and deposited most of the money from the day's sales for the night. Many stores in Monroe weren't usually open after six, except the month before Christmas, and it was still summer. The two men went to the stand-up desks on the sides of the foyer and used the pens with chains on them to fill out deposit slips and withdrawal slips and do simple arithmetic on the backs.

While they were doing this work as convincingly as possible, the end-of-day business was getting done and the shop clerks were heading out. Behind the bank building were two other men who had arrived in the Chevrolet Malibu today. They were using bicycle locks with jacketed cable to keep the already-locked rear doors of the building shut. Then the two men walked around the building to enter the doors into the foyer.

When the minute hand of the big clock on the wall clicked forward two spaces and back one to say 5:56, the first two men finished writing and brought their slips to the two tellers' windows. The two new men went to the two doors and each took out another bicycle lock, wound the cable through the two door handles until they were closed tightly, and locked them there. They each produced a paper sign that read, "Bank Closed for Fumigation" and stuck it on the glass door facing outward.

Both men—Tony Wagner and Dave Sherman—stepped to the front counter, vaulted over, and ran to the interior hallway of the building behind the tellers' stations. The tellers and the few customers were startled and confused, but they hadn't figured out what could be happening. This seemed to be an emergency. Was there a fire? A heart attack?

What was happening was that Dave and Tony were hurrying along the corridor, sticking their pistols in the faces of the people in the offices, dragging them out into the hallway, and making them sit there on the floor. They patted down the two men and four women and found six phones, which they took. Then they stood over the employees, occasionally aiming a gun at anyone who moved.

In the open foyer of the bank, Lee Wolf and Bob Carpenter raised their pistols and Lee Wolf called out, "Tellers! Take two steps back away from your stations. If an alarm goes off and I hear it, all tellers are going to die. If I don't hear it and cops begin to show up, all tellers are going to die."

He walked along the counter, staring hard at them as he spoke. "All we want is cash. Each of you take one of these laundry bags and fill it with cash." He took three bags out from under his coat and tossed them on the counter. "Do not reach for the bait bags they give you for robbers. This is not your money, and not even the bank's money. It's covered by the FDIC. Do not die or make your friends die for a federal agency."

Bob Carpenter, who was tall and intimidating, went over the counter and held his pistol on the three young women. They were so terrified that Lee Wolf could see their shallow breathing. One of them was wearing a purple silk blouse, and he could see the vibration of her heart beating. None of them was crying, which he took to be good news. He loved terror, but he hated emotions that would slow things down. The three tellers emptied their cash drawers into the laundry bags, and Carpenter looked inside all the bags before he took them and tossed them over the counter to the floor of the foyer.

Lee Wolf said to the nearest teller, "Now you and I are going to the vault."

He went around the counter with his gun aimed at her. She opened the counter to let him step in. He took her by the arm and steered her into the vault. When they were inside, he handed her the fourth bag. "Fill this bag with the cash from in here. The more big bills, the better."

Leah was staring at the map on her phone again. The car had stopped. It was parked behind a building on Second Street. The map on her phone showed a few names of businesses, and the nearest was a bank. A bank robbery? Of course it would be. That was the way several of these homegrown militias had made up for deficits. Why not the SSS?

The intersection was Second and Bullock.

*   *   *

As Lee Wolf stepped to the door of the vault, he caught some move-ment in the corner of his eye and pivoted toward the glass surface beside him, which was the upper part of the separate room contain-ing cubicles where people went to examine the contents of their safe deposit boxes. The lower part was wood. On the inside was a man in a dark blue uniform. He was kneeling on the carpeted floor of the room, where he had been lying in wait below the glass level where people couldn't see him. Wolf knew bank cubicles like this all had automatic locks that would lock whenever the door shut.

Wolf looked at him, and the man raised a big model 1911 mili-tary .45 pistol and fired. The bullet hit the clear wall and pounded a white impact mark on the glass with a circular spiderweb crack around it, but didn't penetrate it. The man realized instantly that the glass, which he must have seen a thousand times if he worked here, was bulletproof. All he had done was alert Lee Wolf to his presence.

When Lee Wolf moved a step to the side to see the guard better, the guard fired again, pulverizing the glass in another spot, blocking Wolf's view. As Wolf stepped along the glass, the guard fired again and again, turning large sections of the pane into white opaque circles so Wolf couldn't see him clearly.

Wolf had already seen all he needed to. He had identified the pistol, and he could count. As soon as the guard fired his seventh round, Wolf knew he would have to release the single-stack maga-zine and replace it with a full one. Wolf knelt on the floor by the wooden side and fired four shots through the wood, then peered at the guard over the wooden section and through a clear inch of the glass. The man had been hit at least twice, once in the head.

Wolf rose to his feet as the girl turned to run. His hand shot out, snatched a handful of her long hair, and jerked her back to him. "I'm not going to be shy about shooting you too, darlin.' Now get me that bag of money." He swung her around and pushed her back into the vault.

He stood by the door and looked around the foyer. He could see that most people were still standing in a compact herd under Bob Carpenter's eye, some of them unsuccessfully trying to crane their necks to see the guard's body.

He stepped back to the vault and looked in at the girl, who had dumped the contents of a carton in the bag. He didn't care at this point whether she had found him many thousands of dollars or dumped a lot of old deposit receipts in there. The time was rapidly getting used up. He knew from bank robbers he'd met in prison that the second you stepped in and announced it was a robbery, it was like starting a timer. You had to be out before the timer reached its end, or you were finished. He took the bag from the girl and stepped out to the foyer.

He shouted, "All right, boys! Time to go!"

He heard running feet, and in a moment the others were in the foyer too, shouldering the laundry bags full of money.

They stood by the door watching the bank employees and customers while Tony Wagner unlocked the bicycle lock, and then they all backed out. Tony reattached the lock to hold together the door handles on the outside and ran to catch up with the others.

As Leah Hawkins drove toward the bank, she held her phone in her hand and stared at the screen. The car was still there. But as she watched, it began to move, going backward. Then it went forward. They were leaving.

She was still a mile behind them, and they were turning again, heading west. They were going toward the river.

She had to beat them to the bridge. She could see that the entrance to the bridge was at DeSiard Street. She had seen it on the way into town. The bridge was old. It was long, and it had a swing-bridge section in the middle. She didn't know if it still swung open and closed, or if that was some obsolete feature that wasn't used anymore. All she could do was head there and hope she got there first.

Somewhere in the distance she heard sirens. It occurred to her, not for the first time, that she was one of a limited number of people who welcomed that wailing sound.

DeSiard Street was ahead of her—three short blocks, then turn left.

Leah drove hard and in a moment she was on DeSiard Street and accelerating again. She could see the bridge clearly now. There was a long, nearly flat approach, paved like a road onto the water of the wide river. It narrowed to two lanes a distance ahead. It was a few minutes after six, and she was seeing traffic that was probably heavier than it was for most of the day on both the westbound and eastbound lanes.

Leah drove up the approach to where the pavement narrowed a bit, and then all the way along the gradual incline to the center of the bridge. She reached to the dashboard, turned on her emergency blinking lights, and slowed down. As she slowed, cars raced past her on the left, and the ones in her lane slowed with her, waiting for a chance to pass. But before long, the rush of the oncoming traffic to the left, with cars coming every couple of seconds, made the line of cars behind her too long. People stopped passing.

Leah came to a complete stop, brought her untraceable pistol from her purse, stuck it in her belt, flung her door open, jumped out, and slammed the door. She stepped to the right side of the bridge's pavement, where there was a little space to stand, and pressed the lock button on her key fob.

As she stepped away, drivers in cars stuck behind her abandoned car honked their horns over and over in a frantic rhythm or leaned on them, tried in vain to swerve to the left to get around her car, fumed, and swore.

lights of the dozen or more police cars were now visible to everyone on the bridge, and most could see the armed uniformed cops advancing up the bridge between the lines of cars toward them.

When Leah was only one car length behind the Malibu and two lanes to the left, she could see the faces of the men in the car. She recognized Lee Wolf in the driver's seat.

She stayed low and ran to the next lane, keeping in the blind spot so Wolf didn't pick her up in his mirror or his peripheral vision. At the moment he was focused on the rearview mirror, where he could see police officers making their way up the bridge between lanes of stalled cars toward him. He appeared to be talking, giving his companions instructions for ambush-shooting the approaching police officers. Leah approached across the front of the car beside the Malibu.

Suddenly Wolf seemed to sense it was time to look around him, and he turned to his left just as Leah bobbed up ten feet away from him with her gun aimed at his head, and fired.

Wolf's blood, a bit of brain tissue, and tiny shards of cranial bone sprayed the inside of the car. A half second later, Leah was at the side window with her gun aimed at the tall man in the passenger seat. She flung his door open and shouted, "Get out!" She yelled louder. "Get out with your hands up! If there's a gun in your hand, you're dead too!" She yelled louder than she had ever yelled in her life. "Out of the car!"

The three men had already begun trying to get out, speckled with Wolf's blood and not inclined to try to shoot anyone. As they came out, Leah hastily patted each of them down, but found their only weapons were on the car seats.

Leah shouted, "Keep your hands high in the air at all times as you walk down the bridge toward those officers. Do it now!" She gave the one nearest her a push in that direction, then gave each of the others a push that sent the man a few feet. She kept the pistol aimed at the men for the first twenty feet.

Leah lowered her Glock and the crowd of people in their cars began to applaud. A couple of the people yelled, "Great work, Officer!" and "You got them!" Leah waved, and began to trot the other way toward the center of the bridge, where she had left her car. After a hundred feet or so, she raised her speed and ran between cars, speeding up to a full run as she went.

By the time she reached the rental car, she was winded and sweating. The lane was clear ahead of her, since she was the sole cause of the traffic jam, so she got in and drove fast toward the west.

38

July 19 was always a somber, quiet day in Weldonville, Colorado. It had been seven years since the first bad July 19, but to most people in town, it felt as though that night had been so big that it couldn't be confined to a specific year. Every day when they woke up, the memory of the dreadful events reached their minds with the return to consciousness and became real all over again. For Weldonville there were two times: the time before and the time after.

The time before was the world they'd been born into, where their childhoods had taken place, and their parents and grandparents and aunts and uncles had towered over them and taught them how a person was supposed to be. For Leah Hawkins, it had also been the time when people first noticed her ability to dominate the boards for the rebound and then make the three-point shot at the other basket a few seconds later. There was the glory of being the first real female athletic phenomenon in that part of the state, and then the parade of college recruiters had arrived. Next came college, and the bright, early days of her career. It was the time when she first fell in love.

Leah had stopped being resentful about the awful circumstances of that love some time ago—being the other woman, the long-term mistress her married lover had to hide. She was just glad that love had happened, that she'd had those times with Mark. She had not blamed him even then because the circumstances had not been his fault any more than hers, and Mark had, after all, died at her side trying to protect her. That had been on July 19, the final moment of that other lifetime.

After she had visited Marcia Ballard this morning, she had been busy doing practical tasks, and now she was waiting, sitting at one of the best round tables at Steele's food stand across from the city park, her place shaded by one of the giant oaks. She was having a root beer float, something she hadn't had in years. That was one blessing Leah had never fully appreciated when she was younger. She had complained to the silent universe about being a tall, skinny, big-footed scarecrow, awkward except when she was on a court or a field. But the compensation was that she could still eat anything without consequences.

She looked up at the oaks. She had noticed during her errands this morning that some of the saplings the city had planted on empty lots where houses had burned down seven years ago were already fifteen-foot trees. Someday they would be as big as these, and the reason for their planting would be forgotten.

A couple walked up the sidewalk past the stand and the man, Carlos Estrada, noticed her and stopped. "Hi, Chief."

"Hi, Carlos," she said. She stood and hugged him and then hugged his wife. "Hi, Lois." She added, "You know it's not 'Chief' anymore though. I've been retired for years."

"I know." Carlos looked down for a second, then up. "And I know this is a hard day. But I, uh—"

"It is for everybody," Leah interrupted. She patted his shoulder. Then her eyes focused on something in the distance, far behind his head. "I'm sorry to be distracted, but Ken has the kids at the movies, and I think I see them coming out of the Tivoli. They'll be looking for me."

Carlos turned and said, "Yep. That looks like them." Ken Long was as tall as Leah, and he had the three children walking with him. Carlos said, "Well, it's always good see you, Chief." He and his wife walked on down the sidewalk toward their car.

"Bye, you two. Drive carefully."

Leah watched her family's approach. They had come to her as part of the post–July 19 world. She had first learned of Ken's existence as a name on a list, the father and ex-husband of three victims. Now he was the husband she wished her parents could have lived to know.

Sometimes it felt to her as though she had learned everything she knew after she and Ken had adopted the kids, because she had known none of it before. Other times she thought maybe she was just trying to mimic what she had loved having her own parents do. The kids were the new world, and her job and Ken's was to take care that they grew and learned, then launch them into a future she and Ken would probably only see at its beginning.

Raymond, the eldest, walked with his father, both of them talking seriously about something, which she guessed was probably the capabilities of several kinds of dinosaurs. He was starting to carry himself like Ken, even to sound like him. God, they grew up fast.

When Ken reached her, she kissed him and took the younger kids, Bill and Kristen, by their hands. "Let's go, you guys," she said. "I've got your clothes and swimming suits and jackets and stuff packed in the car, and the car is in the lot behind city hall."

"Are we going straight to McClellan's?" her son Raymond asked.

"Yes," she said. "How were the dinosaurs?"

"Pretty good," he said. "They have a couple of new ones in this."

Leah knitted her brows. "New ones?"

"Yeah."

Ken shrugged. "You know, genetic research."

Leah smiled as they reached the car. She clicked the key fob to open the doors and then scooped Bill up into his car seat and put

Kristen in hers, and locked the fasteners. Then she handed Ken the keys while she watched Raymond click his seat belt closed and then gave it a tug of her own to test it before she got into the passenger seat.

Ken drove to the Parkman House, the restaurant where Ray McClellan had tended bar when he'd first returned to Weldonville after retiring from the ATF. He and Marjorie had bought it, attached a comfortable fifteen-room hotel with high ceilings, thick beams, and stone fireplaces to the historic structure, and called that part McClellan's Inn. Marjorie had been one of the Clays who had inherited the local hardware business after the murder of her parents and uncle, and the project had provided work for some of the Clays' employees at a slow time.

When Ken pulled into the parking lot and he and Leah began to extricate the kids from the confinement of their car seats, they saw Ray and Marjorie come out the side door of the restaurant.

The children took their first steps at a run, but Ken yelled, "Freeze!" They all did. "Do not run across the parking lot," he said. "Cars pull in here too fast all the time." They all stepped off the edge of the pavement and ran across the grass to where Ray and Marjorie McClellan waited.

Marjorie said to the kids, "We've been waiting for you people. It's been months."

"That's right," said Ray McClellan. "And I notice that all three of you got shorter." He turned to Marjorie. "Aren't they supposed to be growing?"

"We are!" Raymond said. "We're all taller."

"You're tall enough," said Marjorie. "You're already Longs. We set aside a room for you Longs that opens onto the courtyard where the pool is. We'll get you settled, and then you can change for a swim. That okay, Mom?"

"Sounds great," Leah said.

The whole group set off for the room near the pool, with Ken and Leah trailing behind carrying the duffel bags full of clothes. When they were settled and had changed, Marjorie led them back to the pool. "All right, ladies and gentlemen." She pointed at a young man and young woman in bright red bathing suits. "These two lifeguards are Felicity and John. They are qualified, certified, and thoroughly tested by the state of Colorado. What they say goes." The two young lifeguards got into the water to help the children descend into the shallowest part of the pool.

Leah and Ken Long stood in the water, not quite relinquishing their children to the lifeguards, and Marjorie and Ray sat down beside them, dangling their legs in the pool. Leah said, "Thanks so much for doing this again, Marjorie. It makes me think about the things I want to remember and not the rest of it."

"I know what you mean. It's the anniversary of the deaths of all the people I loved. That's true for Kristen, too, and Bill. If you guys didn't come, we'd all be crying in public. How long are you all here before you go back to New York this time?"

"We're here until school starts."

"Good. We'll have some fun with the kids. Some grown-up evenings too."

"You and Ray have to come out and stay with us at the ranch while we're here. You won't have to be in charge of anything, and nobody will have to drive home after a few drinks. I lived here all my life without spending a day on a ranch, but I married a guy from New York, so now I have a ranch. We might as well use it to keep from earning a DUI. And you have to come visit us in New York again in the fall when the tourists move up to the mountains to break their legs."

"I promise."

"Oh, look." Leah pointed. Bill Halvorsen was standing by the hotel door, still straight-spined and muscular after seven years out of the marines. He was holding it open while Kristen came out to join him. Each of them had a toddler cradled on one arm and a bag slung over the other shoulder. They waved at the group and walked toward them along the side of the pool.

Leah said, "Look at them. Sometimes I wonder if I'm just not capable of remembering between times how good they look. Especially her."

Marjorie sighed. "Being a beauty made her a great partner in our detective agency. But it wasn't always a blessing in her life. I think the first time she ever felt happy about what she sees in the mirror was after he turned up. It was like she found out who it was for."

Leah, Ken, Ray, and Marjorie climbed up on the deck as the Halvorsens walked into their midst. Leah and Marjorie took the two little children, Nick and Stephanie, in their arms and fawned over them and rocked and bounced them to make them laugh, while the others hugged Kristen and Bill.

Ray McClellan looked across the pool at the window into the bar and waved at someone, and then a man came out carrying a tray of drinks. Ray said, "I've placed an order for the drinks that each of you usually have when you come. If your order has changed since I wrote them down, please tell Walt, or you'll drink the consequences until you do."

Kristen picked up a glass from the tray and handed it to her husband, then took the one that was meant for her. "Thank you for doing this again, Ray and Marjorie," she said. "On the nineteenth, I always feel grateful when I see certain people." She lifted her glass toward Leah and drank. She and the others said no more, just turned their attention to the children, who were unaware that anything had just been said.